MY NAME IS ADAM

Also by Elias Khoury in English translation

Gate of the Sun
Yalo
As Though She Were Sleeping
White Masks
The Broken Mirrors: Sinalcol

Elias Khoury

MY NAME IS ADAM

CHILDREN OF THE GHETTO:
VOLUME I

Translated from the Arabic by
Humphrey Davies

MACLEHOSE PRESS
QUERCUS · LONDON

First published in the Arabic language as *Awlad al-ghittu. Ismi Adam*
by Dar al-Adab, Beirut, 2012
First published in Great Britain in 2018 by

MacLehose Press
an imprint of Quercus
Carmelite House
50 Victoria Embankment
London EC4Y 0DZ

An Hachette UK company

This book has been selected to receive financial assistance from English PEN's
PEN Translates! programme. English PEN exists to promote literature and our
understanding of it, to uphold writers' freedoms around the world, to campaign against
the persecution and imprisonment of writers for stating their views, and to promote
the friendly co-operation of writers and the free exchange of ideas.

A CIP catalogue record for this book is available from the British Library.

ISBN (TPB) 978 0 85705 751 8
ISBN (Ebook) 978 0 85705 750 1

10 9 8 7 6 5 4 3 2 1

Designed and typeset in Minion by Libanus Press
Printed and bound in Denmark by Nørhaven

To Jad Tabet and Anton Shammas

"Say: 'Are they equal – those who know and those who know not?'"

Koran, "Companies", Verse 9

These notebooks came into my possession by coincidence, and I hesitated at length before deciding to send them to Dar al-Adab in Beirut for publication. To be honest, the reason for my hesitation lay in that ambiguous feeling that combines admiration and envy, love and hate. I had met the writer and hero of these texts, Adam Dannoun – or Danoun – in New York, where I teach at the university. I remember I told my Korean student how good-looking I thought he was. It was towards the end of February 2005, if my memory serves me correctly. We had gone out to eat falafel after the graduate seminar and observed the man carefully and cheerfully preparing his sandwiches. He was tall and a little on the thin side, his shoulders broad and slightly stooped. White hairs had grown among the chestnut on his head, making it look as though wreathed with a shining corona, the brightness coming, I think, from his grey eyes, which shaded into green. I told my student I understood now why she was so taken with this Israeli restaurant, and that it had nothing to do with the food but was because of its owner. I was wrong, though: that might have been the best falafel sandwich I have ever tasted. We Beirutis claim to be the best falafel-sandwich makers in the world, and the Palestinians say the Israelis stole falafel from them, which is correct, but I think both sides are wrong because falafel is the oldest cooked food known to man, being pharaonic when you really get down to it, and so on and so forth.

The name of the restaurant was the Palm Tree, and when the handsome man with the pale oval face and the dimple sketched on his

9

chin came over to us and began talking to my student in Hebrew, Sarang Lee, answering in English, turned to me and introduced us. The man then started speaking to me in Arabic and Sarang said, in English, how much she liked his Palestinian dialect and he replied with something in Hebrew that I didn't understand.

When we stepped out again into the cold, Sarang Lee suggested a drink. I was taken aback, because I don't go out with my students; I still recall the warning given to me by my Armenian friend Baron Hagop – the one to whom Edward Said awarded the title "King of Sex" – about what they call "harassment" here. He said if a female student were to claim I had harassed her, it would be enough to ruin me and destroy my academic career.

I agreed to have a drink with Sarang Lee because I could tell from the look in her eyes that she had something to say. We had a glass of white wine at the Lanterna café, my Armenian friend's favourite and the one habitually used by Hanna el-Akkari, a former Popular Front fighter; we often used to go there for a drink and to reminisce about the old days, when we dreamed of revolution.

I said to Sarang Lee with a laugh, raising my glass to her, "We don't usually drink wine after falafel," and waited for her to speak. She said nothing, however, and after a seemingly interminable silence, I asked her if she was in love. Immediately, the twenty-two-year-old girl's eyes shone with tears. I can't say for sure that she cried, but that is what I thought happened, at least. Then she said she didn't know, but she loved me too.

The word "love" set off a tremor in my heart that was immediately put a stop to by "too", since the latter meant she loved the Israeli but didn't want to hurt my feelings. I had no love in me at the time, especially not for a girl who was countless years younger than me. All the same, I had found in my young student's academic excellence, her shyness, and her exquisite Asian beauty, something that led me to pay special attention to her. That day, I found I had been strung along. Though "strung along" isn't the right term here: the girl had never sent me anything but signals of ordinary admiration, such as any student might her teacher. I asked her what she'd said to the "old man" and she smiled and said he wasn't old and was "the same age as you, my dear professor", adding, with gentle malice, "unless, that is, you consider yourself old". I ignored her remark and asked what the man had said. She replied, "He said he was speaking Galilean for your sake, as my professor, because it was close to Lebanese." She also said there was some mystery there, because, having spent her childhood in Tel Aviv, she knew Israel well but couldn't work out the man's precise identity – was he a Palestinian pretending to be an Israeli, or the reverse? – but that, in any case, he was a very special person.

As Sarang Lee pronounced the words "very special", her eyes gleamed with love. I couldn't think of anything to say because I had a feeling something strange was going on, and indeed, at another meeting, she let me in on the secret, telling me that the man wasn't Israeli: "It's true he has an Israeli passport but he's Palestinian, from around Lydda I think, but he likes ambiguities and doesn't mind people thinking he's Israeli."

I never again met this man who "liked ambiguities" socially, but my student would tell me curious tales about him, saying she thought he was a womaniser, but charming. I could not have cared less for these anecdotes about the Israeli who spoke perfect Arabic, or the ambiguous Palestinian who spoke Hebrew as though it was his own tongue, or his charm. I was jealous of him, though it was an unspoken jealousy. I don't know why it occurred to me that he might be an agent of Israel's Mossad and that that might be the reason for all his ambiguities and disguises, but I didn't care. That was the sole reason I wanted my student to keep away from him, but when, through a slip of the tongue, I put my foot in it and told her of my suspicions, she got angry and left the Cornelia Street Café. We'd taken to meeting there once every two weeks on average, it being a little out of the way of prying eyes, on Washington Square, which is the centre, practically speaking, of New York University, where I work.

Once, Sarang Lee told me Adam didn't like me and had said he had doubts about this teacher of hers. He went further, in fact. She said she didn't want to tell me (though she did) that he had doubts about my intentions towards her and that when she'd defended me and said I'd never made even the slightest allusion to the possibility of starting an affair, the guy got angry and said he wasn't talking about that sort of thing, he meant something more important, and asked her if she'd read my novel Gate of the Sun, saying writers couldn't be trusted and one day she might come across herself as a heroine in one of my novels.

Her reaction amazed me: she asked coyly if she'd make a good heroine for a novel!

I don't want to talk about myself, and if Sarang Lee hadn't been the cause of these notebooks reaching me, I would never have mentioned my relationship with her, which at no time went any further than flirtatious glances. All the same, I was surprised that the idea of being the heroine of a novel attracted my young friend; and, unfortunately, she actually did end up being a heroine, though not at my hands but at those of my rival. I asked her what he'd said about Gate of the Sun but all she said was that he hadn't liked it, and it was left to me to discover his attitude on my own, when the Israeli movie Intersecting Glances was shown at Cinema Village on 12th Street.

I'm not going to give an account of what happened at the cinema *or of the anger that seized me, because I have no right to parasitise the stories of the author of these notebooks – not to mention that the reader will read the story as Adam Dannoun tells it and can judge between us, just as Sarang Lee will read her story, or fragments of it, in this book, if it gets translated into English. She will then discover that the Israeli who wasn't an Israeli didn't love her, because he thought she didn't love him, and that this misunderstanding, which left its mark on the falafel-seller's life, had saved the Korean girl from a relationship that would have ruined hers.*

When Sarang Lee brought me the notebooks, she said the man had died in a fire. It seems he'd dozed off while smoking in bed; the recording tapes that filled his bookshelves caught fire, and by the time the fire department arrived, he was dead. I expressed my doubts and said the story mimicked exactly the manner of death, in New York, of Rashed Hussein, the great Palestinian poet and translator into Arabic of Bialik. She too said she thought Adam had committed suicide, staging his death to make it an exact replica of Hussein's, because he was an admirer of the poet and had learned his verses by heart. She added that a week before his death he'd given her a short letter containing his will and asked her to read it only if something happened to him. I asked her to let me read the letter but she refused. She wept bitterly as she related how she, along with Nahum, his Israeli partner in the falafel restaurant, had carried out his wishes, cremating his body and throwing his ashes into the Hudson. She'd been surprised, however, to find that the file containing these notebooks had survived the fire. The file's blue edges were burnt and it was completely buried under the ashes, but the notebooks were untouched, the texts, written in black ink, seemingly illumined by the flames. Refusing to carry out Adam's will, she hadn't burnt the file containing the notebooks; she'd taken it home with her, tried but failed to decipher the Arabic runes, and decided therefore to give it to me, extracting a promise that I would do nothing with it without her knowledge.

Sarang Lee probably thought that I'd do what she'd been unable to, and, given the problem at the cinema, burn the papers, because in a fit of that lack of control that has so often cost me dear, I'd screamed in Adam's face that he was a nobody who criticised my book because he understood nothing, and that I'd written a story, not history, and couldn't know the actual fate of characters I'd made up. I don't know why the guy insisted that he knew the characters in my novel, but he started raving like a madman and it was only when I read these texts that I came to understand what he was talking about.

That day, when Adam left the cinema Sarang Lee had run after him, while I quivered with rage. I told my friend Chaim that the man was a liar, claiming to his girlfriends that he was Israeli when in fact he was Palestinian, and that this identity of his was his main argument against my novel – as though I had no right to write about Palestine just because I wasn't born of Palestinian parents!

The notebooks given to me by Sarang Lee were ordinary, ruled, Five Star university notebooks, the pages held together by a spiral binding. On the first page of each, we find a calendar, for the years 2003, 2004, 2005, 2006 and 2007, and they can be bought from any stationery store in New York. It seemed likely that the author was planning to write a work long enough to need all these notebooks with their coloured covers.

I read them all three times and had no idea what to do with them. Even today, seven years later, I don't know why I eventually decided to go back to the notebooks. I then reread them with eyes from which the passage of time had erased all my hatred for the man, substituting sorrow. I grieved for him and grieved for myself, and after much hesitation made up my mind to publish the notebooks as though they were the text I wished I had written myself.

The undeniable truth is that I faced a major problem that made me hesitate at length before taking this decision.

A satanic idea had taken hold of me – to steal the book and publish it under my own name, thus realising my dream of writing a sequel to Gate of the Sun, *something I'd found myself incapable of doing. What was I supposed to write about after the murder of Shams and the passing of Nahila? With their deaths, my pen ran dry and I felt I'd lost the ability to write. I entered the depressed state known in Arabic literature as "the lover's demise", in which death chokes the lover the moment the beloved vanishes, and it took Daniel Habeel Abyad, hero of my novel* Yalo, *to rescue me, because he forced me to study Syriac, and in learning that new alphabet I rediscovered love, as a gateway to betrayal.*

Plagiarising the book didn't mean that I would publish the text word for word as I'd found it. It meant rewriting it, treating it as primary material. I told myself I wouldn't be the first to do so. Indeed, I believe – and this is what I teach my students – that all writing is a kind of rewriting, and that plagiarism is permitted to those who are capable of it. What the Arab critics referred to as "the thefts of al-Mutanabbi" may be the model for the kind of plagiarism that is on a par with, if not superior to, creation. Similarly, Sholokhov, author of the masterpiece And Quiet Flows the Don, *one of the greatest works of Russian literature, has been accused of having stolen the manuscript during the Russian Civil War, an allegation that has had no impact on the novel's importance or its author's place in the history of modern Russian literature.*

After trying to rewrite the text a number of times, however, I found that I couldn't go on: Instead of being a thief I'd become a copyist, and instead of working on the text I felt it had started to exert a hold over me; I began to feel that my life was dissolving and becoming part of the life of the man, and of his story, and it seemed to be on the verge of taking me over so completely that I feared losing my soul and entering into the maze of his memory. I decided, therefore, to abandon the idea completely.

The reader will notice that these notebooks contain texts that are incomplete, a mating of novel and autobiography, of reality and fiction, and a blending of literary criticism with literature. I don't know how to categorise the text, in terms of either form or content: it mixes writing with outlining and blends narration and contemplation, truth and imagination, as though the words have become mirrors to themselves, and so on and so forth.

Finally, I wish to stress that this book contains the manuscript in its entirety, as it reached me via Sarang Lee. I have not added a single word to it beyond the chapter headings, which I believe are needed to guide the reader. By the same token, I have deleted nothing from it. I have even retained, as is, the savage criticism that the author directs against my own novel, convinced as I am that the respected reader will see it as an infringement of my rights and an injustice to me and my book.

I have changed the order of the notebooks, hesitating, however, before the one with the red cover, which begins with what is apparently the outline of the novel about Wuddah al-Yaman that the author seems in the end to have decided not to write. This I initially decided to publish separately, taking it as the plan for a novel about love whose hero is that Omayyad poet; then I dropped the idea, after discovering that this concept ran through, and was woven into, all the notebooks. I also hesitated before the numerous analytical passages, as the author, rather than deleting them, had left them in place, either because it had never occurred to him that his book would be published, or because he'd thought he'd be able to revise it first.

At first, I decided to put these passages, which are more like sketches, into the footnotes. Then I thought I should print them in bold in a different font. However, I dropped both ideas, convinced that I had no right to do so and that through these passages the reader could join in the intertextual game and explore, as I did while reading the manuscript, the aesthetics of beginnings and the magical nature of the relationship between the writer and his text. Similarly, I have made the preface, which I found on its own in a notebook with a blue cover and which is a short text resembling a will, into an introduction to the work.

The manuscript had no title, and I actually compiled a list of possibilities before eventually arriving at the idea of making the author's name the title, which thus became The Notebooks of Adam Dannoun. That way, the author of the book would have succeeded in doing what other authors have failed to, namely, transforming himself into a hero of a tale that he himself had lived and loved.

I changed my mind at the last moment, however, just before sending the manuscript to the publisher. I decided that the book should expose a truth to which no-one previously had paid any attention, namely that the Palestinian women and men who had managed to remain in their land were the children of the little ghettoes into which they had been forced by the new state that had taken over their country, erasing its name.

I decided therefore to give the book the title Children of the Ghetto, thus making a contribution, insignificant as it may be, to the writing of a novel that I am myself incapable of writing.

In conclusion, I apologise to Sarang Lee for failing to consult her on the publication of these notebooks as a novel written by Adam Dannoun, while being certain, at the same time, that she will be delighted to find herself numbered among its heroes.

Elias Khoury
New York/Beirut, 12 July, 2015

THE WILL

I sit alone in my fifth-floor room, watching the snow falling on New York. I don't know how to describe my feelings about this rectangular window in whose glass I see my soul refracting. It has become my mirror, in which my image loses itself amongst the other crowding images of this city. I know New York is my last stop. I shall die here and my body will be burnt and my ashes scattered in the Hudson River. This is what I shall request in writing in my will: I have no grave in a country no longer mine that I should ask to be buried there, in the arms of the spirits of my ancestors. In this river, I shall embrace the spirits of strangers and encounter those who find, in the meeting of stranger with stranger, a lineage to replace one they've lost. (I realise I've just turned two lines of Imru' al-Qays's poetry quite unpoetically into prose but I don't care: no-one is going to read these words after my death because I shall ask in my will that these notebooks be burnt along with me, so that they too can be thrown into the river. Such is the fate of man, and of words: words die too, leaving behind them an expiring wail like the one our souls give out as they disappear into the fog of the end.)

I've made this window my mirror so that I don't have to look at my face in the actual mirror – my face dissolves into the other faces, my features vanish, and thus I fashion an end for the end that has chosen me and put an end to the dream of writing a novel that I don't know how to write or even why I should. The novel was lost to me the moment I thought I'd found it. That is how things are lost. It's how Dalia, the woman who vanished from my life at the very moment when I thought the time had come for me to write my life in her eyes, and who'd agreed we should have a child and start, was lost. The beginning, or what we thought was the beginning, was the end. However, the apparent end, which led me to leave my country, seemed more like a false start, when I imagined I could find a substitute for life in writing it. This delusion seized me when the Israeli film director, who was my friend because he spoke the language I'd resolved to forget, suggested that every individual's life deserves to be a novel or a film.

I've put my notebooks in this file and I shall ask that they be burnt and their ashes placed in a bottle, and I shall ask my young friend to mix their ashes with mine before everything is thrown into the river. Strange, my relationship with this young woman who came out of nowhere, and remained in the nowhere from which she came! Did she love me, or did she love her New York University professor? Or did she love the idea of love, and use it as a substitute for the two of us?

When I decided to emigrate to New York, I was determined to forget everything. I even decided, at the moment when I obtained my U.S. citizenship, that I'd change my name, though it looks as though I'll die before that happens. Death is a right, and the right that death owes me is my death. I'm not ill. Nothing requires that I think of death so unceasingly. Normally, it is the sick and the elderly who die, and I am neither. I'm over fifty and on life's last lap, as they say. My lust for life has become sluggish due to a woman who decided, in a moment of insanity, to abandon me and her love for me – and she was right: we have to make sure we abandon things before they abandon us. I, though, have begun to rediscover how lust creeps into our joints – and I don't just mean sex, I mean everything, but especially the lust for vodka and wine that sweeps over me, so that I feel a numbness in my lips, and my ribcage shudders as I sip the first drop.

A renewed lust for life and residence on the shores of death are a paradox that throws me into confusion, but I know that death will be victorious in the end, because death does not have the right to be defeated.

The death whose phantom I see before me isn't born out of despair at anything. I live in the post-despair age and am neither despairing nor lonely. I have fashioned my own despair and made of it a shade under which to take refuge, one that protects me from a descent into naivety and futility. My loneliness, on the other hand, has been my own choice: as soon as I finish work, I return to my room and start writing. My loneliness is my writing, and shall be my only title. I had failed to write the novel that I wanted to, so I decided to write a great metaphor, a universal metaphor fashioned by an obscure Arab poet who lived in the Omayyad period and died a hero's death – and then suddenly I discovered that metaphors are futile. New York has taught me that nothing in our world is original or authentic. Everything has become a metaphor, or so it seems to me. Why should I write yet another metaphor to add to the others?

At first, I wrote the metaphor that I'd chosen to express the story of the country from which I'd come. Later, having decided that metaphors were futile, I didn't tear up what I'd written, but reworked parts of it to allow me to recount the circumstances in which the idea had been born, and the reasons for it. Then, in an absolute fury, I decided to abandon the metaphor altogether,

23

stop writing the novel, and devote myself to recovering my own story, so that I could write the unadorned truth, stripped of all symbols and metaphors. No doubt I've failed to realise my new goal but I have uncovered much that had escaped my memory or sunk into its folds. Memory is a well that never runs dry and it both reveals and conceals, either so that we may forget when we do not forget, or so that we may fail to forget when we do, I know not!

I don't recall ever reading anything about the relationship between anger and writing but my decision to write my own story was a result of rage, a savage rage that overwhelmed my being and that had two, unconnected, causes. One was my meeting with Blind Ma'moun, who took me by surprise with his ambiguous story about my parents which meant nothing to me at first but which began to assume terrifying proportions following the visit of Israeli director Chaim Zilbermann to the restaurant and his invitation to attend the showing of his film "Intersecting Glances". There, and this was the second cause of my rage, I witnessed the story of my friend Dalia being torn to pieces, followed by the author of the novel *Gate of the Sun* standing next to the bald Israeli director, introducing himself as an expert on the story of Palestine, and lying.

Both of them told lots of lies, and I couldn't restrain myself from shouting and leaving the cinema, Sarang Lee at my side. She took hold of my arm and led me to the café, but instead of supporting me, she started explaining that I was in the wrong.

It's true. I was in the wrong, and what I've written is a record of my mistakes. I've noted here both my rage and my errors. I told myself it was my duty, that I have to end my life with a story. We live to be turned into stories, no more and no less! This is why I wrote so much, only to discover that silence is more eloquent than words and that I want these words to be burnt.

All the same, I feel like a coward. I'm incapable of committing suicide, incapable of driving these notebooks to commit suicide, and incapable of going back to my country to recover my soul – as Karma, the Palestinian woman I got to know as a sister whom my mother hadn't borne, and who then disappeared from my life, advised me to do. I ran into Karma again by coincidence here in New York and promised her I would, but I don't know, I may not be sincere. Probably I'm not sincere but I'm not sure, which is why I gave Sarang Lee a short letter and asked her not to open it unless something should happen to me, and why I charged her with the job I'd been unable to carry out and asked her to burn these notebooks after my death.

I'm not certain I really want the flames to consume these papers, but it's too late now, which is better. I am sure that the yellow moon which has illumined a small part of the darkness of my soul will do what she thinks is right.

I hesitated at length before making up my mind not to send these papers to any Arab publishing house, not because I don't believe that what I've written is important but out of despair at the relationship between writing and the world of publishing, where writers rush to seek immortality for their names, or any relationship at all with immortality. I don't believe in immortality, of souls or of words: it's all vanity. The vanity of vanities, as Our Lord Solomon wrote, is us. I don't know how poets and authors can dare to write, after *The Song of Songs* and *Ecclesiastes*! The writer who was a prophet, a king and a poet, the lover who loved all women, the mighty ruler who reigned over the kingdoms of the jinn, wrote that "all is vanity", so why add my vanity to his?

I'm sitting alone now. My window is open onto the mirrors of the snow. I inhale the whiteness and listen to the crying of the winds that bluster down the streets of New York. I sip a drop of wine and take the smoke of my cigarette deep into my lungs. I open my notebooks, read, and feel thorns in my throat. I close the window and shut my eyes. My story is like thorns, my life is words, and my words are gusts of wind.

THE COFFER OF LOVE

(concept paper for a novel, first draft)

Waddah al-Yaman

(POINT OF ENTRY 1)

He was a poet, a lover and a martyr to love.

This is how I see Waddah al-Yaman, a poet over whose lineage, and very existence, the critics and the transmitters of his verses differ. To me, though, he represents the most extreme sacrifice of which love is capable – a silent death. The poet kept silent because he was trying to protect his beloved, and the coffer of his death, in which the caliph al-Walid ibn Abd al-Malik interred him, was the coffer of his love.

The title of the novel will be *The Coffer of Love* and I'm not going to play the allegory game with it. Love is the most sublime of all the emotions – their lord and master, indeed – and is what gives things meaning. Only love, and words, give meaning to life, which has none.

I refuse to write an allegory, for the reader who sees in the story of Waddah al-Yaman a symbol of Palestine will simply reduce it to a human metaphor for the Palestinians and all the world's persecuted, including the Jews.

I don't want to go on about semantics – I'm not confident of my ability to write anything on the topic – but whenever I'd read in the faces of my Israeli friends, or in Israeli texts, contempt for, or criticism of, the Jews of Europe for being driven to the slaughter like sheep, I'd feel I was suffocating. I think the image transforms them into heroes and the hollow criticism directed at them only points to the folly of those who think that the power they possess today will last for ever; indeed, that contempt may have been the first sign of the racism that would later spread like an epidemic through Israeli political society.

That discussion is of no interest to me. I love the image of the slaughtered sheep – an emotion I may have acquired from my Christian mother who, whenever she looked at the picture of her brother Daoud, who'd been lost to exile, would say he looked like a sheep because there was something about his features of the Lord Jesus, peace be upon him.

The idea for the story had nothing to do, however, with the "sheep that is driven to the slaughter and never opens its mouth", as per the Prophet Isaiah; rather, it was conceived when I saw Tawfiq Saleh's movie "The Duped", a Syrian production directed by an Egyptian and based on the novel *Men in the Sun* by Ghassan Kanafani, a Palestinian. The movie shook me to the core; it made me reread the book and decide to write this story.

I didn't like the cry at the end of the novel. The three Palestinians who got into a water tanker, driven by a man whose name and appearance are shrouded in mystery, died of suffocation in the tank, in which they were supposed to be smuggled from Basra in Iraq to the "paradise" of Kuwait. They died in that inferno before crossing the Iraq–Kuwait border and they did nothing, causing the novel to scream into the driver's ears that near-stifled "Why?" The Egyptian director, Tawfiq Saleh, changed the ending, though, so that instead of us asking the three Palestinians why they hadn't banged on the side of the tank, as in the novel, we instead see their hands banging on the sides of film and tank alike.

In both mediums, however, the banging is meaningless as it would have been impossible for the Kuwaiti border officials, barricaded inside their offices, their ears deafened by the sound of the air conditioners, to hear anything, thus making the real question not the silence of the Palestinians but the deafness of the world to their cries.

I'd thought the perspective from which I would write my novel would be different: I wouldn't devote a single word to Palestine and that would save me from the slippery slope that turned Kanafani's novel into an allegory whose elements you have to deconstruct to get to what the author wanted to say.

I don't feel comfortable with messages in literature. Literature is like love: it loses its meaning when turned into a medium for something else that goes beyond it, because nothing goes beyond love, and nothing has more meaning than the stirrings of the human soul whose pulse is to be felt in literature.

I repeat: literature exists without reference to any meaning located outside it, and I want Palestine to become a text that exists without reference to its current historical conditionality, because, based on my long experience of that country, I've come to believe that nothing lasts but the relationship to the *adim* – the skin – of the land, from which derives the name of Adam, peace be upon him, that they gave me when I was born. My name, going back to Our Lord Adam, was the first signifier, and it alludes to a man's relationship to his death.

Waddah al-Yaman fashioned an astonishing love story, one not lived by any lover before or since. He was unique among his kind – a poet who played with words, rested on rhymes, rode rhythm. In the end, he decided to keep silent to save his beloved and died as die the heroes of unwritten stories.

It never occurred to him to bang on the sides of the coffer, and I, unlike Kanafani, will never ask him that wretched "Why?"

I shall let him die and shall live his last moments in the coffer with him, and I shall give his mistress – for whom Arabic literature provides no name other than the conventional Umm al-Banin, or "Mother of the Sons" – a name, and so make of her death a final cry of love that will ensure the story a place in the ranks of those of "the lover's demise". This mistress – the caliph's wife – was, I hereby declare, called Rawd, meaning "meadow". I give her that name because the poet's love for her began with a confusion over names, in that, following the death of his first beloved, Rawda, he found in Umm al-Banin both his meadow and his grave, and the two beloveds, both killed and both killers, became confused in his mind, and he himself, through the silence that he chose as the correlate of his verse, became the victim, for the only correlate of poetry are the interstices of silence, whose rhythms are matched precisely to those of the soul.

The Life and Sufferings of the Poet
Waddah al-Yaman
(POINT OF ENTRY 2)

Said the transmitter:

> "*O Rawda of Waddah,*
> *Waddah of Yemen you have exhausted and distressed!*
> *Revive then your lover with a draught*
> *of a clear wine by dirt unsoiled,*
> *Its scent that of quince,*
> *its taste that of wine from the cask, made of grapes unpressed.*
> *Two doves on a branch*
> *make me yearn for you to slake my thirst.*
> *The husband calls to his mate*
> *and each feeds the other with homely bliss.*"

So declaimed the lover to his beloved, but the poem got mixed up in the poet's head: of which Rawda did he write? Had the two women with the same name become one?

What is love? And how can passion so overwhelm us that we become its plaything and go to our fate unresisting?

What is this mystery, which caused a poet – who had gone almost insane as a result of his forced separation from his beloved Rawda and his collapse on seeing her in the valley of the lepers – to leave his homeland in the Arabian Peninsula for Syria, only to meet his end in a new love story?

Did his love of Rawda, the first, die when he encountered Rawd, the second?

How does love begin, and how does it disappear and die?

Ibn Hazm al-Andalusi, God have mercy on him, said, "Love is what the philosophers would call an accident, and an accident cannot be susceptible to other accidents. At the same time, it is an attribute, and attributes cannot be further qualified. The following discussion of love's accidents and attributes will, therefore, be metaphorical, and will put the attribute in the place of the thing that it qualifies." In classical Arabic literature, this "attribute", which swallows the thing described and thus becomes it, has led lovers to their destiny, and destiny is another name for fate, and fate is death. Love itself, however, does not become a destiny, nor is fate transformed into death, unless the poet weaves from it verses, turning the heart and its spasms into words, and eyes and their allure into mirrors. There is no love without an ode to love, no ode without a story that can be written in its margins, at which point the marginalia become a text and the original text a destiny. This is what the poets believed and this is what led lovers to tragedies, for their odes became tokens of their madness and their madness an embodiment of their passion.

Among the hundreds of books on love in the classical Arabic library, I feel a special closeness to *The Dove's Neck Ring*, compiled by Ibn Hazm in Seville, a province of Andalus, in 418 A.H. / A.D. 1027. In this book, which presents love's pain in prose narratives, and lovers' suffering in garlands of odes, I came across the most accurate definition of this emotion that consumes the mind and takes over the memory, turning imagination into a sort of sickness, a bane into a balm.

Ibn Hazm says, "Love, may God exalt you, begins in jest and

ends in seriousness. Its aspects are so majestic that they are too subtle to be described and its true nature can thus be known only through the experience of it." These words captivated me with their wisdom and their despair. Like everything said about this kind of emotion, however, the topic can be defined only in negative terms, for love can only be described through the endurance of pain, while pain has no names and no attributes.

What caught my attention in the description written by the learned scholar of Andalus was the relationship between "jest" and "seriousness", which sums up the relationship between love's beginning and its ending. Probably what the author meant by seriousness was the lived experience, the pain, and, perhaps, the death, but it never occurred to him to deal with a more critical issue, namely the ending of love. Suddenly, the lover finds himself emptied of love, like a vessel whose water has been poured out. This is a seriousness that exceeds that described by the transmitters of love stories. They all halt at the separation, or at that parting of which al-Mutanabbi wrote that it leads at its most extreme to death. Nobody, however, has dared to open the door onto that greatest mystery lurking in the murk of the human soul, the one that obscures the moment when everything vanishes, the one whose pain exceeds all other. I'm not speaking here of the pain of the abandoned lover, of which the bellies of novels and other books are full, but of the pain of the lover who loses his love for no clear cause and finds himself empty and trivial and discovers within himself a deep despair – inspired by the self, not by others or by death.

It is around this despair that I shall write the story of my beautiful poet, Waddah al-Yaman – the tale of his love for two women and of how he died twice over.

Had I the daring of those who write autobiographies, I would write of my own sorrow and pain. I wouldn't do so because Dalia left me when debilitated by the film she was making about her friend Assaf who committed suicide, but because, with no warning – with no warning, I swear to God! – and for no clear cause, I woke up one day from a heavy sleep, one swimming in the humidity and the suffocating heat of Jaffa, to find that my love, which had lasted ten whole years, had evaporated. I felt that all things were vanity. How could I not have been patient, after all those years during which I'd suffered pain, jealousy and fear, with the woman in whom I had seen all that was most beautiful, most pure, and most tender? Dalia was the light of my eyes. I beheld how she radiated love, and glowed, and I could see light and grope my way through the shadows cast by that light and by joy. Logically, I should have been patient with her in her moment of greatest trial, when it was revealed how her friend Assaf had died. He was fifteen years her junior and was to her like a son whom she'd brought up. She used to tell me of his fragility and say that within him was an artist who wouldn't be able to bear his compulsory military service in the Israeli army. And in the midst of her work on a film about a friend of Assaf's who was the first Israeli to be killed in the second Palestinian *intifada*, Assaf committed suicide, leaving a videotape similar to those left by Palestinian suicide bombers before they go to their death. That day, Dalia had a nervous breakdown and told me, as we discussed her decision to stop working in the cinema, that she didn't love me and was going to disappear from my life for ever.

I knew she loved me, that what she had told me was just an expression of the crisis in our relationship and that it was up to me to wait for her, and that in fact is what I'd decided to do. I knew love is the art of waiting, had practised that art throughout the years of my relationship with Dalia, and was prepared to do so again and enter the worlds of patience and latency, but I suddenly felt, as I sipped my early-morning coffee and dreamed of a cold shower to remove the traces of the humid night from my eyes and body, that I was mediocre and empty and that I would never love the woman again, or want to wait for her. In fact, I wanted to escape this place that was suffocating me and forget the woman, whose magic had suddenly vanished as though it had never been.

I was struck by grief, not because I'd lost her when she went off I know not where, but because I'd lost myself. I discovered that the greatest pain comes not from love but from its loss, and that I had entered the maelstrom in which the self despairs of itself, which would lead me six months later to emigrate to America and to work in this restaurant. That's another story, of interest to no-one, differing from the rest only in that it doesn't interest me either, because it was just a way of using time to kill time, or so I thought until the phantom of Waddah al-Yaman returned to occupy my imagination as my desired image, my dream that had gone unrealised both in writing and in love.

Who was Waddah al-Yaman?

I first met with Waddah al-Yaman in a book. It was 1978 and I was teaching literature and language at the Haifa school. I was teaching the boys the rules of Arabic grammar and struggling with the dual endings, unable to comprehend why they hadn't been dropped from Arabic as they had from all other ancient languages and not knowing how to rescue myself from the trap of that tongue whose music enchanted me but whose rules I found myself incapable of teaching because I'd ejected them from my memory the moment I joined the Hebrew Literature department at Haifa University. A colleague advised me to read *The Book of Songs* by Abu al-Faraj al-Isfahani, and in that unrivalled encyclopaedia of verse and song I encountered my poet.

Or rather, no. Before encountering him, I'd mastered the dual and fallen in love with it, discovering that the gateway to the language of the Arabs and their poetry was that relationship between the "I" and its shadow that had been wrought by Arabic's master poet, Imru' al-Qays al-Kindi al-Yamani, our grandsire, teacher and caravan-leader to the paradise of music and verse.

Imru' al-Qays wasn't a lover like those who came after him, and it is claimed, though only God knows, that the poet never even existed, an opinion advanced by the dean of Arabic Literature, Taha Hussein, in his *On Pre-Islamic Poetry*. Likewise, that the famous story about his lost kingdom was simply an indirect expression of the story of a certain notable of Kinda and his relationship with Islam. Even the existence of a noble saying by the Prophet Muhammad that "the King Errant" would lead the poets into hellfire failed to budge the Egyptian writer – regarded as a founding father of Arab cultural modernism – from his conviction.

I don't care whether Imru' al-Qays was real or invented – what would "real" mean here anyway? We have a story associated with this poet and we have his poems, which is enough to make him real, more real in fact than reality itself. It follows that I fail to understand how writers can defend their heroes by saying they're fictional and not factual. Phooey to them! I consider Hamlet to be more real than Shakespeare, the Idiot more tangible than Dostoevsky, Yunis more factual than that Lebanese writer who distorted his image in *Gate of the Sun*, etc. (Here I will have to make a footnote to say that I know Khalil Ayoub, narrator of *Gate of the Sun*, personally. Indeed, I'd go so far as to say that I know all the characters in the novels I like just as well as I know Khalil Ayoub.)

Imru' al-Qays taught me the dual, by which the poet's ego is divided in two, becoming the mirror of a self that refracts against the poet's shadows in the desert, and the dialogue between ego and ego becomes the starting point for the relationship between words and music.

Getting to know Imru' al-Qays wasn't enough for me. I journeyed through the *Book of Songs* as though on a visit to my memory and observed how my very self had become the receptacle for a literary, poetic and linguistic storm that shook my being to the core and also turned me into two men dwelling in one body. Suddenly, the Arab asleep within me encountered the Israeli citizen who would move from teaching to writing for a small Israeli newspaper published in Tel Aviv. That too is a story that has nothing to do with our current topic and that I believe to be of strictly personal significance.

In the *Songs*, I came across Waddah al-Yaman, but the only thing about him that caught my attention was his beauty. His is one of the rare instances in the classical literature in which a man is described as beautiful, and his beauty was of such powerful impact that the man was obliged to cover his face. The poetry of his to be found in his collected works, however, falls short of the level achieved by the love poetry of his day. His meagre output cannot be compared to that of Qays ibn al-Mulawwah al-Majnun – "the Madman" – or Jamil, or Umar ibn Abi Rabia, and even though I read the moving story of his death, I failed to notice its significance and importance; I read through the story without paying it much attention, thinking it a fabrication of the imagination and tending to the view that Waddah al-Yaman wasn't a real poet but a romantic love story to which some verses had been added to provide its hero with a certain nobility. (In those days it was enough for a man to be a poet to attain a social rank that raised him above others.)

The ancient Arabs built their literary legend on the triad poet–prophet–king. This schema began with Imru' al-Qays, who was a poet and a king, and reached its apogee with al-Mutanabbi, who was a poet and a prophet and aspired to kingship. The traces of this schema remain engraved on Arabic poetry, like a watermark, to this day.

Our relationships with poets begin with a love of their verses. Without such love, the poet loses his personal presence in our lives and we forget his story, or so I believed until I met the Palestinian poet Rashed Hussein. I first became acquainted with Rashed through Mahmoud Darwish's poem "He Was What He Became" and was startled by Darwish's daring in comparing the man to a field of potatoes and maize, telling myself that a man who was like a field of potatoes would have to be a great poet indeed. I read Rashed's three collections of verse and felt let down: I liked his poetry but felt it was pre-poetry, that he was paving the way for the other poets who came after him and writing the sort of spelling-out of the self that precedes mastery of the language in which it is expressed.

When, though, I looked at the picture of the poet on the cover of a book published in America and edited by Kamal Boullata and Mirene Ghossein, I was amazed – a beautiful man carrying within him a brilliance that shone out through his eyes and a poet who wrote his own story by dying by fire in a small apartment in New York.

I found the book at the Strand bookstore on 12th Street in Manhattan in the midst of a display of second-hand books at the entrance and I paid just one dollar for it. The story of this Palestinian poet's death in a fire caused by alcohol and his burning cigarette drove me to reread his poems, and I felt that his story was his poetry, and that the sorrow manifested through his words was simply an introduction to the story of his death.

Rashed Hussein didn't die from love or because of it. He died of despair, and his despair then resembles mine now. The poet died a hero of his own story. I, on the other hand, don't have the courage to commit suicide, which is why I cannot write my own story the way heroes do. On the contrary, I have to write their stories in order to come close to myself, and by making up stories conceal my inability to be a hero.

It was from this perspective that I rediscovered Waddah al-Yaman, and the story of his love and death, which had seemed to me naive thirty years earlier, took on a new meaning, not just as a metaphor that could serve to express the events of the Palestinian Nakba, as that first reading had seemed to indicate, with the lover choosing silence to protect his beloved, but as an expression of what follows the despair that comes when love dies and dissipates. Thus, the poet's death in silence becomes the meaning of the meaning, or the moment at which life acquires meaning through death.

I shall have to write the story twice. The first time as the story of the demise of the lover who seeks to protect his beloved's life and honour, the second as the story of the death that comes to give vanishing emotions a meaning.

Waddah al-Yaman's story, like that of other lovesick swains, began with love. He fell in love with a young woman and wrote of her and for her, so to avoid scandal her family married her off to someone else, and the poet went insane. In its early stages,

Waddah's story resembles that of "Mad-over-Layla". Qays ibn al-Mulawwah went insane not because he loved, but because he spoke his love and proclaimed it, the story thus becoming part of his poetry, the man evaporating and being so thoroughly subsumed into it that many scholars have expressed doubt as to his existence, regarding him as mere legend and claiming that most of his verse is misattributed.

Waddah al-Yaman was a poet who went mad, and his story almost fell into the oblivion of the lepers' valley, where his first beloved was buried alive. Waddah al-Yaman's greatness, however, lies in his ability to transcend the clamour of words and reveal the eloquence of silence. This is why he died in the cruel way that he did, proclaiming silence as the highest level of speech because it holds within it the eloquence of life, which exceeds in its expressive capacity any rhetorical form that language can devise.

(Note: It seems that instead of writing his story, I'm analysing a story that has never been written, which is one of the drawbacks of the profession I chose for myself. I decided for no clear reason, and after obtaining my qualification in Hebrew literature from the University of Tel Aviv, to become a teacher. And instead of my being attached to a Hebrew school, they sent me to the Wadi al-Nisnas school in Haifa and gave me Arabic literature to teach. In flight from the dolors and incoveniences of that profession, I went to Tel Aviv, where I worked in journalism and ended up being neither one thing nor the other, which is another story that this isn't the place for.)

The Madness of the Lover
(POINT OF ENTRY 3)

Said the transmitter:

"How am I to describe Waddah al-Yaman to you? I fear my words may lead you where I do not want to go, and instead of being a guide to my poet become a trap, and that you will think that the man, whose beauty bewitched the women of his age, was effeminate. (I use the word 'beauty' here rather than 'good looks' in view of the fact that writers of the modern age commonly use the latter to refer to male beauty, 'beauty' having come to be thought of, for reasons I know not, as feminine or effeminate. Given that the word 'beauty' is indeed feminine, I can describe beauty only in feminine terms, for it is both effeminate and feminising, like literature, which only becomes literature when feminised by language, and when it has been given the transparency of water, and the bashfulness of eyes.)"

The man was in love, and love is the opposite of manliness. It takes what we give the name of manliness – generally a collection of empty claims fatal to the emotions – to its extreme, where it dissolves in the femininity of water and attires itself in the translucent whiteness of death.

If Waddah al-Yaman were to speak, he would describe to us the whiteness in which he drowned and how he discovered in the darkness of the coffer of his love a whiteness words cannot encompass.

Said the transmitter:

"Waddah, meaning Luminous, was an epithet he acquired due to his beauty and brilliance. His real name was Abd al-Rahman ibn Ismail ibn Abd Kulal. Many stories are told of his strange beauty. He had a fair complexion, reddish hair, a comely face, fine features and a distant gaze, as though light shone through his eyes.

"The transmitters differ as to his lineage. One story claims he was a descendant of 'the Sons', i.e. of the Persians whom Sayf ibn Dhi Yazan called to his aid against the Abyssinians in Yemen; another that his father died when he was a child and that his mother then married a Persian, which is where the confusion lies. In reality, the man was a Himyarite on his father's and grandfather's side, a Kindite on his grandmother's."

The transmitters trace the story of the epithet that became his name to the conflict that arose, between his mother's husband on the one hand and his paternal uncle and grandmother on the other, over which tribe he should belong to. They went (as the author of *The Songs* relates) to the ruler, and he ruled in favour of Waddah's uncle. "And when the ruler ruled in favour of the Himyarites, he passed his hand over the boy's head and was taken by his beauty, and he said, 'Go, for thou art *Waddah al-Yaman* – Yemen's luminous child – not a follower of Dhi Yazan!'"

The lack of clarity over his origins had an effect on his story as a poet. This began when he fell prey to passion and became enamoured of Rawda, but this love of her and the madness to which it drove him were not the end of it, as another woman was to appear in his life and make of his death a mirror of the confusion that perplexed both transmitters and critics.

From the moment the ruler gave the youth who had been known as Abd al-Rahman ibn Ismail the name Waddah al-Yaman, his life changed and he came to have two names, a name for oblivion and a name for remembrance: Abd al-Rahman was forgotten and he became Waddah. Legends were woven around his beauty, one of which claims that for fear of its disruptive effect on women, he used to go about wearing a mask.

Said the transmitter:

"Waddah al-Yaman, as well as the Masked Man of Kinda, and Abu Zubayd al-Ta'i, used to attend the festivals of the Arabs wearing masks, covering their faces for fear of the evil eye and to guard themselves, they were so beautiful, against the women."

The story began when the young man tore off his mask and stood before a brook, drinking in with his eyes a beauty that presented itself to him as the image, reflected in water, of a young woman, who looked, as she gathered up the skirts of her dress to reveal legs like marble, like some nymph emerging from the stream and carrying in her eyes the tremulous shadows made upon its surface by a ben tree.

Rawda, a girl of sixteen, belonged to the Kinda, tribe of the kings of the Arabs, from which came Imru' al-Qays, greatest of the poets of the Arabic language. The girl raised her skirts and put her feet in the water. When the poet noticed her, he tore off his mask and stood spellbound by the magic of her beauty.

Love stories usually elide the beginning at the very time that they pretend to recount it. What the transmitters fail to mention is that Waddah al-Yaman's mask fell from his face when he ran towards the image of the girl reflected in the water. He reached the brook, bent to drink, and the girl had no choice but to withdraw and take refuge in the shadows of the ben tree. As the water rose in his hands towards his mouth, he noticed that the girl didn't rise with it, so he turned around, but he couldn't see her, so he sat down at the edge of the brook to wait.

Probably the girl rebuked him and asked him to leave, so he asked her to appear so that he could see her. He said he was Waddah al-Yaman and that his mask had fallen off because of her, and he asked her to come forward so that he might see her but she refused. Indeed, she reviled him for his impertinence, and so on and so forth.

The first encounter was one of vituperation, and not, as the poets would have it, of epiphany. The girl wasn't bowled over by Waddah's beauty and paid no attention to his beautiful words. She emerged from her hiding place and looked at him with the contempt of a woman who knows she has before her a man who has built his reputation on his attractiveness, and she said he was not as beautiful as she had expected and left.

(Note: The first encounter between Waddah and Rawda resembles that of another Omayyad poet and his beloved. Jamil ibn Maamar, who took his beloved's name as his second and became known as Jamil-Buthayna, refers to his first encounter with her in terms of a quarrel that reached the point of insult:

The first thing that led to affection between us
at Wadi Baghid, dear Buthayna, was an altercation –
We made some comment and she answered right back –
for every query, dear Buthayna, has its refutation.

This similarity puzzles the critics as it implies that what is passed down is not a factual report but a text containing a good measure of imagination and depending on the replication of a ready-made formula. In return, though, in my opinion, it confirms the importance of the fictional story, its superiority to the factual report, and its ability to convey the diversity of human experience – unlike the true report, which pales in comparison and may have no significance worth mentioning, though that's something else I don't want to get into now.)

Returning to my poet, I must tell you that his first encounter with Rawda took place at the Yemeni village of al-Khasib, in an area known for its abundance of water, verdant plains and fields of wild flowers scattered here and there. It is said, though only God knows, that Waddah felt the tingle of poetry fermenting in his veins and wrote numerous verses but didn't dare to recite them publicly because the poetry was as yet only incompletely formed in his heart and sensibility, and that the daemon, or spirit-companion, or faery, of poetry that dictates to poets their verses had yet to appear to him. (That was what people thought then, and the poets believed them and took to waiting for their faeries to turn up and trim the meanings and the music inside them into shape.) So he went to al-Khasib in search of his absent spirit-companion and sat down in the shade of a ben tree, shaded in turn by a holm oak, to wait for it, the water of the brook before him reflecting in its mirrors the colours of the land; and that was where he saw her and that was where he bent over the water to drink her reflected shadow.

That day, the beautiful Himyarite youth became a poet, and that day he drew his beloved with words.

The young man returned to the brook the next day and saw her again, as though she were waiting for him, and recited to her his first ode, which became his path to the Kindite girl's heart, and the story began.

Like all lovers' stories of the period, it was loaded onto the poem's back, for verse isn't just the Arabs' collected poetical works, it is also the repository of their legends. Without it, there are no stories, and without the stories the poetry withers and dies away.

Now begins the tragedy, for Rawda's parents weren't simply hostile to the poet, they actually married their daughter off to another man. And the story doesn't end there: the marriage to an older man brought about Rawda's death in that appalling fashion and led the poet to lose his wits.

Waddah drew a picture of Rawda in his verse. She was full-breasted, pure of mien, polished of forehead (the latter embellished with blonde hair the colour of the tail of a bay horse), her eyebrows perfectly arched, her eyes as dark as night, her nose chiselled, her arms plump, her hands soft, her waist narrow . . . a sixteen-year-old girl, forced to marry a man of sixty and be his fourth wife – the final stop on the itinerary of his pleasures before pleasure itself dried up and the stooped body fell apart.

Before the marriage, the poet had believed that the story was the truth and that it had swathed him in the character of Antara al-Absi, the poet and knight who fought to reach his beloved, Abla, and whose sword was his sign, his verse his new lineage – a poet who was a slave turned, by virtue of his verse, into a lord and a lord turned into a knight, the poet's dark skin, once a barrier between him and the lords of his tribe, becoming his mark of distinction, his blackness a foil for the whiteness of his blade.

Waddah believed the story. He was the slim youth who had encountered his beloved, after which they would pick wild flowers and gather truffles, which he would grill for her, and he would drink to her health and suck the wild flowers from her lips while declaiming poetry to her about his love.

Rawda passed a message to him that her seven brothers had shut her away, that his poetry, which had achieved worldwide

fame, had made her an object of scandal, and that she feared
for him:

> *"Don't hang around our house!" said she –*
> *"A jealous man is my father."*
> *Said I, "Then I'll wait for a moment of inadvertence,*
> *and my sword is resolute, a hacker."*
> *Said she, "Around me next are seven brothers."*
> *Said I, "I am a conqueror, an overcomer."*
> *Said she, "You've exhausted all our arguments!*
> *Come, then, when sleeps the night reveller*
> *And fall upon us as falls the dew*
> *on a night when there is no proscriber and no scolder."*

Rawda listened to his poem and was intoxicated. She watched
as the poetry of this Waddah transformed itself into a robe for her
woven from the silk of words, and she put it on and it became
her second body, and instead of telling him not to come because
her brothers were getting ready to kill him, she made an arrange-
ment with him to come the evening of that very day and told
him she'd be waiting for him in her tent. All he had to do was creep
into the encampment by night and she would come out to him.

The lovers believed the poetry and called the truth a lie!

That night, Waddah al-Yaman fell into an ambush set by the
seven brothers. When the poet found himself within death's
grasp, he tugged on his horse's reins and decided to flee, at which
point he heard a ringing laugh and a voice asking him sarcastically
about the "hacker" of a sword that the poet had mentioned in
his poem, which was now on everyone's lips and tongue. The poet
then turned back, realising that his verse had killed him, and

plunged into his brief battle, which ended with him perforated with wounds, prostrate in the desert, moaning in his blood.

The story says that Abu Zubayd al-Ta'i passed the poet as he lay dying and took him on his mount to his people, where he stayed for a year, on his back, suffering bouts of fever in which he beheld the phantom of his beloved, slain at the hands of the seven brothers, the blood pouring from her every part.

When the fever left him, the wound to his belly had healed over, and he was cured, he discovered that the fever's nightmares had been less cruel than the reality of his healed state. They told him Rawda had been married off to an older man who had, it seemed, concealed from her family that he was a leper, and that the husband had died a few days after the marriage. Rawda, though, had been afflicted with the accursed disease and her family had thrown her into the lepers' valley, where the sick live in total isolation, receiving only crumbs of food donated by well-doers and waiting to die while suffering bodily torment and spiritual anguish.

Waddah didn't write any verses about his visit to his beloved in the lepers' valley. He mentioned that he visited her but didn't mention what he saw or what she said to him or he to her. All we know about the visit is that, on his return, the poet tore his clothes, rolled in the dust, and went mad, and that he stopped writing poetry.

Said the transmitter:

"Yemeni men of learning familiar with the reports of Waddah and Rawda told me that Waddah was on a journey with his friends and that along the way he asked them to halt and for a while left the path they were on, then came back to them in tears. They asked him what was wrong and he said, 'I turned from the path to see Rawda, and found that she had become a leper and had been thrown out of her town. So I did what I could to help her and gave her some of my money,' and he started weeping out of sorrow for her."

In another version of the report, the poet recovered from his wounds a year after taking to his bed and left for the area of al-Khasib in search of his beloved. On the way there, a company of people saw him and told him Rawda had been stricken with leprosy and thrown into the lepers' valley, so he went there in search of her, declaiming:

O Rawda of Waddah, O best of Rawdas,
  for your family, should they bestow on us a place to stay,
Your ransom is a Waddah whom you drove mad –
  so, if you wish to cure, then cure, and if you wish to slay, then slay.

The poet reached the valley only to be taken aback when he found his resolve giving way. He'd gone to Rawda with the resolve of a knight, intending to die with her. He'd made a decision: he would vanquish death with his love. But when he saw her and how the light in those beautiful eyes had gone dead, how her skin peeled and her eyebrows sagged, he was overtaken by fear, his chivalrous urges evaporated, and he felt a desire to flee. Rawda approached him, holding out her arms and moaning softly, so he took some money from his pocket, threw it at her, and began to back away. The woman, skin peeling, body wasted, stretched out her arms to the man standing in front of her as though she wanted to fly, but instead of flying upwards she collapsed as though felled. She covered her face with her hands and her head began swaying from side to side, as though she wanted to say and not say.

The woman didn't bend down to pick up the money. She let her beloved retreat and sat down on the ground, then dismissed him with a gesture of her hand.

The transmitter doesn't say what the poet said about his trip to see his beloved and how he'd fled the place at a run, flinging his love aside out of fear of death, escaping to save his life from love.

Thereafter, the poet ceased to be Waddah of Yaman and became Waddah the Madman, lost in the wastes, eating weeds and sleeping under the open sky. The beautiful young man's mask became a token of his fear of himself and of others. All that was left of the love were the poems, and of the passion the memories, which putrefied like the body of a leper.

The only hope of the poet's escaping his wilderness and his ever-deeper descent into incoherence and insanity lay in his urge to make the pilgrimage to God's Holy House in Mecca, to make the circumambulation and to throw the stones, and thereby perhaps reclaim his soul from the devil that had made it his dwelling place.

When I read this story, as told in Arabic literature, I thought that the story of Waddah and Rawda was a retelling of the story of Qays, or "Mad-over-Layla", the parents of whose beloved refused to let him marry her because he'd written about her in poems, a refusal that drove him to insanity, for which he attempted to find a cure by making the pilgrimage to Mecca. However, I was wrong.

The error arose from the transmitter's neglect of what befell the poet when he met his beloved in the lepers' valley. This neglect was deliberate, as what happened disturbed the schema of the victim-lover transformed into a source for an oral heritage that tells how love leads to the death, or madness, of lovers.

Waddah al-Yaman's madness reveals another face of insanity,

that brought about by fear of the consequences of love, or fear of life, which is another name for fear of death.

Love ends in madness. Despite this, madness, or the attempt to cure it by making pilgrimage and praying, ushers in the beginning of a new chapter in the story of Waddah al-Yaman.

Confusions over the Name
(POINT OF ENTRY 4)

Said the transmitter:

"Umm al-Banin, daughter of Abd al-Aziz ibn Marwan, asked permission of al-Walid ibn Abd al-Malik to make the pilgrimage and he granted it, he being then the caliph, she his wife. She arrived, bringing with her slave girls of a beauty never before seen, and al-Walid wrote threatening all poets with dire consequences should any of them mention her name or that of anyone in her entourage. She arrived and was seen by the people, and the philanderers and poets came out to see her, and her eye fell on Waddah al-Yaman, and she fell in love."

What occurred between this woman and the poet who appeared to those who saw him in Mecca as a bag of bones, a phantom, aimlessly wandering, his glances unfocused as though he could not see, his lips cracked from thirst, forever bursting into prayer, falling to the ground, sluggishly rising again and looking about him as though fearful of the wraiths of love that pursued him, the words crumbling on his lips as Rawda's skin had crumbled from leprosy?

And what could this woman have hoped to gain by dallying with poetry and poets?

It is said, though God alone knows, that Umm al-Banin wanted to play the game of love-through-poetry, as was the fashion among noble-born women of Quraysh at the time, and to feel that she'd entered the annals of the Arabs in the form of an ode written in praise of her beauty. She hoped the poets would write erotic verse about her as they had about her sister-in-law Fatima, daughter of Abd al-Malik and wife of Umar ibn Abd al-Aziz, and about Sakina, daughter of al-Husein, and as they did about every noble-born Arab woman. She therefore asked Kuthayyir-Azza and Waddah al-Yaman to mention her in their verse. Kuthayyir was scared and limited his verses to one of her slave girls, whose name was Ghadira. The verses of Waddah al-Yaman, however, became his shroud, and another door leading to his tragedy.

The new story began in jest and ended in seriousness, *à la* Ibn Hazm.

The jest was from the caliph's wife, who took the game to its outer limits. The seriousness fell to the lot of our poet, who awoke from the daze of his madness into a yet greater daze, entering with this woman into the labyrinths of the name.

The story says that Umm al-Banin had first wanted Kuthayyir-Azza, a poet celebrated for his love of a woman called Azza, which had transported him to such an extreme of lovelornness that he'd abandoned his own second name and taken that of his beloved. Furthermore, he'd followed her to Egypt, where she lived with her husband, finding expression for his love by walking in her footsteps.

The caliph's wife had learned by heart a poem of Kuthayyir's in which he speaks of his beloved as though she were divine—

Were they to hear Azza, as I have, speaking,
*   they'd drop to their knees before her in prostration—*

and she asked the poet to deify her too. The poet to whom this line is attributed stood before Umm al-Banin, shaking with fear.

He told her that he didn't dare, and she replied that she couldn't believe it. He said he feared the caliph's wrath and had no desire to purchase death with a poem.

No, that's not how it went.

The story says that Kuthayyir was famous for his ugliness – a short man with a hideous face, and stupid – and people used to make fun of him. Azza fled him, and everything he said about his affair with her came from the workings of his own imagination. Despite this, Umm al-Banin wanted him for the purity of his style and his expressive power. When the slave girl Ghadira brought him to her, she was revolted by his ugliness and refused to remove her veil.

Kuthayyir abased himself before the woman, asking her to excuse him the assignment or the two lines he'd compose for her would cost him his life. The woman got on her high horse and said he was a liar and the transmitters of his verse were liars too, because it was Waddah al-Yaman who had deified his beloved and Kuthayyir had simply stolen al-Waddah's poem and changed Rawda's name to Azza's. Then she drove him from her parlour.

This is where the first chapter of the woman's jesting comes to an end, leaving her with the feeling that her visit to the Hejaz had been a failure and that she would never return home with an ode to immortalise her name in the corpus of Arabic poetry and the collections of lovers' verse.

(Note: The issue that puzzles me as I read this story is the obsession of the powerful with literature. What was this infatuation with poetry that made kings, princes and governors captives of the never-ending search for the word that would enroll them in the world of literature? Why were they so convinced that literature was a door to immortality that Seif al-Dawla, Prince of Aleppo, was willing to allow al-Mutanabbi to sit beside him and recite his verses and even allow the poet to praise himself in the same text in which he praised his patron?

Should this impel us to take another look at the post-classical critics' attack on praise poetry as a form of humiliation for the poet, who had to sacrifice his pride and dignity to make money? Does the former supposition mean that the phenomenon of the eulogy points not to a failure in the poetry but, more accurately, to a failure in the authority, which found itself obliged to submit to the word in its search for immortality, which can be forged only through literature and art?

This is the delusion, and the weakness, of power, for immortality is a delusion of the living, not a concern of the dead, albeit the living can read their inevitable deaths only within the framework of what they can grasp rationally and understand. This is why they deal with their deaths as though they were going to live for ever and seek immortality for their names in the register of the living – because of the register of the dead they know nothing.

Kings seek their immortality in poetry, but poetry isn't good enough for poets, who want to turn it into prophecy, or something like it, so that they can add immortality of name to immortality of authority and then manipulate people and rule their lives from behind the veil of death.

A vicious circle of illusion and the search for further illusion.)

Umm al-Banin discovered that this, the most beautiful of Arab men, was given to circumambulating the Holy House. She hesitated, however, to become involved with him, because of his madness. After all, she'd gone there to gambol on the shores of love, not fall prey to the attractions of a man of whose beauty so much had been made, one who was an embodiment of the beauty of Joseph (who almost met his end as a result of his affair with Zuleika, as recounted in the Noble Book). She had heard, moreover, that the man had gone mad following his beloved's forced marriage and affliction with leprosy. The seductive qualities of poetry were, however, too strong to resist, and she decided there was no point in sending her slave girl to him, as she had done with Kuthayyir, and that she would have to make her own way to "Crazy Waddah".

She went to him with her face unveiled. She left her bed-chamber wearing a slave girl's clothes and accompanied by her slave Ghadira, and she walked unveiled through the alleys of Mecca, the way slave girls did in those days, searching for her prey. The slave pointed out where the young man with the cracked lips walked, dazed, through the streets, as though seeing nothing. She approached him and asked him his name. The man turned, saw a face effulgent with beauty and desire, but bowed his head and looked at the ground.

Waddah stood rooted to the spot. The woman's beauty dazzled him, and he sensed for an instant a thrill of desire. Then he went his way. She caught up with him and gave him a pitcher of water.

"You are thirsty," she said. "Take this and drink. Your lips seek water."

He mumbled that all the water in the world couldn't quench his thirst.

The lovely woman didn't catch what he said but she held the pitcher out to him and he saw her soft hands and the gleam of her fingertips and said, "No," making as though to leave.

The woman grasped him by the wrist and cried out, "I am Rawd!"

Where had Rawda sprung from, that she should suddenly

appear at the place where he was seeking to cure his insanity with disoriented wandering and minister to his morbid fear of love with love?

"You are Waddah al-Yaman," said the woman. "Come!"

The man followed the two women without knowing what he was doing. Was he alive or dead? Was he seeing things as they really were or had the phantom of his beloved Rawda appeared before him?

When he reached where the woman was staying and saw the beautiful slave girls around her, he understood that God had accepted his prayer and that he was meeting his beloved once more, reunited with her in death.

He sat before her and drank until he was satisfied, then recited three lines of verse:

God knows, did I desire to find within myself
    yet more of love for Rawda, I'd find no augmentation.
The monks of Madyan, as I've observed,
    weep for fear of Hell, yet maintain a seated station.
Were they to hear her, as I have, speaking,
    they'd drop to their knees before her in prostration.

She asked him about his cracked lips, and he said he'd decided to treat the thirst of love with the thirst of lips. He said nothing resembles love so much as thirst for water because love is the water of the soul, and he'd decided to punish himself because he'd abandoned his beloved when he saw her diseased body cracking open and her soul wandering blindly among the shadows of death.

The words came.

From the man who hadn't said a single word since he'd found

himself confronted with his beloved's illness and who people believed had been struck with insanity in the shape of silence, the words flowed like water, while the woman, who had wanted only to dally with poetry and poets, found herself captive to a feeling she'd never known before because she was living it for the first time in her life.

She began to laugh and cry, approach and withdraw, listen to the poetry and drink in the words, stretch out her hand to Waddah and fly with him, as he with her.

She questioned him and he questioned her. She kissed him and he kissed her, and instead of asking him to write verse about her, she became herself the poem. She surrendered to the rhythm that enfolded her and entered into the rhyming magic that we call passion, and she understood why the Omayyad poet al-Farazdaq, on passing a mosque in Kufa and hearing a man reciting from the Suspended Ode of Labid, had prostrated himself. Asked why, he replied, "Your vocation is the prostration of the Koran, mine the prostration of poetry."

That day, the woman came to know the prostration of poetry, so she prostrated herself, and she came to learn the meaning of love, so she loved.

What happened that day?

Did things really get mixed up in the poet's head, making him believe he was face to face with his beloved Rawda, now cured? Or had his heart – fickle like those of all sons of Adam – found in this woman a new love that made him forget the old?

And was that new woman's name really "Rawd", as she claimed?

Fickleness was a curse with which our friend had been stricken without realising. Probably, Waddah felt the story was enough in itself. He saw himself at the peak of passion's mountain, the only way down from which leads to the valley of death, and he chose this ending, reminiscent of that of a hero in a story. He went mad, or pretended to, thereby elaborating a new chapter among the stories of those who lose their wits to love. When Qays's, or Mad-over-Layla's, beloved married, his love for her increased, for it was now joined by jealousy, transforming the embers into fire, obsession into insanity. Nothing sets love afire like jealousy – as though love needs that extra fire to turn the lover into a mass of flames and feelings and take him to an abasement beyond which there can be no other.

There can be no passion without this abasement, which breaks manhood down and forces the lover to turn into a simpleton, or a sucker, or a mixture of both.

Fate, however, willed that Waddah's story should take a different turn. The moment he saw Rawda's corroded body, the fires of jealousy died in his heart, and this made his story of mourning and despair different from those of his fellow lovers, because he discovered that as life rots in the beloved's body so love rots too.

Waddah al-Yaman went to Mecca to complete the story's circle by circumambulating the Black Stone, announcing, by so doing, that he had decided to bury himself inside his story.

Waddah al-Yaman didn't know that what he thought was the end of the story was in fact its beginning, that his tragic tale was just starting when he met the woman whom people called Umm al-Banin and who, face unveiled, barred his path in a Meccan alley-way so that she might invite him to the coffer of his death and of his love by proclaiming she was Rawd.

Were Waddah al-Yaman to speak, he'd tell us how the name

shook him to the core as it left the woman's lips, and how he felt it wrap itself around the woman's body, making it into a new form for his beloved.

Was this memory's trickery or its magic?

Waddah al-Yaman had no idea how the face before him had become the face of his beloved. He heard the name, and the features sketched themselves anew and the Rawd of now became the Rawda of then and the passion entered a new phase, one that none of the earlier poets of the age had entered.

Though here, perhaps, we should reference the story that brought about the death of Imru' al-Qays, namely, his love for the daughter of the Emperor of Byzantium. The poet and monarch of Kinda went to the emperor to ask for his support against his father's killers, but instead of returning in a royal procession to reclaim his lost throne, he returned with a poisoned cloak, given him by the emperor. The poet had fallen in love with the daughter of Byzantium's monarch, and his reward was a poisoned cloak that covered his body with sores like those of a leper. He died near Antioch, or according to another report, near Homs, and was buried next to a nameless woman stranger at the foot of a mound known as Jabal Assib.

Was the cloak the King Errant's coffer?

And was the first Rawda's leprosy a reiteration of the sores of Imru' al-Qays?

Waddah al-Yaman didn't dare compare himself to Imru' al-Qays, and it never crossed his mind to recite the King Errant's two famous lines, addressed to the woman lying at his side:

Neighbour, our graves lie close
        and what Assib once erected I dwell within.

Neighbour, we're two strangers here together,
and every stranger to every other is kin.

Did Waddah al-Yaman, at his death, confuse Qays ibn al-Mulawwah with Imru' al-Qays?

Such a confusion would probably have angered the two poets: the first was an Udhri poet who loved just one woman and adopted her name, the second a poet, king, drunkard and debauchee, to whom no woman was ever more than a passing fancy.

Stories, however, like lives, have their fates, which cannot be reversed.

The Coffer of Death
(POINT OF ENTRY 5)

Said the transmitter:

"No-one knows how the game turned to tragedy. The encounter with the caliph's wife who had left the palace with her face unveiled, dressed like a slave girl, was almost dreamlike.

"Waddah al-Yaman could believe neither his ears nor his eyes. He heard her say, 'I am Rawd!' and saw her as though seeing his murdered beloved, and his life became a dream from which he awoke only in the coffer of love, which the transmitters would refer to as the coffer of death."

Umm al-Banin was a dream. That's how the other poet, Ubaydallah ibn Qays al-Ruqayyat, saw her. But what was the relationship between this other Omayyad poet, Umm al-Banin, and her love story?

Ubaydallah ibn Qays al-Ruqayyat was poet to so many women that, instead of adopting the name of his first love, Ruqayya, according to the custom of the poets of the day, he took its plural, making Ruqayya into Ruqayyat. The man wasn't faithful to one woman, and it's likely that to him love was no more than the "ordered speech" of verse-making. He was, however, the master of a new genre of poetry to which the critics gave the name "the satirical love lyric". Its apogee was his love poetry addressed to Umm al-Banin, wife of the caliph al-Walid ibn Abd al-Malik, through which he sought to enrage and make a public spectacle of her husband.

This poet isn't going to find a place for himself in the story of Waddah al-Yaman. His love poem to Umm al-Banin, though scandalous and obscene by the standards of the day, played no role in deciding the fate of Waddah or that of the story's heroine. If I weren't such an admirer of that poem of his, I wouldn't have spent any time on it at all. In fact, I prefer to believe that al-Ruqayyat wasn't the author of the poem in question, that its attribution to him was due to the political struggles of the period, and that its true author must have been Waddah al-Yaman. Its svelte and magical lines must have been the message that preceded the latter to Damascus, to which he would go in search of his beloved after the queen returned to her own country.

Some may say I'm imitating Hammad, the great verse transmitter of the Abbasid age, who stands accused by the critics of having made up thousands of the lines of verse that he attributed to the pre-Islamic poets, as well as of attributing poems to people who didn't write them. Such a comparison makes no sense to me: I don't possess the talent of Hammad, who, if everything that is attributed to him were really his, would have been the greatest poet of the Arabic language bar none. By the same token, all I'm doing is following my intuition, which tells me that this poem will play a decisive role in settling the fate of the poet of the coffer.

After his meeting with her, the second Rawda, or Umm al-Banin, was transformed into a kind of dream. Before he left her tent, she asked him to come to Damascus and promised she would intercede on his behalf with her husband the caliph, after which he could write eulogies to him and live under his protection.

The second Rawda returned to Damascus, and Waddah fell captive to a new passion.

Was the first Rawda expunged, the new woman taking her

place? Or did the poet combine the two into one woman, as the writer of these lines tends to believe?

I prefer to suppose that he combined them, since the effort needed to accept the first supposition puts me off: exchanging a woman who had died, or was in the process of dying, of that particular disease of hers for another, strikes me as an act so immoral it would ruin the story and make it difficult to write. The literature of love cannot mirror human cruelty, which would reach a new zenith if the emotions were to be brutalised through a swap of the sort we are discussing here. Such an act would raise many questions as to the meaning of love; it might even turn love into an empty and meaningless word.

All the same, such things do in fact happen, which is why I'm confused.

The ancient transmitters of Waddah's story paid no attention to the apparent swap, and the shift of the Yemeni poet from a first love that ended with the beloved woman's death to a second that would end up killing the lover created no problem for them. They didn't question the meaning of this shift from an old passion to a new, both of them fatal. Were the transmitters seeking to establish a secondary parallelism that would point to the fact that love takes place between two deaths?

In our story, things are not so. Waddah was stricken with something akin to madness, and his encounter with the first Rawda in the lepers' valley, where he saw how his beloved's skin had cracked and her spirit been broken, was the moment that made him indifferent to everything and incapable of distinguishing between truth and illusion, or fact and fiction.

At the moment when Umm al-Banin, or the second Rawda, appeared, things got mixed up in his head. Once again, he found himself unable to tell where or who he was, or whom he was with, up to the moment when he found himself in the coffer.

Now let's get back to the story, where we discover that, on Umm al-Banin's return to Damascus, the poet became strangely enraptured with sleep and love, or with love while asleep, if one can speak of such a thing – a rapture that took the form of sleeping fits. No sooner would the poet wake than he'd fall asleep again. In the world of sleep, which became his refuge, he discovered tranquillity and love, and in his waking moments, when he would drink milk and chew on dates, poetry would come to him in the form of memories from his dozings. Stammering as he declaimed his poem – because he wasn't composing verse, he was remembering verse he'd composed while asleep – he would say of Rawda and Umm al-Banin, who had now become one person:

> For Umm al-Banin, when
> > her passion draws her close –
> In my sleep I saw her,
> > and while I took her said this verse:
> No sooner had I taken my pleasure in her
> > and her sweet lips had towards me turned
> Than I drank of her saliva till
> > my thirst was quenched, and I gave her to drink in turn,
> And I remained her happy bedfellow,
> > she pleasing me, I pleasing her,
> Making her laugh and making her cry,
> > being her vestment and stripping her bare.

When people told him, "Fool! Don't you know these verses will lead to your death?" he'd shrug his shoulders to show how little he cared.

Some transmitters state that this and other love poems like it weren't written by Waddah al-Yaman but by *jinn*: there was a *jinni* who had tasted the bitterness and terror of love and decided to make fun of it, so he'd appear to Waddah during his sleeping fits and dictate his poems on Umm al-Banin to him. Others set these poems within the framework of the bruising political struggles between the Omayyads and their enemies and attribute them to other poets. It was in this context that Ubaydallah Qays al-Ruqayyat made his appearance in the story and that the poem was attributed to him.

What matters as far as we're concerned is that word of these poems reached Umm al-Banin, who was now living in Damascus; she discovered that her game had turned serious, and that the only thing she now wanted was her beloved.

All she did about it was order her slave girl Ghadira to address her by her new name of Rawd. Now she had two names – Rawd for her poet and her slave and Umm al-Banin for everyone else.

Did the sleeping poem arouse her desires, causing her to send a message to the poet and invite him to come to Damascus?

How did the woman come to possess the daring needed for the adventure, once these love poems had found their way on every tongue and it had been reported to her that her husband the caliph had decided to kill the Yemeni poet?

Did she invite him in order to kill him?

Only death releases the lover from the one he loves. It is the only eraser that can transform life into a shadow, leaving on the soul the marks of obedience and submission.

Did Rawd, or Umm al-Banin, know that by inviting the poet to Damascus she was forcing the story to its climax, allowing death to then come along and extinguish the flame?

I don't believe the woman could have found a way to contact her poet and invite him to come to her. Probably, Waddah decided to go because he'd heard the call of love coming to him from the depths of her pain at their separation.

The story has it that the poet confided his decision to his friend Abu Zubayd al-Ta'i, and the man wrenched the mask from his face and wept. Then he told the poet he would go with him to Syria to bear witness to the death that awaited him there.

Waddah al-Yaman smiled and responded to his friend with two lines from the poetry of Imru' al-Qays:

> My friend wept on seeing the road ahead
>   and on being assured that to meet Caesar we were resolved.
> "Let your eye not weep," I told him. "We do but
>   seek to regain a kingdom, or to die and be absolved."

Waddah al-Yaman said, "I'm no king seeking his kingdom, and if I'm slain it'll be by the eyes of the woman who brought me back to life."

Waddah reached Damascus in the spring. The plum blossom was opening along the banks of the seven rivers that traverse the city and the white of the almond branches glittered under the sun. Snow could be seen on the peak of Mount Hermon, which enfolds the Lands of Syria in its white mantle.

In the city, which seemed to the poet like God's paradise on earth, Waddah al-Yaman lodged at an inn by night and wandered the roads by day, and he began to melt and dissolve and walk in circles around the palace of al-Walid.

Said the transmitter:

"Al-Waddah's mind had been dazzled by her and it began to

melt and dissolve, and after suffering long from this tribulation, he left for Syria, where he took to walking in circles each day around the palace of al-Walid ibn Abd al-Malik. However, he was unable to come up with a stratagem for entering the palace until he happened to see the blonde slave girl. He quickly struck up a friendship with her and asked her, 'Do you know Umm al-Banin?' 'Do not be so foolish as to ask after my mistress!' said the girl. 'But she is my cousin,' he said, 'and would be happy to know where I am, were you to tell her.' 'I shall tell her,' said the girl.

"The slave girl left and informed Umm al-Banin, who exclaimed, 'Oh my! Is he alive?' 'He is,' the girl said. 'Tell him,' said Umm al-Banin, "'Stay where you are until my messenger comes to you. I shall rack my brains till I come up with a trick to help you.'"

"So she schemed until in the end she got him in to where she was in a coffer. He stayed with her for a while, and whenever she felt it was safe, she would take him out and he would sit with her, and when she feared they might be seen, she would put him back in."

In this coffer would be written the final chapter in the story of the poet whose beauty bewitched women and whose silent death in the coffer of love became his poem, a poem written in stifled breaths and through surrender to a death unlike any other.

In the coffer of love, the world would evaporate into thin air, words disintegrate, feelings be erased, and the whiteness of death fill the blackness of the pit into which the poet had been thrown.

Which is where the story begins.

The Night of the Queen

(POINT OF ENTRY 6)

(Note 1: In this chapter, the story reaches its climax. The issue my version must put forward has nothing to do with the sterile discussion that revolved and revolves, anciently and today, around the story's historical veracity. Perhaps this insistence on searching for the truth was one of the elements that prevented the emergence of a story-based literature among the Arabs, or ensured that it emerged obliquely, previous to a sudden and astonishing explosion of the imagination in the form of *The Thousand and One Nights*. It is noteworthy that Taha Hussein, leader and Grand Old Man of the modernists, fell into this trap set by the ancients: instead of analysing the stories and legends of the ancient poets, he set out to refute them scientifically and thus, having decided to expunge the story from literature, wasted his talent and erudition on proving things that didn't need proving (as though literature could ever work without a story, when stories are its kernel!). It's bizarre that the G.O.M., in a moment of rationalist exuberance, obliterated pre-Islamic poetry as a source for the Arabic language, positing instead the Koran as its ultimate wellspring. The man's rationalism and materialism dropped him into a hole that the ancient Arab critics, starting with Qudama ibn Jaafar, had sought to avoid, so as to liberate the language from Koranic sacralism. The linguists and critics had regarded pre-Islamic poetry as a source for the understanding of the Koran, thus giving language precedence over the sacred. Taha Hussein's rationalist extremism, however, led him into the trap, making it the other face of religious superstition – an issue that deserves separate treatment.)

(Note 2: The issue my version will deal with is that of the relationship of death to love. The tale of how Waddah al-Yaman entered his coffer of death is well known and has been told dozens of times, echoes of it reaching modern Arabic poetry, as when the Yemeni poet Abdallah al-Bardawni alluded to it in his two wonderful lines:

> What shall I tell of Sanaa, my father?
>   A pretty town, its lovers consumption and mange!
> It died for nothing in Waddah's coffer
>   but the love and the joy in its guts never change.

The issue isn't how Waddah came to enter the coffer of his death, a story I shall tell just to get the facts straight, even if that involves a certain amount of repetition; the issue lies in the moments separating life from death: how did Waddah reread his life in the whiteness of the dark, how did he recover his first Rawda, the beloved whom he'd left to die in the valley of the lepers, and how did his love for Umm al-Banin evaporate?

It was his despair of love, which had turned into despair of life itself, that led him to silence.)

The transmitter says that Waddah didn't believe the blonde slave girl. He saw before him a blonde woman who had wrapped her body in a yellow cloak. Her eyes were small and swallowed up by thick eyelids that made them look like two little almonds. She went up to him and asked him who he was. The Yemeni was walking on the banks of the River Barada, making his way around the caliph's palace at a distance, not daring to go closer and unable to bear being further. He was walking around aimlessly, madly declaiming the poems from his sleeping fits that had stuck in his memory and repeating the name of Rawd, who had appeared to him at Mecca in a kind of epiphany.

The man had begun to doubt himself and his memory. Had his night with Umm al-Banin been real or imagined? What difference did it make, he asked himself, when after the night he'd spent in Umm al-Banin's bedchamber making love to her, he'd recovered the self that had deserted him in the lepers' valley and had seen how the leprosy had eaten away at his soul and how love had dawned within him as beauty does in women in love?

And he decided to go to her.

Nevertheless, after the exhausting journey to Syria (its sky washed by spring with an effulgent blue), the poet felt that the desert was seeping into him and that the thirst that rose up from his innards had set his lips afire, and he felt he was a stranger, and alone.

The poet told himself he'd gone there to die and he sat and waited in the shade of a Damascene jasmine. He closed his eyes and suddenly the daemon of poetry came to him:

In Syria my soul refused to mend –
    memory of the dwelling place of tribe and lover held me in thrall,
Capturing my heart – it pitched its tent where they pitched theirs
    and now can scarce resist their call.
Would that the winds might be a messenger to you
    be they from north or from south!

He felt a hand take his and pull him up. He stood and walked like one sleeping. He found himself in darkness. Everything was dark inside the vestibule to which the hand led him. He walked and walked, stumbling with trembling steps, knowing he was going to his death in her presence.

The story has it that the story began in the queen's wing.

Andalus had yet to be born in poetry at the time of Waddah al-Yaman, but he sensed the Andalus of desire. He felt that he was in a familiar place, like the Andalusian throb in the throat that has made of that land a repository for the mysteries of a strange mixture of homeland and exile. I'm no expert on Andalusian literature, but when I read the poetry of Ibn Zaydun or Wallada or al-Muatamid, and when I lose myself in the music of the *muwashshahat*, I feel as though I'm walking along a narrow ledge overlooking the valley of death – a poetry written in the midst of loss, and a memory that transcends nostalgia to arrive at a joy that is mixed with grief.

That is how I imagined Waddah as he walked into that darkened vestibule, holding the slave girl's hand, his face reflecting a mixture of fear, joy, anticipation and curiosity.

The only thing like love is love.

A tempest that recomposes the world, as though things were born swathed in mystery and ambiguity and are now beheld anew, as if they hadn't existed before love gushed from the water of the eyes. He walked in darkness, his eyes closed, enveloped in vertigo. When he opened his eyes and saw her, he smelled the fragrance of the water and laurel that spread from the long black hair that flowed down to her ankles. He halted, dazzled by the whiteness that shone from her bare wrists, and found himself prostrate before the poetry of her eyes.

The story has it that Waddah and Rawd lived for three months in their private Andalus. They spent the time alone, sipping the golden wine of Baalbek while he recited poetry to her.

During his stay in al-Walid's palace, Waddah discovered two blacknesses – the blackness of her hair, which covered her full white body with the night of love, and the blackness of the Damascene coffer in which she would hide him whenever danger approached.

The story goes that the poet spent long hours in the coffer and grew used to sleeping on the Damascene silk that his queen had spread over the coffer's bottom, and that the owner of the hair would slip in at night and whisper to him the words the poet had spread over the ground for the barefoot queen to walk upon.

The story does not, however, tell of the torments of Waddah.

True, when the queen was visited by her master the caliph, she would avoid meeting with him in the room containing the coffer. The eunuch would come to her to announce the news of the caliph's visit, and she would hurry off to another suite, there to bathe, perfume herself and wait, and would not return until after the dawn call to prayer.

Once, however, she returned to the room containing the coffer in the company of her master.

He heard her say, "Why do you want this room, sire?" and heard him reply that in that room he could smell the scent of Syrian wood.

He told her that this room smelled different from the rest of the rooms.

She said it was the smell of love.

"But I smell wine," he said.

"I drink to extinguish my jealous desire for you when I imagine you whoring with your many slave girls," she said.

"You are the most beautiful of my whores," he said. "Come!"

He heard the man guffaw as he ordered her to take off her

clothes and listened to her as she sighed before him.

How could Waddah recount these terrible moments? Probably, he would never have found the words to do so, and, had he done so, would have found no-one to listen to him, and, if he had, no-one would have believed that strange feeling in which jealousy blended with lust, hatred with love.

She would moan before her master as she did with him, repeating the expression that used to set him on fire whenever he entered her, and crying out, "God!" then falling silent for a moment before saying, "*Rahimo!*", which sounded to him like "Mercy!", and then repeating the two phrases times without number, before sobbing into the spurting of her water.

(Note: When Waddah heard the word *rahimo*, he felt amazement at the mistress who would ask her lover for mercy at the very moment that love reached its climax, almost as though she were performing an act of worship. Once, he asked her why she asked for his mercy when it was he who lived in the shade of her love and compassion. The queen smiled and said that she'd heard the word for the first time from her slave girl Ghadira, who was the daughter of an Assyrian prince and had been taken captive in a raid on northern Iraq and who said that *rahimo* meant "love" in Syriac. That day, Waddah learned that *rahma*, meaning "mercy"; *rahimo*, meaning "love"; and *tarahum*, meaning "mutual respect" all come from one root, which is the woman's *rahim*, or womb, and he decided to write a poem on the relationship of *tarahum* to love and on the woman's *rahim*, that inexhaustible wellspring of tenderness. Fate, however, failed to grant him the time, and mercy still awaits its poet.)

The same phrases, the *rahimo* that sprang from the cry of love, the sobbing that cradled the heart, and the white woman's writings – he'd see them with his ears and ignite with fury, and see them with his closed eyes and ignite with desire.

Waddah didn't sleep that night until he heard the muezzin announce the birth of dawn. He fell asleep without sleeping, and when he woke, his mistress was no longer there to open the coffer for him and invite him to eat. He remained concealed in his hunger and thirst, and when she opened the coffer in the evening he didn't see her eyes, which were cast down, while her body trembled and her voice choked in her throat.

That night, she put food and drink out for him and went away to sleep in another room.

The Coffer of Silence
(POINT OF ENTRY 7)

(Note: Do I have the right to skip the three months Waddah spent in the queen's palace and pause at only two moments – the poet's progress to the queen, and the confusion of his feelings as he listened to her sleeping with the caliph – before getting to, or with the aim of getting to, his tragic end?

I doubt if that way of doing things is appropriate to a novel; it's more like a cinematic treatment, when the writer of the screenplay divides the time up into scenes that summarise things so as to take the viewer to the place where endings are constructed. In other words, such treatments set little store by anything but the beginning and the end and ignore the daily life that reinterprets these and gives them meaning. A novel, on the other hand, interprets life itself through the imagination so that the reader may live the relationship between the beginning and the end as a journey, not a fate.

All the same, when the author finds himself caught up in making metaphors, he's obliged to make use of such short cuts and finds himself in a situation similar to that of the poets, though minus their greatest stylistic aide, namely music. I have no choice, however. It's Waddah's story and can only be written as a poetic story, which is to say as a metaphor. The ending, therefore, has to carry all the possible meanings within it and sum life up within the time spent inside the coffer, which was no more than half an hour.)

(Note: In relating this final chapter of the story, I shall have recourse to a number of books in addition to *The Songs*, my basic reference. I have referred to two books by modern writers – *The Tragedy of the Poet Waddah*, by Muhammad Bahjat al-Athari and Ahmad Hasan al-Zayyat, published by Ahd Press, Baghdad, 1935, to which I owe much of the credit for my reading of Waddah's story and for helping me to liberate myself from the sterile discussion around truth and imagination to which its pages are devoted, and Taha Hussein's *Wednesday Talk* – and among the ancients, to *The Book of Murdered Men* by Ali ibn Sulayman al-Akhfash, the *History of Baghdad* by al-Khatib al-Baghdadi, and *The Book of Eloquence and Exposition* by al-Jahiz.)

Said the transmitter:

"The lovers never spoke of that sad night. The queen commanded him to forget. She said forgetfulness was the cure for those who controlled neither their livings nor their lives. She said she feared for him and for herself.

"The poet forgot, or resolved to forget, the night, and things went back to the way they had been, or so the lovers tried to convince themselves. Two changes, however, occurred in the outward relationship between them. The first was the appearance in the story of the factor of fear. What the queen did not tell her poet was that she'd felt that the caliph had smelled betrayal. The disappearance of Waddah from Yemen and the Hejaz and the transmitters' failure to recite any new poems by him may have aroused his suspicions. Plus, the caliph's insistence on making love to her in the room containing Waddah's coffer because it 'smelled different', made her behave as one permanently afraid. She no longer laughed out loud, she stopped singing his poems while strumming on the oud, and she drank less wine, out of fear that her husband might suddenly turn up. Henceforth, the only thing she appeared to want from her poet was his body, as though the spirits of dead lovers that had fluttered about the coffer room had abandoned the place, never to return. The second change manifested itself in the poet's ceasing to write poetry. When she asked him if his daemon had abandoned him, he said that the words halted in consternation and became impossible to pronounce when faced with the poem of her body, which had been written by the Creator, Mighty and Sublime. She nodded but didn't believe him."

How can love live with fear, and without poetry?

Said the transmitter:

"Umm al-Banin loved Waddah. She would send for him and he would come to her and stay with her, and when she felt afraid, she would hide him in a coffer of hers and close the lid on him.

"Al-Walid was presented with a necklace of great worth. It pleased him and he thought it handsome, so he called one of his servants and sent him with it to Umm al-Banin, telling him, 'Say to her, "This necklace pleased me, so I thought you were the more worthy of it."'

"The servant went in to see her unannounced while Waddah was with her, so she put him in the coffer but he saw her do so. He gave her al-Walid's message and thrust the necklace at her. Then he said, 'Mistress, give me a gemstone from it!'

"'I will not, you son of an uncircumcised woman! What would you do with such a thing?' she said.

"So the servant left, full of ire against her, and went back to al-Walid and informed him. Al-Walid said, 'You're a liar!' and ordered that he be beheaded. Then he put on his slippers and went to see Umm al-Banin, who was sitting in the same room, combing her hair. The servant had described to him the coffer into which she had put the poet so he sat down on it and said to her, 'Umm al-Banin, did you like the necklace I sent you?' 'All these beautiful things,' she said, 'are a part of your bounty to me, and so is the necklace, my lord.'

"Then he said, 'What makes you like this room more than your other rooms, and why do you prefer it?'

"She said, 'I sit in it and prefer it because all my belongings are here, and I find whatever I need within easy reach.'

"He said, 'And these Damascene coffers, what do you put in them?'

"She said, 'I put my things in them, sir.'

"He said, 'Give me one of these coffers.'

"She said, 'They are all yours, Commander of the Faithful.'

"He said, 'I don't want them all. I want just one.'

"She said, 'Take whichever you want.'

"He said, 'This one I'm sitting on.'

"She said, 'Take another. That one has things in it that I need.'

"He said, 'I don't want another.'

"She said, 'Take it, Commander of the Faithful.'

"Then he summoned the servants and ordered them to pick it up, which they did, and they took it to his audience chamber, where they put it down. Next, he summoned slaves of his, and ordered them to dig a deep well shaft in the audience chamber, and the carpet was moved aside and a well was dug, down to the water level.

"Then he called for the coffer to be brought and said, 'You there! A report has reached us. If it is true, we have now enshrouded you and buried you and buried all trace of you until the end of time, and if it is false, we have buried nothing but a wooden box, and what could matter less?'

"The coffer was tossed into the well, earth poured on top of it, the ground levelled, the carpet put back in place, and Caliph al-Walid sat upon it. From then until this day, no trace of Waddah has been found."

This text poses numerous questions. However, what keeps me awake at night is one: why did Waddah remain silent in his coffer; why didn't he call out and ask for mercy?

This is the question that makes me want to convert this manuscript into a novel. My novel will lead to the coffer, like Ghassan Kanafani's *Men in the Sun*, which led its heroes to the tank of a water truck so that it could ask them "Why?" Kanafani's question came from outside the tank but mine will be part of the gloom inside it, where the darkness of the soul mixes with the darkness of the world. Likewise, I shan't ask any questions of my poet, who has now become my friend. What he experienced went beyond question and answer. The four-dimensional experience of love, death, the death of love, and love of death that Waddah lived leaves me companionless before the eloquence of silence and death and makes me incapable of pulling his story in the direction of a direct meaning, political or moral, the way Kanafani did with his heroes.

Before getting to the scene in which the poet is carried off live in the coffer of his love, which has now come to resemble a coffin, however, I would like to consider the story's other protagonists – al-Walid, Umm al-Banin, and the slave who was killed.

As far as the slave and his fate are concerned, it was part and parcel of the customs of the day in that the deaths of slaves, like their lives, were meaningless outside the framework of their relationships with their masters. The slave lives and dies according to the same logic, and when he learns a secret to which he has no right to be privy, it is his fate to die.

The slave in this story is simply a tool to link the plot to its climax, meaning its ending. That is his function. In my novel, however, I shall delete him, so as to turn the story of the coffer into a progress, one that began with a night of lovemaking in the room where the coffer was and where the caliph sensed something was amiss and that continued up to the moment when he felt he had to go to the room, where he would see, with his own two eyes, the end of Waddah's garment poking out from his hiding place inside the coffer.

Deletion of the slave will, however, complicate the issue and, logically, should lead to the slaying of Umm al-Banin as well, as it is difficult if not impossible to have the caliph see with his own eyes the evidence of his wife's betrayal and be satisfied with killing only her lover. That is why there has to be a witness whose testimony may, on the one hand, be doubted, and yet, on the other, is easy to kill off without consequences.

The existence of the slave opens the field to the possibility of doubt as to the veracity of his testimony and, at the same time, allows the king, whose heart had been ignited by jealousy with a love that had, he knew not how, disoriented him, to pardon Umm al-Banin and make do with the slaying of her lover, or the story of the slaying of her lover.

Al-Walid owned countless slave girls, and love had never been part of the lexicon of his life. A woman was a body that constituted an extension of his sexual desires. Umm al-Banin, on the other hand, his wife and the mother of his children, held a twofold meaning for him – that of the mother, whom he wished to see surrounded by the sanctities of motherhood, and that of the body, which, on rare occasions, became part of the female body in general, though holding a special excitement for him owing to her shyness and her drowsiness. When he had sex with her in the room that held the coffer, she took him aback with her moaning and her words. He emerged confused by an ambiguous sensation, to which he refused to give the name of love. Then, when he thought about it, he remembered the verses of Waddah that were on everyone's lips and tongue, and felt jealous because he imagined that the woman must have been thinking of her poet while with him.

Al-Walid spoke the truth when he said to the coffer, "You in there! We've heard a tale about you. If it's true, we have now buried all tales about you and wiped all trace of you from the face of the earth, and if it's a lie, there's nothing wrong with our burying a wooden box." The caliph had made up his mind not to believe the slave even though he believed him, because he had, at the same time, made up his mind to bury what the transmitters and the people were passing around about Waddah's love for his wife.

Burying the coffer was, for the caliph, a symbolic act by which he hoped to kill the story and bury it in earth and water.

And it is here, at the moment of its killing, that the story will claim its victory. The tyrannical monarch has authority over slaves and objects. He can kill people and lay waste to the land. But when he tries to kill a story, he turns into a minor character within it and loses his power and freedom of action.

If the king hadn't buried the coffer, Waddah's story would have remained just a part of the tapestry of stories without number about poets who rhapsodised over the wives of kings and noblemen and whose stories end at that point, and it would have had no special significance. The jealousy, however, that ignited in the caliph's heart, and the love that it gave rise to, made him do what none before had done and, instead of killing the story, become part of it. The strange thing is that the monarch's love for Umm al-Banin evaporated at the very moment that he buried the coffer. As the ancient Arabs used to say, "Only death can erase love."

As to Umm al-Banin, who gave up her poetical name of Rawd and went back to being just a near-forgotten wife of the caliph, two tales are told of her: the first says the woman went on with her life in the palace and decided to forget, and that she turned to religion and never asked the caliph about her buried coffer. In this version, the author of *The Songs* relates (quoting Ibn al-Kalbi) that "Umm al-Banin never saw anything in the face of al-Walid that gave any clue as to the matter, up to the day that death parted them."

In another version, the woman experienced torments. When Ghadira told her how al-Walid had buried the coffer and what he'd said as he did so, she fainted.

Life started to lose all its savour. She prayed and asked for forgiveness but felt that her prayers were going nowhere, as though the heavens had closed their doors to the words of a woman destroyed by sorrow and guilt. The poet's death demolished her life.

Ghadira reported that her mistress constantly felt as though she was suffocating. She said the air had become as solid as rock and she couldn't breathe rock. She would open her mouth, begging for air, but there was no air. She began to be surrounded by emptiness: she would look and not see, weep without tears. She told Ghadira that her bowels had dried out and that all she hoped for from life was the angel of death.

Did she go to the caliph's audience chamber one night when it was empty and when she felt her end approaching, because, as it is said, she wanted to embrace with her death the death of her poet, or did she throw herself on the floor of the chamber and commit suicide?

Neither *The Songs* nor any of the other ancient books that

recount the story of Waddah al-Yaman speak of the woman's suicide, for the woman is of no interest to the transmitters once the poet has died – and here lies a defect in this story that I have to correct, as I'm loath to agree that the woman (in this case the caliph's wife and poet's mistress) was merely a tool that permitted the transmission of Waddah's story as the tale of a man who was buried alive with his story. I shall, therefore, as a postscript to my novel, attempt to recover and write the story of the queen's suicide.

Unfortunately, though, however much the heroes may multiply, the stories concentrate, in the end, on just one. I shall, therefore, be obliged, despite my intense interest in the queen's end, to focus on the poet. Writing has to take a specific point of view. Despite its importance, incidents similar to the queen's suicide are to be found in many novels and plays, while the method by which Waddah met his death is unique, has been used only once, and is what allows the text to approach what we may call the essence of the meaning of love.

Said the transmitter:

"Waddah was shivering in the coffer. The queen had told him she thought the slave had seen her as she was closing the lid of the box and had noticed the end of his garment. She'd said she'd refused to give him a gemstone from the necklace because she was certain he would blackmail her: no slave had ever before raised his eyes to look at her, so why else would he dare to do so? How would she have been able to deal with him afterwards if she'd given in to his demand? She said too that he'd never have the courage to tell on her because he wouldn't by so doing kill her, he'd kill only her lover, and would, indeed, bring destruction upon himself as well."

Waddah said she'd been wrong, and she asked him to lower his voice. He said the cat was out of the bag because the slave would tell his fellow slaves before telling the caliph, or while he was on his way to him.

She told him to shut up.

He tried to open the lid of the coffer but she locked it and told him, "No. You have to stay in there."

He tried to persuade her to flee the place, but he knew that was impossible in daylight and it was only midday. He knew as well that this woman, to whom he'd written poetry, would never leave the palace because she was the heroine of the story and she had to behave the way heroines are supposed to.

It was then that Waddah understood that the woman would become a story and realised that he'd lost two women and two stories. When he arrived at the outskirts of the third story, he realised that he'd lost himself too.

Said the transmitter:

"When Umm al-Banin heard the caliph's footsteps, she stood in front of the mirror that was on the wall close to the coffer and combed her hair. When he drew close to her and put his hand on her shoulder, she flinched, before turning and saying, 'How did my lord enter? You scared me!'

"'You're scared of me?' asked the caliph.

"'All your subjects live in awe of you, master, and I am but one of your slaves.'"

The king observed the lie and the betrayal, but the calm of the avenger descended upon him, and he asked her why she liked that room more than her other ones. Then he asked her about the three Damascene coffers that had been placed in the same room. Then he asked her about the necklace he'd sent with the slave. After he'd heard her answers, silence reigned.

Waddah was curled up on his right side in the coffer waiting for the end. The poet imagined a scene in which the lid opened and he saw the caliph's beard shaking with anger and the drawn sword in his hand as he ordered him to come out.

The poet visualised death as a sword plus eyes like flints emitting sparks and a woman curled up at the end of the room, and he decided to die like a true knight. He would come out with head held high and announce that he was requesting his lord think of him as a martyr to love.

The lid of the coffer remained, however, closed. He heard the caliph asking her for it, and a cold sweat started to bathe his eyes. Time stopped, as though the movement of the planets in the heavens had slowed, as though the darkness of the coffer had turned day into night.

He waited for the hands that would take hold of him but they did not come. Instead, he heard a whispering, the droplets of sweat in his eyes drew things in blurry shapes, and the thought came to him that death appears to the dying in the shape of little white crowns covering everything.

He heard footsteps and began to feel himself rise. He clung with his body to the bottom of the coffer so that he wouldn't roll about and decided to lie on his back and grasped that the reason why the best way to lay a corpse on its wooden stretcher, after it has been washed and wrapped in its shroud, is flat on its back is so that it doesn't fall off before reaching the hole that is its final destination.

The numbness rose from his legs to his shoulders, and he felt the touch of the oak against his arms. The wood was smooth and silky, and something like ants came out of it and spread throughout the coffer. His heart started to beat hard, its sound growing louder, and the coffer swayed as though this beating, which had transformed his fear into a stifled scream, was about to cause it to drop. He told his heart to be silent. He put out his hand and grasped his heart and made it go silent, but the throbbing was transferred to his ears and sounds coming from the outside lost their meaning.

They put the coffer on the ground, and he heard the voice of the caliph ordering his slaves to dig, so he understood that he was about to be buried alive. He closed his eyes and surrendered to a drowsy torpor.

The time that elapsed between the start of the digging and his hearing the king's voice whispering to the coffer was no less than half an hour, but it passed in what seemed like seconds. Only death is like love in its ability to reduce time, and to produce the illusion of not passing even as it passes.

The caliph's voice reached him softly, interspersed with hissing high-notes: "You in there! A report has reached us. If it is true, we have now enshrouded you and buried you and all your works until the end of time" – and the poet decided to die.

The whole story lies here.

Did Waddah die choking on water because he'd decided to protect the story?

The man realised that he couldn't escape death, so became suddenly calm. His body stopped sweating, the trembling that had afflicted him from the moment he had heard the king's footsteps stilled, the little crowns that had filled his eyes disappeared, and he saw the darkness that surrounded him. He became aware of the water that was creeping through the wood towards him. He curled up on himself like a foetus and the life within him began to be choked off.

In that moment of serenity, facing surrender to the darkness of death, Waddah decided to remain silent, like "a sheep that is driven to the slaughter and never opens its mouth", as the prophet says. He decided to be Rawd's sheep because he wanted to protect his beloved with his silence, for any sign that he was inside the coffer would lead to her death.

He knew he would die whatever happened and understood that the only way to protect the story of his love was to suppress the instinct for life inside him.

Or did he die enshrouded in silence because he became filled with strange feelings that made him indifferent to the cruelty of his death?

Waddah had no idea when it had begun. Of course, we can always simplify matters and suppose that the monarch's visit to the room with the coffer knocked the poet off kilter, which is true: he'd felt that he was just a small footnote, not only to the life of that woman who had made him her prisoner and a prisoner of her palace, but to life itself. True, he'd been convinced by her argument that he should forget that *rahimo!* that she uttered while having sex with the caliph, and at the same time he'd tried to set aside the idea that he was a prisoner, and isolated, and had lost his poetry, which now had only one person to listen to it, which was Rawd. He'd persuaded himself that his coffer was not a grave for his poetry, as poetry was communication, union with the beloved is the ultimate goal of all communication, and his poetry had become his way of achieving union with the beloved. Everyone had forgotten him, and the transmitters had stopped passing on the most beautiful of his verses, the ones he had written in Syria (which is why we find only the early poems in his collected works, and why the books fail to list him as a major poet) but he'd been happy: what he'd written had become a second body for the beloved.

Suddenly, however, he'd felt as though he were suffocating. Ten days before his death, he stopped making love. Umm al-Banin spent most of her time with him but he lost first his words and then his desire. The woman didn't say anything to him. She respected his silence and his distractedness, but persisted in using the perfume that he liked and would kiss him when she arrived and when she left, feeling the taste of his cold lips and saying nothing.

The moment the coffer rose into the air, Waddah realised that the evaporation of his love had robbed his life of its meaning, and that the death of love is death.

He did not think about anything. He surrendered to the torpor of the end and became aware that death is not, as they claim, the price of love, but the price of the ending of love.

At that hour, called "the fearsome hour" because it contains within it man's terror at the end of everything, the poet felt no fear. He didn't hope that the lid of the coffer would open and let in the fresh air. He forgot that during his stay in the palace with the queen and the long periods he'd spent in the coffer he'd felt that his chest was shrinking and his lungs shrivelling and that the moment he was let out, and before asking for water, he would open his mouth to drink in the air.

At that moment, he felt that the coffer had become as wide as the world. Breezes sported through it, and he listened as his heartbeats gradually died away.

He forgot Umm al-Banin and Rawda, who became as though they had never been, curled himself up in the box, which had begun to fill, and entered the lethargy of the water.

And so ended the story of the most beautiful lover in the history of love as known to the Arabs.

(Note: The story appears to have two, contradictory, climaxes, but I don't find myself obliged to choose between them, a fact that may be attributed to my decision to refuse to offer an allegorical–expository version of it. The transmitters of this story have fallen without exception into such an expository mode and chosen one of two easy solutions: either to end the story with the words of the king – in which case all that the reader knows of Waddah's fate is his death, while his terrible experience within the coffer is overlooked; in this way, the writing of the story becomes part of the-victors'-writing-of-history, and thus we betray literature, whose first task is to upend that formula and make the story the history of the vanquished – or to regard the story as a silly myth and a political forgery directed against the Omayyads. I'm against both options, because the explicative version would turn Waddah into a symbol, which is impossible: it is a condition of the symbolic figure that he can be replicated, as was the case with Mad-over-Layla. All I know is that Waddah's story wasn't replicated in the past and never will be in the future. Likewise, to regard the story as a myth or a lie, one told as part of the war between the Omayyads and their enemies, is to turn it into a purely gratuitous tale. I hate such tales because they lose their meaning with time, while the story of Waddah hasn't lost its meaning; on the contrary, it has increased in radiance and uniqueness.

On the other hand, entering the coffer with the poet to write the story from within the darkness of the box places me before two further options, between which I am neither able nor in the mood to choose.

Did the poet keep silent in order to protect his beloved, in which case his story is an epitome of self-sacrifice and self-abnegation? Or did he keep silent because he no longer cared about life itself after the obliteration of love in the refusal of the lips to either speak or kiss, thus finding in death a fitting form for the ending of his love?

My perplexities over memory bring me back to Sheikh Usama al-Humsi, whom my mother brought to the house to make me memorise the Koran as a way of preserving my Arabic when the tiny minority of the inhabitants of Lydda who remained in the city came to fear that everything Arabic was on the verge of becoming extinct under the new state that had taken over Palestine. Whenever I put a difficult question concerning Islamic law to my sheikh and teacher, he would give me two different answers, and when I asked him which was correct, he would reply, "There are two points of view, and only God knows which is right."

I end this manuscript with that same expression of my revered sheikh's, in the hope that I can write my novel from two points of view and leave time to rewrite it as it wills.)

ADAM DANNOUN

Prayers of Refuge

Say: "I take refuge with the Lord of men, the King of men, the God of men, from the evil of the slinking whisperer, who whispers in the breasts of men, of jinn and men."

I left the cinema consumed by rage and sought sanctuary in the two "prayers of refuge".

Say: "I take refuge with the Lord of the Daybreak, from the evil of what He has created, from the evil of darkness when it gathers, from the evil of the women who blow on knots, from the evil of an envier when he envies."

It was a strange scene. In that New York cinema I saw my life being torn to shreds before my eyes and the corpses of my friends dragged from my memory and dissected in front of every-one. I felt rage, and then the rage evaporated into a slight dizziness accompanied by nausea and a feeling that I was about to vomit. No-one has the right to turn memory into a corpse and then dissect it and rip its joints apart in front of everybody just to make a movie.

What kind of a way to behave is that?

I remember that Sarang Lee came after me, running, and took me to the café, where she explained that I was in the wrong, and that it was inappropriate for me to insult the director and the author. When she got to the bit where she told me I'd looked like a psychopath, claiming that I knew the heroes of the film and the novel personally, I found myself standing up, kicking the iron table in the Lanterna Café's glass-roofed garden, and walking out into the street.

The ground was covered in muddy snow. The temperature was five below zero, and I walked without buttoning my overcoat, exposing my chest to New York's whistling, bone-chilling wind.

Something inside me was on fire, my chest was burning, and a strange craving for air swept over me, as though my chest had been locked shut and my lungs were no longer capable of inhaling. At the same moment, my pores all closed and my head started ringing with a kind of senseless jabbering.

I don't remember what happened exactly. I went into a bar, drank a lot of vodka, and went out again into the street, where I walked without thinking about where I was going. I don't know how I found myself in my little apartment on 96th Street. Had I really walked all that way from Lower Manhattan to my home or taken a cab or what? I had no idea. All I know is that I recovered from my daze when I fell on the bathroom floor, banged my head on the edge of the basin and saw blood. I washed my face and forehead and got into bed to sleep. In the morning, I found myself in the middle of a pool of blood that had spread over the pillow, and couldn't get out of bed because I was overcome by dizziness.

Sarang Lee told me she'd given up on trying to get in touch with me by telephone, so two days later she came to my house, knocked on the door and then opened it. Entering, she was scared by my pallor and the blood congealed on the pillow and the sheet, as well as by the bouts of feverish ranting that would seize me. She said she hadn't understood a word I'd said because my speech was slurred. She got me a doctor and stayed with me for four days, until I began to emerge from the fever.

Six days were enough for my life to turn upside down and put paid to the novel that I'd begun writing.

I'd long dreamed of writing a novel. One novel would be enough to say something no-one had ever said before. I'm the son of a story that has no tongue, and I want to be the one to make it speak; when I found the story, and took up residence in Waddah al-Yaman's coffer, that damned movie came along and expelled me from the coffer of metaphor which I'd hoped would be the grave of my story and the cave from which it could once more shine forth. The scales fell from my eyes and I saw that I was alone, looking for my shadow, which I had lost. My shadow had disappeared and been erased, and it became my task, before I could write, to find it again, so that I could lean upon it.

The fever was devouring me and I was trying to explain to my young friend, in stumbling English, who I was. I told her everything and watched my life forming into a story before me, and my story was long. Was she listening to me, or could her eyes not see the story because she couldn't understand what I was saying?

She told me my speech had been slurred and that I'd talked without stopping and would jump from one subject to another, beginning in English, then switching into Arabic or into a mixture of Arabic and Hebrew, and drinking a lot of water. She spoke of tears she'd seen in my eyes and said she'd tried the whole time to calm me down.

Odd. I remember things differently. I remember seeing everything clearly and being amazed at what I saw. I could recall everything. I saw the remnants of the people of Lydda living in a ghetto fenced off with wire by the Israelis, and I smelled death. I even saw before me the words in which my mother recounted to me the story of my birth, as though I were remembering them.

I recalled everything, and today I sit down to write what I remembered and saw, convinced that memory is too heavy a burden for any to carry and that forgetfulness was brought into being to liberate us from it.

From that moment, the weight of my memory began to exhaust me, and I decided to write it, so that I could forget it.

People think that writing is a cure for forgetfulness and the vessel of memory, but they're wrong. Writing is the form appropriate to forgetfulness, which is why I've decided to review my entire project and, instead of killing memory with metaphor as I tried to through my aborted work on a novel about Waddah al-Yaman, I shall transform it, as I write it, into a corpse made out of words.

I am not Waddah al-Yaman, I will not die in the coffer, and my beloved is neither Rawda nor Umm al-Banin.

True, I did love two women: the first died and my love for the second died in my heart. Between those two, I loved a number of other women; or at least, did not love them but had relationships with them that were like love but quickly crumbled. What remains, though, in my memory, of the heart's blood that I lost is connected to just two women, the first of whom was born in Saffourieh in Galilee and died in Haifa at the age of twenty-two, the second of whom was a Polish Iraqi born in al-Ramla who moved to Tel Aviv to live and study and who did not die, but love for whom died in my heart for no clear reason except that love dies, which is what drove me into the depression of writing.

Unlike Waddah al-Yaman, I entered no coffer, though now I discover that I've lived my whole life inside a coffer of fear, which, in order to escape, I must not just write, but break.

This is why I've decided to change everything.

What happened at the cinema?

Now, reviewing those moments, I can't understand what brought about the state I was in during my six days of raving. It wasn't worth it. I should have left the cinema quietly and without making a fuss, gone back home, and immersed myself in *The Songs*, as I do every day. I return from my job at the restaurant, wash the smell of frying oil from my body, and become clean, so as to be worthy of the blessing of reading the verses and the stories of the poets.

The truth is ... (I have to stop using this word. It doesn't express the truth of things, because no-one knows the truth about that forest of tangled branches called the soul. Our souls are worlds spotted with darkness and no-one knows the truth about them, and when inspiration or anything of the sort possesses the poet, he thinks he's got to the truth, but inspiration is abundant and multiple, as is the truth.)

The truth is that the movie and the discussion that followed triggered something inside me that was waiting to explode. I won't say my memory exploded, its water flowing like blood at an explosion of the arteries, but what happened was something like that.

The water of my memory drowned the metaphor and erased the symbol, which is why I now feel that I have to write the truth – naked, shocking, contradictory and cruel – as I lived it.

I have decided to adopt a genre that all my life I have rejected. My problem with many novels was always my feeling that the writer was borrowing the novel form to write a part of his autobiography but from an oblique angle. I used to regard that kind of literature as a trick and an easy way out, and I still do. That's why I've eliminated all references to my own life story, even where it concerns the woman with whom I was on the verge of sharing my life and death. I refuse to behave as lovers do at the beginning, when they tell each other the stories of their lives. I told Dalia I had no story to tell her. The dusky girl whose desire shone on her wrists would, when intoxicated with love, overflow with words, then ask that I tell. She used to say that my silence was the sign of the deficiency of my love, and I'd say nothing. How was I to tell her a story that had no tongue? How was I to tell her about the invisible child I'd been and the journey of my life that had hidden itself under a magic cap of invisibility? My mother used to tell me to put on the cap so I'd disappear and no-one could see me, because we had to live as invisible people if we weren't to be thrown out of our country, or be killed.

I never let Dalia in on my story because my tongue had been cut off. I never even told her about Hanan, who died in Haifa.

Now, though, I find myself swimming in words and depression, and I take off my magic invisible cap and don't care, which is a sign of the end.

I want to clarify things to myself first. What I write now, and what I shall write, isn't a novel or an autobiography and it isn't addressed to anyone. It would be logical not to have it published as a book, but I don't know. I shall let my self address itself as it desires, without rules, I shan't change the names to make myself think that I'm writing a work of literature, and I shan't cobble together a framework. I shall tell things as I told them to my young friend.

I don't like what the critics call "the dramatisation of the self" as a novel form, and I don't like autobiographies despite my extreme admiration of Jabra Ibrahim Jabra's book *The First Well*, which I consider to be the most beautiful thing written by that elegant and admirable Jerusalemite.

I think literature shouldn't be like life. It should be a pure literature dedicated to language and its beauties, which are without
limit.

This is neither a novel nor a story nor an autobiography.

And it isn't literature.

I lost the opportunity to make literature when I decided to
break open Waddah al-Yaman's coffer, and I must pay the price
and let the ink flow as it will.

I have to begin at the beginning, but every beginning has its
own beginning, so where am I to begin?

I was standing behind the counter watching the two young
Egyptian men who were preparing the falafel and shawarma
sandwiches for the numerous customers with whom the little
Palm Tree restaurant had filled, when Chaim Zilbermann walked
into the restaurant that I'd been managing for more than two
years. I love the man. I loved him first for his way of devouring
food: when he eats a dish of hummus, I feel as though he relishes
the interplay between the garlic, the tahini, the lemon and the
ground chickpeas. This large bald man became my personal
taster, on whom I'd try out the different mutations that I would
introduce into the various dishes. He was the first to taste the
fried-eggplant-mixed-with-tahini-and-yoghurt sandwich, which
became one of the reasons for the restaurant's success.

I loved him too because he loved the Middle East, which he'd
left because of his feeling that there was no place for him in a
country that had occupied another, a feeling brought about by
what happened between him and the donkey in the October, or
Yom Kippur, War of 1973.

I loved him thirdly because he was a film director with a conscience and made fascinating documentaries.

My friendship with him gained depth when I met his Jewish-American wife, Tally, who did not feel the cold in New York, a woman who concealed behind her mild manner a depth of human feeling that I only discovered when she told me the story of her love for Chaim.

The fifty-year-old became my friend. We spoke Hebrew together and would recall the Middle Eastern sun and talk about politics, and sometimes we would go out with his wife to the Italian pizza restaurant *Tre Giovanni* where we'd drink red wine. I would observe his embarrassment when faced by the pizza, which he didn't dare to eat in front of his wife because he claimed he was on a diet, so Tally and I would eat while the poor man made do with devouring a plate of chicken salad and stealing sad glances at our tasty food.

Chaim hadn't come that day to eat, and when I made him a jumbo falafel sandwich, he took it with an annoyed expression and said, as he wolfed it down, that he wasn't hungry.

That was his habit: he would come to the restaurant, and when I offered him food he would look at it with annoyance because it didn't fit his diet, and then eat it with aggressive appetite.

That day he had come to tell me he'd got me two tickets for the opening of his new movie.

I said one was enough, and he said he'd be going out after the movie with Tally and a few friends and would like to make the acquaintance of the young woman whom he'd seen here in my company on many occasions, and he winked at me before bursting into laughter.

Next day, I was surprised when Sarang Lee invited me to the same film. I told her I'd received a ticket from the director and had an extra one for her, and she said she'd go with me even though she didn't need my ticket because her Lebanese professor had also invited her.

I didn't ask her what the professor had to do with the movie. I surmised it was one of the things the faculty did to get out of teaching. This was something I'd been told by a customer of mine, a Palestinian living in Ramallah and teaching history at Birzeit University who also worked as a visiting professor at the university here and with whom I had old history that went back to Jaffa, though this isn't the time to tell it. Dr Hanna Jiryis used movies a lot in his class and when I asked him why, he gave me a lecture about the importance of the image in the post-modern period. I guessed that the man, who loved the Big Apple (as New Yorkers call their city), had chosen an easier way to enjoy it than burying himself in books, devoting himself instead to his hobby of hunting girls with his cappuccino machine.

It was Chaim who told me of this obsession of Hanna's, and how the professor would take him to Café Reggio to show him the oldest cappuccino machine in America.

I thought the professor who'd invited my friend to the movie must likewise have fallen in love with cappuccino and that he too must now be playing the game played by Hanna, whose coffee-making talents were made clear to me by the girls he brought with him to the restaurant before going on with them to cappuccino paradise in his lovely home overlooking Washington Square, where the university professors resided.

But I was wrong.

I didn't hate Chaim afterwards. It was nothing to do with him and I'm convinced his motives were good and his attempt to make a film about the beginnings of the Second Intifada was his way of expressing his anger at the Occupation.

I can't blame anyone; instead, I blame the incompleteness of the truth. Art, no matter how hard it tries, will never get to the bottom of all aspects of reality; it follows that there's no point in talking of "realism" in art. My friend's mistake lay in thinking that the exhausting research he'd undertaken had brought him to the complete truth.

The truth was known to only one person, called Dalia, and it was she who told it to me before deciding to abandon me and her project for a movie about Assaf after she watched the videotape that no-one else ever saw.

My anger was directed at the writer, the one who'd come before to the restaurant with Sarang Lee and to whom she'd introduced me. I think the man must have been disappointed when I failed to welcome him in his own right and made no reference to his novels. Sarang Lee claimed that my anger was due to my jealousy of the man because, like all men, I could only think about one thing. But that isn't true. Over whom and of whom should I be jealous?

How could I feel jealous over a girl with whom I hadn't had an affair and with whom I never for a moment wanted to have an affair? True, a few times we'd been on the verge of one but something had always told me, No!

The mistaken journey began in Tel Aviv.

I ran into Nahum Hirschman by accident on the street in Tel Aviv in January 2003. I was leaving the theatre after watching Eugène Ionesco's play "The Bald Soprano" for the fourth time. My head reverberating with the meanings fashioned by the Romanian playwright from the meaninglessness of words, I found Nahum Hirschman in front of me. This Nahum was a friend of mine from our days as students together at university. I'd given him the title of the Soldier of the White Lilies because I'd seen in him a double of the Israeli soldier in Mahmoud Darwish's poem who dreamed of peace and wanted to leave Israel. Nahum had implemented that decision and disappeared. We'd graduated together from the Department of Hebrew Literature at Haifa University. I'd started working as a teacher in Haifa, while he'd gone to America.

At that meeting, I decided to emigrate to the States.

He offered me a job at his New York restaurant, which was facing financial difficulties. I went in as a partner, using the money I'd got together to get married, and became a falafel-seller, as well as a proper chef, thanks to the additions I made to the restaurant's fast-food menu, among them the large *manaqish* to which we gave the name "oriental pizza". We added *manaqish* with *kishk* too, which also sold very well, as well as the eggplant *makdous*, which became one of our most famous sandwiches and consisted of eggplant stuffed with walnuts and garlic pickled in olive oil. Nahum gave this the name of "olive-oil eggplant" in English and *hatsil makhdus* in Hebrew.

I say "mistaken" but it was the correct mistake as I had no alternative. "My paths had become strait," as the Arabs say, meaning I could no longer find a foothold in my own country. The paths there had ended up leading me into the wilderness and I could hear the voice of my mother saying I'd end up getting lost there, like her brother, my uncle Daoud, whom I resembled so much.

I had to find a new place so I could come to an end. Usually, people emigrate in order to begin a new life. My decision to do so was a search for the end. I told myself, as I said farewell to my house in Jaffa's Ajami quarter, that the end resembles the beginning and that when I set off in search of my end, it must become a metaphor for the beginning, and that both words deserve to be entered into the Arabs' dictionaries of antitheses, in which a single word means both a thing and its opposite.

I considered my job at the falafel restaurant the best choice if I was to escape the circles of culture and the cultured and devote myself to writing my novel. It had nothing to do with criteria of failure and success: I was a successful journalist, writing my weekly article on Arabic music and tickling an oriental Israeli memory that is a blend of nostalgia and exoticism. Gone were the days of Noah's Café, where Egyptian-Jewish musicians who had emigrated to Israel used to meet to play their painful memory in exile and recover Egypt, which they'd lost for ever, and in their place had come the days of the Israeli Orient, which may be divided into two halves – one consisting of religion, which had become the refuge of the scattered souls of the Moroccans and Yemenis who had emigrated to Israel, the other of exoticism, which sees in the Orient a pillow for its desires.

I was successful, and I was an Israeli like other Israelis. I didn't conceal my Palestinian identity but kept it out of sight, in the ghetto where I was born. I'm a son of the ghetto, and the ghetto had granted me immunity of Warsaw (which is another tale I shall tell at the right time).

I decided to leave the immunity of the Warsaw Ghetto behind me and to abandon al-Sitt Umm Kulsoum, her songs, and my analyses of eastern art, which were the means by which I'd managed to occupy a weekly column at the newspaper.

I didn't say goodbye to anyone: there was no-one to say good-bye to. For the past ten years, I'd made do with Dalia's friends, deluding myself that I'd won. I did indeed beat the German artist whose pictures filled the Tel Aviv galleries with Dalia's features. I paid no attention to her presence in the pictures till she told me that her relationship with the painter had ended the moment the wall of colours between them had broken down. She said she'd become tired of living in pictures and decided to take off the veil of colours, which had become a burden on her soul. I believed her. The painter wasn't really German but in that small circle around Dalia we called him that because he was tall and blond, had bulging muscles, and looked like a German. I don't know why they broke up: I fell in love with Dalia before discovering she was the painter Amnon's girlfriend. I met her by accident at the Isaiah Bar in Tel Aviv, a small place frequented by left-wing intellectuals.

Suddenly, I saw her in front of me. She was standing as though she were her own shadow. I saw a woman's shadow but couldn't see a woman. She had a mysterious translucence and gave the impression that you could see things through her, and she was as beautiful as silence (if that is the proper expression to describe a woman covered with her own shadow and a silence that spoke without words).

She approached the bar and sat down next to me. She was cloaked in her own self, concealed behind the diaphanous veil of sadness that covered her face. I thought she asked me something, or said she knew me; that's what I believed during the ten years of my relationship with her, but now my memory springs to life to tell another truth: the woman didn't ask a question; when I spoke to her as though I were answering a question she'd asked, she didn't even turn towards me.

Everything happened quickly. I talked and talked and watched my words ripping open her silence and stealing between her closed lips. Then she spoke. I don't remember what she said but I saw words drawing themselves over her grey eyes.

We drank a lot that evening, then walked aimlessly in the street, and I found myself embracing her and kissing her.

I don't believe in love at first sight, but I fell in love with her and told her, as I held her to me in front of the building where she lived, that I loved her, and I heard her laugh and say it was the wine.

Two days later she behaved as though she didn't know me, I have no idea why. She was sitting in the same bar, surrounded by a group of men. I went up to her shyly, then sat down without being invited. I felt uncomfortable, but love made me see things wrongly. I'd hardly got over my embarrassment before I found Amnon talking to me pleasantly, and we got into a discussion about the relationship of painting to music. The man was fond of Umm Kulsoum and said that when he was painting a woman he would listen to the singer, not understanding anything but intoxicated by the voice, which entered through his pores. He said the person who'd introduced him to Umm Kulsoum had taught him what it meant for music to be sensual and for the voice to rise from the depths of desire. He said Umm Kulsoum had introduced a flavour of the Orient into his pictures and it was through her that he'd discovered Iraq!

I couldn't grasp the relationship between Umm Kulsoum and Iraq. For me, Umm Kulsoum is the Nile, shimmering with the depths that lie hidden beneath its calm surface. Umm Kulsoum is the Nile when it overflows with desires, simultaneously watering and devouring the land. I made no comment, however, and later I found out that the "Iraq" of which he spoke was simply the symbolic name of the woman with whom I was going to fall in love.

How did Dalia come into my life?

What did I want from a girl who said she was Iraqi and that

through me she could catch the scent of coffee mixed with cardamom? I don't take my coffee with cardamom and I get dizzy when I smell it. Later I discovered that she was searching, through me, for something mysterious, something that had been born in her depths the moment that the wall of colours between her and the German painter had been broken.

I didn't believe her when she told me her affair with him had been broken off. I would feel his ghostly presence everywhere, and a mysterious jealousy, which for ten years I suppressed, intoxicated me.

The woman was fashioned out of the brown spaces that radiated inside the blue of the pictures painted by the German with the same detail as the nudes of Matisse, and she exited my life as stealthily as she had entered it.

She said, sketching her mysterious smile on her lips, that she'd decided to go, because life had lost its meaning.

I answered with a shrug of my shoulders.

That was our last meeting. Instead of waiting for her, my love for her, which had enveloped me, fell away. I became like a tree that the autumn has stripped of its leaves and discovered that she had said what I hadn't dared even to think, and that she had left me because I had left her.

I'm not going to recount my story with Dalia now, not because I want to put it off, but because it's shorthand for all the stories of which my life is made up, and she will crop up everywhere. Even her absence fills places with its ambiguous presence.

When I remember the Lydda ghetto, in which I was born, I feel as though she'd lived the story with me – and then scoff at my memory and scoff at the love that so often made me remind Dalia of events she hadn't lived through. Perhaps that's love – living what we haven't lived as though we had – and when love ends, the memories are transformed into scents we can no longer recall.

Now I live the memory of the fragrance that once was and that appears to me like a dream approaching from afar, as though the life that I have lived has been no more than a rehearsal for the death that awaits me.

Intersections

My present problem is my inability to concentrate and the incoherence of my thoughts. Usually, writers are at a loss as to how to
begin, because the beginnings of their novels define their endings.
I'm not a writer, and I'm not in the process of writing a novel. I let
my memory say what it likes and its images generate themselves
unordered, which is why I don't care about the ending, which I
shall not, in any case, write. Anyone who, like me, wants to tell his
tale should be aware that he will never write the ending, because
he doesn't know it.

My problem is simpler. Now that I've abandoned the idea of
writing the novel about Waddah al-Yaman, the issue has resolved
itself, and all I have to do is to get into the substance and ignore
the breath of poetry with which Waddah's story filled the first
pages of this text, setting me on a wandering course, lost among
meditations and memories, and making me abandon the search
for a beginning that would fit the ending.

The substance is straightforward and simple.

It was 10 February, 2005. I left my work at the restaurant at
7 p.m. I went home, had a shower, and then went to the cinema. I
met Sarang Lee at the intersection of Fifth Avenue and 12th Street
and we walked together. In the lobby, I bought myself a cup of
coffee and my friend a bag of popcorn and a Coke. We went in
and found the theatre was crowded.

To this point, Dalia had been completely absent from the

screen of my memory. New York is a great eraser. It has wiped my memory clean and made me enjoy life's little details. "This is the life!" I said to my soul. "Life is living the present as it is." I envied those Americans who have come to terms with life's details. They've forgotten the larger goals. They've forgotten the massacres that were committed on their land. Even the battle cry against Iraq and the hysterical hatred of the French that accompanied that war now seem fabricated, just entertainment.

I'd convinced myself that here it was up to me finally to live and enjoy life. All my affairs with women were ephemeral and I refused to allow them to break through the walls of my soul, which, after Dalia, I'd rebuilt, adding an iron shield that sprouted from my chest. Even Sarang Lee I'd kept outside this shield, and, although I did almost slip into a love that I had regarded from the beginning as forbidden, I managed not to. I put the past of the past in the place of the past and camouflaged myself with the stories of my grandsires, the Arab poets, regarding this blending into the background as just a game, until, on that freezing New York night, things turned upside down.

New York is a rhythmic city. I discovered there that daily life composes itself from an assemblage of voices, which interconnect along numerous trajectories. Don't believe the poets! This isn't just a city of steel and skyscrapers. It is also a city of exquisite miniature components that exist within it as something simultaneously both strange and familiar. A city without memory! One of my Lebanese customers told me it resembled Beirut, though I didn't believe him, unless we are to regard both cities as existing within a memory that has been lost.

I put myself together anew. I became a lone wolf and forgot all the emotions at one go – a man without affiliation or language, a man over fifty beginning his life in its final moments, intoxicated with death.

I made the small kitchen at the restaurant my world and my friend Chaim was so pleased with my dedication that he suggested we open a real restaurant where I would be the chef, but I refused. He said I had no ambition and he was right. Screw ambition! My little world and my little successes are enough for me, with the books I read, the bars I go to, and my ephemeral women.

I decided I'd write as though I were a reader, which is where the true pleasure lies. You open the covers of the book, you fear its mysterious worlds, and then you slowly draw closer to it, like someone standing on the shore, hesitating in front of the water. Then, when you wade out into it, you find you've become a part of its plunging, rising and falling, waves, and you feel you're the real author of the book because it has become your sole property. That's how I lived my first two years in this city. I'd go to movies, enjoy the ballet and music, drink French wine and vodka, and read as though I were writing.

Sarang Lee wasn't part of my world. She was just a breath of fresh air and only entered my life after the crisis I went through, when I decided to rewrite the novel I hadn't yet written and she became the companion of my dying moments.

I don't wish to generalise and say that every writing is a form of death, but that's how I feel now, as I write. Perhaps all writers have these thoughts, I don't know. In my heart of hearts, I believe that writers approach death certain that they will never die and that death is just an artistic game that allows them to access the most extreme emotions. Personally, I disagree. At the instant when I woke from my coma, I felt death had come so close to me that I'd never again be able to free myself from its clutches and that my decision to abandon the story of Waddah al-Yaman to write the story of my relationship to the movie I'd just seen, with the consequent necessity of writing my own life story, was the very moment of death, from which no man can escape.

No soul knows in what land it shall die, as it says in the Precious Book.

What drove me crazy was the mendacity of the truth. That the director should stand up before the beginning of the showing to talk about Palestine, the author of *Gate of the Sun* next to him, didn't provoke me. I regarded it as just a normal situation that called for no special concern. But when the movie began to tell the story of Assaf's suicide following the death of his friend Danny in Gaza at the beginning of the Second Intifada, I felt the fire ignite in my brain; never before that ill-omened day had I felt as though the folds of my brain were on fire and that the blood was about to explode in my veins. I knew the whole story – not just the story of Assaf, whose video, recorded before his suicide, Dalia had shown me, but also the story of Yibna, the town from which the Palestinian martyr Fahmi Abu Ammouna came – from beginning to end.

My grandmother Najiba, who came to visit me once in Haifa, is originally from Yibna. She lived in Lydda and then bolted with the rest of those who fled, only to find herself back in Yibna. She told me everything. I don't know how she rebuilt her relationships with her family in Nuseirat Camp in Gaza, after they were expelled from Yibna, but she knew everything, which was what drove me to visit them countless years later, encountering there my grandmother's brother, Abd al-Ghaffar, whose story deserves to be told.

Was Sarang Lee right? Should I have kept silent, gone to the director to congratulate him, and then greeted the writer with a show of admiration for his work?

How could I possibly admire what I know to be false? I know Khalil Ayoub, narrator and hero of *Gate of the Sun*, and I know his mother. I met Khalil more than once on the shores of the Dead Sea and the man seemed to me more like a poet than a military commander, despite his having been in charge of one of the branches of the Palestinian Preventive Security force before becoming governor of Nablus. As for his mother, Najwa Ibrahim, she was the beautiful nurse I met at the Ramallah hospital when I broke my hand as a result of a car crash and who asked me to help her sell the house in Lydda that she'd inherited from her Bedouin husband.

I didn't tell Sarang Lee the truth, I told her half of it and left the other half for the dark. The truth is that, three days before I went to see the movie, I'd had a terrifying personal experience: I'd run into Blind Ma'moun by chance in New York. This encounter, which I don't know how to write about or whether I shall ever be able to turn into words, reduced me to a limp rag of confusion and grief and tore my soul apart.

Blind Ma'moun, who lived in a room in the garden of our house in the ghetto for seven years and who was so much like a father to me that when he left us I felt like an orphan, suddenly turned up, more than fifty years later, in the form of an elderly man with the halo of a scholar, come from Cairo to New York to lecture on Palestinian literature and expatiate on the image of Rita in the poetry of Mahmoud Darwish.

He was an enthralling speaker, and his ability to switch between Arabic and English was amazing. He approached the podium with hesitant steps, but as soon as he'd taken his place there, with his dark glasses, he was transformed into a combination of Taha Hussein and Edward Said. The blind man's hesitancy disappeared, to be replaced by an absolute command of the language. He began by speaking about the city of Lydda, in which he had lived until he was twenty-five, saying that the tragedy of Lydda had taught him how to read the silence of victims, and he said that Mahmoud Darwish's poetry was fashioned from the gaps of silence that provide the foundations for the rhythms of the meanings.

Instead of listening to him, I heard the voice of my memory, discovered that only poets can awaken the voices of the departed, and saw the child I was in the lanes of Lydda return to me in a pall of tears that gathered at the corners of my eyes and would not fall.

No sooner, however, had I happened across Ma'moun – the friend of my childhood and my teacher who'd betrayed me when I was seven and gone to Egypt to finish his university studies, leaving me on my own with my mother – than I lost everything again, and felt that that "I" on which I had stumbled was a delusion, because, as far as Ma'moun was concerned, I was no more than a story that deserved to find a writer.

That's what he told me, word for word, when I accepted his invitation to have a drink in the lobby of his hotel after the lecture. He told me I'd been with him all these years as a story that would make a good metaphor, one he'd tried to write several times but without success.

He said most stories find no-one to write them and that he was sorry he'd never be able to write mine, even in his memoirs, which he'd decided to get finished soon, before the final parting, which was at the gates.

I didn't ask him for any further clarification as I was overcome with gloom and thought it pointless to look further into a story the witnesses to which had died, with the exception of this last, who was unable to write it.

Ma'moun recounted my story, which was known to no-one except Manal and himself. When he found out that I was surprised by it, he expressed his astonishment that Manal hadn't told me.

He said he'd made her promise to tell me the truth when I reached fifteen, because a person ought to know the truth about himself, not live a delusion.

And he told me.

I listened to him with my eyes, and saw myself as a baby, lying there sleeping on my mother's breast.

Dear God!

Where did the blind man get that story?

Dear God! Suddenly, at the end of my life, I find out that I'm not me and that the "I" that I see in others' mirrors has turned to shards.

Ma'moun said he'd left the town with the rest of those who fled and walked in the column of death under the bullets, the sun and the thirst, but before reaching Naalin he saw me lying there under an olive tree, on the breast of a dead woman.

IIe said I was still a babe-in-arms (Manal estimated that I was no more than four days old), so he decided to pick me up and take me to my family and set off back towards Lydda again, but none of the throngs of displaced people suffering the thirst and the hunger, many of whom disappeared for ever in the wilds, paid me any attention or took me. He said he'd held me high up, shouting to everyone that he'd found this child lying under an olive tree in the arms of its mother, who had departed this life, but no-one stopped to ask questions or take the child from the

119

blind youth's hands. When he reached the city of ghosts that was called Lydda, and found himself at the hospital, a young nurse called Manal came up to him, took me from his hands, and said I would be her son.

"So Manal isn't my mother?" I asked.

"And Hasan Dannoun isn't your father!" he replied.

"And no-one came looking for me?"

"Your real mother was dead, and they probably thought you'd died with her, in the wilds."

"So why you?"

"How should I know? I swear I just picked you up without thinking, and went back to Lydda and got stuck in the ghetto."

"So you're my father."

"If you like, but how should I know? You're the child of the olive tree."

He said he'd given a lot of thought to writing a novel to be called *The Child of the Olive Tree* that would tell, through me, the story of the terrible tragedy suffered by the people of Lydda, but he couldn't do it. He said he was a critic, not a novelist, "And this is a story that needs a novelist, like Ghassan Kanafani or Emile Habibi."

"But how could you see me? You're blind!"

He said the one who'd seen me was his friend Nimr Abu l-Huda, who'd held his hand the whole way, and that when he'd bent down to pick me up, he'd heard Nimr telling him to leave me and go, but he'd taken me and gone back on his own because his friend Nimr had disappeared into the crowds.

I said I didn't believe him, though in fact I did, and the truth is that I felt nothing. All I felt was that Ma'moun had abandoned me when he went to Egypt and that he'd had no right to.

"It's Manal's fault. I said to her, 'Let's get married and

leave, and take the boy with us,' but she said she wouldn't leave Palestine."

The story seemed meaningless to me. I don't care whose son I am. Better the son of the olive tree in whose shade my true mother, whose name I don't know, died than son of a martyr who fell in the war of the Nakba and grandson of a hero of the First World War.

I told Ma'moun that Manal had been right not to tell me and I didn't hold it against her, but that now I'd begun to understand her, though I couldn't understand Ma'moun's own behaviour. How could he have left his son and gone off and never asked about him?

He said he regretted it, but that he hoped I'd accept his invitation to visit him in Egypt.

He told me the whole story and I listened as one listens to a fairy tale, and when I got up to go at three o'clock in the morning, he repeated his invitation to visit him in Cairo.

I flee from a book that was never written and discover that I don't know who I am.

Am I a child of the story?

The children of stories grow up fast and die fast, and I'm the same. All of us are children of the story, because life itself takes us where it will, just as stories do their heroes.

I was part of one story and tried to escape from it, and I found myself instead the captive of another. My new story turned the whisper of the first into silence.

In order to exist, I was supposed not to have existed. That's the trick that fashioned the beginnings of my life and has stayed with me for fifty years. I've put my life together anew six times – once by fleeing my mother and taking a job at the garage of Mr Gabriel, a Jew; a second time by going to Haifa University and living in the company of religious Jews; a third time by reading and analysing Israeli literature; a fourth time by turning myself into a journalist writing on oriental music and Umm Kulsoum; a fifth time through my relationship with Dalia; and a sixth time by emigrating to New York and leaving everything to work in the restaurant. Today is the seventh time, and I'm putting my life together by collecting its pieces, unpicking it and reweaving it, so as to make a new garment that can only be my shroud. Such is writing. Don't believe the claims of litterateurs and artists: art doesn't conquer death, regardless of what Mahmoud Darwish wrote. Art weaves us a shroud of words and colours in which we wrap ourselves, pretend-ing to find hope where there is none.

When a person reaches the moment at which he claims that he's gathering together the pieces of the life, or lives, that he has lived, or supposes himself to have lived, he discovers that his days have streamed by like an elusive dream.

I am a child of the story and of thirst. My story's water never runs dry and my thirst is never quenched.

Thirst

As my mother told the tale, I was born in thirst. Now, as I write about that woman who vanished from my life when I was fifteen, I don't know whether her lips were indeed cracked in parallel, straight lines, or if it is the image of thirst, which has pursued me since childhood, that transforms her thirsty lips whenever I recall her.

She was my mother, and she was Manal, daughter of Atif Suleiman, of the village of Eilaboun in Galilee. When I remember her, I say, "Manal was . . ." for to me she's like the first word in a sentence that was never completed. After I left the house at fifteen to work in Mr Gabriel's garage in Haifa, I discovered that the woman had passed through my life like a sigh of wind, leaving behind her nothing but her world of stories, and that the only things I could remember of her were her cracked lips, her wide almond-shaped eyes deep inside whose pupils trembled a hint of dark brown, two fine, almost invisible, lines on her cheeks, and a deep feeling that I had been abandoned so that I could live alone.

I don't know what brought this woman of Galilee to Lydda, or why she fled from her village to join a hot and humid city under siege. Is that what love is?

She said that one look from Hasan's eyes had been enough to change the course of her life. When she talked to me about Hasan, she would look at me with pitying eyes and say she'd been surprised that "that boy Adam" (meaning me) did not look like his father.

Hasan was tall, dark-skinned and broad-shouldered. His honey-coloured eyes held a flash like lightning, and his smile, which lit up his face, signalled his attitude to life.

She said she'd met him in Eilaboun. He was with a band of the Holy Struggle *fedayeen*. He asked her about the village spring, so she walked with him and instead of her taking him to the spring, he took her to his city.

The woman loved only one man. When she married Abdallah al-Ashhal and we went to live with him in that house – more of a shack – on the flank of Mount Carmel, she told me she didn't love him and that she'd done it for the respectability. I looked at her with strange eyes and said nothing but decided to leave.

I was ten when I decided to leave the woman for ever. I don't know where that "for ever" came from! I do, however, remember that I whispered it to myself and only put my decision into effect five years later. That's another story, the beginning of my own story.

My mother was a woman fashioned of words, the first word of a sentence with no last word but the ghetto, as though she'd been born there. She had no family, no village and no memory. She didn't talk about Eilaboun or her people and only mentioned her earlier life once, when she told me that I looked like Daoud, and my fate would be like his. She said it with dissatisfaction, because I didn't resemble the man she had loved.

"And who's Daoud?" I asked her.

I was seven. I was standing in front of her as she cut my hair.

"You call this hair?!" she asked.

"What's wrong with it?" I asked.

"Fair," she replied, and said she was sad for me because I looked not like my father but like Daoud.

When I asked her who Daoud was, she said my father had been a hero and when she gave birth to me, she'd felt that Hasan had come back to her. She'd wanted to call me Hasan, after him, but Hajj Iliyya Batshoun, head of the residents' committee in the ghetto, said I was the first child born to the ghetto so they had to call me Adam, and that's what happened, against her wishes.

I asked her again about the Daoud whom I looked like but she didn't reply and I had to wait eight years to listen, on that rainy Haifa night, to the tale of Daoud and his endless wanderings.

I don't know why I didn't ask her more! At that moment, I felt poised to escape the trap of the life my stepfather Abdallah had forced on me and was terrified by the violent sea winds that made the entire hovel shake.

It was two in the morning. I hadn't slept that night and was overwhelmed by anxiety; then the rain came, to make me feel entirely alone in this world. I was sitting in the room with the wide rectangular window that my mother used as her sewing workshop, listening to the shloosh of the rain against the glass. I saw her come in wearing her long, light blue nightdress and stand next to the window. She looked at me with half-closed eyes and said in a whisper that she knew I was going to leave.

"From the day I bore you, I knew you were like Daoud."

She told the tale of the man's endless wanderings. She said they'd lost him because the road had swallowed him.

They were driven out of Eilaboun. They walked and walked till they came to Lebanon and at Tyre they looked for him and couldn't find him. They were told he'd been seen in Sidon. His brother went to Sidon and was told he'd been seen in Beirut and in Beirut he was told he was in Tripoli and in Tripoli they said he was in Aleppo and in Aleppo they said he was in Latakia and in Latakia they said he was in Antioch. His brother went back from Latakia to Sidon, saying he could not go on. "Where should I go? Maybe he's at the ends of the earth now. Am I supposed to go to the ends of the earth to catch up with him?" And when it was decided that the inhabitants of Eilaboun should go back to their village, a year after they'd been driven out of it, his brother Subhi stood in the midst of the families that had gathered to wait for the buses and wept and moved others to weep. He said Daoud must still be walking northwards and would keep walking till he reached the end of the world.

Manal said the people of Eilaboun had returned to their village, but Daoud was still lost, "And you look like him. You too will walk to the end of the world and I can't stop you, because you are following your destiny."

She came close to me. I thought she was going to bend over and hug me to her breast but she remained frozen in place. I thought I saw tears on her cheeks but wasn't sure. The combination of the darkness and the pale light from the electric lamp made me see things as shadows.

Now too I see Manal as a shadow drawn in black, and I see that her lips are cracked and thirsty. In the past, I thought her cracked lips were an indelible trace of the days of thirst in the ghetto, but now I see things differently. I believe her lips cracked out of thirst for a kiss. I'm certain that her relationship with my father was a thirst for love that was realised only on the deathbed, and that the other man, who married her because he was desperate for a house in Lydda that he believed she owned, only to discover she owned nothing – that man never once planted a kiss on her lips because he had no idea how to kiss a woman, or he thought that to kiss one was to make her the equal of a man. When I learned that she'd died alone in Eilaboun after her divorce and that in those last days she'd asked to see me, I didn't cry. I was getting drunk in a bar in Tel Aviv and I don't know what devil possessed me but my reaction to the news was to laugh. A grimace of contempt passed over the face of the man who told me he'd been looking for me for ages because they wanted me there in the village to receive condolences, and he turned his back and left, muttering insults.

Now, when I recall the story, I feel water filling my eyes and taste tears on my lips. I cry without crying and my crying has no meaning, for crying too has its time, and its time had passed.

I got up, filled my glass with French red wine, lit a cigarette, opened the window so that I could breathe in the hot New York summer air that pricks the face like needles, and decided to forget the woman again.

I can say that I've lived alone inside the cages of the ghetto made out of my mother's words and stories and her nostalgia for the days of the barbed wire. That story planted itself in my memory as firmly as if I'd lived it and as if the wire that encircled the Sakna quarter, where the hospital where I was born was located and where Lydda was transformed into a detention camp surrounded on all sides by graves, had been my life; it would become my secret story for over fifty years. When I was asked at Haifa University where I was from, I'd always reply with a single word – the ghetto – thinking my colleagues, male and female, would look at me with pity as the son of a Warsaw Ghetto survivor.

I wasn't lying. I know the stories of the Warsaw Ghetto as well as I know the stories of the ghetto of Lydda. Such stories resemble each other, like the dead. The stories of the first I read innumerable times, till they were engraved on my memory, and those of the second were like a brand stamped on my soul – stories I read and stories I heard, not just with my ears but with my body, on which my mother's words were traced.

All the same . . .

I don't want to lie now as I did during my childhood and early youth. Or rather, I didn't lie: when I was asked who I was, I'd run my fingers through my fair curly hair and say one word, and the listener would understand that I was assigning myself to his memory, not my mother's. It was, of course, a silent lie, but only if we believe that the clouds are lying when they don't bring rain. Silence has been the distinguishing mark of my life, and that is what I have in common with my mother. Now, I call the woman my mother, but I don't remember ever calling her by anything but her name, devoid of the water of motherhood.

Manal was young and will remain so for ever. If I were to meet her now, I'd treat her as a child. She was a child who had never left her childhood behind her. She'd fallen in love with a man twenty years her elder as though it were a game, and the game had led her to a tragedy that would draw a permanent mask of childish pain over her face.

I told her I was going. I was a young man. Down had begun to trace the outline of a moustache and I'd decided I could no longer stand life there, next to the garbage dump, where Abdallah al-Ashhal lived with his wife and her son.

He never once called me "son" or addressed a word to me. He'd speak to my mother so that she could speak to me, since I was her son. I knew nothing about the man. I hated the smell of cognac mixed with garbage that wafted from his mouth and clothes. When I later learned his story, pity blended with my hatred of him and of myself. He hated me and hated my mother's insistence on sending me to the school in Wadi al-Nisnas.

As far as I was concerned, it didn't matter either way. Books were doors that I'd open onto the world, and the Hebrew teacher was pleased at how enthralled I was by "the language of paradise", as he called the language of the Torah, which I alone in my class spoke well. It was my door onto the world. I never got into the worlds of children's books, which didn't attract me. In contrast, I entered a wide world fashioned by literature. I memorised the poetry of Bialik and read the novels of Yizhar, was bewitched by Agnon and amazed by Benjamin Tammuz, but my true love was for Russian literature in translation.

"Your son has to work," the man told my mother, one wintry, rainy night.

When it rains in Haifa and the salty sea wind rages, you feel that you, in your house on the flank of Carmel, are in an ark tossed by the waves, and that the dove will drown in the sea.

I told the daughter of the owner of the garage where I'd ended up both working and living, whose name was Rivka, about the dove planted in the water. It was my point of entry into her heart. The girl understood what I meant by the simile only when we went far out to sea together on a fishing boat. There, Rivka discovered the dove and almost drowned in the sea . . . which is another story that deserves to be told.

"I can't spend any more on him. He's big as a donkey now, so he has to work and help me," my stepfather said.

The donkey decided to leave. That night, he didn't sleep a wink, and at two in the morning Manal came to him and he didn't say anything because she already knew.

I was surprised the woman didn't ask me where I was going.

She bent down and kissed me and said it was time, so I understood that she knew and that she wanted me to go.

She went to her room and returned, tiptoeing on her bare feet, then gave me a long letter written in ink that had faded almost to illegibility, along with a sheet of paper written in clear ink.

"These papers," she said, "are your father's will. I'm giving them to you even though he left them for me, because I have no right to them. They are the will your father left you."

I took the papers in my hand and almost laughed.

"You call these papers a will?" I asked.

"We own nothing," she replied, "but words."

Such was our farewell. She said she might have been wrong. "Well, well, maybe it would have been better to bury the will with your father, but at the time, poor us, I had no idea what was going to happen and everything was topsy-turvy. I didn't know what to do and now I'm handing over the sacred trust. You're his son. Do with them as you like."

I put the will in my bag and left, and when I read the pages in the cramped room where I stayed at Mr Ghurbial's garage, I felt for the first time like a character in a novel, not a real person. When the feeling repeated itself forty years later in New York as I listened to my blind friend Ma'moun telling me my story as he had lived it in Lydda and in the midst of the Caravan of Death that had left the city, I felt as though a thunderbolt had split me in two, and no longer knew who I was. It is a story that "if inscribed with needles on men's eyes would serve as a lesson for the wise", as Scheherazade puts it in her book (inviting us to read the story with Ma'moun's blind vision).

The Blind Man and the Goalkeeper

All that remains with me of my childhood is a vague image of two friends with whom I lived through the days of the ghetto, to the rhythm of my mother's stories.

Can I really describe Ma'moun and Ibrahim as friends?

Ibrahim was a friend of Ma'moun's, which is why he became my friend. Ma'moun was the one who put together this trinity of friendship, which was like a ladder in terms of our ages, Ma'moun being eighteen years, Ibrahim five years older than me. Despite this, Ma'moun was able to build a pyramid of friendship. He brought us together in the midst of a melting pot that can be understood only through the sense of loss that had transformed the inhabitants of the city of Lydda into strangers.

Ma'moun was my first friend.

I called the man a friend because he insisted on being so called, though it would have been more appropriate for me to call him a father. I know nothing of his relationship with my mother but I came to consciousness to find him already in our house. True, he called the room he lived in *his* house, but his room was in the courtyard of the house that had become ours after the fall of Lydda, so it was as though he was living with us. With him I learned to see through closed eyes and to read the letters of darkness.

The blind man was like my father. With him I discovered I was living in a world of the imagination, even though it was real and tangible. The things around us were substitutes for other things.

131

Our house wasn't our house but a substitute for the one that had been occupied by people who'd come from Bulgaria. It was that house, which we were not allowed to enter, that my mother called "our house", while she called the one that we lived in "the Kayyali house". Likewise, my father, who had died before I was born, became a father in the story but my day-to-day father was the blind man who taught me and took care of me because my mother was kept busy all day long by her work in the neighbouring citrus grove.

Following the removal of the barbed wire that had defined the borders of the ghetto that the people of the town lived in after the fall of their city and the Dahmash Mosque massacre – after which the vast majority of them were forced into displacement on the Caravan of Death – Ma'moun the Blind became the ghetto's teacher. He was the only one among the young people to have graduated – in 1948, from the Amiriya College in Jaffa – and to have his matriculation certificate, so it was agreed that he should open a school to teach the fifteen or so boys and girls, ranging in age from five to fourteen, who were all that remained of Lydda's younger generation. I went to this bizarre school for two years, until it was closed following the return of normality to the city and the opening of the first official Arab school, which was placed in the charge of a teacher from Nazareth called Mr Awwad Ibrahim.

Ma'moun succeeded in turning his school, which he named the Lydda Oasis, into the only place to preserve some vestiges of the city that had been destroyed.

How the blind youth managed to administer a school consisting of a single schoolroom holding a mixture of ages and levels is an amazing story that made of Ma'moun "the only person in the city who could see", which is how Nurse Ghassan Batheish described him at the celebration held in the square in front of the mosque to bid farewell to Professor Ma'moun, who had decided to travel to Nablus and rejoin his family, and who was to set off from there for Cairo or Beirut to complete his studies.

In those days, no-one opposed the idea of someone leaving Palestine, of which the name was now Israel. Once, with the opening of the official school, the blind professor lost his job because the city's Education Office, citing his disability, refused his request to be appointed as an English-language teacher, he no longer had any reason to stay, far from his family, who had moved out two months before the fall of the city.

Ma'moun had refused to leave and he had lived alone through the siege of Lydda and the massacre. In the mass exodus known as the Caravan of Death, he had decided to go back, having discovered that the humiliation that faced him in exile would not be much different from that which faced him in the occupied city. Once he told the students of his school that he'd decided he would prefer to die from the bullets than of thirst in the desert. There, in the Sakna Quarter, which had become the city's wire-fenced ghetto, he slept in the Great Mosque for two days before finding for Manal the house in whose garden he would live, in a room built originally for storage.

Ma'moun invented a unique teaching method: he divided the students into three groups, a Big Class, a Middle Class and a Little Class. He taught the big students Arabic, English and maths; the big students taught the middle class; and the middle students taught the little ones. The textbooks were brought him by the big students from their raids on abandoned houses, from which he had asked them to bring him whatever textbooks, exercise books and pencils they might come across.

By such means, work at the school was set on a sound footing, and our professor was possessed of an amazing memory, as though he'd learned every book by heart. When teaching us, he seemed to read through his eyelids, which he would move, allowing him to see everything. He corrected using his finger, with which he would draw the words in the air, and nothing escaped him, so much so that the students believed that this blind man wasn't blind at all but sighted and that he placed thick black spectacles over his eyes so that he could read people's secrets.

Ma'moun chose Ibrahim among all the students to be his friend. Ibrahim was a hard-working student, but failed to perform outstandingly in any subject. Despite this, Prof. Ma'moun chose him as his friend because he saw in him the flower of Palestinian youth that would inevitably awaken once the terror of the days of the Nakba was over.

When he left us, to complete his studies, I felt I'd been left an orphan, that my world was coming apart, and that I could no longer see things. After his sudden departure, which I was unable to comprehend, everything lost its meaning, and two months later Ibrahim left us too, telling us, jumping up and down with joy, that his mother had decided to go back and live with her family in Nazareth. Nazareth, as Ibrahim told us, repeating his mother's words, was still an Arab city: "There we can breathe and die, because we'll be among our own people, and there I can realise my dream and become a goalkeeper in a football team."

That day, on which I was seven years old, I felt I was suffocating and alone. I think Manal too must have felt homesick, because she wasn't from there, and both her men had left her on her own, with a small child called Adam. In her marriage to the man who humiliated both her and me, she found herself a doorway that got her out of Lydda and took her to live in Haifa.

In Haifa, I learned how to read the pages of the sea and to become friends with the foam of the waves that beat on the endless shore. There, at the school at Wadi al-Nisnas, I found, in books, my refuge and my world. I was bewitched by the books of the Old Testament, especially the *Lamentations of Jeremiah*, in which I found an echo of the pain that for no clear reason had spread through the tops of my shoulders. My mother took me to the Arab doctor in Wadi al-Nisnas, whose name I no longer remember. He told her there was "nothing wrong with the boy – they're psychological symptoms resulting from trauma". He advised her to take care of me and said the best cure was sea air, and the sea's iodine-rich waters.

I asked my mother what "trauma" meant and she didn't know, but the word gave me a feeling of importance. I used to tell my schoolmates, when I pulled out of a game of leapfrog, that I had "a serious illness called trauma". This led to "Trauma" becoming one of my names at school, and I only found out what it meant at Haifa University when I took a class in the Nazi holocaust during which the professor described the trauma that afflicted Jews who had survived the disaster.

From time to time, the blind man would call me by the name Naji, meaning "Saved", and when I got angry and rejected it because I already bore the name of Adam, the father of humankind, he would pat me on the shoulder and tell me, "Your name is also Naji, and time will teach you what it means to bear two names."

When I complained once to my mother that he'd called me Naji at school, she smiled and said, "Let him say what he wants. He's blind, and the blind see things we don't."

I never asked, during my childhood, why this man lived in our house. I came to consciousness in this world when he was already an inseparable part of it, so I never asked my mother, "Who is Ma'moun?" Just once, when Manal informed me that she'd decided to marry Abdallah al-Ashhal, I asked her why she hadn't married Ma'moun. She didn't reply, and the question remained unanswered. Why did they live together, and what was the nature of their relationship? Did Manal want Ma'moun to be like a father to me, after the death of my real father? And how could the people of the ghetto accept this business of a young man living with a young widow in the same house?

That's the mystery of my mother.

All my life I felt that the woman was concealed behind a great mystery whose walls I was incapable of breaching or making a hole in to peep through. She hid her story in her dark brown eyes and never divulged it to me, and now I behold her walking like a phantom, her feet not touching the ground, roaming our little house on the flank of Mount Carmel and then stopping in front of the door that faced the sea of Haifa and taking the sea air into the depths of her lungs.

A woman of thirst, who filled all the vessels in the house with water because the experience of the ghetto had taught her to fear its absence. Her husband constantly expressed his disgust at her infatuation with water and cursed her for turning the house into a swamp.

Manal, my young mother, who drowned in her tears the day of Ma'moun's departure, didn't cry the night I told her I was leaving home. I couldn't see the effect of my words on her features but I felt she had drowned in her eyes and gone far away. Her eyes were her weapons. She'd open them as wide as they would go, then narrow them as though she were squeezing the whole world inside them and turn away in silence.

Ma'moun, Ibrahim and Manal – this was the trinity that surrounded my childhood and formed my memories of the ghetto. True, by the time I became conscious of the world, the wire had been removed and the people of the ghetto were no longer obliged to get permission from the Israeli officer to leave it, but the wires remained in their lives; indeed, their presence had become stronger.

When, so as to cross into the city, we passed the places where the fence had been, we would bend our backs a little as though passing beneath the barbed wire. Even blind Ma'moun would bend, without anyone telling him that the fence had been there. We would duck and then continue on our way, as though slipping through from one place to another.

The people of the ghetto were one family, and I, Adam Dannoun, was the first child of the ghetto, so they adopted me, one and all. However, the man who became engraved on my memory as a father who didn't beget me was Ma'moun, who surrounded me on every side, taught me to read the darkness, and then left me to my fate and departed.

The Will: Manal

Manal said it was his will and I had to take it with me wherever I might go. She didn't ask me where I was going or how I'd survive on my own or what I planned to do in the future about my education. She just said she'd known the time would come and it seemed it had. We were like two strange ghosts swaying in the Haifa darkness. I stand facing the distant sea, inhale the dampness of the night, and watch my mother withdrawing.

I decided to leave because I couldn't stand her husband any longer. At fifteen, I felt I'd become a man and that my stepfather, who reeked of garbage and cognac, hated me, and I had to make up my mind either to kill him or to go.

That is what I thought then. I was certain it was the right decision: I had to escape that atmosphere. Today, though, I discover, as I write down these stories, that it wasn't my decision, and that I left because my mother had withdrawn.

I can imagine that the cause of her introversion and silence was her inability to have children. Her husband Abdallah never stopped cursing her because she couldn't have children and he wanted a son to carry his name and didn't want as his heir that orphan "whose name you didn't know, so you called him Adam".

He called me "the orphan", and hated my name because it wasn't a name, and my going to school provoked him because it turned me into a burden on him and on society. His problem was not with me, though, but with Manal. He'd married her believing the house in which we lived in the Lydda ghetto belonged to us and he could sell it whenever he wanted. When he found out that our own house was now listed as absentee property, that it belonged to the state and was no longer ours to dispose of, that the Israeli authorities had confiscated it and given it to a Bulgarian immigrant family, and that the house we were living in belonged to the Kayyali family, who had moved to the West Bank, he went crazy.

"The martyr left you nothing, and I hate martyrs," he used to tell her when he was drunk, and I'd see her humiliation, and mine, and could do nothing.

Why didn't I tell her to come with me?

Why didn't she suggest she come with me? She made do with saying goodbye in silence. Then she went into the bedroom, returned with an envelope, gave it to me, saying, "This is your father's will," and left me alone in the dark.

I don't know why I didn't open the envelope that night. I put it among my clothes and carried it with me on all my moves, but I didn't open it until the garage. At that point, I understood nothing, could find no mystery, and thought many times of tearing it up, but didn't dare. Like all Palestinians, who lost everything when they lost their homeland, I throw away nothing connected to our fugitive memory, for we are slaves to that memory. It isn't true what Jabra Ibrahim Jabra says in his novel *The Ship* to the effect that "memory is music". No, memory is a wound in the soul that never closes. You have to learn to live with its pus, oozing from its open sores.

I went back to the will once more and discovered on reading it that it had nothing to do with me. It was a letter Ali Dannoun, my supposed grandfather, had written to his father from Manchuria just before he died. Probably Ali's son Hasan, my father, had inherited the letter from his grandfather, preserved it, and then given it to his wife as he lay dying in the hospital at Lydda, and it was never intended to be a will. I don't know why Manal thought that the letter had to be in my possession and that I had to bear the burden of my martyred grandfather as well as that of my martyred father!

I don't feel I can go on writing. After my encounter with Ma'moun, the significations of things changed and I became like a blind man. This time, the stories were true. Ma'moun told me, as he said goodbye, that the story of Lydda had been inscribed on his eyes and that he hadn't written out the story of his city because the ink with which it was inscribed was colourless, and all we had to do was look into his closed eyes and read.

"I left you, Naji, my beloved, because I had no other choice."

"And what was the name of the babe-in-arms you found beneath the olive tree on its dead mother's breast?" I asked him.

"How should I know? That's why I called you Naji."

"I want my original name," I said.

"Your name, Naji my beloved, is Naji."

I didn't believe him. I don't mean that I didn't believe the story of the olive tree: despite its symbolic importance, it's just part of a story of which I cannot claim to be the sole hero and which shouldn't therefore be allowed to have any impact on what time remains to me. I am I and I don't want to be made into a symbol. I hate symbols, and that was one of the reasons I abandoned my plan to write the story of Waddah al-Yaman. This is why I have to ignore the tale Ma'moun told me, even though I now believe that it played a large role in Manal's marriage and her withdrawal from me. But I don't believe Ma'moun had no choice. Probably the man could not stand being without a job following the closure of his school, so he decided to flee the responsibility for a woman and child with which he had found himself stuck.

But how can I write my story now that Ma'moun has revealed my secret?

My only choice is to return to Waddah al-Yaman, not to follow his story but to bury that of my being found beneath the olive tree in the coffer of love; to leave it immersed there in the water of forgetfulness and never let it float back up to the surface. I shall leave it and go back to my name, for I am Adam of the Ghetto: my father died in the hospital before I was born, my mother conceived me in miraculous fashion when she slept next to the dying man in his bed in the hospital at Lydda, and Iliyya Batshoun, when he saw me swathed in my mother's arms, cried out my name, saying, "An Adam for the ghetto!"

I have placed the story of the olive tree inside Waddah al-Yaman's coffer and turned to the story of the Adam of the Ghetto to give me a chance to say that I shall postpone until its time is come the story of Naji, the one saved in the embrace of his despairing mother, who died of hunger and thirst beneath the olive tree. I am Adam, scion of the family of Dannoun, in the name of one of whose ancestors, a Sufi sheikh, a time-ravaged shrine had been built on the edge of town.

I shall leave the story of Ma'moun and his silent love for Manal and go back to the beginning of the story.

All the same, I ought to have asked Ma'moun about his love for Manal. It's a story that wasn't told in the alleyways of the ghetto and has remained immured in oblivion. It all comes down to the fact that my imaginative memory (fictional elements always creep into, and in large part fashion, our memories) transformed this supposed relationship into a tempestuous love affair, which ended with its hero's departure.

I cannot place this story properly in the sequence of the first days following the city's fall, the expulsion of its inhabitants, and their wandering in the desert. Manal told me nothing, and it would have been unreasonable to expect her to do so. Women are shy, and they prefer to remain, in the eyes of their children, swathed in chastity, the mother being for ever a sacred, inviolable figure. This was the image of mothers that prevailed in my childhood and it's the one that, though it would change with time, has remained firmly embedded in my sensibility.

In those days, the mother had to preserve that halo, created from her love, as something for her children alone. Even the man, or spouse, had to stay somewhere in the darkness. The light was dedicated to the sacred relationship that made "mother" another name for virtue.

Manal said nothing about the matter, and, strangely, I never heard any insinuations from my mates about my mother's relationship with "Prof. Ma'moun". At the time, I regarded Ma'moun's presence in the garden room in our house as quite natural. Similarly, I gave no thought to certain mysteries that I witnessed during my childhood and whose implications became clear to me only when I fell in love with Rivka, the daughter of the owner of the garage where I used to work, and felt a tingling in my lips – the same tingling whose effects I would feel on my mother's as she gave me my goodnight kiss.

I can't forget a certain stormy winter's night when I woke up in a panic at the sound of thunder and of the whiplash of the hail striking against the window and didn't find her next to me in the bed. I got up, shivering with cold, and searched the house for her, but she wasn't there. I sat, cradling myself, on the couch in the living room and cried. I must have dozed off, and when I woke, found myself borne in the arms of my mother, whose clothes were wet with rain, and put back to bed. At that instant, the sky lit up with lightning and I beheld my mother's face. It was bright and beautiful. Everything about it shone. She kissed me on my eyes and I caught the taste of her tingling lips.

She took to disappearing, or I began to notice her night-time disappearances. I wasn't scared any more. I was certain she'd come back and didn't ask her, or even myself, where she went, and I made no connection between Ma'moun's living in the garden room and her absences.

Is this enough for me to assume a story? Of course not. But I sensed mysteries, from whispers at the dinner table, or the accidental touch of hands, or his insistence when he asked her to stop working in the citrus groves of the Jews because his salary from the school was enough for us all.

Manal would always answer him by saying that she wasn't working in the groves of the Jews: "This is our land," she would say, "and soon we'll get it back."

What happened, then, and why did the relationship end as it did?

It isn't true that when I met Ma'moun in New York I didn't ask him about his relationship with my mother because I was embarrassed. I didn't ask because I lost the capacity to speak when I discovered that the man had been dealing with me not as the son he'd abandoned but as a story. I felt anger and grief. I'm a person, not a story—though look at what I'm doing to myself right now! What irony! I'm sitting in my little apartment in New York, piles of writing paper before me, transforming myself into a story and becoming what Ma'moun wanted me to be!

143

It's pitiful, and takes me to the verge of the melodrama that I eschewed when I pooh-poohed the story of the child lying on its mother's breast, abandoned to a wretched fate, saying it was a truth that changed nothing – I had read dozens of similar stories about the children of the Nakba, not to mention that of the child whom Umm Hasan named Naji in *Gate of the Sun*, and I'd heard the story about the baby abandoned to death and worms in a house in Lydda that Saleem told every time my mother spoke of her nostalgia for the days of the ghetto.

Ma'moun said I was a story, but failed to realize that he too might become one and that in order for me to renovate my own story, I would have to reassemble the passages missing from his with my mother, passages I would never be able to find anywhere.

How did the love story of Manal and Ma'moun begin?

It was a love without a story, for stories, if they are to exist, must have a beginning. My mother never tired of recounting the beginning of her love for Hasan Dannoun, the martyr. She said that when she walked ahead of his horse to lead him to the spring, she felt her feet could no longer hold her up. "In his eyes was an irresistible brilliance. He was on the run from the British army, who were rounding up the revolutionaries, and he passed through our village, and I was with a crowd of girls. He stopped and looked at me. He chose me from all the rest to guide him to the spring."

All I could gather from her was that the story of her love for Hasan remained at the beginning, since it ended the moment the girl from Eilaboun thought it had begun. The man, with whom she went without a backwards glance, took her to his mother's house, and left. He married her in a hurry and left, and when he came back, so that the story could begin, he took a bullet in the back and died.

Ma'moun's story, on the other hand, never began because Manal found herself in the middle of it without realising. I can imagine the story the way it appeared to me during the New York nights. Here in New York, when I found myself on my own, I grasped that my mother had lived two aborted loves – the first had died, and the other she was afraid of, so she'd let it go. Two aborted loves – the first born of admiration for the knight riding a hero's horse, the second of pity for the blind man who'd come back, bringing her the present her horseman hadn't been able to give her. Two men combined in the woman's emotions and became one man living in two darknesses – the darkness of the grave for which her horseman had left, and the darkness of the eyes in which her new man lived.

Ma'moun saw things differently, though. Once he asked me to describe colours to him and I was at a loss as to how to answer. Colours are resistant to language because they bear their own language within them. I was a child, and didn't know how to describe things, and with Ma'moun I was astonished at the blind man's ability to describe them down to their finest details.

He said the Arabs were the masters of description: "Our pre-Islamic poetry is an epic of description without equal among the literatures of the world." He also said he was obliged to translate shapes into words in order to be able to interact with them but had no idea how to translate colours into words that could give voice to their descriptions.

This was, as far as I remember, a few months before his departure. I closed my eyes and saw the colour black, cracked apart by white infiltrating from the daylight. I screwed up my lids so as to drown my eyes in it and told him that at least he knew one colour for sure, which was black.

I remember he didn't reply but muttered something indistinct.

When we met in New York after his lecture at the university, he reminded me of that conversation and said I'd been wrong.

"It's a mistake," he said, "that most writers fall into when they write about the blind. I don't live in the colour black because I don't know what you mean by that word. I live in my world, which is unlike yours and which you may, if you wish, describe as a world without colours, though that description has no meaning for me."

He said he could see: "I am the only person in whose depths the tragedy of Lydda is engraved. When the great Lydda massacre of July 1948 occurred, it took a blind man to see it. History is blind, Naji my beloved, and it takes a blind man like me to see it. Now do you understand? I didn't abandon you; I had to go so that the blindness of history could be realised to the full through the three of us – me, you and Manal."

I felt like telling him that Ismail Shammout, who painted the bodies of Palestinian men and women aghast before the terror of the massacre and the expulsion from Lydda, was the one who'd seen, but I didn't. At that meeting, at which we were joined by another man, who caught up with us in the lobby of the Washington Square Hotel at eleven o'clock that night, I found myself powerless to speak.

I'm not going to talk about that other man now. I'm sure Ma'moun invited him so he could wrap the rope of the mirror around my neck and show me the other image of myself, the one embodied in a university professor teaching philosophy at the University of Pennsylvania whom he introduced to me as Dr Naji al-Khatib. Ma'moun had told me about this other Naji, whom Umm Hasan had picked up from where he lay beneath an olive tree and restored to his mother in the village of Cana.

"You're like facing mirrors. Anyone willing to look will see in you two all he needs to read the Nakba," said Ma'moun.

I want to forget about that other Naji for now. I don't like playing games with life. We aren't heroes of novels that our fates and stories should be played around with like that. I'm not a child and I hate heroes. I'm just a man who has tried to live and has discovered the impossibility of doing so. I'm not saying life has no meaning, because meaning has no meaning and looking for it seems to me boring and trivial. I'm a man who's lived all his life in the postponed and the temporary.

Ma'moun left me, which is understandable. It's what fathers usually do. Some of them, in fact, kill their children, which is to be expected and should come as no surprise. Since the story of Our Master Abraham (peace be upon him) and his son, fathers have repeated the act of killing. But not mothers!

Why did Manal let me go? Why didn't she come with me and leave her husband Abdallah al-Ashhal, who was going to divorce her anyway?

Was she afraid of him and his complexes about women? His first wife had left him after they were driven from Haifa to Lebanon. She took his three daughters and slipped over the border and took them back to Haifa. When he himself slipped over the border four years later and caught up with her, he felt miserable because he discovered that his wife was no longer his wife, his daughters had become another man's daughters, and his house was occupied by strangers. He had to live like a thief on the outskirts of the city in which he'd been born, and work at the garbage dump, where he lived and picked his daily bread from leftovers. And in Manal he found the refuge that could never replace his life.

What have I to do with this man's story? His time will come, and what I want to say now is that I don't understand why Manal abandoned me! Did the young woman think she was living a Greek tragedy, whose last word has to go to Fate, not its victims? We Arabs, though, are ignorant in our classical tradition of anything one could call "tragedy". The blind Argentinian writer Jorge Luis Borges scoffed at us for translating the words "tragedy" and "comedy" as though they meant "panegyric" and "satire", translations that cost our philosophers an understanding of Aristotelian aesthetics, which they distorted. The blind Argentinian scoffed at all the sighted Arabs but didn't dare to go near Abu al-Alaa' al-Maarri, not just because the blind man of Maarra understood the meaning of the two words and translated them beautifully but because he sailed off to a faraway place and, in *The Epistle of Forgiveness*, charted the path for literature's magic journey to Heaven and Hell, initiating the discussion between the dead and the living that lies at its heart.

Manal's behaviour probably wasn't tragically inspired but might rather be described as pushing melodrama to its limits. The silence of women in Egyptian movies is a gateway to melodrama, and Manal kept silent and sank deep into melodrama, thereby losing everything. We're not in a movie directed by Adel Imam that has to have either a happy ending to make the audience happy or a sad one to make its tears flow. Here, the ending that a director might imagine in order to bring me, her and Ma'moun together doesn't exist. We're in a real tragedy, whose elements have become twisted together so as to form themselves in our consciousness into a melodrama. It isn't beautiful and leaves no doors open to hope. On the contrary, the story opens onto an unending hell of further stories.

I imagine the love story that brought Manal and Ma'moun

148

together, and become frustrated because my imagination refuses to help me. Ma'moun told me he loved her and left it at that, adding not a single word. She herself said nothing, not because I didn't find the courage to ask her but because her marriage to Abdallah al-Ashhal made her wrap herself in the cloak of silence.

How should I describe her silence?

I was a child living off the crumbs of stories told only in whispers, and after Manal married, the whispers stopped. The woman came to be surrounded by a wall of silence. My memories are probably inaccurate, because her muteness in fact began when Blind Ma'moun left. That day, I watched as a pall of sorrow enveloped her, and when I asked her about him, she'd always answer by saying, "He went home. They all went home." I discovered her silence after her marriage and our move to Haifa. The only way I can explain her marriage today is to say that it was revenge: Manal couldn't find anyone to take revenge on, so she took revenge on herself.

I hated her, felt that she'd abandoned me, and found myself a stranger in the new house we moved to. At the time, I had no idea that we'd been obliged to vacate our house in Lydda. I don't know exactly what happened but the one time Manal told me about why we had moved to Haifa, she said that "they wanted to take the house".

I didn't ask her to whom the pronoun referred for in those days "they" meant one thing. "They" meant the Jews.

They took her first house, then expelled her from her job as a nurse at the hospital because she didn't have a nursing certificate. Then she worked in the olive field and citrus grove that had belonged to her husband Hasan, both of which were then registered as absentee property. And in the end, they took the second house, next door to the hospital, in which she'd taken refuge during the days of the ghetto.

Now, after her death, when I remember her silence, I'm struck by something akin to passionate love. When I tried to describe Dalia as being "as beautiful as silence", she, my Jewish girlfriend, looked at me in amazement and asked me if it was an Arab thing to describe beauty in this way. I replied that I'd read the comparison in a poem whose writer's name I could no longer remember, but she said she didn't like the strange simile. "Silence is the opposite of love," she said.

I don't know why Dalia misunderstood me. I wasn't describing love, I was describing silence. All the same, I told her she was right. That's how lovers turn into idiots, or become naive and agree without thinking. Love for Dalia took me to the gardens of speech but didn't change my opinion on the aesthetics of silence. Beauty has no name, and Manal was beautiful the way she was. Despite which, I lost Manal just as I lost Dalia.

I don't know why, but I'm sad! Sorrow isn't regret but memory, just as memory isn't nostalgia but the mark of a branding iron planted deep within us.

The Will: God's She-camel

I don't know why every time I tried to ignore the papers Manal
had given me as my father's will I'd find myself stuck in the same
trap: I'd rush to the papers, read them, reread them, and then
decide there was no point in bothering with them; they were
worthless, and I should tear them up. But instead of doing so, I'd
put them back in the folder and decide not to write about them,
because they didn't deserve to be part of my life.

Today I'm at a loss: it seems the price of ridding oneself of the
delusion of belonging is to belong.

I remember I was sitting alone in the night of the garage where
I worked and lived when an obscure sadness swept over me. I
shall refer to this fit of sorrow by the name of the city, and give
the sadness that has dogged me all my life its own special name –
"the sadness of Haifa".

The sadness of Haifa has no cause. It doesn't come from anger
at anything or because of the loss of something and it in no way
resembles depression. It's a state that afflicts the soul, palpating
its darkened chambers and settling there, making my solitariness
and self-sufficiency part of the translucence of the sorrowful
moment, a moment that may dissipate after a short while or go
on for days.

I connected Haifa with this state because of the sea. During
the part of my childhood that I spent in the ghetto, I never saw the
sea. When I went with my mother to Haifa and felt my heart gasp

before the blue-streaked whiteness, an obscure feeling struck me that robbed me of the power of speech. Later, I discovered that the only name to fit that feeling was "the sadness of Haifa".

A sadness unlike sadness: the Haifa sea mirrors the sadness of this city that sweeps down from the top of Mount Carmel and then stretches out its wings like a dove swooping over the vastness of the water.

In the midst of this sadness, I went back to my bag, read what Manal called "the will", and decided to forget about it, because it meant nothing to me.

Back then, I believed that it meant nothing to me, but today I don't know.

Today, having drunk my ration of French red wine, I decided to go back to the folder and try to understand.

I contemplated the photo of my father, wrapped in white paper. I couldn't fail to be entranced by the magic of his smile and his wide-open eyes. I put the photo aside and went back to the papers.

I read the four pages, whose edges had crumbled from the damp, and fell into a deep slumber from which I was only rescued by the rain, which had made its way in through my window, open to the humid and stifling heat of New York.

How am I to rewrite this "will", which in no way resembles a will, to make it a part of my life? Why do I have to? Is it because the headline on the newspaper cutting placed inside the folder as part of the will held an irresistible magic? It was the front page of a newspaper put out by captive Ottoman army officers in Krasnoyarsk in Siberia and called *God's She-camel*. At the top of the page was a picture of a camel lost in Siberia and beneath it was written, "A Satirical Literary Critical Weekly". To the right of the page was written a verse from the Koran referring to the miraculous story of God's She-camel, which the Prophet Salih used as a demonstration of his powers when his people challenged him to show them a sign, which in this case took the form of a she-camel producing milk: "O my people, this is the She-camel of God, to be a sign for you. Leave her that she may eat in God's earth, and touch her not with evil, lest you be seized by a nigh chastisement." (Hud, verse 64.)

The only explanation for my going back to the papers is the magic of words. Magic began with words, and when words are written down they pulsate with life's possibilities. So here I am, gazing dumbstruck at words from the past's own past, and finding myself before a story to which I feel myself to be heir simply because I'm its only reader.

This, of course, takes me back to my relationship with reading, which I can't reveal to anyone because it's so hard to believe. Despite the conviction of my teachers at the Wadi al-Nisnas school that I would become a poet or a writer, I have spent the whole of my life unable, or, let us say, unwilling, to write. I satisfied myself with writing articles in Hebrew on the aesthetics of the Arabic musical modes and never attempted to write a single short story; even though my head was awash with stories that I made up for myself, I never wrote them down.

The reason was my infatuation with reading. Don't misunderstand me: my infatuation with reading doesn't imply any feelings on my part of inadequacy before the creations of the writers whose novels and verses I love. On the contrary, the feeling that affects me when I read a beautiful text is of being a partner in its writing or, more accurately, of being its true author. The actual writer becomes no more than a meaningless name or signature.

This feeling took me to faraway places of whose existence I

had never dreamed and made me feel full. I am a writer full of the texts that I have read/written and that I treat as though real, and I exploit the imagination of others to serve my own. From this perspective, I'm the writer who never wrote anything because he wrote everything, and this makes me superior to all the rest of the world's writers, who sense that an arid emptiness surrounds them, while I feel pleasure and a thirst for yet more of the water of words.

You may find what I'm saying strange, and you're right. Even I, to be honest, find it strange, and hard to believe. But your more legitimate question would be, why did I decide, at the end of my life, to write, abandoning the pleasures of fullness for the desert of emptiness?

(I write as though I were addressing someone, even though I know that what I'm writing isn't publishable and will never be published: I have reached such a degree of despair that I will never try to have it printed, no matter how much the glory of being called "a writer" urges me to seek that glory for my own name. All the same, I write like this because I feel I can speak to words, for words are living creatures, capable of listening, provided we address them in the proper way.)

Where were we?

We were trying to tell the story of the will and then we stumbled over the question of the meaning of my decision to write, at the end of my life.

The question does not, of course, concern itself with these personal stories of mine, because they have no shape, and when a text has no shape, it can never be put into a particular literary pigeonhole and, consequently, never be a source of existential anxiety to its writer.

The question, then, concerns itself with my project to write the Waddah al-Yaman novel, the truth of which is that it was never more than a passing urge that I got over quickly, since I'm not the right person to write a major Palestinian metaphor/allegory based on the story of that eternal lover. It was an urge through which I thought I'd be able to fill the emptiness of my days by writing the Long-Awaited Novel.

There's always a Long-Awaited Novel, and it takes a courageous author to decide to stake his reputation on writing it. Palestine has been waiting for such a novel for more than half a century and I'd lose nothing if I gave it a try, so why not let me, Adam Dannoun, son of Hasan, bearer of the will of God's She-camel, be that writer?

The truth is that a much more urgent motive to write was personal and sprang from my relationship with Dalia. It was the idea of the end of love, not its beginning.

However, I've discovered I'm not the writer who has the right to pen the Long-Awaited Novel, because there is no Long-Awaited Novel. All things are vanity. Even the story of Waddah al-Yaman, with all its symbolic incandescence, will never be more than one among hundreds of stories, and not even, for sure, the best of them.

I have decided to devote myself to writing about the transform-ation of writing into a personal game, using this text, with which I feel, as I write it, that I'm rewriting all the novels that I have ever loved, freed of the burden of form and avoiding the need to cross the desert of emptiness that encircles literary writing.

(This ends my response to that question, which I must never bring up again.)

Full stop.

At the bottom of the first page of the newspaper called *God's*

She-camel is an article with the title "The Shrine of the Prophet Dannoun the Egyptian in Palestine". Unsigned, the article gathers some of the sayings of the Sufi for whom the people of Lydda built a shrine in their city. I suspect that the author of the article was my grandfather, the page having being added to the letter that the man wrote on his deathbed in Manchuria and that was delivered to his family by the famous Palestinian historian Aref al-Aref, when he returned from captivity on the Russian front during the First World War.

Next to the newspaper there were two handwritten pieces of paper in which the man tells of his sad death in a strange land, longing for his wife and children, with prayers to God to help the poor so that justice may spread throughout the world, along with stuff about Arabdom, Islam and Palestine.

The writing is so faded as to be almost indecipherable, and the whole story can be found in summary form in the letter's first paragraph:

After the torment of our captivity and hunger in the middle of Siberia, and accompanied by noble brothers from Syria and Palestine, God decreed our release at the hands of the Bolsheviks who no sooner had they succeeded in their revolution than they released us from our captivity. We left the camp, free to wander as we wished, and traversed countries and cities in our desire to return home. Now I am here, afflicted with fever, in a small village in Manchuria, looked after by my dear brothers, but I feel the death tremors passing through my body, and it seems that I am not destined to see my beloved son Hasan, whom I left a babe-in-arms when they forced us into the army. I ask God, the Mighty, the Omnipotent, to consider me a martyr and have requested that I be buried where I die.

We walked them as steps written for us
  And he for whom steps are written will walk them,
And he whose end lies in one land
  Will not meet his with death in another.

You will not read this letter now, Hasan, but when you grow up, your grandfather will give it to you so that you do not forget that your father died a stranger and a wanderer over God's earth, and that before he died he saw a wonderful vision and understood that God, Glorious and Sublime, had chosen him to die in a foreign land. I saw myself bending down to drink milk from the udder of a she-camel wandering aimlessly in Siberia's snowy desert and when I stood up again, saw characters written in light saying, "God's She-camel".

After the vision, there is stuff about the olive field and the small citrus grove and a request to his son that he visit the shrine of the Prophet Dannoun once a year and take part in the feast of Lydda that was held in the church of St George, also known as al-Khudr.

Where was the "will" in all this?

What was the significance of the story of a man who was conscripted into the Ottoman Army, taken prisoner, and died of fever in Manchuria?

Why did Manal give me this letter as my father's will, even though my father wrote none of it and left me nothing?

(Now I understand how the whole game works. Novelists, when they begin writing a new work, are quite sure that they're making the story up from their imaginations. In no time, however, they find themselves faced with events and emotions coming from a hidden place within them and bursting out of their memory. They try to trick their memory by using the imagination or, let's say, they dissolve the memory in the imagination. This is the whole secret of Emile Habibi's game: the man wrote exclusively from memory, having first cut it up into little pieces, which he used the way a mechanic uses second-hand spare parts to mend the engine of a car that has broken down. I'm now at that same place. I decided to write a novel of the imagination about the poet of love in the Omayyad period, making use of the memories of others that I found in books, only to find myself faced with the explosion of my own memory. This is what drove me to abandon the story of al-Waddah, along with the other reasons that I mentioned earlier.

Memory loss is the enemy of the imagination. When a person loses his memory, he becomes incapable of imagining, because the imagination exists as primary material in the memory. Herein lies the secret of my admiration for Anton Shammas's novel *Arabesques*: the writer doesn't trick us or himself; he lets memory gradually expand until it brings him to the peak of the imagination, where he writes that amazing encounter between Michael Abyad and Anton Shammas, whom he treats as the two halves of one man or, let's say, as the completion of the first hemistich of a line of poetry by its second, and in so doing manufactures that amazing moment called literature.)

To get back to my father's will: it isn't a will nor did my father write a word of it. It seems Manal found the papers in the famous little bag from which he was never parted during his travels during the Holy Struggle days in Palestine, so she kept them and decided in her own mind that they were his will. These papers were also the only thing of value she possessed as a memento of the martyr Hasan Dannoun, so she decided to give them to me, to be a thread tying me to my father and grandfather, and so that I'd have a story, like other people.

The story says that my grandfather, Ali son of Hasan Dannoun, born in the village of Deir Tarif in 1888, resided in the city of Lydda, where he owned a small orange grove and a field of olives. In 1913, he married a girl from Yibna called Najiba, who was eighteen years old, and she bore one son, whom his father named Hasan after his grandfather. Hasan's date of birth was 2 July, 1914.

When mobilisation was announced, my grandfather and grandmother fled with their only child and stayed in Yibna with my grandmother's family. He believed that by escaping he would avoid conscription into the Ottoman army, but he was wrong. One month after his arrival in Yibna, a company of Ottoman soldiers arrested him and he was conscripted, and bad luck took him to the Russian front, where he died.

That's all I learned from Manal. Or rather, I found out too that my grandmother Najiba returned with her son to Lydda after her husband's death. The woman refused, with amazing vehemence, her family's decision to marry her to her husband's younger brother, Kamil, as was the custom in those days, and as a result was repudiated by the other members of the family. She worked on the land that her husband had left her and lived in poverty, on her own.

Manal said she wasn't sure if Najiba ever learned of the death of her son, as the man died on 10 July, 1948, while Lydda fell on 12 July of the same year.

"I don't know what happened to my mother-in-law. I went to the hospital and stayed there. The man was very sick, and a doctor there, from the Habash family, I've forgotten his name, told me they needed nurses, so I volunteered and put on the white gown and spent my time next to Hasan until his soul departed, and I stayed there. Your grandmother fled with the rest, I don't know how. Everyone went to Ramallah but no-one saw her there. Your grandmother was stubborn and had a head like a mule. That's what everybody said. I really only knew her for a few months and there was shooting going on. Then we found out that she'd gone to her family's house in Yibna and that was the last we heard of her."

As for the business of my grandfather Ali Dannoun and what happened to him in Siberia, these were things I would never have known if I hadn't run into a man from Ramallah called Dr Hanna Jiryis, who worked at the Centre for Palestine Studies in Beirut before going back to Ramallah and becoming a professor at Birzeit University. Dr Hanna found out, I don't know how, that my grandfather had died in Manchuria during the First World War, and he contacted me and came to see me at my house in al-Ajami in Jaffa. He said he was preparing a study on Aref al-Aref and wanted to ask me some questions about my grandfather.

When the man discovered that I knew nothing, he asked me if my grandfather had left any handwritten papers, and I remembered the will and showed him the newspaper cutting. The moment he saw it, the man was overcome with astonishment. He pleaded with me to give him the cutting and said it would be preserved in the university's archives, where it would be a document of importance for researchers into the history of the Palestinian cause. I refused, however, and told him I couldn't give up my family's heritage. He said I was wrong, because it wasn't a personal heritage but belonged to the memory of the Palestinian people. Faced, however, with my insistence, he accepted that he'd just photocopy the cutting, and things were left at that.

Of course, I regret it now. I shouldn't just have given him the cutting, I should have given him the letter too, since, if I'd done so, my grandfather would have been guaranteed a place, albeit as a footnote, in the history of Palestine. No doubt, the study that was to be published would focus on the great historian Aref al-Aref and not even mention an unfortunate soldier called Ali Dannoun, who died alone, a stranger in a strange land.

When I told the man that it was Aref al-Aref who'd brought my grandmother the letter, his face lit up, and instead of passing things on to him, I listened to him tell me one of the strangest of all Palestinian stories.

The story I heard transported me to the First World War. The Palestinian historian doing research on the life of another historian ran slap into my grandfather Ali Dannoun, the Ottoman soldier who died as a vagabond as he tried to get back to his country after the torments of captivity in Siberia.

The man wanted an answer from me to one question: had my grandfather joined the Turkish Red Brigades (*Türk Kızıl Alay*) that had brought together around a thousand fighters, made contact with the Bolsheviks, and taken part in the fighting against the Whites?

From the letter, I'd gathered that Dannoun sympathised with the Bolsheviks who had released the prisoners after the victory of their revolution but I was unaware that Red Brigades had been formed among the prisoners' ranks. All I knew was that my grandfather had left Russia and joined a convoy of Arab soldiers after he'd been hit by a bullet in the thigh, but the man said nothing about the reason for his injury or where it occurred.

When he read about my grandfather's death in Manchuria, the historian told me, "I've been looking for this man," but he expressed disappointment when he failed to find in my possession the document he'd been hoping for that would have proved that Arab Bolshevism had begun in the prisoner-of-war camps of the

First World War. He said he was hoping to find just one document that would prove his claim, so that he could publish his theory.

He told me of his meeting in Beirut with the son of one of those prisoners, a Damascene from the al-Qarout family who'd told him that his father had become a Bolshevist in Krasnoyarsk in Siberia and had joined the Turkish Red Brigades there. When he returned to Beirut he'd started promoting communist thought, then by chance run into Fu'ad al-Shimali, one of the founders of the Communist Party in Syria and Lebanon, and joined it.

The historian said he'd studied the life of the Ottoman Arab prisoners of war, and started telling me about the detention camp at Krasnoyarsk, near the shore of the Yenisei River in central Siberia. He spoke of the cold and the hunger and the torments suffered by the prisoners, who were forced to work in the mines, and of the towers and wire that surrounded the Wayouni Gorduk camp there.

"And then what?" I asked.

"Then nothing," he replied. "The Bolshevik Revolution occurred, and they fled to join Feisal I."

"So what's it all got to do with me?" I asked.

"I want just one thing from you. Try to find something written by your grandfather so I can prove my theory."

I told him that was all I had and he didn't need any more, given that he had al-Qarout's testimony to prove it.

He said that wasn't enough. History has to rest on written documents, preferably official documents. He said he was sorry Aref al-Aref hadn't written about these Arab Bolsheviks and that, as a result, he'd be unable to prove his theory.

"What kind of nonsense is that?" I asked him. "The whole history of our Nakba is unwritten. Does that mean we don't have a history? That there was no Nakba? Does that make sense?"

He said those were the rules of the discipline of history and we could only face the Zionist historians if we had a properly documented past that they could recognise.

I said I was sorry and suggested we reread my grandfather's letter and add a passage where he tells how he joined the Red Brigades, was wounded in the thigh, and died of gangrene.

"Is that true?" he asked me.

"It's as good as true," I told him.

"That's writers' business," he said, "not historians'."

"What's the difference?" I asked.

He shook his head in disgust and walked off.

Betrayal by the Father

The historian went off, leaving me bewildered.

I wanted to run after him so we could discuss the meaning of truth, because I'm sure, given the fragmentary stories Manal had told me about her first husband, that my father must have been a Marxist sympathiser even if he didn't belong to the Communist Party. That would explain why, in the ranks of the Holy Struggle organisation, they'd referred to him as the Red Warrior.

If I'm to believe my mother, my father's presumed communism was the result of the effect on him of what he'd been told of *his* father's, the martyr's, relationship to Bolshevism.

Why had judicious Dr Hanna Jiryis flown off the handle when I suggested adding a short paragraph to my father's letter, thus solving the problem of the text he was looking for? That way he could put forward his new thesis that the foundation of the Palestine Communist Party was not the doing of Jews alone: Palestinian prisoners of war in Russia who were members of the Turkish Red Brigades had played a role too.

I wasn't suggesting faking history, just filling in the gaps. He said imagination was alright for literature but not for writing history; although, if that's so, how does the historian expect us to write it? Are we supposed to leave it to the Zionists? And who told him that the histories that have been written of Palestine are true and not an out-and-out orgy of fakery?

I should have discussed the matter with him when he came

to the restaurant in New York to eat stewed beans, but I'd forgotten the whole thing, and it only came unstitched from the folds of my memory today, as I sat alone trying to gather together the threads of my life.

What do I want, and who am I?

God protect me from the word "I", as the Arabs say! Looking for myself in these stories that I tell, I find myself in others' mirrors. Each person is the reflection of another, each story the reflection of another. That's what my solitary existence in New York has taught me. When I came to this city in flight from a love that had died, I expected to experience solitude, live with myself, forget that world so crammed with people and events, and sit around in idleness.

"Nothing beats boredom!" I told myself as I set my bags down in my small apartment in New York. Even writing the story of Waddah al-Yaman had been part of what backgammon and card players call "killing time". From the day I let myself into this hell, however, I found myself surrounded by people who'd been hiding in the crevices of my memory, and instead of luxuriating in my boredom, I found myself under duress, forced to set aside time for all these wraiths who hem me in and organise their introduction into this text, so there can be some thread for me to follow.

This world consists of mirrors that, when we break them, shatter into a thousand little pieces that are transformed in turn into new ones that have to be broken. The mirrors that hem me in today are those of my three fathers who abandoned me.

I shall begin at the end, as I was never interested in the issue of the relationship to the father. I came to consciousness as the son of the martyr Hasan Dannoun and a child of the Lydda ghetto, and that is enough. Even my mother's marriage to Abdallah al-Ashhal in no way altered that conviction. I am a descendant of the great Sufi, Dhu al-Nun the Egyptian, as I am a son of the city of al-Khudr, and a citizen of the Arab World – or a Palestinian living in the State of Israel. And when I left my mother's house, I discovered that I was my own son and that all the legends about my father's heroism that she had planted in my head meant nothing to me. I know the man only as a name and a picture, and names and pictures mean nothing until they are transformed into a voice that takes you by surprise when summoned back from some unknown place.

Running into Blind Ma'moun here in New York, and the fragmented stories he told me about my other, real, father, stirred up lots of questions. When those questions encountered the movie that presented a forgery of the truth about Dalia and her friends and made no reference to my grandmother's village of Yibna – as would be proper for a village whose inhabitants were brutally expelled in 1948 – my soul exploded and my memory burst open.

To keep it short, I will just say that when I was taking classes in psychology at Haifa University, I read avidly about the Oedipus complex as fashioned by Freud, not because I felt the father had to be killed, but because, on the contrary, I felt I was devoid of the complex, as someone had taken it upon himself to kill my father before I was born.

Even when my mother married (I was eight at the time, i.e. past the penile stage presided over by the Oedipus complex), I didn't feel jealous of the man. On the contrary, I felt disgust, which has nothing in common with jealousy. I felt pity for my mother at the thought that she could bring herself to sleep next to him.

They don't, however, teach the Oedipus complex's twin – the Abraham complex. I now, based on my personal experience,

166

believe that the Abraham complex is the more firmly rooted in the collective human unconscious. The only place I have come across it is in contemporary Jewish Israeli literature, which has a strong focus on the sacrifice of the son.

(Note: Oddly, the Jewish religion has no feast day dedicated to the sacrifice of Isaac, even though there are so many feast days and despite the foundational centrality of this story of son-sacrifice. The Muslims, on the other hand, have transformed the tale into their greatest celebration, which they name the Feast of the Sacrifice, and at which they perform the duty of pilgrimage and slaughter sheep as a ransom for the son who was saved at the last moment – the eldest son, called Ismail, grandsire of the Arabs. Christians, for their part, have combined the sacrifice of the human son with that of the divine son and it has become their Easter – which, in our country, they call the Great Feast – at which they celebrate the *killing* of the son and his resurrection from the dead.)

Returning to the Abraham complex, I would say the essential point is that of the slaying of the son, while the slaying of the father in the Oedipus story is no more than a reaction to the father's having nailed his little son's feet to a piece of wood and cast him aside to die. Oedipus killed his father only because the father had wanted to kill the son, for fear of the oracle's prophecy and as a step towards its fulfilment.

Now, in my solitude, I discover that all three of my fathers wanted to do away with me. Indeed, symbolically speaking, they did kill me, and I ought to have killed them, in defence of my very existence. I am the murder victim who has to turn into a murderer while feeling pity for his own wretched victims.

I know nothing of my first, meaning my biological, father

(according to Ma'moun's account of how he found me lying on my dead mother's breast), not even his name. It seems that the wife, with her baby son, waited too long to join the march of death, so the man kept going, like all the rest who'd lost members of their families but were sure they'd meet up with them once they got to the areas under Jordanian Army control. And when he reached Naalin, he looked for his wife but couldn't find her, so he joined the ranks of the searchers, who were made the more miserable by the indifference of others to their plight. On that terrible July day, people lost their souls and were transformed into living corpses. Heat and thirst devoured them, and they felt the great fear that frees the survival instinct from all constraints. Sons abandoned fathers, fathers sons. Small children got lost under foot and people died of heat and thirst.

People talk of fear as though it were an individual experience. They speak of knees giving way, of the void within the heart, of the annihilation. But it is the fear that turns into waves that is the greatest – the fear that undulates through thousands who have been cast into the wilderness beneath the lead of bullets and amongst the faces of soldiers gloating at their misfortune, soldiers scattered along the length of the rocky road who take everything the stream of fugitives possesses by way of money and jewellery and gaze at the wandering throngs with indifference.

A wave of fear rises and my father walks alone, a youth of twenty-five who has lost his wife and only child. He walks next to his aged father and keeps turning round to look for his wife. Then the wave sweeps him up and he finds himself alone, wrestling with fear. His thirst is transformed into a feeling that he is choking. He raises his head above the wave to breathe and then is swallowed up again.

I don't want to go looking for excuses for this man of whom I know nothing. The truth is that, ever since I found out about what happened between us, I've felt nothing but pity and contempt for him. I mean, tell me – tell me how he could have abandoned his son, who was no more than four months old, to save his own skin?

I am assuming here that my first father escaped death on that march of death, that he reached Naalin safely and that from there he kept going with the caravan of refugees to Ramallah, but it's not certain, and I am not prepared to go looking for him. Most likely he's dead now, or on the brink of the grave. Meeting him would do neither of us any good. It wouldn't, in fact, even have the savour of a meeting in a melodrama, at which tears flow. It would, in fact, be a meeting of strangers.

Let's suppose the blind youth hadn't rescued me and given me to Manal. Probably, I would have died of hunger. I prefer not to go now into Ma'moun's description of the stiffness of the child he picked up; it makes my skin crawl. Moreover, since Ma'moun told me the story I've had strange headaches and feel as though my "I" is drowning in fog, as if I weren't I.

My first father killed me. He left me to die on a dead woman's breast and fled towards his life. That's my first story with fathers – a cowardly and impotent one, a people herded like sheep towards the wilderness and death, and a child, its body rigid with thirst, lying on its mother's dry breasts.

All I needed was a drop of milk. One drop, which my mother's breasts were incapable of offering me, so I lay on top of them waiting to die. My relationship with death began that torrid day in July, the day I died and Manal had to rub my body with oil and feed me boiled ground lentils with her finger, which she continued to do until the people of the ghetto came across the cow in milk that saved me and the rest of the children from death.

Ma'moun said that the moment when they found the cow was the most beautiful of his life. "Imagine, lad, how we were! To this day I'm convinced that cow was a gift from God, Great and Glorious."

I don't want to submerge myself in the days of the ghetto now: that's a story I need to write from beginning to end, at one go and without digressions. Instead, I've told Ma'moun's version of my first father's story, which has no story, apart from my feeling that I'm a murdered son and that my murderer was my father.

Perhaps in saying this I'm being a bit unjust towards the guy, whom I never knew: he was a victim and I'm the victim of a victim. It's a kind of justification I don't care for. Being a victim doesn't grant one the right to make victims of others – on the contrary, it makes one doubly responsible for them. I tried to explain this so many times to my Israeli Jewish friends, though with no great success. True, to be honest, my beloved Dalia once surprised me by adopting the same idea and, indeed, expressing it eloquently when she said, "The Palestinians are the victims of the victims, and the Jewish victims have no right to behave like their execution-ers. That's why I'm not just Jewish, but Palestinian too."

We were walking that day on the shore at Jaffa, close to the Sea Cemetery, where the Palestinian academic and writer Ibrahim Abu Lughod is buried. I told her about this man whose voice still rings in my ears and of how, when he died, his daughter Leila took him by car from Ramallah to Jerusalem so that his death could be announced in that city and he could claim, as a non-Jewish American, the right to be buried in Israel, which is to say, in the cemetery where his fathers and forefathers lay. An expression of grief passed over Dalia's brown, oval face, and she announced that she'd become a Palestinian.

How and why Dalia came to abandon me and her Palestinian identity is another story, woven from sorrow and ambiguity.

My first father didn't look back, and thus failed to see me being pulled from my mother's womb a second time so that I wouldn't die. I can imagine the man weeping, or pretending to weep, for his only child and proclaiming me a martyr, then marrying a relative, having a boy, and giving him my name.

Though I don't know and don't want to know what that name was.

My name is Adam and I don't care that my first father doesn't know that, because the man means nothing to me. He appeared on the screen of my life as one made up of words spoken by the blind man – without features, like a black spot in my eye.

Maybe I'm doing the man an injustice! I'm basing everything on the assumption that he kept going and didn't make a serious search for me. But what if he had already been killed? What if he was one of the victims of the massacre that took place at the Dahmash Mosque? If that were so, it would mean my mother fled with me on her own.

It's a serious possibility, but I'm in no position to prove it, which is the case with all the other possibilities concerning my first father. All the same, I'd rather not set him among the ranks of the martyrs, because one martyred father is enough.

My second father, Hasan, son of Ali, Dannoun was a real human being, who became familiar to me as a photograph hung on the wall. A young man in his mid-twenties, broad-shouldered, with coal-black hair, eyes so wide they seemed to be drinking in the whole world, and a thick black moustache that covered his upper lip. Manal always spoke of how beautiful he was, and of the magic hidden in his glances. I lived my childhood as the son of this martyr, whose lungs were ripped open as he fought to defend the city of Lydda, and I was supposed to feel proud of being an heir to blood and heroism.

I was supposed to have been given the name Ali, after my grandfather, who was also a martyr, because my father was "Abu Ali" or "Father of Ali" – that's what everyone called him when they came to visit us and stood before his photograph, which was draped with black and topped with the Palestinian *keffiyeh*.

My mother wanted to name me according to my father's wishes but changed her mind and decided to give me the name of the martyr, Hasan. The fates, however, had other plans. Ma'moun told me that when I was a child I had three names: I was Hasan to my mother, Naji to him, and Adam to the people of the ghetto. In the end, it was the third that stuck and that I feel adhering to my skin and my soul. The story of how "Adam" came to stick to me wasn't just a matter of the headman's registering me with that name, following my mother's more-or-less coerced agreement to the ghetto's decision, but because I wanted it. I fitted it and it fitted me.

Adam is the name that best expresses the truth. I grasped that many years later, so it was as though my intuition had told me I wasn't the right person for any other name, or that all names were wrong for me except for this, which refers to the skin, or *adim*, of the earth, meaning its soil (or so the books say). This way, I am a son of the land and have no other fathers.

When I learned the story of my first father, I was shocked, I can't deny it. Then I got over the whole thing, as I could think of no convincing reason for switching my affiliation from the Dannoun family. I had lived my whole life as the son of a man who didn't know he'd become a father because he died before I was born. This spared me the complications of relationships with fathers, especially those who are heroes, like mine.

I have to admit that Manal liberated me from my father through her marriage to Abdallah al-Ashhal. After we moved to live in Haifa, I exited the man's story, even though my mother, who didn't dare hang my father's photograph in the living room of the new house, put it in my room, and when she came to wake me in the morning would stand for ages in front of the photo and continue her muttered discussions with it in a low voice.

I say I exited the man's story, but that's not accurate. I was liberated from the martyr's photograph but never from his seemingly miraculous story that my mother ceaselessly recounted, even after her marriage to Abdallah al-Ashhal and the discovery of her inability to bear children.

How is it that I never asked her, or myself, the most obvious question about that inability? That's how most people are – blind, unable to see the things in their lives that are closest to them.

"Damnation!" said Ma'moun. "So what, man? If she didn't tell you, couldn't you see?"

I should have understood, but I didn't – at least that night, when Manal asked Abdallah to take me to spend the night in the house of one of his relatives, because it was their wedding night, and the man refused because he had no relatives. "And what's all the fuss about? Suddenly you're a virgin? You've got a boy the size of a man!"

I was eight. I went with my mother to Haifa, after she'd gathered a few belongings and clothes into a bundle, and the man was waiting for us in front of his house.

He mocked her and her bundle. "Your trousseau is your

son, who's popped out at me from God knows where?!"

The formalities of the marriage contract were completed without fuss. The sheikh came, bringing two witnesses, and when he'd finished his work, he turned to Manal and asked her to give a ululation of joy. A lifeless trilling, closer to a moan, emerged from her mouth.

And then . . . I don't want to remember! I heard the man shouting that he could feel blood, and cursing because he thought that Manal was having her period, and I heard her whispering to him and swearing that she hadn't realised.

After that, I don't remember. Perhaps I dozed off, or fainted or . . . I don't know what happened.

I should have known, as the blind man said, but I refused to, so here I am now, observing those moments, which well up from a place I didn't know existed. I remember as though I were imagining, or as though the scene were taking place in front of me now.

I'd better get back to my father and ask my memory to erase that scene and throw it onto the garbage dump of oblivion.

The story says my father was wounded at the Battle of Latroun and spent ten days in the hospital at Lydda afterwards.

Manal never tired of telling the story of her dead husband's heroism. She said my father was an aide to the martyr Hasan Salama, whom the Arab Higher Committee had appointed commander of the Central District, meaning the Jaffa–Lydda area, during the War of the Nakba. By a miracle, the two men survived the Haganah's attempt to blow up the position Hasan Salama had taken as his command headquarters, an orphanage located west of Ramallah consisting of a large three-storey building surrounded by an orange grove about two kilometres from the Jewish settlement of Be'er Ya'akov.

Haganah forces succeeded in penetrating the building and blowing it up, and around thirty fighters fell, their remains visible on the walls and in the trees.

My father and his commander survived the slaughter by chance. Manal never stopped thanking the Lord of All Worlds for putting it in the men's heads not to spend the night there.

Fate, however, had other plans, for the two men met their ends as martyrs in quick succession. My father died first, at the Battle of Latroun. Hasan Salama followed him ten days later at the Battle of Ras al-Ein.

The two were alike in everything, and Manal's account of their deaths made them seem like twins, because she mixed them up and they turned into one person with two names and two deaths.

"Honestly, my dear, that's how it happened, and that's what I went through, and God is my witness, I never mourned for the man or for myself. Your father's a martyr in the Gardens of Eternity and God left me behind for you, or why else am I still alive? I stayed so I could raise you and you could grow up and clear the path for me to join him."

As it happened, she cleared the path for me: she went and married that man. I couldn't understand her or come up with any explanation for what she did. Two years later, she told me she didn't love him and was sorry.

"Okay, so why did you marry him?" I asked.

She looked at me with dead eyes and answered dully, "It was fate."

"What do you mean, 'fate'?"

"I mean fate. Heavens above, you don't know what that means? It was my fate and I accepted it because that's the way it was. Honestly, I don't understand why I did it, I just hope God forgives me."

What do she and I have to do with one another? Our present topic is my father. Her story is for later and is going to stay that way because I don't understand it, just as I don't understand why she withdrew from me and put a veil of silence between us, as though she wanted to force me out of her life so she could go to her death without having me on her conscience.

The news of my mother's death reached me when I was thirty-five years old – twenty years, in other words, after we parted. She died having divorced the man and gone back to her family in Eilaboun. I can imagine how she was looked down on in her village, how she became a servant in the family house, which her older brother had inherited, and how she went to her death because she stopped eating. That is what the man who brought me the news told me. He also told me that they wanted me there to receive condolences, but I didn't go, which was one of my many mistakes. I should have gone so as to find out the woman's story, but I was in a different mood then. I'd thrown the past, all of it, into oblivion and got on with my life, or what seemed to be my life, the way I wanted to. Now, though, I regret it. I shouldn't have left my life full of these holes and gaps that have turned today into besieging ghosts.

The ghost of my father comes to me, drawn by my mother's words. I see her wearing a nurse's gown and sitting next to him, rubbing his hands, which tremble with pain. I see her bow her head and bend over him, kissing his dry lips and then lying down on the bed beside him, closing her eyes but not sleeping. I hear her sighs and witness the moan of death blending into the moan of life.

My mother said they brought him to the hospital with blood splattered all over his back. They laid him on his left side because his back was hurting and his chest had been hit, and in the midst of the pain the man asked to see his commander, Hasan Salama, so he could return the gun he'd been given.

My mother said the meeting was quick and without emotion or tears, but enough to make a stone weep. Abu Ali Salama bent over and kissed his friend's brow. My father closed his eyes, which were exhausted with pain, asked his wife to hand him his pistol, and gave it to his friend. The next day, Hasan Dannoun died.

My mother said that the pistol had become a legend. Abu Ali Salama had presented it to Hasan Dannoun for his courage in battle, and when my father was wounded at the Battle of Latroun, he gave it, as he lay dying, back to its owner. Then, when Abu Ali Salama was dying in the hospital at Lydda after being wounded at the Battle of Ras al-Ein, he presented the pistol to Hamza Subh, who had led the battle to recover Ras al-Ein from the Jewish forces. My mother said she knew that Hamza Subh, as he lay wounded and dying after the Battle of al-Nabi Salih near Ramallah, had directed that the pistol be given to the son of Hasan Dannoun, who had not yet been born. When my mother told me this story I was nine and I asked her to give me the pistol. She looked into the distance and said, "You're still too young."

Then, when she gave me the will, in my haste to get to wherever my feet were going to take me, I forgot to ask her for it.

To get back to the subject of my father, I searched for his photograph in the folder. I saw a slim man with hawk-like eyes gazing at the horizon, and I told him that both of us had been tricked. My father was twenty-six when he died, a very young man who could take the part of my son today, though in fact I'm alone and have no children. I asked him what he'd say to switching things around: I'd adopt him, fully aware of what I was doing, instead of him adopting me unaware of what he was doing. I heard his laugh exploding in my ears and he said something, in a voice not unlike mine, though I couldn't understand what it was. His voice resembled the texts in my dreams: I dream I've written something, and when I try to read it, the letters follow one another in succession like little black grains, and I am unable to decipher them. It seems I'm not a real writer, since I believe that writers dream their texts and all they have to do is recall them and write them down when they wake.

I heard him and I didn't. I didn't propose adopting him so that I could kill him, the way fathers do, applying the will and testament of God's Friend, Our Master Abraham. I'm allowed to kill him in his capacity as my father: that's expected and accepted because Freud has convinced us that the killing of fathers is not only possible but necessary. The killing of sons, though (which in my opinion is more integral to human nature), appears in our modern age as a barbaric act to which no-one would agree.

I don't care whether the story of the pistol is true but I've decided to believe it, because it's a beautiful story. Beauty, not reality, is the yardstick of literary veracity. The story of Manal getting pregnant with me, however, I am incapable either of believing or of placing in the context of the relationship between beauty and truth. My mother would have nothing to do with magic or stories about *afreets*, but the story, which she told more than once, of her getting pregnant with me, would work as part of *The Thousand and One Nights*, though not as part of the story of my life.

I've gone into the matter in detail, not for literary reasons but to make sure that the report that Blind Ma'moun stunned me with was true.

I know I am the only son of Hasan Dannoun, and that my

mother didn't know my father until after he was wounded. (I use "know" here in the sense in which it occurs in the Bible in the report of the Virgin Mary's getting pregnant with Jesus, where it's stressed that the Virgin hadn't "known" her husband Joseph, meaning hadn't slept with him.) My mother said she was a bride without a groom and that after she jumped onto my father's horse, went off with him, and was married to him by a sheikh in one of the caves in which the revolutionaries were holed up, a woman came and took her to Lydda. Her husband asked her to wait for him at his mother's house and promised he'd be back soon to build her one of her own. The girl found herself waiting in an old house in an unfamiliar city, living with an elderly woman who never stopped praying.

Manal said she'd only ever seen her husband and beloved drenched in blood. There was a noise outside and she overheard a man telling the old woman her son was at the hospital, wounded.

My mother ran after the man and found herself entering a long corridor and stepping over a pool of her husband's blood. From that moment on, she never left her beloved's side.

"I stayed with him. 'What are you doing, woman?' they asked me. I told them I was his wife. They said, 'Go home. There's nothing for you to do here.' I told them I was a nurse, and then a doctor from the Habash family, God bless him, took pity on me. He was fair-skinned and had a thick moustache like your poor father, and he said, 'Come along, Sister.' So I went with him and he gave me a white tunic and said, 'Now you're a nurse. Stay with the man and take care of him. He's in bad shape.' And that's what happened. I stayed with him and saw his soul depart. God, what a beautiful soul! A martyr's soul is like incense – light white smoke with a delicious smell. I saw Hasan's soul and felt it hover over my head before disappearing. It was telling me to look after you, and till now whenever I long for him I smell the same smell."

The story – not the one my mother tells but the one that most of the people of the ghetto firmly believed – says that the girl from Eilaboun spent ten days next to her dying bridegroom and that she'd steal into his bed at night and sleep next to him, and that she got pregnant by him before he died.

I didn't experience the ghetto. Or at least I did but I don't remember it, because the wire was taken away – without our being allowed to leave – when I was about six months old, so how can I be expected to remember? (The truth is, we never left the ghetto. We stayed in it, but when the barbed wire was removed, they said, "The ghetto's over," though it wasn't. The fact is it encircles us to this day, which is the whole thing in a nutshell.)

Who says it's memory that we remember? Memory is what we feel we're remembering. In that sense, the memory of the ghetto lives on within me. When I used to tell my fellow students at the University of Haifa that I was from the ghetto, I wasn't lying. I was giving them the truth's first cousin, which is always truer than the truth.

I never once wondered how the woman could have become pregnant from a man lying on his bed between life and death, his lungs damaged by bullets, moaning incessantly with pain. I believed her just as everyone else in the ghetto did! In those terrible days, when brother denied brother and son trod father underfoot as they sought to escape death, anything could have been true. Unbelievable things happened. An entire people was driven to its slaughter. More than 50,000 people had found themselves driven along on the march of death that they'd been forced into by the Palmach forces that invaded the city. There were shredded bodies on the walls of the Dahmash Mosque, human remains on the roads, animals running loose, flies devouring the dead and the living.

No-one was interested in looking closely into the story of a woman who found herself alone with the body of her husband the martyr, so they believed her, turned her newborn child into the ghetto's Adam, and celebrated him as the first son of their story, which was walled in by silence.

If the truth be told, I was infatuated with the story of my birth as told by Manal. I believed it, considered it my destiny, and lived my childhood with the image of my father the martyr, who had produced the miracle of my birth from inside his death. All the same, the story long ago evaporated and broke up into little pieces in my heart. My father no longer means anything special to me. He's just a story I had hidden away somewhere secret whose location I've now forgotten. And when, these days, it suddenly rose up again, it turned to dust.

Curiosity and the death instinct drove me to research the dates of the battles that my mother had made the markers of my birth. I discovered that not only was the story a tissue of lies from beginning to end but that Manal's naivety made it extremely easy to expose their fabrication. Here, I'm talking exclusively about my birth. The story of Manal's relationship with Hasan Dannoun and how she was transformed into a nurse at the Lydda hospital and the business of her meeting with a doctor from the Habash family – probably Dr George Habash, the Palestinian leader who was given, and with good reason, the title of Doctor to the Palestinian Revolution – is nothing to do with me, and I tend to believe it because it is beautiful and deserves to be true.

My mother recounted that my father was wounded at the

Battle of Latroun, that he died of his wounds ten days later, that the commander, Hasan Salama, was martyred as a result of being wounded at the Battle of Ras al-Ein, and finally that Hamza Subh, who decided to return the pistol to the son of the martyr Hasan Dannoun, meaning to me, died at the Battle of al-Nabi Salih in Ramallah.

Setting aside the suspicious resemblance between my father's injury and that of Abu Ali Salama, which I'd rather not examine too closely because it may either be true and/or the result of a mix-up in my mother's confused memory (memory being always, as we know, confused!), an investigation of the dates of these battles leads to only one conclusion, namely, that the story of my mother's becoming pregnant with me after my father was wounded cannot possibly be correct.

I was born, according to my mother and my I.D. card, on 14 July, 1948, meaning that my mother had to have conceived me nine months before that date, which is to say at the end of November or the beginning of December 1947, while the Battle of Latroun took place on 15 May, 1948. Thus, if I'm to believe my mother, the "miracle" of her becoming pregnant with me occurred in May, so I would have been born before completing two months in her belly, which is impossible.

My mother wasn't telling the truth. She pretended she'd given birth to me, and Ma'moun, for some reason I don't know, colluded with her. Meanwhile, the people who remained in the city, inside the ghetto, in an atmosphere resembling that of the Day of Resurrection, were in no state to investigate the story of a woman who appeared to them wearing a white tunic, like an angel, carrying another, smaller, angel and claiming that it was the first Palestinian child to be born in the Lydda ghetto.

The idea of one angel carrying another is not of my making, it's Ma'moun's. When he told me the story, he said the people had seen a white girl-child carrying a baby. "Your mother was a child," he said and stopped speaking, and I saw white tears running from his closed eyes and was seized by terror at the sight of dead eyes coursing with tears, as though they had welled up from nowhere. Then he said, "No, not a child. She was an angel carrying an angel."

"Why did she lie, and why did you join her in the lie?" I asked, after long minutes of silence.

"No, your mother didn't lie. She told half the truth."

"So what's the other half?" I asked.

"It's what I'm telling you now," he replied.

"Why was it so?" I asked.

"Why the Nakba?" he answered. "The only thing that could save a young woman from the death that had made a home for itself inside each of the inhabitants of the ghetto was a new life arriving like a miracle, and the miracle took place at my hands, without my meaning to do anything, like all miracles."

What kind of a bind was this? More than fifty years afterwards, the man who claimed to have produced the miracle of my birth had killed off my second father—and that after I'd reached an age at which I'd forgiven that same father for abandoning me, killing my childhood, and handing me over to the heartless man who had become my mother's husband.

I'd hated my second father because he'd killed me, and now here I was watching him being killed, today, in front of my eyes, in the midst of Ma'moun's white tears, while I sat there like an idiot, incapable of saving him.

Ma'moun had come to me when it was all over to destroy the image I'd drawn of myself as the son whose father had killed him, and now here I was, faced with two impotent fathers – the first, who'd abandoned me when Lydda's sky had fallen, and the second, who was just an image in which Manal, alone amidst the puddles of death and sorrow, had sought refuge so as to give a meaning to her life, which had lost all its meanings.

You, though, Ma'moun, my third father, I will not allow to escape the punishment of the son whom you killed and abandoned, fleeing to Egypt to study, and building your life on the ruins of mine!

What strange coincidence was it that led me to Ma'moun, or led Ma'moun to me in my journey from myself and my country to New York?

After Ma'moun had told me what he did, I asked myself what was the meaning of it all. Ma'moun's closed eyes, weeping tears that implanted themselves, coloured white, in my memory, stirred panic within me. We were sitting. He was sipping a glass of scotch, I was drinking vodka, and his friend Naji was sitting in the corner, as though he didn't want to interrupt the conversation. Suddenly, Ma'moun took off his dark glasses and wept. At first, I thought he'd uncovered his obliterated eyes so that he could wipe away his tears, so I held a paper napkin out to him but he didn't notice it. I pressed the napkin into his hand, he took it and put it to his forehead but wiped neither his eyes nor his cheeks with it, as though he wanted his tears to remain graven on his face and to make me a witness to his baptism with them.

They kill like fathers and weep like sons!

It was as though Ma'moun wanted to take over my role, playing executioner and victim at one and the same time while I was merely a witness. He was the Abraham who placed his knife on his son's neck and the Ismail who, abandoned to the thirst of the desert, took refuge in his tears and initiated the baptism that became a mark of being lost and a stranger.

Now I understand why Arabic poetry began with Imru" al-Qays. The wandering, exiled king of Kinda stood over the remains of the campfire and wept, and invited his friends to weep, but he was the opposite of everything the critics said he was. He wasn't the first to open verses, and life, with tears. The first was the slaughtered son who gave the Arabs their particular baptism: the first was Ismail, whose tears were transformed into the water with which he quenched his thirst and that of his mother.

Stop, and let us weep at the memory of a beloved and an abode!

With these words, Arabic poetry began, in the desert that had given birth to the prophets, and I, the fugitive from those prophets' shadows, hate myself for having been provoked by Ma'moun's tears. I felt he was stealing my tears, borrowing my name and story so as to prove his innocence of his crime.

He sits there and brings me his friend, or student, called Naji, to be a witness to my story. This Naji is not a real person. He's a character in a book whom Ma'moun brought along to prove that reality is more fictitious than fiction.

That had been the essence of Ma'moun's lecture on Mahmoud Darwish at the university. He'd presented an astonishing lecture about the character of Rita in Darwish's poems and then gone on to argue that the poet who had loved and married Rita was not Darwish but Rashed Hussein, and that the story of the death of that poet in New York was more tragic than any Palestinian poetry.

But that was wrong.

I kept my mouth shut during the discussion that followed the lecture, on whose exceptional importance all the speakers agreed. No-one objected to the conclusions drawn, apart from Dr Naji, who made a long intervention about the poetry of Mahmoud Darwish that boiled down to fiction being better able to reveal the multiple layers of reality than real events.

Dr Naji sits, hunched-up, in his corner, observing me in my role as the hero of an unwritten story!

What cruelty is this?

After this encounter, it became possible for me to say what I'd always believed but never dared articulate, which is that writers are capable of being the cruellest of all creatures. In their claim to reveal the human condition and expose repression, torture, sadism, murder and so on, they turn themselves into voyeurs who revel in what they imagine and describe!

That's why I shall never write a novel. This isn't a novel, and Ma'moun, with help from my friend the Israeli movie director, opened the door out of this dilemma for me.

Ma'moun was surrounded by darkness and silence, and I found myself drowning in his darkness along with him and could think of nothing to say.

I stood, went up to Ma'moun to shake his hand, and stepped back. Then I turned around, mumbling words of thanks, and left.

A Dream of Words

What does it mean when a dream returns again and again? And what made Dr Hanna Jiryis appear in my dreams?

In Jaffa, I only met the guy once, when he brought me the story of *God's She-camel*. Then I met him several times here at the restaurant in New York; both of us, however, behaved as though our first meeting and our discussion about my grandfather who'd died in Manchuria had never taken place. Probably, the university professor no longer saw in the falafel-seller I'd become an interlocutor worthy of him and his elevated academic standing. The man restricted himself to eating a plate of fava beans in my restaurant once a week and dropping in every now and then with his students to buy eggplant-and-falafel sandwiches. For my part, I restricted myself to watching the various means he employed to seduce girls, using his cappuccino machine.

When the man disappeared, having found a job in a university in America's far west, I only realised after a while and by accident. The man and his *God's She-camel* researches meant nothing to me at the time.

Suddenly, however, he turned up again and, without asking my permission, entered my dreams and became a witness to my crisis over reading and writing.

The dream says I'm sitting in a public garden. It's not clear where this garden is but it's neither New York nor Haifa. It may be in Beirut. I divine that it's Beirut, which I've never visited, from the noise. The garden is small and surrounded by barbed wire, and I am sitting alone and have my papers with me. The barbed wire might be a pointer to the garden's being in the Lydda ghetto, but, logically speaking, there couldn't have been a public garden in the ghetto.

What's Haifa got to do with Beirut? It's true that Haifa's only about eighty miles from Beirut and that under the right weather conditions someone sitting on the beach at Tyre can see Haifa plunging into the sea with the naked eye, but the distance between the two cities cannot be measured in miles. Between them lie rivers of blood and other obstacles that make moving the garden's location from here to there impossible.

It is, on the other hand, a dream, and dreams don't know borders or acknowledge distances. The important thing is that I'm sitting in a public garden surrounded by barbed wire similar to that of the Lydda ghetto. In my hand, I'm holding pieces of paper like those on which I'm writing, or which I'm trying to read.

Suddenly, I see Dr Hanna. He is sitting next to me on the bench, puffing on a Cuban cigar.

I tell him I'll read him the chapter I've written about him and my grandfather.

"How come? You know how to write?" he asks, laughing.

He says only those words, which repeat themselves like an echo, and when I start to read, the rain begins falling heavily – ropes of rain, blocking off the grey horizon and drenching the papers. I watch the ink running and the rain turning black, and I try to pick up the words that have run down onto the ground, and my face and hands become stained with ink.

The dream ends there because I don't remember what happens after that. Did the dream go on or stop? Strange is our relationship to dreams, because we remember only fragments of them, which is for the good: how could someone who remembers the totality of his dreams distinguish between waking and sleeping?

On that occasion, I couldn't read. Instead of the words being erased and turning into clumps of black ants, they dissolved in the water, to the sound of the historian's raucous laughter, mocking me and my writings.

However, the dream came back twice, in different forms, and neither time was there water; instead, the words disappeared into one another, as though they'd swallowed their letters, and the lines began to dance before my eyes so I could no longer pick out a single letter and read it. I averted my eyes from the piece of paper and tried to read using my memory, but my memory couldn't remember.

Did this mean I had to stop writing? Despite my insistence in principle that what I write is unfit for publication and will indeed never be published, at moments of weakness I'm afflicted by a desire to see my name among those of the writers I love, and I dream, during moments that I dare not prolong, that I shall publish this thing that I'm writing.

This dream that came three times served to return me to the path I'd set myself. I don't write to be read by Dr Hanna and his like or to be recognised by Arab and Israeli historians. My tragedy isn't in need of their recognition, and whether they acknowledge it or not, it is engraved on souls and places. The rocks, the trees, the birds, the rivers and the seas speak it – and phooey to the scholarship of scholars, if it is going to remain captive to a mendacious story based on deficient documents!

Sarang Lee drew my attention to another aspect of the matter. When I told her one of my dreams (not, of course, the one with

Dr Hanna), I said I was reading from a book whose title I didn't remember, but I couldn't read, like an illiterate who sees in front of him shapes whose significations he is unable to fathom. She said no-one can read when dreaming, and when I doubted her words, she said that she too had once dreamed that she couldn't read some text and that my dream was common and nothing to worry about, and so on and so forth.

I told her I didn't believe her, and she turned to me and asked me why I didn't consult a psychiatrist.

"Why a psychiatrist?" I asked her.

She laughed shyly, the way she did, covering her mouth with her hand, and said she had noticed that I'd become a little odd since that accursed movie evening, and that I was drinking a lot and smoking non-stop. "Perhaps you need to see a therapist to help you get through the crisis."

I told her I didn't believe in psychoanalysis and didn't care for that kind of nonsense.

We were in the small living room of my apartment. I was sitting in the cane rocking chair that I had come across in a place where they sold used furniture on East Hudson, and Sarang Lee was standing, pouring us coffee. She put it on the table and stretched out on the grey couch. Her skirt rose to above her knees, and I heard her say, "Stretch out like me, close your eyes, and say whatever you like." I closed my eyes and silence reigned. "Why don't you say something?" she said, her eyes still closed. At that instant, I felt a desire for her knees, but instead of leaping up and throwing myself down beside her, I closed my eyes and imagined myself drawing the girl to me and I did not wake from my naughty dream till I felt her hand stroking my cheek as she asked me where my imagination had taken me off to!

Sometimes when she was beside me I'd be silent, when I felt the words were about to turn into thorns in my throat, and she'd respect my silence and not ask me why, waiting till I came back from the place or time I'd travelled to. Then we'd resume our conversation as though nothing had happened.

This time, though, I'd broken with that tradition, which was linked to our friendship, which began three years ago. I suppose I was afraid she'd guessed my feelings, and I felt embarrassed and blushed.

She told me not to be afraid. There was nothing to be embarrassed about in going to a therapist. "The doctor will forget everything you've said the moment you leave the clinic, plus there are strict rules to protect patients."

I told her I didn't believe in psychoanalysis and thought that what they call "psychological" or "spiritual" malaise was just chemical reactions.

"The chemistry of the soul!" she said. "A person is spiritual chemistry, otherwise they wouldn't be a person."

Sarang Lee may have been right. I'm writing now, without realising it, as though I were lying on an analyst's couch and talking spontaneously, though that is not the case. The goal of lying down is to sink deep into the self, so as to reach, by indirect means, the cause of the psychological disturbances one is experiencing. This doesn't apply in my case as I'm not talking, because I'm looking for something and not closing my eyes so as to sink into the self. My eyes are open as wide as they can be so that I can see the entire world in the mirrors of words. These words that I write have become my mirrors. I look into them to discover the world and recompose it. Our lives, Manal, my mother, used to say, pass quickly and lightly, like a dream, and she was right. Life is just like a dream, and the only way to see it is in the mirror of words. Herein, in my view, lies the importance of literature, for literature is the shading in of a world without shadows, in order to reveal its secrets. Such revelation has no object other than to create pleasure, a pure pleasure that looks no further than its own horizon. Do not believe writers with messages! They're just false prophets and failed soothsayers. People with religious messages, on the other hand, are in essence writers who dream of filling in the distance between fiction and reality and who there-fore build a world of delusions that quickly transform themselves into an authority practising repression, terror and control. This is why I have taken literature as my religion and the shadows of the world as my literature; why I have lived my whole life as though leaving one novel or poem simply to enter into a new novel or poem, my eyes becoming repositories for grief, my tragedy transformed into fiction . . . all of it thanks to al-Sitt Umm Kulsoum, though that's another story!

The only person I told of my dream about the words that refused to be read was Sarang Lee, who suggested I consult a thera-pist, failing to understand that my disease isn't psychological and that the battle I entered into with Dr Hanna in my dream costs me so much sleep because it seems to me a compressed version of my stories with my mother, and with Ma'moun, and with Dalia.

Dr Hanna Jiryis is a man of sound judgement, capable of deploying an irrefutable logic. One really shouldn't write a work of history to suit his own tastes or as summary of his own personal experience; on the contrary, the writing of history should be documented and based on facts. My suggestion of adding a paragraph to my grandfather's letter wasn't serious, I just said it as a joke. Today, though, it's become a real issue, because I've decided to write the story of the place where I was born, and herein lies the dilemma – for the story that I shall tell is 100 per cent true and is based on things my mother told me so often that I came to feel I wasn't listening to the stories with my ears but had lived and witnessed them; it's as though it's my memory that's remembering, not my mother's. At the same time, I've made use of a number of books and testimonies, including Isbir Munayyir's writings on Lydda, Raja-e Busaila's memoirs, Michael Palumbo's study of the expulsion of the Palestinians, Ethel Mannin's novel *The Road to Beersheba*, and innumerable studies and books on Palestine that I found in the New York University library, up to and including Aref al-Aref's writings on the Nakba and the studies of Walid Khalidi. I even went specially to see Emmanuel Saba, whom I'd met at the seminar on bringing American war crimes in Iraq to trial that was organised by a group of leftist students and professors at the Cooper Union. I visited him at his home in Brooklyn and invited him to dinner at the Tannourine restaurant, where he told me what I'd already heard from my mother. I remember the voice of his wife Ahlam trembling as we started in on the deluxe Nablus-style *knafeh* and her saying she could taste Palestine on her tongue. I also contacted many people still living in Lydda to collect testimonies from those days, facing in the process many difficulties, as though I were returning to a place I didn't want to go back to – despite which I knew that going back was a condition of my final emergence from the cocoon of that place and its gappy memory.

I won't go on at length about my attempts to document the days of the ghetto. It was a cruel and bitter experience. All the same, I must confess that there are many gaps in the story of those days as I pieced it together, and I can only write a well-ordered account by filling in the blanks in the way I proposed to Dr Hanna, namely, by simultaneously adding and subtracting.

I had to leave out a lot of what I heard because it was full of passionate emotions and constructed out of an unabashed romanticism. Can one reasonably say that a seventy-year-old living in Brooklyn, who spends most of his time organising religious activities among the congregation of St Julian's Greek Orthodox Church, "longs" for the days of the ghetto because they were filled with emotion, affection and solidarity?!

"You 'long'?" I asked him. "Are you serious when you say that, man? Who could long for flies, thirst and all the other crap?" He replied that I hadn't understood him: when he used the word, he didn't mean it in the ordinary sense. He meant "feel nostalgia".

"And what does nostalgia mean?" I asked him.

"Nostalgia means nostalgia, meaning the warmth of memory," he said. "When your soul feels cold, what can you do? The only thing that warms the soul is nostalgia. Even if the memories are hard, it's the only way to get back to the nest that you left and warm yourself with your memories and find refuge in them."

I didn't tell him that his desired refuge was the very cause of my anger, that I had to rid myself of the warmth of memory because it made me feel as though my skin was itching, and that I'd like to rip my memory to pieces so that I could climb out of its cocoon and look towards the future.

"What future are you talking about, dear? The future's behind me now," a woman living in Lydda told me when I phoned to ask about Crazy Karim, whom I'd heard had tried to rape her in the ghetto. "He wasn't crazy or anything, dear. They said he'd gone crazy so that they could let him off the punishment. It was dear old Abu Adnan, God treat him well and have mercy on his grave, who announced that the man was possessed by an infidel *jinni*, and it ended up with a *zikr* ceremony and a lot of hullabaloo, and Karim sat there and acted out the *jinni* leaving him, alive and kicking, and the ululations and the shouting began, and the Jews thought there was an uprising and started firing into the air. Everyone ran away back to their houses, and the *jinni* didn't know what to do so he ran away from the ghetto and we were rid of him. That's what they said, and what could I do? My father said I had to get married, and they married me to Abu Riyad. He was a decrepit old man whose wife and children had fled and disappeared leaving him stuck here. What can I tell you, dear? Days of nothing but bitterness."

The woman wept on the telephone as though we were at a funeral and began telling me the story as though she were recounting the plot of a melodrama. She told me about her beloved, who'd sneaked back over the border for her sake and, when he found out that they'd married her off, decided to kill himself: "But he didn't. 'Life is dear,' as they say, and he went back to Ramallah." She told me how she'd been widowed as a girl, and had had to wait on the old man who had become her husband after he was struck down by hemiplegia, and how the Israeli woman conscript had spat on her as she stood in front of the barbed wire waiting for the men to return with the water barrels, and so on and so forth . . . I wanted something different from her. I wanted her to tell me about the rhythm of daily life, so I asked her about her feelings when the wire was removed, but instead of answering my question, she went on and on deploring her bad luck, as though the Nakba had happened in order to give her, specifically, a hard time; as though all the stories of the ghetto could be summed up in the tragedy of her paralysed husband.

All that had to be left out so that the text didn't sink under nostalgia and grief and the experience lose its flavour, for the truth isn't always believable; sometimes, indeed, it seems concocted and inflated. Writing the truth requires avoiding the melodramatic elements, which have to be eliminated from our life stories if tragedy is not to turn into farce. And just as I've eliminated many details of my life, both knowingly and unknowingly, so shall I eliminate a number of details of daily life in the ghetto, and I won't be any more of a tyrant than memory itself, for memory does the same, continuously and without our realising.

In my work on filling in the gaps I didn't resort to inventing events that didn't happen. Instead, I would move an event from one place to another. Let's suppose that the woman Crazy Karim tried to assault wasn't the one who told me the story of her elderly husband and whose name was Umm Jamil. Now let's suppose that it was my mother Crazy Karim tried to assault and I heard the story from a schoolmate, and that when I asked her about it, she denied it vigorously and said it was just a lot of drivel that Umm Jamil's husband had claimed to have heard after he went senile.

I wouldn't have argued about it with my mother, even though I knew that the man had lost the power of speech after he was struck with hemiplegia. But if I were to follow up on my supposition about the attempted rape of my mother, it would give the story I'm writing a deeper dimension, and Ma'moun would come into the picture as the man who accosted his opponent and defeated him. Looked at from that perspective, his relationship with Manal would take on a new dimension.

I'm not sure yet which version to adopt. I've put both down so as to clarify what I mean by "filling in the gaps", which isn't just a matter of random invention; it's an operation of the greatest complexity.

Naturally, Dr Hanna Jiryis would consider such talk "literature". The man used the word to indicate contempt because he believed literature wasn't something serious. I don't know what he meant by serious, but it would seem that his point of departure was the arrogance of the scholar who can see only facts. The man isn't working in the exact but in the human sciences, which remain, in my humble opinion, not far removed from speculation and which resemble literature in many aspects, though they lack its magic and beauty. Enlarging on his idea, Dr Hanna showed himself up by saying, derisively, that the majority of novel-readers were women. I reject that male-supremacist position, even though it is, to some degree, true. Dr Hanna considers this a fault because, in his view, reading literature is just filling emptiness with more emptiness, while life has taught me that women are the light of the world and for literature to exist it must become feminine and seek inspiration at its Scheherazadian wellspring.

Scheherazade was the first narrator. She gave birth to children and told a thousand stories, every one of which became a person who narrates. I wanted to explain to the judicious scholar of history that Cervantes found his novel written in the language of Scheherazade, and the novel was thus born at his hands through a translation from "the language of the *'ayn*", a language that a bewitching woman had turned into that of storytelling. Such was the claim of the author of Don Quixote. Maybe he was lying; indeed, he probably was lying when he claimed to have bought the manuscript of the book from an Arab bookseller in the market at Toledo, but his lie was truer than the truth itself.

(I don't know why the ancient Arab linguists called their

language "the language of the *ḍād*": the *ḍād* isn't a beautiful or evocative letter, and my admiration for al-Khalil ibn Ahmad al-Farahidi, founder of the science of prosody, has led me to adopt the suggestion he makes in his dictionary *The Book of the 'Ayn*, where he proposes that the *'ayn* should be made the first letter of the alphabet. The same supposition that led to the language being called the language of the *ḍād* holds true for the *'ayn*, as the letter *'ayn* isn't to be found in any other language in the world either, not to mention that it has numerous meanings, ranging from the *'ayn* ("eye") with which we see to the *'ayn* ("spring") that we drink from, and so on and so forth.)

What have I to do with this accursed dream that has been repeated three times, but which I will not allow to repeat itself again?

I shall write the story of the ghetto, not because nostalgia for my country impels me to do so. I am a stranger here in New York, as I was there, in Lydda and Haifa and Jaffa. I shall write of my being a stranger, not of my nostalgia. That is the issue.

THE DAYS OF THE GHETTO

Where Did the Ghetto Come From?
(1)

The inhabitants of the ghetto woke at six in the morning to a burst of gunfire. Bullets slammed into the walls of the houses, competing with the echoes of the loudspeaker that summoned the people to assemble in the square in front of the Great Mosque.

It had been their first night inside the fence built by the victorious Israeli army around the quarter embraced by the mosque, the church and the hospital. They did not know their quarter was called the ghetto. All they knew was that they were still alive and all that remained of the city's inhabitants after the great expulsion. They were a strange mixture of humanity – doctors, male and female nurses, shopkeepers, peasants, refugees from neighbouring villages – whom the sudden onset of fear had brought together and caused to hide in and around the hospital as they fled the bullets that flew over people's heads, driving the city's inhabitants to leave it, on foot, for nowhere.

The people awoke in fear. After the three days of random killing that they called "the massacre", they spent their first night surrounded by a strange silence that was disturbed only by the barking of stray dogs aimlessly roaming the city's streets.

The people of the ghetto slept their first night without bullets. Exhaustion, hunger and thirst made them unaware of the extraordinary numbers of flies that had spread everywhere and were swarming over bodies swimming in sweat and the summer's heat. Later, Manal would call that first night on which she slept without being woken by the sound of machine-gun fire "the night of the flies". She said that, were it not for her little child, whose face she was obliged to cover with her headcloth to prevent the flies from eating its eyes, she would have slept like a log and would not have been bothered by the blowfly bites. "Everyone slept. As they say, son, 'Sleep is an imperious master'."

Everyone slept to the sound of the barking, broken only by a mysterious moaning, then woke to the sound of bullets flying and a summons to assemble in the square in front of the Great Mosque. Once the sleep had begun to lift from their eyes, leaving skewers from the pain of darkness interspersed with threads of light, they walked with the sluggishness of the terror-stricken to the square in front of the mosque, certain that their fate would be no different from that of the fifty thousand inhabitants of Lydda who had been compelled to leave over the past three days. They saw wire surrounding them on all sides and heard the voice of Dr Mikhail Samara exclaim, "It's a cage!" Then they heard him turn to his wife, who was holding her small daughter's hand, and say, "Don't worry. They aren't going to expel us. They've caged us, like animals."

The people emerged, pushing one another out of the way to get to where they had been ordered to assemble. The remaining inhabitants of Lydda had learned their lesson well: these soldiers didn't joke about and were willing, and indeed eager, to kill. The smell of blood had given them an appetite for more.

Dr Samara noticed that the ground was spattered with a mixture of blood and dust, and he smelled death. He turned to Nurse Manal, who was walking next to him, carrying her baby, and asked her to take care not to walk in the blood. "We'll have to hose the ground today with water and clean it away. It's not right to walk on blood."

The people arrived in groups from where they had been hiding in the church, the mosque and the hospital. They looked around them, eye meeting eye, and the only sound was that of footfalls on the ground. The firing stopped and the loudspeaker fell silent. The people squeezed into the square in front of the Great Mosque, where a detail of about ten soldiers was disposed around them, rifles at the ready.

The soldiers had a bizarre appearance – unshaven young men, eyes half closed as though they had slept badly, their khaki uniforms hanging loose on their bodies, smoking voraciously, and looking right and left, as though afraid. Some had covered their heads with Palestinian *keffiyehs* to protect them from the heat, while others wore beaten-up military caps.

The heat was extreme that July dawn. The phantoms walking sluggishly towards the assembly point stuck close to one another, like frightened chickens. About five hundred men, women, and children met at the corner of the mosque square. The scene was comical, or so at least thought one of the bearded Israeli soldiers. He pointed, laughing, at the people huddled together at the corner of the square and said in Hebrew, *"Khavasim, kmo khavasim!"*

"What's he saying?" Manal asked the doctor, who was standing next to her.

"He's just jabbering in Hebrew," Dr Samara said.

"He's saying we're like sheep," said Mufid Shahada, who'd learned Hebrew from working at the nearby Ben Shemen colony.

At that moment, the crack of a bullet was heard, fired close to where the people were assembled, and a large bird fell from the sky and thrashed about as it died in the middle of the stunned crowd.

It was the soldier who had described the assembled people as sheep who had fired into the air, hitting a bird that had been hovering in the sky over the city. Dr Samara bent over the bird, whose death throes were now over, picked it up by its feet, and carried it away from where the people were gathered, only to hear the soldier yelling at him. The doctor came to an immediate standstill and looked right and left, not knowing what he was supposed to do, and the soldier let off a burst of gunfire at his feet. The doctor shuddered, then squatted down and threw the bird from his hand.

The soldier came up and ordered him, with a motion of his rifle, to stand, but the doctor, whose body was still quivering, didn't move. He remained in a squatting position, his eyes closed and his teeth chattering.

The soldier aimed his rifle as though about to shoot, approached the doctor, and grasped him by the arm to make him get up, but the Palestinian doctor refused to be budged. Two other soldiers now came up to him, pulled him by his arms, and made him stand. At the same moment, the Israeli soldiers burst out laughing.

"*Asa bamikhnasayim!*" ("He's pissed himself!") the first soldier yelled.

"*Magia lo lamut!*" ("He's a coward and deserves to die!") the second said.

The soldiers moved away from the doctor, their rifles trained on him. The man collapsed onto the ground again and sat there, making a choking sound as though he was weeping. At that moment, the soldiers heard the voice of the officer telling them not to shoot him. The doctor sat where he was, without moving, through the long hours that the people of the ghetto spent in the courtyard of the mosque waiting for the Israelis' orders.

When the soldiers backed away, leaving the doctor, who had wet himself from fear, sitting where he was, the people looked up and took note of the strange birds circling in the sky, and an obscure fear, unlike that which had drawn itself on their faces during the invasion of the city, seized them. People would remember those birds as one of the signs of the Last Hour. They would feel that they were about to become food for birds of prey and that their fate would be similar to that of the corpses that lay strewn through the city's streets.

The Israeli officer's orders were strict: "*Lo rotseh leshmoa milah*," which one of the soldiers, shouting, translated as "Not a word! Not a sound! Got it?" Silence reigned over the men and women who had gathered in the square in front of the mosque. Nothing cracked the wall of silence that surrounded the people standing there until a baby burst out crying, quickly joined by a group of other children, who turned the place into an orgy of weeping.

(Manal boasted that I was the leader of the band of weepers who broke the silence. She said she didn't know what to do and I was hungry and the milk had dried in her breasts. She pushed her nipples into my mouth but I refused them. She said that the night before she'd cooked me a meal of boiled lentils and made me lick her finger, which she'd wetted with the water from the lentils, and I'd fallen asleep, exhausted from crying, but it hadn't occurred to her in the morning to bring any lentil water because she'd left in a hurry with everyone else to go to the square in front of the mosque. Manal said my crying had severed her heartstrings and, instead of silencing me, she stood there as tears began to pour down her cheeks, to mix with those of her hungry child.)

A soldier came up to Manal and tried to pull the child out of her arms, so Umm Yahya ran up and took the child and began rocking it and gave it her breast. The child suckled and fell silent, and the sound began to die down. Manal wept as she thanked Umm Yahya.

"After that wretched sunbath, some of the inhabitants of the ghetto fled. I don't know how they managed to slip through the barbed wire. The doctor, Mikhail Samara, disappeared with his wife and daughter, and Umm Yahya disappeared with her husband and her four children, and there were others I don't know. It's said they bribed the soldiers, but no-one knows. We didn't give any thought to it at the time, and I don't think there was any bribery. They said they wanted to go to Ramallah, so they opened the gate for them and they went. You, though, poor thing, suckled only once at Umm Yahya's breast, and were raised on lentil water till things got better."

Mothers cradling their babies, men exhausted by exertion and fear, and the smell of death. Later, Dr Mikhail Samara, in a paper he published in the *Journal of Palestine Studies*, would dwell at length on the smell that spread through the city.

(I remember reading Dr Samara's text in the library at Haifa University, where I came across it by chance when I was preparing a paper for the seminar in which I participated on S. Yizhar's *Khirbet Khizeh*, which the Palestinian novelist Tawfiq Fayyad had translated into Arabic and published in the *Journal of Palestinian Affairs*, published by the Centre for Palestinian Research in Beirut.

I thought then and, despite the passage of all these years, still do, that Yizhar's novel is a masterpiece, because it was able to arrive at a deep Aristotelian catharsis in a language appropriate to its day. In it I beheld the image of the New Jew, without the burdens of the ideology of the period of the sabra and the pioneers – an existential Jew creating himself and his mistakes without any guilt complex. It's a pity that the novel has only recently been translated into English; it remains a witness to the depth of the relationship with death that unites the Arabic and the Hebrew languages. Recently, though, I've discovered in this novel new depths and multiple levels – but that's another matter and requires a different context.)

Dr Samara's paper was published, by coincidence, in the same issue of the journal as Yizhar's novel. The paper was devoted to an analysis of the Sabra and Shatila massacre, carried out by the Lebanese Forces under Israeli supervision during Operation Peace for Galilee, which reached its climax on 15 September, 1982, when the Israeli army invaded Beirut following the departure of the fighters of the Palestine Liberation Organisation. The paper focuses on two things. The first is the smell, the second the "dance of death", when the victims were forced to dance before being killed.

I read the paper and I saw before me Dr Samara as depicted by my mother – a thirty-six-year-old who had graduated from the American University in Beirut and come back to Lydda to be deputy director of the city's hospital. The tall, self-confident young man married Sawsan, the most beautiful girl in the city, at the Church of St George, and the wedding was blessed by Teophilos, Greek Patriarch of Jerusalem, who came, resting his weight upon his eighty years, to repay the favour to the young doctor from Lydda who had cured him of a fit of hiccups that had almost carried him off to his grave.

This man, who spoke to people through tilted nostrils and told everyone he'd made up his mind to go to America to complete his studies as a specialist in diseases of the respiratory system, bent down with dignity, picked up the bird, still flapping about in its death throes, so as to get it away from the crowds that had assembled at the southern corner of the mosque courtyard, squatted down on the ground and when the Israeli soldier fired bullets at his feet, wet himself.

When the fall of the city to the Israeli forces had become a certainty, the doctor had ordered all the hospital employees to wear their white gowns and make sure to put the Red Cross emblem on them. He said the soldiers would never dare attack medical staff. In the event, the doctor was shocked by the indifference to such concerns shown by the members of the Israeli force, which belonged to the Palmach's 8th Brigade, and felt ashamed of his cowardice, so he did not raise his head. After that long day of sun came to an end, and when the officer ordered the people to disperse, the doctor couldn't find the strength to get up and he stayed where he was and only departed, with his wife and daughter, after everyone else had left the square.

What brought Dr Samara to Beirut during the Sabra and Shatila massacre?

The paper published in the journal was in essence a lecture given at the annual conference of the Association of Arab-American University Graduates, held in November 1982 in Minneapolis, Minnesota. In the introduction to his paper, the doctor mentions that he went to Beirut at the beginning of August as part of a delegation of Palestinian academics headed by Dr Ibrahim Abu Lughod. He states that his participation in the delegation was at the request of Edward Said, whose requests none could refuse given the author of *Orientalism*'s academic and moral stature. He writes that he had decided to stay on in Beirut following the departure of the Palestinian fighters in order to take part in the reorganisation of Red Crescent work in the devastated city and had found himself stuck in his apartment in Ras Beirut while the Israelis took over the city. Then, when he heard news of the massacre, he'd rushed to the camp, only to find himself faced with death, smell and flies.

The doctor writes:

Leila Shahid phoned me in the morning and started yelling into my ear, relating in agitated words how she had gone with French writer Jean Genet to Shatila Camp, where they had walked among the bloated bodies that filled its alleyways. "What are you doing at home, Doctor? Do something! They're slaughtering them!" When I entered the camp, my first surprise was the smell. The Lydda smell had come back. The smell has no name and can only be recalled when you smell it again, because it wafts up out of the memory. I smelled death before I saw anything. I entered the camp, and the words I had heard from Leila Shahid became echoes reverberating in my brain. I did not know where the buzzing that I could hear was coming from. Then I noticed the swarms of flies, in uncountable numbers, and smelled the Lydda smell – the very same smell, the smell of burnt spice, spreading out from amidst the blowflies, as though time had taken me back thirty-four years, to where I saw myself fall to the ground, nauseous from the smell and unable to get back up.

He recounts the story of his tour through the alleyways in the company of a doctor who was working at the camp's Galilee Hospital.

I pulled back, feeling I was about to fall, supported myself against the wall of the hospital with its flaking paint, and closed my eyes. Then I felt a hand reach out and touch my shoulder. I jumped in terror and beheld before me a tall dark-complexioned young man wearing a doctor's gown. He asked me who I was, and when I told him

*I was a Palestinian-American doctor, he took me by the hand and led me
into the first floor of the hospital, which smelled heavily of chloroform.
He introduced himself, saying he was Dr Khalil Ayoub, gave me a glass
of water, took me with him on a tour of the camp, and told me the tale.*

The style of the paper struck me as being overly personal.
In fact, what I read was not an article, it was a speech given by
Dr Samara in the U.S.A., and before a gathering of American
professors of Arab origin. The text's intimate tone disturbed me
and I couldn't account for its style till I came, years later, to
New York and discovered that what had seemed odd to me was
in fact a peculiarity of life in America, where speeches delivered
on political occasions are given a personal twist to make them
sound more credible. To be honest, I was amazed when I discovered that people here don't lie about their personal lives and that
truth is an absolute moral and social value. Naturally, this isn't
intended as praise or admiration, just a point that anyone who
lives here is bound to ponder. For all that, this penchant for
truth-telling is in no way reflected in American political discourse.
I also believe that an exaggerated concern for truth does away
with one of language's basic elements, since deception is an
ingredient of language: in so far as they are symbols, words deceive
and don't simply express (if and when they do express) but set
traps to hide the truth, even when they're trying to make an honest
declaration of it.

The Palestinian doctor's account of how he came to be seated
on the ground throughout that July day puzzled me. Did he use
the smell to avoid talking about his fear? Or did he remember the
story and recompose it in his mind over the course of thirty-plus
years in such a way that he could forget that he'd been made into
a laughing stock? Or does the whole thing amount to nothing

more than the man's embarrassment at his having wet himself, leading him to refuse to acknowledge the truth? My mother told the story innumerable times and I believe her. All the stories about Lydda that I've heard and collected have one basic source, which is Manal, who, whenever she got to the end of a story from those days in the ghetto, would sigh and say, "We have to forget, but sorrow can't be forgotten."

I believe my mother. I have no choice – the story would otherwise be lost. It's true, Manal didn't tell me the whole truth, perhaps because she pitied me. I'm not talking just about the olive tree beneath which I was found, but about many details of life in the ghetto, which I gathered from people here and there to complete the picture of my childhood. I won't borrow here the French novelist Albert Camus's ambiguous words about the Algerian War, when he said that he chose his mother so he could avoid the deeper question about the choice between the executioner and the victim: my mother is the victim, and I swear if I were forced to choose, I'd opt to be a victim too, which is why I believe her.

(Once, Dalia asked me a perplexing question. She said, "If you could choose between being born a Palestinian or an Israeli Jew, which would you be?"

I told her I would choose her.

"Does that mean you'd choose to be an Israeli?"

I told her, "I tried to be an Israeli but I couldn't. A Palestinian can only choose to be what he is. But who knows?"

She said that if I'd asked her, she would have replied without hesitation that she'd choose to be Palestinian, because she'd prefer to be the victim.

I said she was saying that because the choice was not available, which allowed her to enjoy both the virtues of the victim and the privileges of the executioner.

She said I wasn't understanding her. "Time will teach you to understand me, and when you get to that moment, you'll discover that every human is the child of a permanent exile. That, in my opinion, was the existential condition of the Jews before Israel did away with it in favour of an absurd existence devoid of meaning.")

The doctor recounted that Dr Ayoub had led him through the alleyways of the camp, which were cold and empty now that the Red Cross had collected the hundreds of corpses, sprinkled them with lime, and buried them in a mass grave dug on its outskirts.

He would stop at every turning that led to an alleyway and enumerate the bodies of the dead and describe the strange positions in which he had found them. Once he had finished describing the bloated, piled corpses, he pointed to the swarms of flies everywhere above us, saying they were all that was left of the massacre. Then he led me to the entrance of one of the shacks in the camp and recounted how the armed men had slit the belly of a pregnant woman there.

I do not want to recount at length the information given by Dr Samara in his article. The details of the Sabra and Shatila massacre are well known to all now, especially after Bayan Nuweihid al-Hout's publication of her fundamentally important book. The massacre bore witness not only to the savagery of the murderers and of the Israeli army, which permitted them to carry it out and was their partner in it, lighting the night of the camp with its flares, but also to the ability of humans to lose their souls and become intoxicated with blood.

What amazed me in the doctor's article, however, was his description of the victims' last moments, when they were forced to dance and clap on their final march from the camp to the sports stadium, where some of them were killed.

Dr Samara writes:

Dr Ayoub saw how his words had etched themselves into my features. He took me by the arm and led me back into the Galilee Hospital, saying he wanted to consult me on a medical matter, and he explained his speech therapy theory to me. He said he had discovered he could revive a patient who was in a coma by telling him stories.

"What?" I asked him, and he repeated his idea, saying he had told the patient the story of his life, thus reviving his damaged memory and allowing his soul to awaken through tales of love. He said he had been led to that conclusion by his diagnosis of the patient's condition.

"That's impossible," I said, and explained to him that we had to diagnose the cause of the coma using a brain scan. Usually, a coma was the result of a burst vein, and we could measure how critical the condition was by measuring how far the blood had spread into the brain.

I was amazed at the insistence of the man, who as far as I could tell was the only doctor to be found in that half-ruined place which resembled a hospital only in the smell of insecticides given off by its corridors. He went on with this sterile medical discussion and asked me to visit his patient, who was his father. He said his father had been lying there for seven days and had begun to display some progress as a result of this "speech therapy" that he had come up with off his own bat. This was clearly absurd, as the elderly man was brain dead and there was no hope of his recovery. However, I did learn from this nurse (I found out later from Dr Amjad, director of the Galilee Hospital, which is run by the Palestine Red Crescent in Beirut, that Khalil Ayoub was merely a nurse claiming to be a doctor) that this tableau of the doctor and his patient was no more insane than the death experience through which the people of Sabra and Shatila had passed. This doctor was proclaiming, in his own special way, his dogged devotion to life, making out of his memory and that of his father a passage to possible survival. The others, however, found themselves flailing around in their own blood, for they lived the experience of death while dancing to the orders of their executioners.

Dr Khalil told his story. His voice, interrupted by stretches of silence, shook as he said that the memory of pain was more terrible than pain itself.

"The story doesn't lie in the killing, or in the bodies of the victims, or in the savagery that etched itself on the faces of the killers, which shone under the flares fired by the Israeli army; the memory of pain, Doctor, is death by humiliation. Imagine us dancing – yes, dancing – while we were being killed, and that I danced and was killed but didn't die. The bullet failed to kill me because 'the General' (the killers gave this name to one of their leaders, who habitually hid his eyes behind dark glasses) was busy issuing orders to the bulldozer that was working at digging a mass grave and didn't notice that I'd only been wounded in the shoulder, and that my death was just a ruse. I lay down among the corpses, to conceal my life under the others' deaths. I waited two hours, then got up and ran back to the hospital, where I treated myself.

"That was at 7.30 a.m. on Saturday, 17 September, 1982, which was the last day of the massacre. We heard loudspeakers calling on people to leave their houses and walk in the direction of Cité Sportif. I set out with the rest and we walked. Many gathered. The camp, which had been covered by the silence of death, suddenly split open to reveal huge numbers of people, walking like sheep. We were surrounded by armed men on both sides, and the man with the dark glasses had a loudspeaker in his hand and was issuing orders: 'Clap!' – we clap; 'I can't hear you properly! I want you to clap louder!' – our clapping gets louder; 'Say, "Long live Bashir Gemayel"!' – we say it; 'Say, "God damn Abu

Ammar"!' – we say it; 'I want to hear it louder!' – we raise our voices. We walked and clapped and shouted slogans.

"While this was going on, the armed men were pulling groups of young men to the side of the road, ordering them to lie on the ground face down, and shooting them. It was, Doctor, a march of applause, slogans and slaughter. But that wasn't enough for them. When the procession reached the statue of Abu Hasan Salama, they made us stop, and we heard the loudspeaker ordering us to dance. 'Dance, you sons of whores! I want you to shake it!' A rigid astonishment seized us. No-one moved or made a sound. Total silence, broken by the sound of bullets fired into the air from the barrel of an M16 rifle held by the General. And at the sound of the bullets, we saw Umm Hasan. The seventy-year-old woman, who'd bound her head in a white kerchief, emerged from among the ranks of the people, and her full body, which was covered by a long black dress, began to dance, timidly at first, then gathering speed until she seemed like a circle turning upon itself. How can I describe the scene to you, Doctor? The image of that woman, whose body twisted to the rhythm of the bullets, comes to me covered in tears, and the relative sizes of things become confused. I see her body become thin as a thread, then widen and stretch, the white of her headscarf spreading over the black of her dress, and everything turning. And I see her face, on which the years had etched their stories, reveal a mysterious smile. You don't know Umm Hasan. If you like, I can introduce you to her, she's always coming here to visit Yunis. She's like a mother to me. She's the only certified midwife here, and all the children of the camp have fallen from their mothers' wombs into her hands.

"When we saw Umm Hasan dancing, dancing fever seized us, and everybody danced. To be honest, I danced without making any decision to do so. I found myself dancing, and don't ask me how long we danced

215

because I don't know. Time disappears at two moments only – of dan-
cing and of death – so what's one to do when they coincide? We were
dancing and dying, Doctor, and only became aware of the scars on
the soul after everything was over and we discovered that we'd all
died. You're right – no-one has the right to convert death into numbers.
Fifteen hundred people died here, or so they say, but the number says
nothing, because everybody died here. The entirety of mankind died in
that moment of dance, when some were driven to the execution wall still
dancing. At that moment, they took me. They pulled me from my dance
to my death, but I didn't die. Umm Hasan danced until she fell to the
ground. Then people heard shots and said that the woman had been
killed, but like me and like most of the others, she died and stayed alive."

Dr Samara ended his article with an analysis of the image of
the sheep in terms of what Khalil Ayoub had said, opining that the
man's feelings of humiliation resulted from the people's surrender
to their fate, since they knew they were going to their deaths
but had lost the will to resist and the instinct to live had deserted
them. He then set up a parallel between the way the Nazis treated
the Jews during the Nazi holocaust and the methods used at the
massacre of Sabra and Shatila.

I don't like that kind of comparison. It deprives things of their
meanings and turns mankind's relationship to history into boring
repetition by seeming to equivocate and declare the criminal
innocent by making him just a copy of some other criminal and
by treating war crimes as though they were inevitable. It turns
the victims into numbers by ignoring their singularity and the
singularity of the tragedy of each.

Not to mention that the article angered me from two other
perspectives.

The first was its coincidental publication side by side, in the same issue, with S. Yizhar's novel *Khirbet Khizeh*, which describes the fall of a village in southern Palestine (in all probability Khirbet al-Khisas), its destruction, and the expulsion of its inhabitants. One of the scenes of the novel intersects to an almost incredible degree with one of the scenes from the first day of the Lydda ghetto and with that of Umm Hasan during the massacre of Sabra and Shatila. Any observer, on reading or hearing of the events of that day, will notice this.

The second is the way it is written, which mixes identification with the victim with sympathy for him. The style really embarrassed me, for the text ends on a preachy note like that of a Protestant minister bringing the Good News to the believers.

Dr Samara's text stirred many painful thoughts in me, especially the scene in which Umm Hasan dances at Shatila's wedding of death. This woman, of whose tenderness and love for people Khalil Ayoub told endless stories, and who became the only character whose presence in the Lebanese writer's novel about the village Bab el-Shams, or "Gate of the Sun", caught my imagination – this woman, whose soul, which radiated a beauty that illuminated her wrinkled face, was a treasure house of wisdom, led the dance of death herself. Umm Hasan, the character most filled with humanity, had appeared to me, from the time I first became acquainted with her through words, as though she were written in water, not ink, because of her translucence, through which the soul shone; and here I find her dancing to the rhythm of the killers' bullets!

Umm Hasan led the dance, so everyone danced, and death itself danced. Dear God in Heaven, why did You test the woman who picked up the baby Naji and gave him back to his mother? Why did You test her with this shameful dance?

I never asked Umm Hasan why she danced, because I never met her. How could I have met a dead woman? Her death was the opening scene of the novel *Gate of the Sun*, but, when Khalil told me fragments of his memories of Shatila Camp, he didn't say anything about the dance of death, and I didn't ask him about Umm Hasan. He patted my shoulder, saying that the memory of the massacre had been transformed into gaps of silence in his life and he hadn't even said anything about it to his wife, who was from Hebron, because he had been unable to.

Umm Hasan dances to the rhythm of death. Why didn't the author of *Gate of the Sun* say anything about the incident? Was he unaware of it? Or had he too developed gaps in his memory, like Khalil Ayoub? Or was he too embarrassed?

The dance had no effect on my love for and infatuation with Umm Hasan. On the contrary, it made me love and admire her even more.

(For my part, I refuse to write from a deficient or gappy memory. I'm going to fill in all the gaps in the story and when I lack facts, I shall look for them in the works of others. Thus shall I construct my mirror, with which I shall make myself whole. But what am I to say about Umm Hasan? Am I allowed to say that, after my encounter with Ma'moun in New York, I wished it had been Umm Hasan who'd picked me up off the road of death at Lydda? If that, or something like it, had happened, my life would have been radically different, and today I would feel that I belonged to a mother who gave birth to me even though she didn't, and this feeling of being the child of coincidence, and that my life was composed of the dust of delusion, wouldn't haunt me.)

My reservations concerning this text come to me from some-where else. Dr Samara made a hasty comparison between Sabra and Shatila on the one hand and the Lydda ghetto on the other, and that doesn't work. One might legitimately compare the Lydda massacres and the Shatila massacre, or the march of dancing and death at Shatila with the march of death on which more than fifty thousand human beings, compelled to leave Lydda by force of arms and violence, were driven. And these cases would allow us to analyse at length how the bloodlust rises to the surface of people's souls and changes them into monsters, which is why the Prophet David, in his Psalms, cries out, "Spare us from bloody men, O Lord!" In and of itself, the savagery is just a trivial matter, since, at the end of the day, it can be regulated by law and held in check, though it comes back, or is brought back, on a regular basis. The larger problem is the canine, cynical mentality that lies behind it. This is where the greater crime lies. The killers at Sabra and Shatila were driven by bloodlust and drugs, but the one behind the curtain who held the thread was calm and rational. He needed the massacre in order to achieve a specific political goal, which was to sear into the consciousness of the Palestinians the conviction that their longing and their nostalgia for their land were pointless and could only lead to death by humiliation.

In Lydda, likewise, the formula was clear – from a massacre to expel the city's inhabitants to the caging of those who remained. In this case, though, there was no distance between the ignorant, stupid implementer and the planner, as was the case in Shatila. Here, the planner was the implementer, which is why he was obliged to lie and deny, and the truth had to wait many long years to appear.

The greater savagery isn't a bloody expression of an egotistical reaction. The greater savagery is the organisation of killing and repression without being oneself affected and in accordance with a cold rationalism that strives to realise its goals.

(To write this chapter, I had to go back to the issue of the *Journal of Palestinian Affairs* that I'd read a long time before at the University of Haifa and which I was only able to obtain because of Sarang Lee. She went to New York University's Bobst Library, found the issue, and brought it to me. Supposing I'd relied on my memory alone, I would have written an incomplete chapter, at the heart of which incompleteness would have stood Dr Khalil Ayoub, who appeared in the article in question sixteen years before he did so in *Gate of the Sun*. When I read the article in Haifa, the doctor meant nothing to me as a character, and likewise the story of his father, asleep in his coma, failed to stick in my memory. Dr Samara's analysis of the smell astonished me, and the dance of death gave me goose pimples, but had it not been for Sarang Lee I would have missed the significance of my meeting with Khalil Ayoub in Ramallah in 1997 and the story would have been incomplete.)

(I'm not trying for a complete story, not to mention that what I'm writing here isn't a story but my final rehearsal for death. I'm not probing the past because I feel nostalgia for it – I hate nostalgia. I am, rather, surrendering to my memory, which is settling accounts with me before it too becomes extinct, at the moment of my own extinction and demise.)

(2)

After what happened to Dr Samara, silence reigned over the crowd of people that had assembled at the northern corner of the courtyard in front of the Great Mosque, a silence disturbed only by the buzzing of the flies that hovered above them and came to rest on their faces and necks, and the sound of one or other of the young children, which would die down as soon as it arose.

Time passed slowly over their bodies, which swayed discreetly under the leaden July sun. Long hours, during which the soldiers paced on the other side of the wire with their rifles, watching the mass of humanity.

Manal said she heard the sound of a body hitting the ground. She turned and saw an elderly woman writhing on the earth. No-one dared leave their place. Suddenly, the boy Mufid Shahada went to her, bent over her and tried to revive her. Then he retreated, leaving the ranks of the crowd, and walked towards the barbed wire.

"Go back!" one of the guards shouted, pointing his machine gun at him.

"The woman," said the young man. "The woman's about to die and needs a drop of water."

"I don't have any water," shouted the soldier. "Go back!"

"The ablutions tank, sir! The ablutions tank is full of water. I'm going to go and get a little of it to sprinkle on her face and give her to drink."

"Don't take another step. Go back where you were!"

"But she'll die," muttered the young man as he returned to his place among the crowd.

A wailing arose from the women. It wasn't shouting or weeping, it was a half-suppressed sound that burst out from inside their chests. Manal said it had scared her at first. "Something no-one had ever heard the like of, like the sounds made by *jinn* and *afreets*. A sort of moaning coming from I don't know where. And then suddenly, dear, I swear I don't know how, the moaning started coming from me too without me realising, as though the air we breathe had turned to sound and was coming out of all the women's chests."

At that moment, Ma'moun emerged from the crowd and walked towards the wire. No-one knew the name of this youth, who was eighteen years old, or how he came to be at the hospital, or how he'd found himself in the ghetto.

Ma'moun was wearing shorts and had a black-and-white *keffiyeh* that Manal had given him as they left the hospital tied round his head, and his eyes were covered with dark glasses. He walked towards the barbed wire, to the accompaniment of the shouts of one of the soldiers, who aimed his rifle at him. A slim youth walking with slow steps that tested the ground, with which his feet had no previous acquaintance. He approached, his shadow moving behind him, his arms stretched out before him, and walked towards the soldier who was shouting at him to stop. People heard the sound of the rifle being cocked as it was raised, giving warning of the approaching release of the bullet. A cry of "God is great!" came from the throat of Hatim al-Laqqis, to be taken up, spontaneously and without thought, by Manal, and the whole crowd was transformed into an ad-hoc chorus, all shouting,

"God is great!" with even Dr Samara raising his voice and joining in. The soldier stepped back, and the ten soldiers guarding the wire took up fighting positions. The calls of "God is great!" gradually died away into murmurs. Ma'moun, who could see only through his ears, had felt, at the moment when they had all cried out, that he was the stronger and that no power on earth could prevent him from going wherever he wanted.

The soldier, who had never stopped shouting orders at the blind young man to go back to his place, dropped on one knee and aimed his gun at Ma'moun, but before he could fire, Ma'moun felt a hand shoving him and throwing him to the ground. He fell, and found a voice at his side asking him in a strange accent to go back.

"Go back. They're going to shoot you," said the voice.

"The woman's dying of thirst and we all want to die with her," screamed Ma'moun, as he gathered himself up, shook his hand out of the grasp of the owner of the voice, and ran towards the barbed wire.

The soldiers seemed to have been taken aback by the moaning that had turned into "God is great!" and were then stricken with paralysis before the boy who ran, stumbling over his feet like a blind man, and reached the barbed wire, where he raised his arms, snatched off his dark glasses and screamed at the soldier, "Kill me!"

Hatim, who had run after Ma'moun and knocked him to the ground to protect him from death, told the story more than once, and at each telling his voice would choke when he got to Ma'moun's cry of "Kill me!" and he'd stop speaking, taking deep breaths before continuing.

The story of Hatim al-Laqqis and how the fates brought him from his town of Maroun al-Ras in Lebanon to the Lydda ghetto is itself strange. I'll write it down when it comes back to me.

Hatim said that all he saw was Ma'moun's back and his shadow. He watched, via that shadow, the movement of Ma'moun's hand, stretched out beneath the rays of the July sun, snatching off his glasses. "I heard nothing, I swear. After Ma'moun had screamed with all the strength his throat could muster, he brought his face close to the barbed wire and said something in a low voice. I saw fear on the face of the Israeli soldier, who retreated, then left the place for a few minutes before returning and talking with Ma'moun. Ma'moun then turned towards us, raised his hands in the air, telling everyone, 'Drink!' and moved in the direction of the throng with rapid steps, soon, however, stumbling and tumbling over, his glasses falling from his hand. I ran towards him and he said, 'Please, my glasses.' I picked them up and gave them to him. He took them, wiped the dust from the lenses, and put them back on before standing. In that instant, I saw the whiteness of his eyes, which opened onto whiteness, and guessed that what had scared the Israeli soldier and made him give the order to let us drink from the ablutions tank was that absolute whiteness, unrelieved by a single black spot."

Manal said the crowd ran towards the tank, "And then we discovered, dear, that we didn't have anything in which to scoop the water up so that we could drink, so we started scooping it up in the palms of our hands, and people bent their heads over the water and gulped and gulped. We did it like animals and only noticed at the end, when we'd had quenched out thirst and we started laughing at ourselves."

There was only one tap, which Ma'moun stationed himself next to, warding people off because it was, he said, set aside for the sick and the elderly. Ma'moun asked Hatim and some of the other young men to lift the woman who'd fainted, so she could be given water. Strangely, Dr Samara never moved from his place to help her, so a fifteen-year-old boy called Ghassan Batheish, who worked as a nurse at the hospital, took care of her, first sprinkling water on the woman's face, then giving her water to drink from his hands and standing her up.

Gathered around the ablutions tank, the people looked as though they'd escaped from the ring of terror that had encircled them and forced them to stand unmoving for long hours under a merciless sun that had burnt their faces and bodies. The masses of humanity that had emerged from their hiding places in the hospital, the mosque, and the church, found themselves in a cage fenced in with wire, and discovered that their fate now lay in the hands of a troop of soldiers who seemed not to know what they were doing.

The solid, unspeaking mass, which swayed like Phoenician statues set next to one another in rows, exploded at one go into speech and movement. The people felt they'd recovered something of their souls, which had been swallowed by fear, and the din grew louder till the voice of Fatima, wife of Jamil Salama the baker, arose, calling for bread. The word "bread" carried with it a magic charge, because the people, whose thirst was now assuaged, suddenly felt hungry. They had risen in panic in the morning to the bullets and the loudspeaker, and it hadn't occurred to any of them to put a mouthful of food into their mouths. Fatima's voice awakened the voice of hunger, and they began calling for bread. Ma'moun's hand went up, asking them to be quiet so as to give him a chance to go to the wire and speak with the soldier, but he was rebuked by the voice of Iliyya Batshoun ordering him not to speak.

225

"This isn't the time for kids' play and nonsense!" shouted the short sixty-year-old with the big belly. "First we have to form a committee to represent the people of the town."

"Before a committee," said Ma'moun, "we want to eat."

"Who's that?" shouted Iliyya. "You can't be from here. We don't know you. What's your name, boy?"

"Ma'moun. Ma'moun Khudr."

"You're the son of Salim Khudr, right? Where are your family, son?"

"They went to Naalin."

"So what are you doing here, blind and with no family to look after you? You should have gone with them."

"I don't want to go," said Ma'moun.

Ma'moun felt a hand patting his back and heard Manal's voice saying, "Ma'moun's one of us, Hajj Iliyya, and we're hungry. This won't do, making us stand under the sun since the morning without water or bread."

"You're right, sister," said Iliyya Batshoun, called "Hajj" because every year he insisted on spending Easter Sunday eve in Jerusalem and making a pilgrimage to the Cave of Light in the Church of the Resurrection where he would spend the whole night in vigil, waiting for the outburst of divine light that announces the Saviour's resurrection.

Hajj Iliyya bent over the child Manal was carrying in her arms. "God be praised! That's the son of the martyr, God have mercy on his soul. How old is he, God protect him?"

"A week," said Manal.

"And what have you named him, God preserve him?"

"I have to name him after his father, the martyr Hasan."

"He's the first child to be born here," called out Mufid Shahada.

"We should call him Naji," said Ma'moun.

"He's the first child, so it's like Adam in the Garden of Eden. We should call him Adam," Iliyya said.

"The Garden of Eden?!" Ma'moun said, laughing. "This is Hell, not Heaven, Hajj. His name has to be Naji because God saved him from the massacre."

"Adam's a nice name," Manal said, "but what are we going to do about his father's name?"

"Adam was his father too," said Hajj Iliyya. "All of us are children of Adam, sister."

In the midst of the chaos around the ablutions tank, the inhabitants of the ghetto managed to give the child, as to the manner of whose birth all were ignorant, a name appropriate to the ghetto, which had become the city's new emblem. "His name is Adam," said Hajj Iliyya Batshoun, and when Manal said no more, everyone took it to mean that she had agreed to be mother to him who has no mother. Our Master Adam, peace be upon him, was the first human, the first prophet, and the first poet. He was born without a mother and it was his job, as the story goes, to give birth to his mother and wife, from his ribs. That is why no-one called Manal "Umm Adam", or "Mother of Adam", as our customs dictate, with the name of the woman disappearing and being replaced by "Mother" followed by the name of her first-born son. On the contrary, she retained her original name, thus remaining for ever young, the years growing older within her while she herself remained unchanged.

In the midst of the chaos and the racket around the name that had been given the boy-child who was the firstborn of the ghetto, people heard the sound of renewed shooting. The voices faded away, everyone froze in place, and they saw an Israeli officer, surrounded by three soldiers, passing through the gate in the wire, which he opened with his hands, and advancing.

The officer took hold of the loudspeaker, brought it close to his mouth, and spoke in Arabic: "I am Captain Moshe. You are all required to move away from the water tank immediately."

The crowd began moving as though hypnotised, and no-one opened their mouths. As soon as they had moved away from the tank, Moshe's voice rose again: "Men aged fourteen and over to the right, women to the left."

The men and women began moving. A soldier approached Dr Samara to order him to join the men, but the officer shouted in the face of the soldier, who retreated, and the doctor remained where he was, at a distance from the two groups.

"Bread, sir."

Captain Moshe turned towards the source of the voice and saw Manal holding on to Ma'moun's arm, while Ma'moun tried to escape her grip.

"To the right!" the officer yelled at Ma'moun.

Ma'moun moved in the direction in which Manal led him and said nothing.

The officer passed in front of the crowd of men and chose thirty of them. They were in their early twenties, and he ordered them to step forward and go, with two soldiers, to an army lorry that was waiting for them outside. Then he noticed Ma'moun, who was moving slowly, and ordered him with a wave of his hand to join the thirty. Ma'moun, however, kept walking towards where the other men were gathered, as though paying no attention to the officer's order.

"Are you deaf, you idiot?"

"Ma'moun's blind," Manal yelled.

228

"Blind, deaf, it doesn't matter. Go with them."

Ma'moun stood in the middle of the road confused as to what he was supposed to do. Hajj Iliyya went forward, took Ma'moun by the arm, and led him to where the thirty men the Israeli captain had picked out were gathered.

Manal ran and yelled in the officer's face, "He's blind!"

"Blind?"

One of the soldiers went over to the officer and spoke with him in a low voice. The officer ordered Ma'moun to take off his glasses. Ma'moun removed them and stood, his eyes open onto the whiteness, before the officer, who stepped back and told him to go back to where he'd come from.

The column of thirty men left the enclosed area, and as the people heard the lorry's engine turn, a wail arose from the women. "They're taking them to their death," Fatima, the baker's wife, screamed, waving to her son Ahmad with the white kerchief that she'd pulled off her head, then starting to beat her breast.

When the women's wailing started, so did that of the children, as though their chests too had exploded with tears. Even the men wept. "And if it hadn't been for Hajj Iliyya being so clever, they would have shot us all," Manal said.

"Hold your tongues!" the officer yelled.

At that moment, a woman wearing tattered clothing suddenly appeared, as though from the bowels of the earth, carrying a baby. She lifted the child up high and went towards the officer, crying, "Take her! Take the girl! Take her! I want to die. Take her!"

The thin, white little girl was almost naked.

All that could be seen of her were two large eyes. The woman lifted her child up high, and the child's tiny feet, which seemed to be smeared with something resembling mud, appeared. The woman was screaming and weeping and shit was spreading over her hand; it seemed the child had soiled itself. The mother had lost all control when she saw her only son, who was fourteen, among the young men who'd been led off to the army lorry. Everyone in the crowd was convinced that the thirty young men were going to their execution. This was what the Haganah and Palmach forces did when they entered an Arab village: they chose a group of young men, took them aside and shot them, then fired rounds over the people's heads to force them to leave.

Khalid Hassouna went up to the woman (this Khalid was a dignitary of the town and what he said was listened to with respect). Everyone saw the seventy-year-old man, limping on his left foot, approach the woman to ask her to lower the child.

"Give me the little girl, daughter, and put your trust in God."

Instead of giving him the girl, the woman ran towards the officer, drawing the child back as though making ready to throw her. Signs of disgust drew themselves on the Israeli captain's face, and he yelled at his soldiers to keep the woman away from him.

At this point, ladies and gentlemen, I don't know exactly what happened. Manal told me, but I couldn't believe her, even though she swore by my father's grave that what she said was true and called on Ma'moun to be her witness, and he repeated what she had said, though in a different kind of language and more concisely.

Manal said that the woman was seized by a fit of madness. She lifted her child up high and started dancing. She danced as though listening to a drumbeat in her ears and started circling around the soldiers, who stood there, dumbfounded and immobilised.

She danced with the tears running down her cheeks, scream-ing, "Take her! I want to die!" as the people watched. Even Khalid Hassouna stood there, not knowing what to do, then burst out weeping as he approached the woman, pulled the little girl from her hands, and sat down on the ground.

People asked where the woman's husband was, and she responded promptly, "My husband was killed at the door of the mosque and left me the boy and the little girl. They've taken the boy to kill him, so what am I supposed to do? They should kill me too and get it over with."

Manal didn't know how Khalid Hassouna managed to calm the woman and stop her tears, because at that moment everyone was distracted by Hajj Iliyya yelling in the officer's face.

Hajj Iliyya was known for his calmness and poise. During the siege, he'd been head of the rations committee that had succeeded in ensuring there was enough food for fifty thousand persons – inhabitants of Lydda and refugees from the neighbouring villages – for six months. The sixty-year-old, who owned an orange grove and a field of olives, had been convinced that the siege would continue for a long while, but had also believed, like everyone else, that despite their overwhelming military superiority, the Jews would never be able to expel the Palestinians, who consti-tuted the majority of the inhabitants of their country. Then, when the city fell, and he saw the blood flowing in the streets, he refused to join the throngs of humanity who were forced to leave. He told his wife, children and grandchildren that he would never leave the city of St George and would seek refuge in the hospital, pretend to be sick, and let matters take their course. He didn't try to persuade them to stay with him as he knew that would be impos-sible in the midst of the vicious and deadly chaos that had taken over the city, but he decided that he would stay himself. He told his children he preferred to die there and wanted no more than that. "I have lived a long life and it's enough. I want to die next to al-Khudr. Al-Khudr will never allow the dragon to devour the city."

His eldest son, Iskandar, said he'd gone mad and senile and tried to take him with them by force, but the man refused, yelling in their faces and cursing at them. Then he disappeared into the crowds – to reappear on that day, there, in the ghetto, yelling in the face of the officer to restore Hamid to his mother.

"He's a child. What do you want with him? You killed his father, now leave him with his mother! Have you no shame?"

Hajj Iliyya approached the woman, took the little girl, who hadn't stopped crying, from Khalid Hassouna's hands, took her to the ablutions tank, washed her and dried her with his shirt, and hugged her to his chest. The child's crying died down in the arms of the Hajj, who shouted to her mother, Khuloud, to come and take her daughter from him and stand quietly so he could solve the problem with the Israeli captain.

Little did Hajj Iliyya Batshoun know that his tenderness towards the child would lead to a story he would never have thought possible, given that he'd passed sixty-five. The man was known for his piety and godliness and had raised a large family – five children and nine grandchildren. He was, likewise, so devoted to his wife, Madame Eveline, that his children believed it was she who decided everything, for them and for him. The woman from Jaffa who, at the age of seventeen, had married a man twenty years her senior, had been no innocent, as Iliyya had believed, while for him the marriage was a token of his decision to mend his ways after a youth spent in the bars of Beirut: on the death of his father, who had grown rich through his labours in the

Lydda orange grove and in the orange business, Iliyya renounced his frivolous ways and decided to marry as part of his decision to change his way of life and to devote himself to work.

It is said, though only God knows the truth of the matter, that he found his guidance at the hands of a Lebanese monk who had severed his relationship with the monastery of Deir Mar Saba, located east of Bethlehem overlooking Wadi al-Joz, and taken to wandering in the alleyways of Old Jerusalem, where he became known as Monk Jurji. Hajj Iliyya spoke of him to his wife Eveline only once, when the monk's body was found lying close to Herod's Gate, riddled with bullets. He told her he'd lost his spiritual guide and accused the Jews of killing him. The story of the monk's killing is opaque: the only trace of it one is likely to find is in popular narratives, which have turned him into a hero and a saint. Probably, the clique of Greeks that runs the monastery of Deir Mar Saba and the Orthodox Church of Jerusalem considered the man a heretic and expunged him from their memory.

Eveline attributed the Hajj's ties to the Holy Sepulchre's Cave of Light to the amazing hold that the monk exercised over her husband – for the Hajj would leave his house in Lydda on Good Friday morning and go to Jerusalem, where he would remain, fasting, at the doorway of the cave till dawn on the Sunday, after which he would return home, shining, and celebrate the Great Feast with his wife and children.

This man, who had surrendered himself to the God of his Lebanese monk and to his wife Eveline, making her the unchallenged authority in the house, and who was regarded as one of Lydda's best minds and most notable men, played an essential role during the battles that raged around Lydda in 1948, and would go on to become head of the Popular Committee formed by the people of the ghetto, which directed its relations with the Israeli army of occupation and managed the difficult daily life inside the barbed wire.

And this same elderly man would unexpectedly find love and drown in its tempestuous sea, and all of it in front of everyone, at the door of the Church of St George, in the Lydda ghetto.

Manal said it was the foolishness of a sixty-year-old.

Ma'moun said it was love, and love was blind.

Khalid Hassouna said it was a madness brought on by the madness of the Nakba.

Whatever people said, what happened would become one of the great stories of the ghetto, because the man proclaimed himself a Muslim and married Khuloud "according to the custom of God and His Messenger", and when the possibility of family reunion appeared on the horizon, his eldest son, who'd left along with the rest of the family to live in al-Birah in the West Bank, was astonished to find that his father ignored Madame Eveline's letters, in which she demanded to be reunited with him and brought back to Lydda. As to what happened when his wife and children learned of his marriage, and the reaction of Hamid, Khuloud's son and the brother of Huda, after he returned from captivity, those are indeed stories that deserve to be told.

Iliyya Batshoun became a Muslim without surrendering himself entirely to his new religion. He designed a new tradition to follow at Easter that was no different from what he'd learned to do from the Lebanese monk, beginning his fast after noon on Good Friday and ending it at dawn on Easter Sunday at the Church of St George, which he now referred to as the Shrine of al-Khudr. His funeral, following his death in 1953, was unique and unlike any that Palestine had seen before.

Iliyya Batshoun left the little girl in her mother's arms and hurried over to the Israeli captain, begging and demanding that Hamid be let go. He said it was shameful, that the child was only fourteen, that it wasn't allowed, but the captain's features never changed; his face was as though carved in stone. Iliyya turned around and called on Khalid Hassouna to join him in negotiating with the Israeli captain.

Manal said the negotiations were tough. "Of course, we couldn't hear anything, but it was clear that the Hajj, who was the town's model of dignity, was humiliated before the officer. His head was lowered and he raised both his hands as though imploring him. I don't know what they said. We were standing, and the hunger was eating us alive. They went on for more than half an hour, and then the captain raised the loudspeaker and informed us of his decisions."

"Listen well!

"First, we have asked Mr Iliyya Batshoun and Mr Khalid Hassouna to form a committee to represent the people of the city before the military governor.

"Second, no-one is allowed to go through the gate without the permission of the military governor.

"Third, the inhabitants may use the houses located inside the wire, under the supervision of the local committee.

"Fourth, the Israeli army is not responsible for providing the inhabitants with food and drink. This is the responsibility of the inhabitants and we will accept no further discussion of the matter.

"Fifth, the committee is required to take a census of the inhabitants and present a complete list of their names, ages and trades tomorrow at ten a.m.

"Sixth, everyone is required to assemble in this place at ten a.m. tomorrow and await further instructions."

Having delivered his speech, the officer withdrew with his men to beyond the wire, and the soldiers relaxed, shouldered their rifles, and sat on the ground, eating their food with the appetite of those who haven't eaten for hours. The people, exhausted by hunger, slowly left.

(3)

"Where are we to go?" asked Khuloud, who was carrying her daughter Huda in her arms.

"Put your faith in God, sister," Hajj Iliyya said. "Go back to where you slept last night, and then we'll sort things out, God willing."

It was six in the evening. After a long and gruelling day of waiting, the people started to leave the square in front of the Great Mosque. They looked more like shadows, enveloped in silence. "I swear, Naji," Ma'moun told me, "that day, for the first time in my life, I heard the sound of silence." Describing to me how the people had begun to set off for nowhere, Ma'moun said, "The Israeli captain was clear: 'You can live in any house you want, so long as it's inside the wire.'"

"And what about us?" I asked him.

Ma'moun said he was the one who'd found the house and told Manal, "You two live in the house, and I'll stay in the room in the garden. That way, I'll be with you."

(The blind man, who had discovered the sound of silence and its various rhythms, would transform the subject of this discovery into the basis for the lecture on the poetry of Mahmoud Darwish that he gave here, at New York University, where he read the rhythms of meaning into the interstices of silence, announcing that the hallmark of the literature of the Palestinian Nakba was that it had "fashioned from the silence of the victim interstices that reconstructed the poetic image". Even though, like most of the audience who listened to the lecture at the library of the Kevorkian Center, located at the intersection of Sullivan Street and Washington Square, I couldn't get my mind around what he meant, Ma'moun's words had an impact on my heart, not simply because his analysis was astonishing, but because it took me back to the square in front of the mosque, where the silence of the victims rose up, drowning out the voices of the Israeli soldiers.

The eloquence of the silence of the victims in the square in front of the Great Mosque made me think of the eloquence of the dance in the village square at Fasouta, in Galilee. I saw the dust of silence spreading, covering everyone – dust like that which rose from beneath the feet of the people of Fasouta as they surrendered to the Israeli army with their northern *dabke*, the dust hiding both them and the soldiers, veiling them so that conqueror and conquered were equally absent and concealed – a terrifying moment, described by Anton Shammas in his wonderful novel *Arabesques*.)

The silence was broken suddenly when Iliyya Batshoun was heard asking the people to wait, so that the committee that was to take charge of the quarter's affairs could be formed and distribute the people among the houses located within the ghetto's ring of fencing. No-one paid him any attention, however. The people wanted to get into the houses, not to take up residence in them but to look for food.

Khalid Hassouna went over to Hajj Iliyya and they spoke in low voices. Then Khalid's voice was heard again, announcing the names of the committee members.

"Listen, everyone! The committee is composed of Iliyya Batshoun, chairman; Khalid Hassouna, deputy chairman; Ibrahim Hamza, Mustafa al-Kayyali and Ghassan Batheish."

"Any objections?" asked Hajj Iliyya.

Mufid Shahada raised his hand. "I object," the young man said. "There has to be someone on the committee who knows Hebrew so he can communicate with them."

"You know Hebrew?" asked Hajj Iliyya.

"*Ken*," answered Mufid. "I used to go up to deliver the vegetables to the Jewish *kubbaniyya* at Ben Shemen and I got to know a few words there. I mean, I can communicate with them, and there's Dr Lehman too. He's my friend and my dad's, and he gave my dad a letter saying so."

"Where's your dad, boy?"

"My dad went off with the rest. First of all, he refused to leave the house. The soldiers came and said, 'Get out and go to Abdallah!' There were two of them and they were wearing *keffiyehs*. My dad gave them the letter. The first soldier took it and read it but instead of coming to an understanding with us, he scowled and said, 'Go on, get out of here!' and spat and cursed at Dr Lehman. The second soldier took the letter and was about to tear it up, but I said, 'Please give it to me, God preserve you!' and took it and started running, and I heard them laughing. I didn't look back. I ran and found I'd ended up here, at the church, and got separated from my family, but I still have the letter."

"So where are your dad and your family now?"

"I don't know."

"Where's the letter?"

"I have the letter with me. I took it from the soldier and ran."

Mufid pulled the letter carefully from his pocket and flourished it.

"This letter's no use to us!" said Iliyya Batshoun, but Khalid Hassouna had a different view. He said it might reassure the

Israelis. "The important thing, my boy, is that you take care of the letter. It might come in handy."

"Give me the letter, my boy," said Iliyya Batshoun.

"I'm not giving it to anybody. Dr Lehman said to give it to Mula and he'd take care of us."

"Who's Mula?"

"I don't know."

Despite all his efforts, Mufid Shahada wasn't included in the committee. Ma'moun said the committee ought to include a woman and proposed Manal, as the widow of the martyr Hasan Dannoun, but Hajj Iliyya refused, saying a woman's place was at home. "You want us to behave like the Jews? No, my boy. Women are honour, and honour must be guarded."

"The important thing is, the committee has been formed, and we've got people who can represent us and defend our interests before the Jews," said Ghassan Batheish, who worked as a nurse at the hospital and whose membership of the committee had been accepted at the suggestion of Dr Mustafa Zahlan. Dr Zahlan had rejected the participation of any of the doctors in the committee because its work might take a political turn, which would compromise the sanctity of the medical profession and of the Hippocratic oath – which made it a sacred profession, above politics; as a result, roles were reversed in the little quarter, with decision-making power in the hands of a nurse, Ghassan Batheish, who would become a legend in the ghetto because he took Ibrahim al-Nimr with him to the committee's meeting with Moshe and thus turned Hatim al-Laqqis's idea into reality when al-Nimr was able to persuade the Israeli officer in charge to allow a group of the young men to fetch water in barrels from a nearby citrus grove.

The committee held its first meeting then and there in the

middle of the square and discussed the need for a plan to distribute the people among the empty houses, with the aim of lightening the pressure on, above all, the hospital, and, in second place, the mosque and the church. Iliyya Batshoun yelled at the people to wait for the committee's decisions, but no-one took any notice. The hunger, thirst and sun that had worked their way into people's bodies after that long day of waiting made them incapable of understanding what was going on, and all they wanted was to leave and search for a crust of bread and a drop of water.

At that moment, the ghetto's first tragedy occurred, and the shock of that seventeen-year-old boy would remain engraved on people's sensibility. Ma'moun couldn't keep himself from weeping as he told me, here in New York, his memories of his emotions and those of my mother, fifty years after the boy was killed in that pitiful way. His memory swept him back to that first day, when Mufid Shahada died, suspended from the barbed wire like a sparrow with a broken neck and scattered feathers, and then fell, his arms outstretched.

"The people called him the sparrow," said Ma'moun, "and his death was the start of the relationship between the people of the ghetto and death.

"The death couldn't be calculated: wherever you looked, you saw nothing else. I'm not talking here about the bodies we had to pick up from the streets and the houses and then bury or, in the end, burn. No, I'm talking about the phantom of the fear of death and disease that haunted the ghetto and turned our lives into no more than a little comma in the registry of the dead. What can I tell you? The city had died. Has anyone before seen the corpse of a city? I swear, the death of the people was nothing. The disintegrating bodies can't be compared to the disintegration of

241

the corpses of the houses and the crumbling of the streets and pavements. Do you remember Salah al-Din Street? I saw how the street had died when they let us out of the ghetto in groups to gather up the bodies. I swear to God, none of us dared put his whole weight on his foot because he'd feel that the asphalt was giving way beneath him. The asphalt had become a corpse, and we had to walk over it slowly so as not to disturb it in its death while we looked for our own dead."

Ma'moun, recalling Mufid Shahada, said that when the memory of death seizes a person in its grip it paralyses all his faculties. "We had to learn, my son, to live at the mercy of memory, which, when it wakes, is like a raging wind that breaks our souls into little pieces and rips our bodies apart."

"And how about you?" he asked me. "How's your relationship with memory?"

I told him, "I don't like memories and I hate nostalgia for the past, because I have no past about which to feel nostalgic. Even the tatters of that past were shredded in front of me when you told me the story of how you picked up the child that was I from beneath the olive tree, so how can you expect me to remember? When you don't remember whose son you are, memory becomes a trick. I don't want to fall into the trap of memory! Leave me alone, my friend, to live my life. Why did you follow me all this way? What do you want from me?"

Ma'moun didn't answer. I saw the ghost of an embarrassed smile pass over his lips, and he said that our memories are a storm we have to weather or we will be turned into corpses. "Only death, my boy, has no memory."

I was not prepared to argue with the elderly blind man who sat before me in the lobby of the Washington Square Hotel, not out of pity for him, for my heart had been freed from all pity after he'd decreed that my memory should be null and void and confessed to conniving with Manal in fabricating me and turning me into a lie. It wasn't out of pity, it was out of despair. Despair, ladies and gentlemen, is indeed the moment when our human nature reaches its highest point, approaching divinity. The gods must certainly experience despair, and they have nothing to face it with; even suicide is impossible for them, since he who never sleeps never dies and the gods neither sleep nor die and are denied the ability to kill themselves.

To get back to the story. I don't know what happens to me when I try to write. It's as though I'm not the one doing the writing, or the words are just passing through me on their way to wherever they're going. It's what we call "musing", which is another name for what Western critics call "stream of conscious-ness". I am not, however, writing a stream of consciousness. The fact is, I don't care for forms. I let the words run through my fingers and limn the darkness of their black letters on the white page, and I watch my soul as it breaks up under the raging of a memory that I had decided to abandon – and that now suddenly devours me, for no better reason than my decision to tell the truth in the face of those shared lies that took over the auditorium at Cinema Village when the Israeli director and the Lebanese writer colluded to disfigure the image of the woman who had become the victim of the movie she'd wanted to make.

My love for the woman was extinguished, for some reason I don't know or am afraid to acknowledge, but my admiration for her has no bounds. Perhaps my love died because I was afraid of that admiration and of my discovery that the woman had become a victim of her own movie. Dalia was a true artist, and an artist doesn't manufacture works or write texts. The artist is merely a powerless vector. This is why the writer ends up not writing but being written. Was that not Gogol's fate? Didn't Emile Habibi end up believing what he'd written more than his own life? Didn't Ghassan Kanafani's stories get mixed up with his mortal remains?

Dalia was of that same stripe of humanity, which is why she was incapable of making me feel she was mine, even though I'm sure now that she loved me. But I was afraid, and fear paralyses love, and when Dalia left me I was afraid of the ending of love, so I ran away. My heart ran away from me, a wall arose in my breast, and I felt in some obscure way that I had to flee before the death of her love for me could catch me unawares. It may have been this that extinguished the desire in my heart and made me discover that love had drained away and vanished under the cold water of the shower, driving me to flee from myself and my memory and recompose myself as a seller of falafel trying to write a novel about a little-known poet who was enveloped by silence, in life as in death. And the writing led me where it wanted, and I found myself emerging from the coffer of Waddah al-Yaman to climb into the coffer of my own story, and was obliged to go back to the beginning.

The beginning led me to recall everything I'd forgotten, and the beginning was the ghetto, where I was born, or so I had been told. And at the start of the ghetto, the boy died, hanging on the wire, where his body continued to tremble in the people's memory.

The story says that, while the members of the committee were busy organising the allocation of the deserted houses, Mufid Shahada ran towards the wires waving a piece of paper with Hebrew written on it shouting, "Mister! Mister!"

The boy ran up to the barbed wire and began trying to climb it.

"*Tahzor le-ahor! Asur!*" yelled a soldier, proclaiming that it was forbidden to approach the fence.

Climbing the wire was impossible. It had been laid down in a hurry to make a boundary around the area and was rebuilt and reinforced three days later, at which point the closed-off site would resemble nothing so much as a roofless cage, and Iliyya Batshoun would make his celebrated remark, "This isn't a ghetto, it's a cage, and we're like chickens. They treat us like chickens in a cage but, damn them, what misers they are! People feed chickens, but they've left us with nothing."

Mufid Shahada ran, waving the paper in his hand.

"*Rotseeh ledber* with Mr Mula!" he shouted in Hebrew. "I want to speak to him!"

A soldier came forward, brandishing his rifle. "Go away! Away!" he yelled.

"Mr Mula," said Mufid. "*Yesh li mikhtav* for Mr Mula."

The soldier hesitated a little when he heard the boy was holding a letter for Mr Mula.

"*Ken*, Mula's my friend and I have a letter for him.'

The sight of the boy was pitiful indeed. He stood alone, a carefully folded piece of paper in his hand, which he waved at the soldiers, asking them to take the letter to his friend Mr Mula.

The soldier, who had come up to the fence, reached out to take it.

"*Lo, lo!*" yelled Mufid. "Not for you. *Rotseh ani Mula.* Tell Mr Mula that Mufid *ha'ben shel* Ghassan Shahada – Mufid, Ghassan Shahada's boy, who used to bring the vegetables to Ben Shemen with his father – Mufid's here and he asks you, please, Mr Mula, I want to go to our house and I want my dad and my mum and my brothers and my sisters. Send me back to them. Is this any way to behave, mister? My granddad told my dad, 'Don't believe the Jews, they have no honour,' but my dad said, 'No, Mr Siegfried wouldn't lie and he said, "You're under our protection."' Siegfried Lehman was my friend and my dad's and he asked my dad to put me in school with the Jewish children at Ben Shemen. Mr Siegfried said Mula was his student and wouldn't do anything against his teacher's instructions. He gave my dad the letter and said, 'Don't show it to anyone except Mr Mula!' My dad gave it to the soldiers who came to us at home and then they threw us out. I want Mula."

Another soldier came up, reached his hand through the wire and snatched the piece of paper from Mufid Shahada. The soldier retreated and began reading the letter, while Mufid waited, his body against the wire, a slight smile on his face.

"Jewish agent!" somebody shouted.

"Agent and son of an agent! They've been collaborating with the Jews since for ever. We should have shot his father," said another.

The boy, though, seemed not to hear the threatening language being used or the muttering that could be heard, and didn't turn to look at the people standing there, unmoving, waiting.

At that moment, Dr Samara, who was still sitting where he had been, under the sun, spoke up. The doctor hadn't moved from his place all day long. Even when the people were allowed to go to the ablutions tank to wet their parched tongues with water, the doctor stayed where he was and refused to respond to his wife's plea to go with her and his daughter to drink.

I don't know how thirst came to be engraved in the man's memory, because he doesn't allude to the subject in his article.

"Thirst breaks voices, and speech comes to resemble a death rattle." That's what Ma'moun said when he told me, fifty years later, the story of the caravan of death that set off into the wilderness that awaited it, taking with it most of the city's inhabitants.

"Calm down, everyone!" said the doctor in a hoarse voice almost no-one had heard before. "Let's see what happens. Maybe Mula will let us go."

But Mula didn't come. Shmuel Cohen, known as Mula, was the commander of the Palmach's Third Battalion, which had occupied the city. The man, who had studied at Ben Shemen, was known for his love of classical music and was familiar with every house in Lydda and its villages as a result of his visits with his humanitarian mentor, Siegfried Lehman, builder of a settlement to foster coexistence between Jews and Palestinians – this same Shmuel Cohen was the military commander who implemented the mass expulsion of the inhabitants of the city of al-Khudr and committed there the worst massacre of the 1948 War of the Nakba.

Mula wasn't there, or refused to go near the wire, or who knows. What is certain is that he knew Mufid Shahada and his father and he knew that Ghassan Shahada, the vegetable-seller, who considered himself a friend of the founder of the settlement for the children of the survivors of the pogroms of eastern Europe, had always said, "There's no call to be enemies." The people of Ben Shemen were different. When the great earthquake struck on 11 July, 1927, they rushed with their teacher to help the people of Lydda. "There's no call to be enemies, everyone."

Mula never appeared, and Mufid Shahada remained, unmoving, at the wire, waiting. Then the boy fell. It looked as though he'd fallen from above, his arms outstretched, as though attached to a non-existent cross. His head hit the ground and he stopped moving.

It is said that the Israeli soldier tore the letter up, ground it into the earth with his boot, and said something in Hebrew that Mufid didn't understand. The boy's knowledge of Hebrew didn't go beyond a few words that he'd picked out of people's mouths as he passed through the Ben Shemen colony with his father. When the soldier spoke, saying, "That time is past. Today between you and us there is only the sword!" the boy didn't understand, though he did understand the language of the soldier's boot when it trod on the torn scraps of the letter.

It is said that when the boy heard the soldier's words, he cried out in a mighty voice, "Where art thou, Khudr, our master? Come! Behold what has become of us!"

It is said that when the soldier heard Mufid's words, he rained blows on the boy's head with the butt of his rifle, and the boy didn't protect himself with his hands; on the contrary, his arms remained outstretched before the wire and the blood on his head took on the shape of a crown of thorns. Then, suddenly, he fell.

It is said the soldier didn't hit the boy with the butt of his rifle but pushed him to get him away from the wire and that Mufid, instead of stepping back, lost his balance and fell.

It is said the soldier neither pushed the boy nor hit him but that he fell because he suffered sunstroke after standing for ten uninterrupted hours under the blazing July sun. That is what Shmarya Guttman, the city's military governor, said during a meeting with the members of the committee. Hajj Iliyya Batshoun had requested the meeting to present an official protest in the name of the people of Lydda demanding that the Israeli soldier who'd beaten the boy with his rifle butt be held to account.

Guttman said, "Listen, Hajj. I want to cooperate with you and fulfil all requests that I find justified, but we can't start like this. Forget putting the soldier on trial. He's a hero of the Palmach.

The soldier didn't kill Mufid – Mufid fell and died. Plus, there are hundreds of dead bodies strewn around the streets of Lydda. I don't want to hear any more demands of this kind. And tomorrow I'll inform you how the work will begin."

Wherein lies the truth of the death of Mufid, who would remain in the ghetto's memory as its first martyr?

Things are said and people say things.

Nothing is sure except that Mufid Shahada died with open hands and closed eyes beneath the setting sun, his head in a pool of blood.

I lay all the possible causes of the boy's death out in front of me, and I wonder about the truth, only to discover that my wondering has no meaning.

Ma'moun was right, and Manal too was right.

Ma'moun said the matter was of no importance. He said he'd seen the boy fall down and die but couldn't remember the cause of that death. "Death is more important than what causes it," the blind man said.

Manal said, "Don't waste your time! It's all death. Death's like death. What difference does it make if the soldier hit him or kicked him or he fell and the sun killed him? It's all death."

Ma'moun said, "You're right: the causes multiply but death is one."

Manal said, "What a waste! He died because he believed the letter. Good God, he'd seen what happened to his father! The man gave him Lehman's letter and they jeered at him and forced him to get out, along with everyone else. Why Mufid was so stupid, I swear I don't know."

Ma'moun said the boy must have known some secret. Maybe they killed him to kill the secret along with him.

Things are said and people say things.

I'm sitting in my little home in New York. From my window I watch the silence of the snow covering the sounds of the city and wonder what it is I'm doing now. Am I looking for the truth, or filling the emptiness of my life with questions to which I have no answers?

(If I were to tell Dr Hanna Jiryis this story, he'd forbid me to write it. I imagine him standing with his stooped shoulders, smiling that smile of his that combines mockery and pity and saying I can't refer to a letter supposedly written by Dr Lehman if I don't have a copy of it.

And when I tell him that everyone who stayed in Lydda knows the story, he'll respond that it doesn't matter; what matters is that if we are to write history, we need written documents.

"But I'm not writing history!" I answer him.

"What are you writing then?" he asks.

"I don't know. Something like literature.'

"Nonsense!" he says. "Give up all this nonsense, so that the weeping can stop for a little and we can see what happened and why!"

Thank God, Dr Hanna isn't here and I can go on with the story as it is, and not bother with a document that exists only in the memory!)

The people of the ghetto made up their minds that all three versions were correct, that the differences among them were merely an optical illusion, and that the optical illusion had nothing to do with eyes and their malfunctions: people have a third eye whose name is the eye of memory, which is invisible and defines what we see, after which we organise its elements, deleting and restoring so as to make a succession of tableaux.

In the case of Lydda, the tableau of the boy's death, as preserved by the eye of memory, is, of necessity, silent. In all likelihood, no-one heard a word of the conversation that took place between Mufid Shahada and the Israeli soldier at the wire. People saw a scene dappled by shadows, a silent scene transformed by the rays of the retreating sun into something opaque and drained of colour. The background to the scene is formed of the people's mutterings, which rise and fall like a musical accompaniment to the sun, whose shadows are withdrawing from the square and departing. People's eyes saw shapes and couldn't distinguish individual objects, for the eyes of the people of the ghetto were thirsty and thirsty eyes don't see clearly.

Recounting the story of the caravan of death, Ma'moun said, "Thirst only reaches its peak when it strikes the eyes. The moment the water of the eyes dries up, one becomes fragile, like a dry stick."

How could he, a blind man, feel the thirst of the eyes? Do eyes that have been obliterated also feel thirst? Why did he tell me that thirsty eyes cease to be able to see, beholding things as though covered in a thick milky fog, and thus lose their ability to distinguish?

Probably, the people of the ghetto, despite having been allowed to drink from the ablutions tank of the mosque, were afflicted with thirst of the eyes, from whose symptoms they would continue to suffer for a long time, facts becoming mixed up in their memory with optical illusions. This would explain why each of them retained his own version of Mufid's death – so much so that when I visited Lydda at the age of thirty (because of the nurse Najwa Ibrahim who had asked me to help her sell her house there and whom I discovered later was the mother of Khalil Ayoub), I heard a different story. Mrs Karima Salihi claimed that the boy had climbed up the barbed wire and that he died because the Israeli soldier had fired a single shot at his head:

"He had his arms open and was speaking Hebrew. Then I saw him lying on the ground. Poor boy! I don't know what he was thinking of, climbing up. All I know is that when I saw him he was like a little bird hanging from the wire. His body was shuddering as the soul left it, and he didn't fall to the ground, he stayed hanging there. Hajj Iliyya went to the mosque and fetched a chair and a blind young man, whose name I don't remember, stood on it, took the poor boy down, and laid him on the ground. Then they buried him."

I listened to her in disbelief, as no-one who'd witnessed the incident had said they'd heard the sound of a shot. I was certain the story she was telling was a figment of her imagination, or of the alterations that affect orally transmitted stories. But I said nothing. I concluded the deal for the sale of Umm Khalil's house and left.

These varying versions of the death of Mufid do not deny the truth that the boy died on the wire, and that the Israeli army, which had corralled the remaining inhabitants of Lydda into the ghetto, was as responsible for the killing of the sparrow-boy as it was for the massacre that killed hundreds of the city's inhabitants.

I don't believe that the multiplicity of versions is attributable solely to the fact that they were never written down. Basically, it should be attributed instead to the victims' attempts to adapt themselves to the new reality by viewing the succession of tragic events through the third eye, which sees only what a person can bear to see. This is the basic cause of the confusions in stories about the Nakba. The solution doesn't lie in writing them down, because you can't organise the stories of the past in writing and extract a harmonious narrative from them when the Nakba is an ongoing process that hasn't ceased for the last fifty years and has yet to be transformed into a past that has truly passed.

What story will my biological father, whom I don't know, tell if we suppose that he was living in Jenin camp and lost two sons when the Israeli army invaded the camp in 2002 during the Second Intifada? Will he tell the story of a child who was abandoned, discarded in the open country while still a baby? Or will he tell the story of two sons felled by Israeli bullets fifty years later? Will he say that he forgot me and forgot my mother? Or that he tried to save himself and abandoned us both? Or that he's still looking for me? Or never even mention my story, because it has become a source of shame to him when compared with the story of the two heroic sons martyred while fighting the army of occupation? My father will forget my story in order to justify his life, for nothing can justify abandoning little children and leaving them lying on the corpses of their mothers under the olive trees. And all I have to do, if I want to get on with my life, is to forget.

The boy from Lydda believed the Israeli pedagogue, thinking that the sharing of bread and salt was stronger than war and more important than a land said to be promised. He had, therefore, to die, and his death had to leave that wretched handful of the people of Lydda in fear, despair and uncertainty.

(4)

Night upon night and darkness out of darkness: that is how I am obliged to describe the night of the city in that July heat that filled space with shadow. Though I don't remember. No matter how hard I try to bore into its depths, my memory refuses ever to take me to the night of the baby I was in July 1948.

My memory is words spoken by my mother, and my mother's words had no order. The woman never sat me down next to her to tell me the story all in one go. She told me fragments and little pieces, as though weaving the tale as they came along. The words had no fixed occasions but erupted from the night of memory. She wasn't telling the story to me—I was there because I was there. She didn't think of me as a listener; probably, she thought I didn't understand what was being said. She'd give me paper and pencil to draw with and talk at length with Ma'moun. I see them absorbed in rehearsing the memory of death, "rehearsing" being the word that best describes this constant activity of theirs.

After they'd eaten dinner, they'd sit in the shadow of a pale candle and weave memory. Their present was their memory, as though they weren't actually living but were fashioning the remembrance of a life that had been denied to them. This is how I would define the Palestinian experience, or, let's say, this is how I lived it. My life was a kind of present that I treated as memories, as though things only take on meaning in the context of that permanent feeling that the present is escaping and cannot be grasped, that it is just experiences that serve to take us down into memory's depths.

It is "memory for forgetfulness", as Mahmoud Darwish wrote in his semi-fictional personal narrative of the siege of Beirut in 1982. What the poet who wrote "Why did you leave the horse alone?" failed to note, however, was that his Beirut present was a possibility only because it was constructed within the framework of a political and social entity that was in the process of being founded and, as such, was eligible for transformation into memory. In those days of the ghetto, though, we lived in a maelstrom of present memory and a present that resembled memory, and through catastrophe after catastrophe. My story with this story that I'm trying to write is full of the ghosts of darkness, of speech exchanged between a man and a woman before a child whose presence they see as an absence. They wove the story without meaning to. They were rehearsing living in a world that offered them nothing: lovers without love, companions with no road to walk; their relationship was just a past without a present, so they fashioned out of memory a bed for a love that never was, or seemed as though it never was.

I gather together the threads of what they said and it feels as though I'm listening to rustles and whispers, and I discover that all stories are like this or, to put it more precisely, that this is how stories are born – in fits and starts, whispered, near-silent – and that when the writer starts to mould them to fit a pattern, he kills their soul and turns them into memory for forgetfulness.

What was said on those dark nights, nights so dark that they can be compared only to themselves, as when the Arabs write of "the most nocturnal of nights"?

The story says that the night when the boy Mufid Shahada was killed was starless. When the people of the ghetto tell the story of those days, they speak of the stars disappearing in the month of July. They say, with their direct way of speaking, that "the stars fled the city's skies because they couldn't bear to witness the death that turned into shrouds borne by the youths of Lydda to the collective graves".

"Stars are the eyes of the sky," said Khuloud as she recounted how her madness on the morning of the second day had been not madness but a fear of the intense darkness that enveloped the city's sky. "When the stars disappear, the sky disappears. Are we to live in a land without a sky?" Well, no, Khuloud didn't say those exact words, but she said something like them. "I went mad with fear and stood by the window and saw Mufid Shahada's body lying there and it was uncovered. I swear by God Almighty, they wouldn't allow us to cover it. I thought, now they'll come and take it and bury it. Nobody came. I stood there as though nailed to the ground. I don't know what came over me. And everything was dark. I looked at the stars. My grandfather, God rest his soul, used to say the stars are the eyes of the sky, and I saw that the sky had gone blind. A sky without eyes, and the young lad dead and lying on the ground, and nothing to cover him but the dark."

Manal related that what she'd seen couldn't be believed, "like stories of *jinn* and *afreets*". She said that at the instant the boy fell, the light withdrew and darkness descended on the place.

"All of a sudden, when he fell, the sun went out." She said darkness wasn't supposed to fall like that: the dark should blend with the light before devouring it. The instant Mufid died, though, the light withdrew and the dark descended, as though the darkness was his shroud, when he could find none to enshroud him.

Iliyya Batshoun, as head of the ghetto committee, went out

into the square in front of the mosque and walked towards the wire, asking everyone to help him carry the body so that it could be buried. No-one, though, dared to leave his shelter, as the people had heard the sound of the Israeli rifles being cocked and the voice of the soldier ordering Iliyya to leave the square and go back where he came from.

"We have to bury him," said Iliyya in a hoarse voice.

"Tomorrow," said the soldier.

"That won't do! Please, let me drag him to the house."

The only person to go up to Iliyya was Khuloud, who was carrying her little girl in her arms.

"Go back to the house!" Iliyya yelled at her.

But Khuloud refused to go back. She sat on the ground and began moaning, while Iliyya stood there not knowing what to do.

"Both of you, go back to the house!" the soldier yelled.

Khalid Hassouna approached. He took Khuloud by the hand and told her to stand up. The woman stood and walked ahead of two men, stumbling through the darkness, to spend the night sitting at the window, keeping watch over Mufid Shahada's corpse.

"Did it ever occur to you that one morning the sun might not rise?" Ma'moun asked me.

"I don't understand," I said.

He repeated the question as a reply, saying that that night was the first time he feared the dark. "Can you believe that a blind man would be afraid of a blackness whose meaning he doesn't know?"

He said Manal had sown the fear in his heart when she informed him of the blind sky and said she was afraid the sun wouldn't rise.

I smiled when I heard Ma'moun's figure of speech. I don't know how he saw my smile, but he said he knew I was making fun of him and of the expression he'd used. "But Manal, my boy, was

257

right. Till now the sun hasn't risen. A whole people is still, to this day, living in darkness."

Manal spoke of the mournful funeral that took place the following morning, saying that she'd learned the meaning of sorrow when she saw the young men wrap Mufid's body in a white blanket and carry him into the mosque.

In the Great Mosque, the corpse was laid out on the ground and nobody knew what to do.

"Where's the sheikh?" Iliyya Batshoun yelled. "This won't do!"

"Where do you want me to find you a sheikh?" Khalid Hassouna said. "The sheikh ran away with all the rest."

Hatim al-Laqqis came forward holding a Koran and recited a passage from the chapter "The Merciful".

Hatim faltered as he recited, so Ma'moun took over from him:

The All-Merciful has taught the Koran. He created man and He has taught him the Explanation. The sun and the moon are to a reckoning, and the stars and the trees bow themselves; and heaven – He raised it up, and set the Balance. (Transgress not in the Balance, and weigh with justice, and skimp not in the Balance.) And earth – He set it down for all beings, therein fruits, and palm-trees with sheaths, and grain in the blade, and fragrant herbs. O which of your Lord's bounties will you and you deny? He created man of a clay like the potter's, and He created the jinn of a smokeless fire. O which of your Lord's bounties will you and you deny? Lord of the Two Easts, Lord of the Two Wests, O which of your Lord's bounties will you and you deny?

Suddenly, Iliyya Batshoun's voice rose in prayer. The sixty-year-old stood behind the body, held his hands out, and began to recite his prayer in Greek, and before he reached the final amen, the people beheld a strange sight: Sheikh Usama al-Humsi

258

appeared from no-one knew where. He approached, pulled Ma'moun from his place, and asked if the body had been washed.

"The martyr needs no washing other than that of his own blood," Khalid Hassouna said. "So let God then accept him as a martyr."

The sheikh looked at Khalid Hassouna with disconcerted eyes and said nothing. The seventy-year-old sheikh of Lydda, who had disappeared and whom everyone thought must have been forced to join the caravan of death, looked different now that he had shaved off his long white beard, cast off his *tarbush* and turban, and stood there in front of the throng, in blue trousers and a white shirt.

"*We are God's and to Him we return,*" he said, and the throng behind him repeated the words.

Ma'moun cried out in a mighty voice, "*Count not those who were slain in God's way as dead, but rather living with their Lord, by Him provided!*"

The sheikh took a step back, looked at the crowd that had gathered in the mosque's courtyard, and said, "Say after me, 'God is great!'" After this had been done four times, he said, "Now we can bury him."

A group of the young men picked up the blanket that had become a shroud and walked with it around the square in front of the mosque. They saw Khuloud scatter rice over it and heard her let out a trill of celebration.

"Where shall we bury him?" Ghassan Batheish asked.

"In the Muslim cemetery," Iliyya said.

A small procession set itself in motion and approached the barbed wire. It is said that those carrying the body were forced to set it on the ground while long and complicated negotiations took place between the committee and the Israeli officer, who said he didn't have the authority to give them permission to leave the ghetto. He proposed they dig a grave in the courtyard of the mosque, and said he was prepared to give them the necessary implements.

"That won't do!" Iliyya Batshoun yelled. "The lad has to be buried in the cemetery!"

The officer said he couldn't go against military orders and the head of the committee said he couldn't renounce the rights of the dead.

He tried to explain to the officer that he was aware that he belonged to a defeated people and that "the price of defeat is the renunciation of all our rights – even our houses aren't ours any longer – but we cannot renounce the right of the dead to be buried with dignity".

The officer responded, "You renounced nothing. We took everything with our own hands. Please, let's not have any more of such talk. I carry out the orders that come to me from above and you have to obey my orders."

(This conversation took place in halting English, and Iliyya Batshoun translated it to everyone the next day, when he informed them of the gist of the Israeli decrees and organised the work teams demanded by Mula, the commander of the Israeli forces.)

The people stood for a long time under the burning sun, and the waiting seemed endless, but Iliyya Batshoun had made up his mind that there was no room for retreat. "They'll kill us all the way they killed Mufid, and if we can't defend our lives, let's at least defend our death."

The fact is that the Israeli officer was embarrassed and did not know what he was supposed to do, as a single bullet from his rifle would have persuaded the committee members to obey his orders – so said Mula, "the Liberator of Lod", as they called him in Israel. After long hours spent waiting by the people guarding the body, during which it began to decompose, the commander appeared and summoned Iliyya Batshoun to his office, which he'd set up in the Dahmash family house, close to the ghetto square.

"When I found out that it was Mula, the officer who'd had Mufid killed for wanting to give him the letter, I told him everything. I told him about the letter that one of the soldiers had torn up and trodden on, in which Dr Lehman had asked for special treatment for the Shahada family and all the people of Lydda, and said that we were requesting him to let us give the victim a fitting burial."

Iliyya said that the officer was deeply affected when he learned that his soldiers had been the cause of Mufid's death and said, "It's war. You know we have no option but victory."

Iliyya begged him to allow them to bury the boy in the cemetery but the commander said it was a difficult matter because the roads of the city weren't safe and were full of corpses!

In the end, however, he agreed. He allowed five men to carry the body to the cemetery, where they would be accompanied by three soldiers, and they had to get it over with quickly. He said he agreed for humanitarian reasons and to honour the wishes of Dr Lehman, who had raised him according to the highest moral values.

And that is what happened.

The funeral procession was led by Ghassan Batheish. They lifted the boy up, took him on a circuit of the square and then left, accompanied by the soldiers, in the midst of a silence broken only by Khuloud and her sobbing.

I heard about what Khuloud did from a number of people, and

all confirmed that she picked up her child and joined the procession dancing, and when the soldiers prevented her from crossing the wire with the small procession, she raised her daughter up high, wagged her to and fro to make her look as though she was dancing, and asked the soldiers to take her. This time too, Iliyya Batshoun rebuked her, and he dragged her back to the house in which he'd decided he would live.

Did Israeli novelist S. Yizhar write Khuloud's story into his novel *Khirbet Khizeh*? Israeli sources indicate that the Israeli novel, which was published in 1949 and became the sole Israeli literary record of the expulsion of the Palestinians from their country in 1948, recounts a real incident that happened in southern Palestine, in which the writer took part in his capacity as intelligence officer of the battalion carrying out the operation. At dawn on 27 November, 1948, a number of units of the 151st and 152nd battalions launched attacks on the Palestinian villages located between al-Majdal and Beit Hanoun, destroying and ethnically cleansing the villages of Hamama, al-Jora, Khirbet al-Khisas, Naaliya, al-Jiya, Barbara, Harabya and Deir Sineid.

The village described by the Israeli novelist is probably Khirbet al-Khisas. This is confirmed by the officer in charge of operations at the Coastal Sector headquarters, Captain Yehuda Be'eiri, who signed the expulsion order. In an interview published in Ma'ariv on 17 February, 1978, he says, "I have no doubt that 'Khirbet Khizeh' is Khirbet al-Khisas itself, or one of the other villages covered by this operation, for which I signed the same order . . . and by the way, there's no point in looking for the remains of these villages because, like dozens of other Arab villages in this area and all over the country, they no longer exist and I doubt if any mention of them survives."

Yizhar didn't write Khuloud's story, but it seems that what he witnessed in Khirbet Khizeh was typical of something that happened in more than one place. I shall reproduce Yizhar's text here as it appears in the Arabic translation of his novel, which I read in the *Journal of Palestinian Affairs*, since, no matter how hard I try, I shall never attain the eloquence of an eyewitness who participated in the crime, and who drew an astonishing conclusion, namely, that the Palestinians had become the Jews of the Jews:

Then a woman came toward us clutching a skinny baby, lugging it like an unwanted object. A gray-hued, gaunt, sickly, undersized infant. Her mother held her in her rags and waved and danced her in front of us as she said to us with something that was neither mockery nor disgust, and not crazed weeping, but, perhaps, all three together: "Do you want her? Take her, take her and keep her!" We screwed up our faces in revulsion, and seeing this, she apparently took it as a sign of success and continued to dangle the pitiful creature, bound in filthy rags, in one hand, while with the other she pounded her chest, "Here, take her, give her bread, take her and keep her!" Until someone thought better and said to her sternly, Yallah, yallah and even raised his hand – I don't know why – and she fled, half-laughing half-weeping, and entered the puddle, dancing the baby in her hands, laughing and weeping brokenly.

That is how Yizhar described the woman, whose name he didn't know. What can I write to cap his text? I know the name of the woman who danced, and made her baby dance – twice – in the Lydda ghetto. Indeed, I know her whole story after she married Iliyya Batshoun, but what happened? What does dancing have to do with death?

They told me that Khuloud danced on her wedding day and astonished everyone in the ghetto with her ability to turn and twist to the rhythms of oriental music, but what does the dance of love have to do with the dance of death? Or is dance the most extreme form of expression, used once all others have been exhausted?

I was doing research on Yizhar, and his novel led me to Dr Mikhail Samara, who led me to Umm Hasan dancing on the march of death at the massacre of Shatila, and from there I went to Khuloud's dance, which the Israeli novelist didn't write about though he wrote about something similar when describing the expulsion of the peasants from their village and the demolition of their houses. What interests me about this novel isn't its admission of the crime, important though that is, but its ability to trace the outline of the mute Palestinian, who was to become one of the staples of Israeli literature, and to infer the underlying meaning of the founding of the Zionist state, which is that for the Jews to become a people like other peoples – "other peoples" here meaning European peoples – they had first to invent their own Jews. What Yizhar presents in his description of the Khuloud of Khirbet Khizeh, or of Khirbet al-Khisas – call it what you will – is the Old Testament scene to which the Palestinian peasants, in their disaster, were subsumed: "And with all these blind, lame, old, and stumbling people, and the women and children all together like some place in the Bible that describes something like this, I don't remember where," Yizhar writes.

Yizhar proclaimed the need for the Jewish people to fashion their Jews in their own image, an image that they had decided to rid themselves of when they entered the realm of the "civilised peoples". This is Yizhar's genius. The matter isn't one of Aristotelian catharsis, as some have written. Its locus is elsewhere. This Old Testament scene, which now vanishes into the mists of history, had to exist in order for the new Israeli age to begin.

The narrator of *Khirbet Khizeh* wonders, "I wanted to discover if among all these people there was a single Jeremiah mourning and burning, forging a mouth of fury in his heart, crying out in stifled tones to the old God in Heaven, atop the trucks of exile . . ."

Do the Palestinians now have to find themselves a prophet of lamentations and defeats like Jeremiah if they are to enter the turning point in history that their catastrophe fashioned for them?

Yizhar proclaimed us the Jews of Israel's Jews. That was the message of his novel. But what do I want to get out of this whole story? Should I lament my people as Jeremiah lamented his? Should all Palestinian writing about the Nakba be a variation on the lamentations forged by the prophet of defeat? Or what?

I feel as though I am writing in an ancient language that dies beneath my pen. All these allusions to legend inspire feelings of disgust in me. Uglier even than the death of language is our inability to find a grave for it to rest in, so that it can decompose and return to dust. Language isn't formed of dust; it is the opposite of all other creatures that die. The problem of language is its corpse, because it stays with us. We reject it, so it comes back in different shapes and we find ourselves chewing its corpse in our mouths.

I couldn't avoid Yizhar Smilansky's description of Khuloud, or a woman resembling her, any more than I could avoid reading the hidden text in Dr Samara's lecture. The Nakba reduced the Palestinian doctor to silence. He wrote about it only in fragments and it was up to the Israeli novelist to finish the story.

A moment, though. The Israeli novelist traced the outline of the mute Palestinian. The muteness of the Palestinian is a necessary condition for what we may call "the awakening of the Israeli conscience", which means in turn that this preoccupation is in essence a preoccupation of Jewish self-awareness and has nothing to do with its victims. Such literature leads us either to equate the executioner with the victim whose consciousness he now possesses or the victim with the executioner whose place he has assumed!

I intended to write about the long night that besieged the people of Lydda in their ghetto, but the story has somehow led me I know not where. I don't want to adopt the Israeli writer's thesis, assimilate the story to the lamentations of the Old Testament, and tinge the tragedy of the people among whom I lived with the flavour of legend so as to justify their defeat, humiliation and shame. Legends are no substitute for history and I'm not going to fall into the trap of supposing that the miracle of the Hebrew state is its ability to turn legend into history and that we must either adopt their legend or find one of our own in which to take refuge. The language of the return to legend is dead, part of the death of language that transforms words from points of light and guidance on a white page into blind words resembling the extinguished stars of the night of Lydda.

I meant to write about the burial of Mufid's body in the Islamic cemetery and the story told by Ghassan Batheish about the woman who slept among the graves, but found myself before the corpse of a language for which we can find no grave because it has taken up residence on our tongues and is killing us. I'm exhausted now. I feel as though words are no longer capable of saying anything and that I'm like that woman who took refuge in the cemetery for fear of death. The woman hid her life among the dead, and I hide mine among the corpses of words.

(5)

Who was the woman, and what brought her to the cemetery?

I never knew the woman's name, to be able to recall it now. My mother, Manal, gave her the title of "the Old Woman of the Grave" and told me nothing about her. After three days, the young men succeeded in bringing her to the ghetto, where she took up residence in a small room next to the church but lived in constant fear. My mother said that the fear had traced itself in the wrinkles of her neck and that she never stopped yawning.

It seems she was afraid of falling asleep, convinced that death would sneak into her slumbers and carry her off.

"Strange! Does it make sense? A woman on the verge of ninety behaving as though she was going to live for ever? Everyone else had died, but she clung on to the rope of life as though . . . I don't know what to say. And every day she'd ask permission to visit the cemetery, till the Israeli officer got sick of her and said if she liked graves so much, he'd take care of it for her. Then she could go and be buried there and not come back."

And when she died, the people of the ghetto discovered that they knew nothing about her or her family, though the Lebanese boy, Hatim al-Laqqis, discovered her secret and the secret of the jewellery that was buried in the grave where the woman had hidden during the massacre and where the young men had found her before bringing her to the ghetto. The trove that Hatim brought and set before the members of the committee led to his being detained, interrogated and added to the second detachment of prisoners, who left for the detention camp two months after the ghetto was set up.

Ma'moun said that the uncovering of the secret of the treasure, which consisted of around fifty Ottoman golden guineas that Hatim al-Laqqis found by chance buried in the tomb of the Yahya family, opened the ghetto's eyes to the growth of the phenomenon of collaborators among them. Iliyya Batshoun attributed the publicising of his marriage to Khuloud, and the insulting letter he received from his son Iskandar, to a collaborator having leaked the news to his family. He suspected Crazy Karim, the one who was said to have tried to rape my mother, though Manal denied it vehemently and said Karim was to be pitied and couldn't possibly be a collaborator.

When Ghassan Batheish and the four young men who'd buried Mufid Shahada in the cemetery returned, their faces were pale and long. None of them could speak; they appeared dumbstruck. Iliyya Batshoun and the other members of the committee went to Ghassan Batheish to hear the details of the burial. No-one knows what they heard but on leaving the short meeting, which lasted no more than half an hour, they too were struck dumb. Khalid Hassouna was unable to tell his wife anything, and Iliyya Batshoun went to Khuloud and sat in silence the whole night long; the woman said Iliyya didn't sleep at all that night and that his body shook with the horror of what he had heard.

The woman of whom we speak wasn't the reason for the terror that traced itself on the faces of the ghetto's people the next morning. Her story was just one of those of eight aged women and men who had hidden in the fields and cemeteries and whom the young men came upon while working in the city and brought to the ghetto.

Ghassan Batheish couldn't recount what had happened. The words emerged from between his lips broken and stammering, and when he managed to pull himself together and speak he uttered just two words: "flies" and "corpses". He said the streets were full of bodies, bodies scattered here and there, bloated by death and stiffened beneath the rays of the sun, and that when they passed the Dahmash Mosque, swarms of blowflies had fallen upon them, flies that stuck to the body and refused to go away, stinging and sucking blood. The committee members saw the blue spots on the man's arms and he said he'd treated himself with spirit and that his whole body was on fire. He said he was afraid of the flies and asked Iliyya Batshoun to talk to the military governor and find a way for the inhabitants to leave the city.

"If we stay, the flies will devour us and we'll be afflicted by deadly diseases," the nurse said.

When Hassouna asked about the number of bodies, the youth began to emit a strange sobbing sound, his body shook, and he raised his hand and said, "Everyone died. All of us are dead, uncle. Bodies too many to count. We couldn't count the bodies. Dear God, dear God, what are we to do?"

"There is no god but God," said Hassouna, and he left with stumbling footsteps.

Iliyya Batshoun said he'd go and ask Dr Zahran to come and treat the young men for the fly bites, and he left.

Everyone would forget the fly bites the next morning, when the young men were rounded up and divided into five work teams. From then on, the people would get used to the fly bites, and spend long days in daily encounter with the disintegrating victims.

Memory Gaps

From here, in my little apartment in New York, things seem simpler, but it is a simplicity full of cruelty and meaninglessness. What does it mean for a city to die flailing in the blood of its sons and daughters?

In the beginning, meaning during my childhood in Lydda, the fall of the city meant the end of the world. Tales of the massacres and of the disintegrating bodies and body parts strewn over the walls of the Dahmash Mosque were, in the lexicon of the people of the ghetto, an indirect reference to the end of the world. The city had had its limbs chopped off, and its inhabitants and those who had taken refuge there were now like orphans.

"We are the Orphans of the Ghetto," I said to the Hebrew teacher at the school in Haifa, when he asked me who I was.

The teacher smiled and asked me to reformulate the expression. "We, my dear child, are the Children of the Cactus. That is how we should introduce ourselves."

My mother used to say that cactus tasted bitter.

I am not speaking here of my personal status as an orphan owing to my father having been killed. I am speaking of the people of the ghetto, old and young, who came to resemble nothing so much as orphaned children.

An orphaned people, lost, its tragedy its inability to forget because it has no present.

However, after going to Haifa, working in Mr Gabriel's garage, and perfecting my Hebrew, the issue changed. I decided to forget. I had left my memory hanging up in our shack in Haifa, fled the slopes of Mount Carmel where my mother had gone to live with her husband, and decided to be someone else. In the word "ghetto" I found my own special way around the problem of acquiring a shadow in a country whose inhabitants had lost theirs. Don't ask me how I survived, how I reinvented myself and adapted myself to the mirror that I constructed, piece by piece, sticking the little bits together with the glue of forgetfulness, and how I lived my life as though it was my own. I decided to neither inherit nor bequeath. I decided there would be no wife and no children and lived as though I was my own phantom, appearing only to disappear, my single pleasure being to put one over on life with my articles on Arabic music, which had become fashionable owing to what I call "the identity pangs" felt by oriental Jews, especially those of Arab origin. Then Dalia appeared in my life and smashed the mirror and ground its splinters underfoot and said she loved me as I was and wanted me with my memory intact and would marry me. And after I'd come to believe her and allowed myself to be swept away by love, she left me and went off to join her sorrows and made me discover the death of love so that I went from one extreme to the other – from the terror of memory to the beauty of forgetfulness. Now the stories of the Lydda ghetto turned out to have been only a rehearsal for the fiction of the Warsaw Ghetto, in which I played the son of one of its survivors, who'd died when I was a baby, after which my mother, having suffered a nervous breakdown in whose aftermath she had been taken to a psychiatric hospital, had abandoned me while still a child.

I invented a father called Yitzhak, who'd escaped from the

Warsaw Ghetto when he was seventeen, leaving behind an aged, ailing mother, then found himself in Istanbul, and finally came to a stop in Tel Aviv, where he married the daughter of a Russian immigrant and had me. My father died in the so-called War of Independence and left my mother alone with her madness, which was full of the nightmares of fear. The story I made up said that Sarah, my mother, spent her remaining years in the psychiatric hospital in Acre and that I never saw her again. I didn't even know she'd died until three years after the event, when the woman who looked after me at Kibbutz Zippori in the north told me the news. The woman's name was Rachel Rabinowitz and she became a mother who hadn't borne me. This woman taught me to stop asking questions about my family and turned me into a boy who'd come from the sea and become the adopted son of this land, his muscles suckling at the sun, which tanned his body with a dappled brown, like a brand on his white skin.

(As you can see, I've turned my own story upside down and transformed it into a Jewish one: my father, Hasan Dannoun, died in the War of the Nakba; my mother lived in a shack in Haifa with her husband – her silence was a sign of the madness of regret that devoured her life – and I became my own son. It was enough for me simply to turn one story upside down to find I'd landed in another. I didn't even need to make up the details because as far as I could see they were identical.)

I decided to write about the fall of Lydda because my story has to begin somewhere, even though I have no memory of the city's fall on 12 July, 1948. The tales I heard from others won't serve to present a complete picture of that terrible day, which Dr Mustafa Zahlan used to call the Day of Desolation.

None of the people of Lydda has a complete picture of the

city's fall, but I decided to collect the fragments and write a story full of bloody stains and memory gaps.

Let me begin with the fall of the city, because stories begin with falls – this is what the scriptures tell us. Does not the story of Adam, grandsire of mankind, begin with his fall from Paradise and the transformation of a demigod blessed with immortality into a mortal, obliged to live life awaiting death?

Adam was an image God created from mud, and an image has no shadow. Adam lived in Paradise without shadows and neither knew nor awaited death. His fall transformed him into a mortal, which is to say, into a being who dies and knows that the secret of life is death.

This is how the story of humankind, as the three Abrahamic religions tell it, began. The fall carries with it a morbid nostalgia for a past that will never return. The story of Adam bequeathed us this nostalgia, and when I begin with the fall, I am adopting, without realising, the assumption that Palestine was a paradise before it fell into the hands of the Israeli invaders. But that is absolutely false. Lydda most certainly was not a paradise and Palestine wasn't Heaven. And I hate nostalgia absolutely.

All the same, beginnings have infinite possibilities, meaning that each beginning takes us to a new one.

The crime followed the fall, and with the crime history began. Human history does not begin with Adam but with Cain, who killed his brother and so bequeathed mankind the blood curse, which had to be complemented by the Flood, which created mankind over again. However, the children of Noah inherited the memory of blood despite themselves and thus it was that Abraham had made up his mind to kill his son as per divine command, and so on and so forth until things end up with the death of the

Messiah-Son on the cross, which the gospels paint as the end of the bloodbath, though nothing in fact has ended.

My story too began with a double crime – the crime of Mula and his soldiers that turned Lydda into a field of killing and corpses and forced the expulsion of its people and their despatch to exile and death; and that of my father, who left me as a babe-in-arms on the corpse of my mother, whose milk had dried in her breasts.

I will not blame my father: he was merely a victim, deserving of pity; and it appears that I can't blame Mula and his men as I have been told I must not blame the Jews because they too were victims. I am not the victim of just one victim, as Edward Said would have it: I'm the victim of two. This is my present condition, as I have just now discovered it to be, when it's too late.

All the same, what if I decide to blame my father and hold him responsible? It then follows that I have the right to blame the Jews, or else logic no longer means anything. Let me blame both victims, without falling into the trap of making them equal: there is a big difference between a father who loses his son on Lydda's march of death and an organised and rational military operation that took the decision to terrorise people so that it could expel them from their land.

But then again, what am I to do with my fictitious father Yitzhak Danoun, whom I invented to find a lineage for myself in their country, in which I have become what in the Israeli lexicon is termed a "present absentee"?

My fictitious father has nothing to do with the matter. His only sin was to be a Polish Jew who lived in the Warsaw Ghetto, from which he was able to escape, making a difficult journey that took him in the end to Istanbul, where he had no choice but to board a ship that carried him to the Promised Land.

I shall not speak of what happened to the man in the Warsaw Ghetto. I shall let that story reveal itself in the context of the love that brought me together with Dalia and made me develop a deep friendship with her grandfather, a Polish Jew who also bore the brand of the Warsaw Ghetto on his memory. This fictitious father of mine would find himself in Palestine, marry my mother, the Russian Jewess, and decide on the eve of the so-called War of Independence to emigrate to France to continue his engineering studies. On his way from Tel Aviv to Jerusalem, he would discover that the world had been turned upside down, and when he reached West Jerusalem, a military police squad would take him off to join the Haganah, where he would be attached to a unit of the Alexandroni Brigade and meet his death in the operation to take Haifa.

The labour of making myself up exhausted me, even though, to be honest, it was a job I enjoyed. I read lots of books about the Warsaw Ghetto, went there with a group of students, received my baptism at Auschwitz, and lived the same terror lived by that third father of mine who never fathered me. I was compelled, likewise, to study the reasons leading to the fall of Haifa, reading a book on the history of the Haganah and tracing an image of that father as a hero of the liberation – though the image soon began to fall apart when I read the writings of the Israeli New Historians; and when I came across the article "The Fall of Haifa" by Palestinian historian Walid Khalidi in *Middle East Forum* (December 1959) I suffered a disappointment deeper than the sorrow I'd felt when I read Ghassan Kanafani's novel *Return to Haifa*.

Kanafani describes the tragic meeting between the Palestinian "Said S." and his son, whom he'd left in Haifa as a baby, only to discover that the son had become an Israeli soldier and bore a new name. For a moment, I thought the Palestinian novelist was talking about me, though the idea quickly dissipated. Adam, meaning me, is more complex than Khaldoun/Dov: Adam became an Israeli by choice and made up his story as a life strategy, whereas Dov – "Khaldoun" before the fates imposed on him the role of victim/executioner – had no choice and became an Israeli soldier involuntarily. I am obliged to suppose that the person isn't the issue. I may be closer to the character called Said in Emile Habibi's masterpiece *The Pessoptimist* – though even that supposition isn't true: Habibi based Said on the character of Candide in order to convey the experience of "resistance-through-collaboration" and "collaboration-through-resistance" and is a symbolic character embodying in abbreviated form the sufferings of the Palestinian in the State of Israel. Me, though, I neither collaborated nor resisted; I'm not based on any model, my story sums up nothing but itself, and I don't want to be a symbol.

My disappointment on reading Khalidi came from my feeling of how deceptive the heroism was. I'd wanted my Jewish father to be a real hero, fighting with a small band of soldiers against a mighty army and beating it, but discovered that my father wasn't a soldier in the army of a David who killed the giant Goliath with a stone from his sling. My father was a soldier in the army of Goliath, which won because the Palestinians hadn't found their David, and three hundred Palestinian fighters were defeated by more than two thousand five hundred Jewish soldiers, with General Stockwell, commander of the British garrison in Haifa, playing a clear role in their victory.

My fictitious father Yitzhak Danoun was a victim, like my fallacious father Hasan Dannoun. They died as victims, leaving a foetus groping around in its mother's belly, and they converge, albeit indirectly, with my biological father, who fled from Lydda and lost his wife and his young child.

I will never forgive any of these three fathers of mine but I can't prevent myself from feeling sympathy for them. Their common factor is that they were victims and that they died, or disappeared, as victims.

Mula and Colonel Moshe Carmel (commander of the attack on Haifa), on the other hand, were not. The leader of the operation to occupy Haifa – the name of which was changed from Misparyim, meaning "scissors", to Khametz, meaning "yeast", on the eve of Passover, when the house has to be cleansed of yeast, so as to convert the Jewish religious symbol into one of the cleansing of the city of its Palestinian inhabitants – and the leader of Operation Dani for the cleansing of Lydda have in common that they were executioners, by which token my three fathers cannot be "victims of the victims".

I could make Hasan Dannoun meet Yitzhak Danoun and have them form a duo worthy of tears, but we are not – if my teacher Edward Said will excuse me – "victims of the victims". We, and the poor Jews they brought from the Nazi concentration camps to the battleground in Palestine, are the victims of the killers who betrayed the language of the Jewish victim when they crushed the Palestinians without mercy.

Hold on, though! Perhaps what I've just said contains a degree of overstatement, due to my emotional reaction. If we were to suppose that my fictitious Jewish father perished in the battles to occupy Lydda after the death of my father Hasan Dannoun the Martyr, or during the operation to expel my biological father whose name I don't know, my Palestinian parents would then be, somehow or other, the victims of my Jewish father who was himself a victim. By that token, Edward Said's view would be right.

In other words, the issue is susceptible to more than one inter-pretation, and God alone, as the Arabs say, knows the answer!

In my story, I chose to have my father die in Haifa so that I could make Haifa my city. The idea came to me in the garage of Mr Gabriel, who used to talk to me about his brother Shlomo, who was killed on Wednesday, 21 April, 1948, during the attack launched by Haganah forces on Dar al-Najjada overlooking Wadi Rashmaya in Haifa. Mr Gabriel said that I looked like Shlomo and that if I hadn't been an Arab, he would have found in me his lost brother.

I decided to be that lost brother but Mr Gabriel didn't believe me and threw me out of my job at the garage, which was because of the love story that Gabriel put an end to when he discovered I was having an affair with his only daughter, Rivka.

My Grandfather Who Was a Prophet

"In this city, the world will witness the return of Jesus son of Mary, peace be upon him, which is why God has written that our torments shall be the beginning of the road."

I remember hearing these words, or something like them, at the start of my relationship with the city, when I was six. They put us into a bus, loaded us with Israeli flags, and took us to al-Ramla to attend the military parade on the occasion of Israel's "Independence Day".

I remember we cried, and the teacher who accompanied us to the festivities, Mrs Olga Naddaf, had a cane in her hand and tried hysterically to make us behave. By the time we reached al-Ramla, our faces were covered in tears and the signs of fear were coursing through our bodies. That was in 1954, if my memory serves me right. A yellow bus, into which were squashed the pupils of the Lydda Arabic School, which had been established in the ghetto district, close to the Great Mosque, after Prof. Ma'moun's school had been split up when the head of the municipality issued a decree for its closure.

I don't know what had got into the teacher and why she never stopped beating and threatening us. I remember her saying we had to stand quietly, wave the little flags, and not talk or be naughty, and explaining to us that it was a holiday for our new state and that we had to respect the white-and-blue flag with a six-pointed star in the middle. I remember that when we got onto the bus we

279

were happy to be going on a trip because it was the first time we'd been outside the city. I don't remember, though, exactly what happened on the bus to make the woman rain blows on us.

The important thing is that our behaviour made "Independence Day" synonymous with the cane, and that we arrived at the ceremony in tears.

That is all I remember. Now that I've read about the impressive ceremony, which was attended by Ben Gurion, flanked by the great men of the state, and learned that the aim of putting on an Israeli military parade in an Arab city was to make the Palestinians realise that things had changed, that there was no going back, and that the country was now the property of the victors, I understand the hysteria of the woman, who was forty and had found herself alone in the ghetto.

The ceremony was awe-inspiring. How can I describe the feelings of the child I then was as he stood with everyone else, carrying the flag and with his eyes glued on the columns of military vehicles rolling down the city's main street, followed by columns of infantry; and when the balloons with Hebrew writing on them flew into the air, the children's eyes flew after them. The balloons filled the city's sky with wonder, and when a boy asked the teacher to translate the writing on them for us, Miss Olga Naddaf hesitated for a moment and then, in correct Hebrew, spoke the words "*Tsahal Magen*", meaning "The Israeli Army Protects". The teacher spoke the words in the two languages and tears fell on her cheeks. Then she looked at the dilapidated houses and asked, "Where are the people?"

The city's sky was filled with the words "*Tsahal Magen*", and we felt obscurely that the teacher's tears were translating them into another, unspoken, language; we fell into a silence that stayed with us throughout the return journey on the bus from al-Ramla to the ghetto.

That other language, fashioned by the tears of the hard-hearted teacher, wasn't a translation from the Hebrew into Arabic, it was a translation into the language of silence, whose letters only the inhabitants of the ghetto knew how to read – a language fashioned from the rubble of words that form themselves only as whispers and mumbles, whose words contained broken bits of letters, and which was expressed using signs sketched by hands, or by eyes that had lost their brilliance. That day I began to understand my mother's whispers and unfinished stories. To tell the truth, though, my life's journey, which I have fashioned from forgetfulness, rendered me unable to make sense of the symbols of that language, and I had to wait fifty years to recover my language, here in the silence that fences me in in New York.

That year, a week after "Independence Day", Ma'moun took me to attend the Friday prayer at the Great Mosque, the first time I went there. Ma'moun said I was a man now and had to learn how to pray.

At the mosque, the words of Sheikh Abd al-Hayy Maqsoud seemed to me like a continuation of the al-Ramla trip. The man's sermon concentrated on "Independence Day" and on the splendid scene of the Defence Force marching through al-Ramla. Then he uttered his celebrated sentence about the return of Jesus, son of Mary, and followed it with words taken from Islamic historians that I spent years looking for before finally stumbling upon them.

The first historian was al-Muqaddisi, who writes in *The Best of Dispositions Concerning the Provinces and Their Positions* as follows: "Lydda, which is a mile from al-Ramla, has a mosque in which many of the people of al-Qasaba and the surrounding villages congregate, and a magnificent church, at whose door the Antichrist will be slain."

The second historian was Ibn Asakir, in *The Great History*, which reports of the Prophet that he spoke of the Antichrist and said that those Jews who are of his people will be his helpers, and that he then said, "Jesus – the son of Mary – and the other Muslims who are with him, will kill him at the gate of Lydda."

The sheikh said, "We must pay allegiance to this new state because it will not be worse than the invaders who have preceded it; indeed, God, Mighty and Sublime, has established it here so that the killing of Jesus the Antichrist at the hands of the followers of the Arab prophet should be an event that is witnessed, by which peace will spread throughout the world."

The sheikh took my childhood deep into the history of the blood with which the city has been dyed since its foundation – a city that bore four names before settling on its present one, having been in Pharaonic days Ratan, in Roman Deuspolis, in Arab al-Lidd, and in those of the Franks the City of St George; then it was al-Lidd again, before the Israelis gave it the name of Lod.

It is the city of the miraculous church, site of the tomb of St George, whom the Arabs call al-Khudr, whose tales have filled our imaginations – the brave knight who died under torture when he refused to abandon his faith and the man of legend who killed the dragon and saved the girls of the city from certain death.

In the Palestinian popular memory, the prophet al-Khudr, or al-Khudr the Green, is a combination of two men – St George, who was a Roman officer who embraced Christianity, and the Prophet Elijah, who killed four hundred and fifty of the prophets of Baal with the jawbone of an ass in defence of his faith in the One, the Only. The slayer of the dragon that was devouring the city's virgin girls and the slayer of the false prophets are two mythical heroes who have become mixed up in our memory and thus make of Lydda a city protected by storytelling. It was in honour of this combined prophet-cum-holy-man that the Church of St George, demolished after al-Zahir Baybars reconquered the city in 1267 and rebuilt in 1870 on a portion of the demolished building, next door to the Great Mosque, was erected.

The Great Mosque itself was built by Baybars, the Mamluk sultan, who ordered the following words to be inscribed on the marble plaque above the mosque's main door:

In the name of God, the Merciful, the Compassionate: this blessed mosque was built at the command of Our Lord the Sultan, Resplendent King, Foundation Stone of This World and the Next, Abu al-Fath Baybars the Righteous, Friend of the Believers, may God make great his victories and forgive him his sins. The work of construction and its supervision were undertaken by the slave in want of God's mercy Alaa al-Din Ali al-Sawwaq, may God forgive him his sins, in the month of Ramadan 666 [1268].

Every Friday morning, Manal would take me to the shrine of the Prophet Dannoun, light three candles, and sit, weeping silently, instructing me to sit beside her. "This is the shrine of the pure saint your grandsire," she would say. "When things go badly, come here and talk to the Prophet Dannoun. Ask him whatever you want and he will grant your requests."

Manal stopped visiting the shrine after her marriage and move to Haifa, and when she tried, on the first Feast of the Sacrifice that we spent in Haifa, to take me to visit it, she met with a beating from her husband Abdallah.

Manal woke me at four in the morning and told me to get dressed because we were going to Lydda to visit the tomb of my father, then make a stop at the shrine. I listened, in the dawn's darkness, to her pleadings and then witnessed the beating to which she was subjected.

She said she was going to visit the holy man's shrine for my sake, because the Prophet Dannoun was my great-grandsire; her voice was low and full of gaps. She said she wouldn't go to Hasan's tomb, "only the saint's, I swear, only the saint's". She was weeping and clenching her teeth so that she wouldn't make a sound. Then her moaning became audible and I began to hear the slaps and her weeping grew louder. She said she'd forgotten Hasan and didn't think about him but was just going for me.

I could hear her voice, choking and imploring, from behind the locked bedroom door, but I couldn't hear his. It was as though she was talking to herself. I went closer and put my ears to the door and heard the beating. The slaps followed one another in succession and the woman was moaning. Now, as I recall the incident, I don't know whether the man was saying nothing or whether I couldn't hear him or whether I've erased his voice and his words from my memory. All the same, when my mother came out of the room and said that the trip to Lydda was off, I saw that her face was covered in bruises. I looked at her, and said in a low voice, "I'll kill him." Then, suddenly, I saw him in front of me with the pomegranate switch in his hand, and he rained blows on me, cursing me, and then started hitting us both, my mother weeping and hugging me to ward off the blows and me embarrassed and shamed.

That day, when I was nine years old, I discovered that I was capable of killing and that killing is a form of expression that may on occasion be necessary. The strange thing is that the first person I decided to kill wasn't an Israeli but a Palestinian, and that the stories and the bitterness of the ghetto never drove me to think of murder, maybe because I was young then, or maybe because talk isn't enough on its own: the decision to kill is taken first by the eyes.

This is what I tried to explain to Dalia when we were discussing suicide operations. I told her I could see the ghosts of the dead in the eyes of the young, would-be suicides, which are haunted with killing and its opposite. Killing is directed towards the Other: you kill the Other so as not to die yourself. A suicide operation, however, is a double death. This desire to kill isn't the offspring of memories of the Nakba, as some think; it is the lived Nakba, for Israel has turned the lives of three generations of Palestinians into a never-ending catastrophe. The Israelis, who, with the stupidity of those with power, wagered on the Palestinians forgetting the stories of their Nakba, went and imposed on them a continuous Nakba. Every day, Israel continues to practise the subjection of the Palestinians to catastrophe, not just in the West Bank, Gaza and Jerusalem, but in Israel itself. As a result, the generation that was supposed to forget its fathers' and grandfathers' stories of their Nakba, today lives with both its own and theirs before its eyes.

I won't say that in my life killing was merely a passing urge that never repeated itself and that came about only because of Abdallah al-Ashhal's savagery as he beat my mother and me on the eve of the Great Feast. Moments have come and gone when I have felt the need to take life. My words, stifled in my chest, and my identity that I hid, have made me experience states of anger that could be satisfied only by doing so. The second man I thought of killing was Rivka's father, Gabriel. Thereafter, the impulse has come again and again – I can't even count how often now – but I've never in fact killed anyone and can still say I'm innocent, even though I believe that symbolic killing, or the desire to do it, is no different from murder itself.

All the same, I have never killed anyone, and it never occurred to me, as it did to so many of my contemporaries, to join the Palestinian armed struggle. I wanted to be a citizen of this state and forget. I invented a new memory for myself and rode it, sliding, to the end, to the point where I no longer knew who exactly I was. Am I the son of Manal and Hasan Dannoun, or the son of Yitzhak Danoun and his sick wife, or am I merely a story, fashioned out of words?

Dalia was supposed to pluck me out of my story. I told her what she was doing wouldn't do, because I'd chosen to be in order not to be and she was destroying me and destroying our relationship. All the same, she insisted on knowing everything. She even took me to Lydda in the hope of stumbling across my story because she wanted our relationship to be built on the truth and not on stories. At the last, we ended up as we did: Dalia disappeared when she stumbled over her own truth, my love for her dissipated in my heart, and she left me flailing in the torments of loss, which I am trying now to fill with words.

I attempted to explain to Dalia that the truth means nothing. She accused me of sophistry because I was trying to find excuses for the Israelis, and my constant talk of the need for forgiveness concealed my inability to face up to the fact that the victim must seek revenge.

Naturally, that wasn't true. Indeed, it was part of the permanent misunderstanding that is a characteristic of love, but that isn't my present topic.

My present topic is that feeling of my ability to kill, which made my body tremble. I felt no hatred for Abdallah al-Ashhal, I was just aware of a sort of thirst. Killing isn't necessarily an act that is accompanied by hatred. On the contrary, it comes from our depths, when they're seized by a thirst for blood.

What I've written above about killing is simply fortuitous: I had meant to talk about my forefather, or the person Manal claimed was my forefather, and his shrine, which stood on the outskirts of the city. There, before the yellow sandstone that gave off the smell of incense, dead plants, and voices raised in prayer, I realised that humans are spiritual beings and that their relationship with the dead is the one thing that gives people a feeling that life has meaning.

To the shrine we would go – me, my mother and Ma'moun. Manal would kneel, murmuring prayers; Ma'moun would stand, gazing into space; and I would feel a thrill running through my body.

Manal would light three candles and place them in front of what is believed to be the saint's tomb, then step aside reverently, bowing her head, which was covered in a white shawl, go down on her knees, open an exercise book in which she had written out the sayings of this righteous saint to whom the people had chosen to ascribe the status of prophet, and read in a barely audible whisper. Her reading began and ended with "patience": "Patience is silence in the face of disaster, and making a show of wealth when poverty strikes." Then followed excerpts from the man's life and works:

Those who worry most are the most immoral.

Let him who would be modest direct his soul towards God's majesty and it will melt and become limpid, and he who gazes on God's might will find that the might of his soul has departed, for all souls are needy in His dread presence.

Never have I beheld anything more likely to inspire a desire for sincere devotion than solitude, for when one secludes himself, he sees naught but God Almighty, and when he sees naught but that, he is activated by God's wisdom alone. Whoever has come to love the rite of seclusion has attached himself to the pillar of sincere devotion and has taken firm hold of one of the main cornerstones of truthful speech.

I would listen to my mother's murmurs and see how Ma'moun's eyes moved as though he were reading her half-closed lips – words sanctified by a mystical attachment to the divine, by abstention from the pleasures of this world, and by desire for a solitude in which to seek an encounter with God.

I didn't understand what was being said, but would feel a coolness invade my spine. Ma'moun had taken upon himself the task of making me learn these excerpts by heart, as a complement to my memorisation of the Koran. I don't know what happened to the exercise book after I left. Did Manal take it with her to her village, and did she continue to read excerpts from it when she prayed in Eilaboun's Church of the Virgin? Or did she throw away the words of our family prophet when she returned to the bosom of the Virgin Mary, whom she used to refer to as the Mother of Light, saying of the belly that had borne Jesus of Nazareth that it was the Cave of Light?

These stories float on the water of my memory. I'm trying to draw a map of pain before going into the memory of that pain that made its home in that city of mine that I left while still young, only to discover, when I visited it with Dalia, that Lydda too had left itself and was living in a state of permanent mourning of which it would never be cured.

My relationship with my forefather the prophet was severed for ever after the frenzy of beating to which Manal and I were subjected. When I looked for him in books, I found out that he was Egyptian and had died in 245 A.H. His name was Thawban ibn Ibrahim and his sobriquet was Abu al-Fayd, or Father of Abundance. Some, though, say his name was al-Fayd ibn Ibrahim, that he was a Nubian widely known as Dhu al-Nun, and was a guard at an Egyptian temple at Akhmim. It is said that Dhu al-Nun knew the language of the Ancient Egyptians, which he had learned from the writing on the walls of the temple. It is a fact that this Egyptian Sufi and man of letters visited a number of countries, including Palestine, but it is equally certain that the shrine of the Prophet Dannoun (whom some call Our Master Dannoun the Egyptian or Dhu al-Nun), located in Lydda south of the Great Mosque, has nothing to do with the Egyptian Sufi.

A shrine fabricated from A to Z out of untruths to hold a family story that has no basis in reality – this Dannoun wasn't the forefather of my father Hasan Dannoun as my mother used to say, and quite possibly never even visited Lydda, and no-one knows why a shrine was built for him in our city. Very likely, in fact, he was just part of that downpour of prophets that rained on our land after the end of the Frankish Wars, which they call the Crusades, filling Palestine with shrines and tombs.

This obsession with shrines – from those of the Prophet Rubin and of the prophets Salih and Musa to that of my supposed forefather – is part of our country's infatuation with holiness and holy things. Since the story of Moses' flight from the pharaoh of Egypt, the Land of Palestine has never ceased making up stories of prophets, to the point that the people have become no more than the stories' transmitters.

The shrine of the Prophet Dannoun is one of sixteen shrines to be found in Lydda – of the Prophet Miqdad, of Salman al-Farisi,

of the Prophet Kardousha, of Abu al-Huda, of Uweidat, of the
Prophet Simeon, of Muhammad the Peasant, of Ahmad al-Salihi,
of Husein al-Alami, of Sheikh Salih the Syndic, of Yaaqoub the
Persian, etc., etc. – not to mention the Church of al-Khudr, or
St George, and the shrine of my grandsire.

Holy men and prophets, known and unknown, took up residence in Lydda to receive the tears of its inhabitants and help
them to face their disasters, from the locusts that invaded the city
in 1916 to the earthquake that struck on 11 July, 1927.

All these prophets, however, were unable to prevent the disaster of 1948. They stayed in their graves awaiting divine succour
and left the tears of the women of Lydda to fossilise on the lintels
of their shrines, most of which have now disappeared.

In Lydda, there were two main streets – King Feisal Street,
which runs from the municipal building south to the Ramallah
Road, and Saladin Street, which crosses King Feisal Street and
starts from Zahir Jandas Bridge. Two streets – the first for defeat,
being named after the King of Syria whose state was torn to shreds
following the Battle of Meisaloun, the second for victory, bearing
the name of Saladin, the liberator of Jerusalem from the Franks.
Even though Saladin the Ayoubid was unable to liberate Lydda,
our city, like many others in Palestine, made a shrine for this
military commander who almost achieved the status of a holy
man – in the form of a principal street, to remind people that
Palestine had known in the past an invasion similar to that of the
Zionists and that the fate of the new invaders would be no different from that of their predecessors.

I don't like this return to the past, as it seems to me a way of
escaping from the present. That doesn't mean I'm not an admirer
of Saladin and his victories. I just think that going back to the past

and insisting on the idea of its rebirth has prevented the Arabs from fashioning their present, starting with a critical reading of it.

The idea of rebirth scares me in and of itself. Who says the living can withstand the resurrection of the dead? Rebirth is a myth fit for literature and religion but not for an historical project. Who says the golden past of the Arabs was golden? Who says the Baghdad of the Abbasids was a city of justice? The founder of the Abbasid dynasty was known as Abu al-Abbas the Spiller of Blood. Haroun al-Rashid, who seems so kindly in *The Thousand and One Nights*, was the architect of the catastrophe that overtook the Barmacides. Who says our model should be a tyrannical state against which the Zanj rebelled because of the extreme oppression to which it subjected them? Even Saladin? No! No, I don't believe I dare recount to you the massacres that Saladin carried out against other Muslims: it might cost me my self-confidence.

As you can see, I too, despite my harsh words, have fallen into the trap of consecrating the past, albeit in an indirect and unconscious way, which is the problem.

Dalia told me that what I call "the Arab problem" is also the Jewish problem, because the latter succeeded in resurrecting their state from the ruins of their myths.

And Dalia, as usual, was right. But who says that the Israeli model, which carries the seeds of its own destruction within it, has to be repeated? And why do the Arabs, and especially the Palestinians, have to cling to the ropes of a past that has passed and will not return?

I told Dalia that our greatest problem was our fear of criticising the past, on the grounds that if we were to lose the delusion of descent we would lose everything.

The woman, who hid her love behind her bewildering smile,

said, however, that all peoples were that way, that politics was simply the offspring of myth, and that the blessing bestowed by the past was a condition for the construction of the monuments of the present.

I meant to say one thing but have slid off into another. Words slide us around wherever they want. They are the soap of the soul, with which we wash ourselves and on which we slip. On my visit to Lydda with Dalia, we met an elderly Yemeni Jewish man who'd found the Promised Land in the village of Deir Tarif, now named Bet Arif. While the man was pointing out the demolished houses of the Palestinian village and how the old names had been expunged to be replaced by new, Hebrew, names, Saladin popped up from I know not where. The man was telling me about Tsahal Street in Lydda, where his only son lived. I told him that the name of the street to which he referred was Saladin Street, not Tsahal Street, and when I pronounced the name, the man regarded me disapprovingly. The sympathetic look disappeared from his eyes to be replaced by one of suspicion and grimness, and I heard Dalia saying we had better go now.

"What's Saladin got to do with this place?" she asked. "You cost us the chance of talking to the guy."

I said, "I don't know." I tried to explain to her that I'd just wanted to put the record straight: Herzl Street was Umar ibn al-Khattab Street, Tsahal Street was Saladin Street, and so on and so forth. Saladin had returned not as the liberator of Jerusalem but as the site of the massacre that scattered its victims' bodies along its sides – those bodies whose remains had to be collected and buried by the people of the ghetto, before the military governor forced them to burn them.

As you can see, my resentment at the idea of rebirth, with which the poets of Arab Modernism slew us and which played a role in the rise to power in more than one Arab country of a tyrannical nationalism, does not mean accepting the abandonment of the name of Saladin Street. In my memory, it has become the street of the dead, and I dare not abandon the dead. I just wanted to tell our ancestors to leave us alone, so we can live and pull together what vestiges of life the world has left to us.

Adam, which is to say me, speaks here as a Palestinian, which is something that puzzles me now because my life's journey – and life, as Sinbad taught us, is just a journey from death to stories and from stories back to death – was supposed to be less confused and to unfold along the trajectory I'd planned for it from the moment I started work at Mr Gabriel's garage. It took, however, an unexpected turn. Dalia did not awaken the sleeping Palestinian in my soul, but she saw him. It was enough for this hidden being that I had deliberately concealed to be seen with the eyes of love for it to awake from its long coma and bring me back to the beginning of things.

What does it mean, "the beginning"? Is there a pattern that unites the child I was with the older man I have become? I think again of the child who was born in the midst of the massacre of the ghetto and feel he's a stranger to me. Then I look at the youth who studied contemporary Hebrew literature at the University of Haifa and remember his adventures and these things look to me like half-erased scenes from a movie I saw long ago. I try to restore the image of the journalist, marginal intellectual and bohemian who lived in the Ajami district in Jaffa but ended up living semi-permanently in the Yemeni district in Tel Aviv, but find its limbs have been amputated, and on and on . . . up to my new period in New York, where I try, with the indirect help of Sarang Lee, to

293

convince myself I'm writing a novel unlike any other because it belongs to a literary genre for which I do not know a name and of whose very existence I am unsure.

I don't think I'm telling the truth now – its sister, perhaps, meaning that I'm trying to use my writing to get out of the fix I'm in. Things are simpler than all this meaningless sophistry. If I had it in me to say things directly, I'd say that my crisis began not with Dalia's leaving but with her appearing. The departure was nothing but a frank proclamation of my personal crisis. With her, and with her grandfather, the Polish survivor of Auschwitz, I'd taken the lie to its peak, and after the peak can only come the abyss. In the end, I discovered my inability to reconcile the two persons that I was and rearrange them into a single person. Dalia told me, as she watched the movie she'd made about Assaf, that I had to choose, as there was no longer space to treat life as a game. She'd made her choice and was passing into silence.

That's how she left. And she made me discover in her silence, which covered the final chapter of my life, that the love that was born in the course of a game had come to an end, and that I had to go, so that my soul would not dissolve in grief.

The beginning of life was the massacre, and I have to gather together the scraps of its stories just as Ma'moun gathered the remains of the victims in the ghetto's long night, and to draw the map of pain as it was drawn on the face of Manal, my mother.

The Map of Pain

Manal's face appears, forming the first image on the map of pain that I am trying now to summon up – a map drawn with the barbed wire that marked the borders of the ghetto in which the remaining inhabitants of Lydda lived in a cage whose limits were set by echoes of death from all four directions. Even the sky looked as though it had been covered with an invisible film that blocked the light.

It is a map that starts in the Hospital District, which embraces the Great Mosque and the church, extends to the body parts stuck to the walls of the Dahmash Mosque and the corpses that were scattered along the roads, turning Saladin Street into a street of blowflies, reaches the cemetery, and makes a turn into the interiors of the houses in which decomposing corpses and children whose bodies were bloated with hunger and death were to be found.

The map of pain is a story of thirst, of barrels of water rolled from Ibrahim al-Nimr's citrus grove, of the wounded waiting for medicine, and of the warmth of mourning that became a substitute for a life devoured by the unknown.

This map begins at the face of my mother, at Ma'moun's closed eyes, at Khuloud's dance, and Hatim al-Laqqis's calls for help before he vanished, at the stories of the captives returning from the cages, at the people bowing in front of the military governor, at the houses occupied by strangers, and on and on.

All I know of these stories is that accursed "and on and on", because I experienced them only as my first days of life and we never remember the beginning of things, which is why we resort to inventing it. Here, however, I am not inventing anything. On the contrary, I remember the stories as I heard them and felt them, and fill the large gaps by looking into the memories of others, mixing all of this with my own words and a certain amount of imagination, which serves more to throw the gaps into prominence than to erase them.

I want my story to uncover its own gaps, because I'm not writing a witness report, I'm writing a story derived from the scraps of stories that I patch together with the glue of pain and arrange using the probabilities of memory. This ghetto, in which I was born and which I believed in my youth to be the card up my sleeve and my passport for a flight from my fate, has turned out in the end to be the be-all and end-all of my fate.

I'm not a historian and don't pretend to be one – despite my respect and esteem for the works of the historians – for I feel that history is a blind monster. When I think now of the things that my friends the communists used to say about the historical inevitability that leads to the liberation of peoples, I feel pity, for anyone who lived his childhood in Lydda and came to awareness in Mr Gabriel's garage in Haifa can only see historical optimism as stupid. This doesn't mean I'm against popular uprisings. On the contrary, I'm against those who are against them. But with years and experience I've discovered that the revolutionary is a person of despair and that despair is the most noble of emotions because it liberates us from illusions and makes of our revolutionary vision a gratuitous act, like art.

I write the story to restore my memory and engrave it on that of an imagined reader whom these words will never reach, because

I'm not sure I want them to go that far. What, though, is the meaning of memory? For an incident or a person to remain in the memory, he must be transformed into a line of writing wrapped in a kind of fog. What do we remember of our loved ones who have departed? What do we remember of the stolen moments of love?

All we remember is death, because death too is a book. Indeed, it is *the* book.

All we remember are states of opacity such as pain. Pain is a half-erased memory that we get pleasure from recalling because all that remains of it is a word made up of four letters that refers only to itself, a word drawn on the paper of memory or fashioned from the echo of its sound when uttered.

Engraving on memory is a way of forgetting. In the course of forgetting we remember, so memory floats on the surface of our life like words stammered and interrupted.

The map of pain begins at the face of Manal, my mother. That is where I have to begin, though I find great difficulty in writing about it – not because I've forgotten it but, on the contrary, because I've been unable to forget it. A face limned by grief – wide brown eyes, long black eyelashes, eyebrows drawn by a thin black pencil, and lips pressed together as though biting back the pain.

The two small grooves etched on the cheeks were, and will ever remain, the whole story. I saw them and I see them now. Two lines resembling the course of a river whose water has dried. Two thin lines that I'm now sure no-one but me ever noticed. My mother never gave away the secret of those lines to any but me. I'm the only one who saw – despite which I turned my back and went, and left Manal, my mother and my little darling, to her fate.

I had to go: I read my departure in her eyes. She was certain her marriage would lead to the destruction of us both and made no objection to my leaving to save myself. I did not, however, under-stand her eyes. Now, I can make justifications and find an excuse for myself in my youth, but it's not true. I must have read her death in her eyes but I was a coward, so I fled. Instead of suggesting that she leave with me or forcing her to do so, I took the will and went on my way.

I'm not a traitor. Or yes, perhaps—the day I left her I wasn't a traitor but now I feel the prick of betrayal. "The woman's eyelashes pierce my soul," as Adonis wrote in one of the most beautiful of his early poems. I wish I'd recited the poem to her, so that I could see the cherries dripping from her lips! When I was with her, though, I was speechless and incapable of expressing my emotions.

> *They said: She left, the field by rapture*
> *confused, the wheat swelling plump.*
> *Harmony was reborn through her gait*
> *and her canter and her strutting, and her quivering legs*
> *beckoned, so that the sunset turned towards her*
> *with yearning and the goats bleated.*
> *What the branding mark? What the strung beads?*
> *Why did the brown ancients not insist*
> *on riddles, not play the soothsayer, not use symbols?*
> *Her glances pierce,*
> *her eyelids are a chord and a summer*
> *song, and her shift is cherries.*

Such poetry is inappropriate for mothers; nevertheless, every time she returns to my memory, I smell the wheat that would be scattered from Manal's clothes and lodge itself in my soul.

Women are like cities: each has its own smell, which rises

from memory, and Manal's was that of wheat, maybe because my mother carried with her from her forebears the smell of the black earth of the plains of Houran, or perhaps because her duskiness, which shone in the sun, made one think of wheat fields, golden-glowing and swaying.

Do I have the right? Can I permit myself to write you the way I want to, now?

Now I admit what I didn't dare admit to Dalia: when I told her she was "as beautiful as silence", I was thinking of Manal. Dalia bears no resemblance to Manal, despite which she reminded me of my mother. That was the reason for my fear and my endless flight from her. I disagree with the theory that says men seek their mothers in their sweethearts, which is bullshit. I wasn't seeking anything when I met the woman. I was messing around with love and love fell upon me and I became a captive, a lovesick swain.

Dalia could never have been Manal, but my idiotic memory now blends the two women and makes me say things about my mother that are inappropriate for a son and that, in the end, are just drivel.

I have to be careful now. I don't know if my emotions are real, or just a lust for writing. I recall that woman on whose face the map of pain was drawn and feel an irresistible desire to gaze into the depths of her eyes, and then clasp her to my breast.

Manal, today, is a lost child, and I am the man who abandoned her in a heedless moment. I am growing old, and her absence, followed by her death, left her a child, one like the virgins of Jerusalem of whom Solomon the Wise speaks in his *Songs*. A virgin the water of whose love had dried up in her heart, whose tears had turned to stone upon her cheeks, whom the three men she had loved had abandoned, and who then fled from her husband after she had divined that her son would depart.

(I have spoken of Abdallah al-Ashhal as a monster, but I'm being unfair to him. I'm unfair to him and know that it must be so: we have to be unfair to someone if our lives are to resemble lives. Yes, I'm unfair to him, for "injustice is a trait of men's souls", as al-Mutanabbi wrote. With his daughter Karma, the monster that appeared to me in the person of Abdallah al-Ashhal seemed more like a human being deserving of pity and regret, and my unfairness to him, like his to me, as simply an expression of impotence and frustration. That, however, is another story.)

I just wanted to describe, today, the longing I feel for my mother, accompanied by an overwhelming tenderness towards her pain-spattered silence – only to discover that here too I was playing a part, through my reliance on a language that has been exhausted by repetition.

The essence of the matter is that I wanted to talk about what came after the tears that drew the map of pain on Manal's face, and I spoke drivel because my inability to express myself made me resort to words that have become stuck in the language.

I never saw her cry. Her voice would quaver and take her to the verge of tears, though I never saw them. It was as though the woman had gone to a pain beyond weeping and therein lay the relationship between her eyes and a city that had lost its smell.

She said she'd come from the smell of wild thyme in Eilaboun to the smell of lemon- and orange-blossom in Lydda. "I travelled, my dear, from smell to smell. I was accustomed to the smell of thyme, which opens the heart, but when I came here I discovered lemon and encountered 'the perfume of the soul', as your poor father used to call it."

Manal said the city had lost its smell after the killing of Hasan Dannoun and the entry of the Israeli army over the body parts of the slain. "Can you imagine what it means, a city without a smell?" She said that when a person dies they lose their own smell and a different, strange, one settles upon them. Thus the dead are rendered identical in their odourlessness, and then are taken over by a smell that is everywhere the same, which is the smell of death.

She said Lydda lost its smell. "When they gathered us in the square in front of the mosque inside the barbed-wire fence, the smell of the city died. The perfume of lemon blossom disappeared and the smell of the dead, which arose from all four directions, settled upon us."

She said and she said. I try to recall her words but cannot. However, I read her secret in her eyes and the name of that woman's secret is "beyond weeping".

I only understood what "beyond weeping" meant when I watched on television the pictures of the corpses that had piled up at the massacre of Sabra and Shatila. I admit I felt unable to weep that day. The tears turned to stone in my eyes and a fire, which ignited in my intestines, swept through me. The words stuck in my throat, and I became as though feverish, everything in me shaking: I shuddered with the cold that spread through my joints and I suffocated from the heat that paralysed me.

That is "beyond weeping". The eyes are so dry they grow hard, the saliva in one's mouth disappears, and the ears fill with ringing and echoes.

Manal lived her whole life beyond weeping.

She said she'd wept a lot, but that weeping isn't mute because it can only have existence through language. One weeps because one wants to communicate a message to others, and when the weeper is met with gloating eyes and indifferent, expressionless faces, the water dries in his eyes.

"Not us, I swear! We couldn't weep because the tears in our eyes had dried up. They disappeared because there was no medicine for the pain we were living. Tears, my dear, are a medicine, like olive oil. We rub the body with oil and the soul with tears."

Manal didn't actually say this, though not because she took pity on her young son and wanted to protect him from the impact of her words – in the ghetto, there was no room for pity to spread its wings: the people there had snatched their lives from the mouth of death, and those who have survived death feel no pity.

Manal didn't say it because she didn't say much, even when she spoke! What I'm telling you on her authority is just what I was able to gather from the crumbs that she uttered. Manal would listen to what she'd said via the echo of her voice, which would then turn, on Ma'moun's tongue, into words. Ma'moun would talk, recounting excerpts from my mother's memory, and I became accustomed to accepting the game of attributing his words to her. The echo, not the voice, recounted my story. Now, when her voice brings the rhythms of silence, I hear the voice of Ma'moun and I weave the beginning of the story.

Listening to Ma'moun at his lecture at New York University, however, I could no longer recognise his voice. The voice of the blind academic, issuing from a microphone placed in front of him, sounded strange. It was a voice full of the hoarseness of age, coming from inside a throat in which whispers blended with shouts and which seemed to emerge from a deep well.

At that moment, I knew for sure that Ma'moun's ghetto voice had not been real. It too had been an echo of the pain.

302

The Abyss

The inhabitants of the ghetto awoke from the coma into which they'd fallen after the long day of sun in the courtyard of the Great Mosque to find themselves in the abyss. There is no more precise word than that, which Ma'moun used constantly when he delivered his lessons to his students.

"Read, you son of the abyss!" he used to shout at Salim, who would stumble when reading excerpts from Jurji Zaydan's historical novels, which our teacher made some of our main set texts, believing as he did that our Arab identity was threatened with extinction in the new state.

There was no relation whatsoever between Salim's inability to read as a result of his obsession with football and the words "the abyss" as spat out by Ma'moun, who would grind his teeth when saying them as though cursing the world and everyone in it. Ma'moun's "abyss" was another name for the cage in which lived the inhabitants of what would later be known by the single term "the ghetto", or "the Arab ghetto".

The ghetto was fenced with barbed wire and had a single gate, guarded by three soldiers. Some of the inhabitants had been distributed among the houses that had been left behind by their owners, Iliyya Batshoun supervising what he called "the fair allocation of dwellings". There weren't enough private residences, though, so the head of the committee decided to put families in the houses and ask individuals to live in the hospital, the mosque

303

and the church. Things were more complicated, however.

This distribution plan was simply a proposal. Some families, finding themselves without shelter, were forced to live in the mosque and the church. As a result, a number of apartments, divided from one another by no more than a few sheets and blankets, were created within the courtyard of the mosque and the church compound.

It was a society in which everything was mixed up with everything else. Even the houses were somehow shared with everyone, since, because of the shortage of food and the crippling water crisis, the inhabitants of the ghetto were obliged to live communally. The result was the creation of a society, peculiar to the Arabs of the ghetto, in which boundaries were erased.

This description of the situation in the shadow of whose stories I lived may seem deceptive, in that it may give the impression of a harmonious communal life – and indeed, one of the Israeli soldiers, observing it, was led to say that the ghetto was "like a kibbutz". The reality, however, was as far as could be from such an ideal communal life, since the people of the ghetto, despite their attempts to adapt to the cage into which they had been placed, were constantly discovering, to their surprise, that their disaster had no bottom to hit and that they were forced, each day, to find new ways to eke out their existence.

The rehousing took place without disputes, as they were convinced that they were living through a temporary situation that must quickly come to an end and that nothing was real, as though the ghetto was just a nightmare from which everyone was trying to wake.

How did the nightmare begin? What happened on that sunny day in the month of July, 1948?

Lydda fell on 11 and 12 July, 1948. When I write "fell", I feel as though the city fell into a chasm. In fact, I don't regard that word as appropriate for the occupation of cities in war. Armies invade cities, they don't make them fall. This in principle, and to be scrupulous. In the case of Lydda, however, the city wasn't occupied: it toppled, fell to pieces and was wiped out. The city that I left for Haifa as a boy bore no resemblance to that which people described to me. Lydda was once a city. The place I left consisted of its mortal remains, limbs severed.

People remember that the weather was hot and humid and that they understood nothing. Suddenly, they saw Israeli armoured columns moving through the streets, shooting. The city's defenders vanished in a flash and the people were turned into a wave of humanity staggering in the face of bullets and death.

In order to be objective and truthful, I have used exclusively Israeli sources to understand how the city fell, and anyway there is no Palestinian military source in existence that documents the battle for Lydda (which is not surprising given how scattered the Palestinians were in exile). The attacking Israeli army consisted of an organised force numbering six thousand armed men, while the defenders consisted of armed groups, haphazardly organised, drawn from the city and surrounding villages.

After the fall of Jaffa on 14 May, 1948, the people of Lydda were convinced they had been left to their fate in the path of an army that was their superior in every way. The question that puzzles me now is why didn't the people flee and thus avoid the massacre, given that they knew they had no practical possibility of repulsing the impending attack. As you can see, this is the opposite of the question that used to keep me awake in my youth, when I felt shame at the story of the displacement of the refugees, which was one of the reasons why I deliberately disguised myself and my identity. I don't want now to discuss the issue of how I played around with my identity: that kind of behaviour is the story of my life, not one that I'm writing as an example or a symbol the way our mentor Emile Habibi did with the pessoptimism of his hero Said.

My question is, why didn't they flee?

I'm on life's last lap now, where the wisdom of death holds sway and the fatuous belief that we will live for ever evaporates. I feel we should turn the questions upside down. Otherwise, we shall become an echo of the Zionist lie that transformed the expulsion of an entire people into a shameful smear on the history of those expelled, absolving the criminal of any moral responsibility and weaving the untruth that the Palestinians left their lands on the orders of their commanders, leaving the field empty for the entrance of the Arab armies that were going to occupy Palestine and wipe out the Jews.

Palestinian historian Walid Khalidi has refuted that lie and Israeli historian Ilan Pappé has demonstrated that what happened in Palestine was ethnic cleansing. That issue is behind us. What disconcerted me, though, in the course of my work collecting the scattered stories of Lydda and other Palestinian cities and villages during the War of the Nakba, was a different question, given that it is logical for civilians to flee during battles and that it is what has happened in all wars in all parts of the world.

What I wish I could ask Manal is why they didn't flee before the Israeli army entered Lydda! What made them wait for the massacre?

Lydda was in the same situation as all the other cities and villages of Palestine. The people awaited death and only left their homes to the rhythm of Israeli orders to do so.

I do not say this boastfully, for blood, death and mistreatment are not tokens of pride. I'm just recounting what I experienced and what I heard from the people who witnessed those days. I ask this now as a question. I'm not offering it as an answer but as a story that would make a fitting start to the as yet unwritten history of the crime.

I should have asked Ma'moun the question but instead of speaking up on the night at the Washington Square Hotel, I was struck dumb. Ma'moun rendered me speechless when he told me the story of the child whom he picked up off its mother's body, and I behaved like a fool and surrendered to a story that was like a myth. Throughout, I was as though drunk, seeing things double: Ma'moun turned into two men before my eyes, one of them sitting in the rocking chair in the lobby of the New York hotel, the other spying on us from a chair placed at the other end of the atrium. What an idiot I was! I, the one who turned his back on Manal and her stories and made up his life as he pleased, now find myself tied down by a story that would make a fittingly melodramatic point of entry for the telling of the tragedy of the Palestinians, but it's certainly not one that fits me.

I'm not Waddah al-Yaman. I played the death game with the poet because I saw in his silence a metaphor for the victim who's tied down by love and paralysed by the possibility that that love has been lost. And when Ma'moun wrapped me in a shroud of silence and I saw the world as double, I decided to flee from the metaphor in order to write my own story.

My story, though – and herein lies the paradox – needs those of others, if it is to take shape in words, and the others whom I seek have died, or disappeared and been transformed into parts of me. I sense them, and I sense that my body has become too cramped for us all and that I can no longer bear the sound of their voices.

I haven't answered the question I've posed and I don't think I'll arrive at a true answer no matter how hard I look. My question does, however, reverse the terms of the question's equation. Why, Manal, when you sensed that Lydda was about to fall and nothing could be done about it, didn't you flee? Why did you stay in the hospital after your husband died? Why didn't you go back to your family in Eilaboun or run off to Ramallah?

I see Manal in my mind's eye. I see my little mother hiding behind the mask of her face and I hear the whisper of her voice as she tells me to close my eyes so that I can go in my dreams to wherever I wish. That woman was the apple of my eye – that's how I shall remember her to my dying day. Her voice embeds itself deeply in my eyes as she tells me to close them so I can sleep. She didn't tell me the stories other mothers do: she'd ask me what I wanted to dream and when I didn't answer start telling me my dream about the sea, taking me to the sand on the shore and describing the coloured fish so that my night would be tinged with the smell of salt and I'd hear the waves that hide in seashells, and sleep.

I see Manal and say that I want her to tell me why she didn't flee just before the fall of the city and why she chose to remain afterwards. Was it because she was unaware of what was going on around her? Did the Palestinians live their story as though it was a dream they didn't believe?

The latter isn't my answer to the question, even though it seems plausible, since, when disaster strikes, no-one ever believes it. Instead, people behave as though they weren't at a crossroads. They close their eyes and go on with their lives until they discover that their long dream has swallowed them.

Lydda fell on Sunday and Monday, 11 and 12 July, 1948. On the third day began the comprehensive expulsion of the inhabitants of the city and those from the nearby villages who had taken refuge there. On the evening of the fourth day Ma'moun brought me back to the city, where I stayed with my mother in the Church of St George before being taken the following day to the hospital.

Ma'moun recounted the story of the expulsion and the march of death dozens of times, and the Palestinian painter Ismail Shammout has painted it, making of the images of the victims a symbol of the wandering Palestinian, as described by Raja-e Buseila in an astonishing text in English published in an issue of *Arab Studies Quarterly* (3:2, Spring 1981), edited by Ibrahim Abu Lughod. The stories of the fall and of the people who stayed in the city and what happened to them are recounted in only two books. The first is by Fawzi al-Asmar and entitled *To Be an Arab in Israel* (1975), the second by Isbir Munayyir and entitled *Lydda During the Mandate and Occupation Periods* (1997). I read both books more than once, and whenever the stories of grief emerged from between the cracks of the words, I would hear my mother's voice. Both books are autobiographical and recount the story as a pointer to desolation and grief, which is what I intend not to do. It is not my concern to uncover the crimes committed by the Israeli forces that invaded Lydda and destroyed it. My story isn't an attempt to prove something. What I'm trying to do now is to take my own story back to its beginning.

It opens with the fall of Lydda. My mother never said exactly when I was born. Was I born before or after the city fell? When she told stories of the first days of the ghetto, she would, however, picture herself as a mother holding her baby. Ma'moun confirmed this when he told the story of me under the olive tree: he said I was a baby but didn't specify my age, and I didn't ask him. I am going to suppose that my birth occurred in the ghetto, even though I'm sure it must have taken place at least a month before the ghetto came into existence.

Let me go back to the beginning.

The beginning says that the Israeli forces that took part in Operation Dani, whose objective was to encircle Lydda and al-Ramla and bring them down, took the village of Yazour as their command base, said forces being composed of the following brigades:

The 8th Armoured Brigade under the command of Yitzhak Sadeh; the Yiftach Brigade, belonging to Palmach, under the command of Mula Cohen; the Kiryati Brigade under the command of Michael Ben-Gal; the Alexandroni Brigade under the command of Dan Epstein; plus the air force, which had been tasked with bombing the two cities. The operation was led by Yigal Allon, with Yitzhak Rabin as deputy, and six thousand Israeli soldiers participated.

The question isn't why or how Lydda and al-Ramla fell, since their fall was inevitable given the large discrepancy in size between the opposing forces. The Israeli army deployed elite forces whose numbers, organisation and weapons were vastly superior to those of the defenders, who consisted of about one thousand Palestinian irregulars, charged with the defence of Lydda and its villages, alongside a small unit of the Jordanian army whose command decided there was no point in fighting; that unit then withdrew to concentrate its defences at Latroun so as to block the attackers' route and prevent them from entering Ramallah.

Between 11 and 12 July, 1948, Lydda was throttled. All the villages surrounding it had collapsed, their inhabitants moving to the city, which came to resemble a large refugee camp. To the north of the city, the villages of Deir Tarif and Haditha had fallen, as had the airport, and to the south, the villages of Annaba, Jamzu, Danyal and al-Dahiriya. Lydda was besieged from the north, the south and the east.

A city under siege. Those who'd fled to it from their destroyed villages wandered aimlessly in its streets, the fighters sensing the coming defeat and discovering that they possessed none of the elements needed to hang on except resolve, which was starting to crumble and collapse in the face of that sense of defeat.

Lydda's Day of Judgment did not begin with the invasion of the city by the 89th Battalion under Moshe Dayan, whose armoured cars came from the direction of Ben Shemen, but with the droves of refugees who invaded the city bringing stories of the horror they had experienced and of how the Israeli army had forced them to leave their villages without burying their dead.

The sound of the guns and the bullets blended with the roar of the planes bombing the city. The planes occupied the sky, pouring out their lava, and a sense of disaster enfolded them all. At around five in the afternoon of Sunday, 11 July, an Israeli force advanced from the east, from the area of the Ben Shemen colony; it was composed of an armoured-car column and went through the city from east to west, firing randomly at everything.

Moshe Dayan could boast to his fellow commanders of Operation Dani that his column had concluded the battle in just one hour, which was the time it took the Israeli column to cross from Ben Shemen to the Great Mosque. And he was right: Dayan's column decided the battle in favour of the Haganah, because it transformed the occupation of Lydda from a battle into a massacre.

No exact count exists of the number of Palestinians killed by this column that randomly spewed bullets and flung hand grenades at everyone whom it happened to find in its way, but when we recall that the streets and squares of Lydda were crammed with thousands of refugees fleeing their villages, we can understand what happened and why the potential of the city's fighters to resist its occupation evaporated. Some sources have spoken of Dayan's column killing a hundred Palestinians, male and female. Let us assume that this figure is correct even though the young men of the ghetto who worked to collect and bury the corpses assert that the number was far higher. Nevertheless, while assuming, as I say, that the number is correct, it does not indicate the number of those injured. Statisticians of war usually calculate the number of the wounded by multiplying by five, meaning that we are faced with around five hundred wounded in addition to the hundred killed. This was sufficient to spread panic among the people who had taken refuge in Lydda, only to discover that they had fled from the fire of their villages to the fire of death.

The 89th Battalion's column was symbolic, as it was the Yiftach Brigade, under the command of Mula Cohen, that actually occupied the city and whose forces were able to spread through it, and the massacre carried out by the 89th Battalion was complemented by the massacre at the Dahmash Mosque and by the random killings carried out on the Tuesday, the day of the great expulsion, when the column of death which left Lydda for exile was formed.

The Israeli decision was clear: all inhabitants of the city were to be expelled. The Israeli lie to United Nations mediator Count Bernadotte, to the effect that the exodus of the people from Lydda was the result of an agreement made at the Church of St George on Tuesday, 13 July between the city's notables and the Israeli military governor Shmarya Guttman, has no basis whatsoever in truth. Palestinian historian Aref al-Aref organised a meeting in Ramallah between Bernadotte and the notables of Lydda, who denied any knowledge of such an agreement and told the international mediator the story of the compulsory expulsion from the city. That meeting was one of the factors that led Bernadotte to put forward his proposal that the refugees must return, which led to his assassination at the hands of the Zionists.

On Monday, 12 July, the city's inhabitants awoke to panic. The Israelis were everywhere and the wave of humanity was drowning in blood. The people of the city didn't know what to do. Some sought protection in their houses while others, including the refugees, decided to gather at the Great Mosque, the Dahmash Mosque, and the church, believing that the invaders' army would respect the inviolability of places of worship. They were, however, wrong.

Was the Dahmash Mosque massacre a mistake? And what does it mean to seek shelter in the idea of a mistake, when the number of victims was more than one hundred and twenty-five, of all ages? Does the claim that it was a mistake absolve of responsibility the one who made that mistake?

Such questions appear to be irrelevant, because to sift through the details of specific massacres is pointless in the context of a comprehensive massacre to which an entire people has been subjected.

I know that the word "massacre" falls unpleasantly on the ear in today's world, which views Israel as the offspring of the Holocaust and as heir to the Jewish pain brought about by savage persecution and mass extermination. Despite this, I can use no other word, for not only is it appropriate to what happened in Palestine in 1948, it is also coextensive with the Nakba that has been ongoing for fifty years in the form of a continuing massacre that has not ceased even now.

I, the sacrificial son of the city, now admit that I discovered the truth of this never-ending Nakba only when I learned to speak. To arrive at that knowledge, I was obliged to read a lot, to meet with numerous people and to cudgel my memory, and here I am now, writing it down, because, having finally reached that bend in life where the living, arrived at the foothills of non-existence, may speak as it is fit that the dead should speak, I too have become capable of speech.

I admit too that my mother never told me the stories of those three days of "the abyss". Her stories began with the ghetto and she didn't describe the whirlwind of death that invaded the city first. My mother was not alone in this. It was the same with everyone, as if the victims had decided unconsciously that the words could not be spoken and that their only means to survive in the abyss of death was silence.

No-one recounted these stories that I am trying to write down. They are word motes and memory shards. I approach them with my faltering language and instead of picking them up and washing the dust of sorrow off them, I blend into them and become a part of their dust.

Lame Ahmad claimed to have been the sole survivor of the Dahmash Mosque massacre and said that he'd found protection from death among the dead who fell on top of him. Then, when everything had gone quiet, he'd sneaked into the hospital, where he was treated for a bullet in the right foot, but because of the chaos that struck the hospital when the nurses and doctors were forced to leave it for the Great Mosque before being allowed to return on the second day, he didn't receive the proper treatment.

Lame Ahmad would be one of the third group of young men from the ghetto who were taken as prisoners, after which he never returned to Lydda; it seems the price of his release from the camp at Sarafand was that he go to Ramallah, where he joined his sister. Ahmad had remained in Lydda after the massacre because he'd died there, or so at least his sister, who was in her house with her husband and children when she learned that all the other members of her family had died at the Dahmash Mosque, in which they'd taken refuge, had supposed.

Lame Ahmad didn't like the epithet that the inhabitants of the ghetto applied to him. He told Hajj Iliyya Batshoun, when the head of the ghetto committee asked him his and his family's names, that all the members of his family had died, and that he too was dead. "Think of me as a dead man, friend. I died and I don't know what happened to me and I found myself in the hospital and my name had become Lame Ahmad."

The man didn't object to the name "Ahmad" that the doctor had given him as he pulled the splinter from the bottom of his foot without anaesthetic. He bellowed like an ox being slaughtered and didn't respond to questions.

Everyone used to call him Ahmad, but Ma'moun, who returned from the camp at Sarafand three weeks after he was taken there as a prisoner, bringing terrible stories of his time in captivity, recounted that Lame Ahmad had woken out of his borrowed name when he'd witnessed an Israeli soldier order one of the prisoners to walk in the direction of an olive tree at the side of the road and stone it, at which he fired on him and executed him.

Ma'moun recounted that on the night of that crime, as the prisoners huddled together, Ahmad had approached and told him his story.

"The young man," Ma'moun said, "was Marwan Abu al-Loz, and the poor guy believed that he'd died in the mosque with the rest of his family, and when I asked him how he'd reached the hospital he'd said he didn't remember. He'd thought that the days he spent at the hospital were a form of 'the torment of the grave', of which he'd heard from his grandmother. That's why he'd refused to speak and hadn't tried to correct the name that Dr Zahlan had given him there. I asked him what had happened at the mosque. He said that all he could remember was the sound of the explosions and the shooting. 'Though I do remember the soldier with his blond beard who was holding a strange-looking rifle from which he fired a shot, and the people starting to fly in all directions.' He said he'd flown, then fallen, and the body parts had started falling on top of him and he'd heard the sound of more than one rocket before he died."

"But you didn't die, and here you are talking!" said Ma'moun.

"No, I died," said Lame Ahmad, before remembering that he was Marwan Abu al-Loz. "I swear I felt I'd died. What can I tell you? The dead don't talk. It started raining death, that's what I thought, and the sounds were loud. Everything was exploding and I exploded and then it all went quiet."

Ma'moun recounted that the strange rifle that Marwan had seen was a P.I.A.T., a weapon that fired armour-piercing projectiles, and that soldiers of the Yiftach Brigade had entered the mosque, fired the P.I.A.T. projectiles, and followed them with bursts of machine-gun fire, and that everybody in the mosque had died.

Ma'moun recounted that the members of the work detail he was on that was charged with collecting bodies preparatory to their burial were struck with consternation when they entered the Dahmash Mosque. He said he hadn't understood what had happened. The place was filled with the smell of death. His comrades left the mosque suddenly without telling him and he found himself alone and discovered, without anyone having to tell him, that body parts were stuck to the walls.

Ma'moun told Marwan's story countless times. "The doctor called him 'the Lame', but the youth was deaf and went for a whole month able to hear only a ringing sound. When he started hearing again, he discovered that people's voices no longer sounded as they had in the past and he decided to stop speaking."

Ma'moun's experience with one of the work details that was charged with collecting bodies and burying them made him a comrade of the dead. That was how his lecture at New York University commenced, after which he moved on to his topic, "The Interstices of Silence", and said that the key to reading the literature of the Nakba was what wasn't said. He said that all the verse of Mahmoud Darwish should be read through its references to the expulsion from the village of al-Birwa and hid more than they revealed, and that it was the role of criticism to give voice to the silence, not the sounds, of the words.

The massacre at the Dahmash Mosque isn't the issue, for when all the streets of the city have become a deathtrap, words turn to stone.

Lame Ahmad, or Marwan Abu al-Loz, said he was going to look for his sister, who hadn't taken refuge with the rest of his family in the Dahmash Mosque. He was sure she'd survived, along with her husband and their two children, and was living now in some camp in the West Bank.

After the two massacres, that by the 89th Brigade and that of the Dahmash Mosque, the Israeli soldiers were seized by bloodlust and started shooting at everything. They ordered the inhabitants to leave their houses and the refugees who had come to Lydda their makeshift camps and pointed to the road leading to Ramallah. "Go to Abdallah!" they shouted as they fired over their heads. They banged on the doors of the houses brandishing their weapons and ordering people to leave with nothing but the clothes on their backs. "Leave everything! Go!" they shouted as they fired. I'm not going to recount the tales I heard of women being raped or of random killings inside the houses as these are all things known to their victims and as they have remained silent who am I to recount them? Today I understand their silence as pride and grief, and I add my silence to theirs.

There is no point in telling these tales now, but the members of the teams of Lydda's youth collecting the corpses came across the bodies of babies, women and men inside the houses, most of whom had been shot.

I know I don't possess the documents to prove my words. My documents are the testimonies of people most of whom are dead. I'm scared that tomorrow a historian like Dr Hanna Jiryis will come along with his scholarly discourse that declares that when we cannot prove our words there's no point in writing them, or an Israeli historian and writer like Tom Segev will turn up with his "irrefutable" argument that the "doyen" of Israeli historians, Benny Morris, made no mention of these events in his book on the refugee problem, and if that historian – who, after all he'd said, made a U-turn and started calling for the Palestinians to be put in cages – hadn't mentioned them, then they didn't happen, or as good as!

I believe that the victims of this massacre didn't tell its tales because these were etched into their souls and went with them everywhere throughout their lives of misery, and they could see no need to demonstrate the self-evident truth of what they had lived through. Furthermore, they wanted to forget them, and that is their right, for how is a person supposed to carry his corpse on his back while continuing to live an ordinary life?

(And I had forgotten. I lived my whole life by forgetting and I found my road by substituting another person for myself. I invented my shadow and lost its story, since everyone believed the shadow was the original. It never occurred to me that one day it would desert me; on the contrary, I was certain that, when the time came, it would be my shroud. And when I decided to withdraw from the battle after Dalia left me and I left my love of her, I came to New York to seek reclusion, my shadow at my side, between falafel patties and Waddah al-Yaman. I let lots of people think that I wasn't I – even Sarang Lee thought so – till my secret came out in front of her when the original and the shadow ran headlong into one another in the cinema and then together broke into splinters in the lobby of the Washington Square Hotel. I came in retreat, raising the white flag, and now I suddenly discover that the final battle awaits me here, that I have to enter it with equipment that I haven't mastered, and that my road to the road's end will be the restoration of the original through memory.)

The people left surrounded by screaming and terror. "Lydda leaves Lydda as the soul leaves the body" – this is how I see it through the eyes of Ghassan Batheish, who stood in front of the hospital as the column took on the form of a spate of people rushing through the bullets, the terror and the blood. The nurse, who hadn't dared leave the hospital to make sure his father and mother were alright, searched for his parents among the faces of the fugitives, which were obscured by the sound of bullets interspersed with moaning. Suddenly, he saw his mother's face bobbing among the others and he rushed forward, only to find himself in the midst of a maelstrom of lost people. The wave of humanity swallowed the face, which had appeared to him at a distance, his mother vanished among the throngs, and he decided to return to the hospital, but the pressure of the crowd was pushing him towards what seemed to be a slope. He stretched his arms out in front of him, like someone trying to swim, and fell to the ground, where he felt that he was suffocating and that feet were treading on him. He cried out for help, but his voice was lost among the other jostling voices and he began to sink into the stickiness of the blood that lay in pools on the asphalt. He saw a hand stretched out towards him, grasped it and raised his head above the waves, then fell back to the ground, discovering that he was sliding and that the blood was about to swallow him. He tried to stand but couldn't. He began crawling on his hands and knees. His eyes drowned in the sun spots that were reflected off the blood that had spread over the street and from which burst fiery red skewers. He wept. He fell on his left side and felt feet tread on his face. He fell into a deep slumber, then came to to find two hands holding on to his and trying to pull him up. He saw that he was standing once more in the middle of the current of screams blended with firing and started rowing with his arms in an attempt to move over the surface of the current of moans in the direction of the hospital.

Ghassan Batheish remembers only the river of people and the moaning rising from the stones of the places through which they passed. He didn't witness the massacre and would realise what had happened only when he was assigned to one of the teams collecting the corpses from the streets and houses. When he entered his house, on Wednesday, 21 July, 1948, he would discover that the face that had appeared to him amongst the throngs hadn't been that of his mother. Ghassan's mother had remained in the house and had disobeyed the invading army's orders to leave the city because she couldn't leave her disabled husband, who had suffered a stroke that had left him immobile. Ghassan hadn't thought of that fact and would say that he'd forgotten his father when he leaped into the midst of the human river and almost drowned beneath its feet. His mother wasn't among the throngs that were organised into the column of the lost, and what he'd seen was just his hopes, which would be dashed when he smelled the strange smell in the house. He stood there hesitating, as though lost, and refused at first to enter, but when the young men went in, Hatim al-Laqqis pulled him by the arm and he found himself inside. There he saw his mother, with no face. She was lying on the tiles, wrapped in her own remains. His father was lying on the bed, covered in his black blood.

The Maze

(1)

By the time three days had passed, the people of the ghetto had discovered they would have to get used to a new and strange way of life. Things started to take on a familiar form, and the sense of loss began to disappear in the face of the facts of the present. People recovered from their shock to find that this ghetto was now their home. The barbed wire that surrounded the place became a part of the scenery through which they became acquainted with the boundaries of their new city, which now consisted of a small fenced rectangle with a single gate guarded by three soldiers. The scene of young children being bathed by their mothers in front of the tank at the Great Mosque became the only source of relaxation, when laughter would ring out, accompanied by the shouts of the mothers.

Manal didn't know what the word "ghetto" meant or where it came from. All she knew was that the people of Lydda heard it from the Israeli soldiers, so they thought it meant "the Palestinian quarter", or "the quarter of the Arabs", to use the name employed by the Israelis to describe the country's original inhabitants. Only Ma'moun knew. He recounted that he'd explained the matter to Iliyya Batshoun, but the guy had laughed at him and thought he was being a smart alec.

"The ghetto is what they call the Jewish districts in Europe," said Ma'moun. "These idiots don't know that we don't have ghettoes in our towns and call the Jewish districts 'the Jewish Quarter', just like any other quarter of our cities, so it makes no sense."

"You're telling me we're Jews now?" Manal asked him naively. "Impossible. God forbid! We're Muslims."

"And Christians," added Iliyya.

"Listen, guys," said Ma'moun. "These people know nothing. They think they're in Europe. They've come and they've brought the ghetto with them so they can put us in it."

Nevertheless, even though everyone was convinced that Ma'moun knew what he was talking about because he had his matriculation certificate from Amiriya College in Jaffa, the general conviction among the fenced-in city's people continued to be that "the ghetto" meant the Arab Quarter and that as of now, following the forced migration of the majority of the city's inhabitants, they had become merely a small minority living in a closed ghetto that the Israelis had decided was to be the cage in which the Palestinians would have to get used to living.

And in fact, after leaving my mother's house in Haifa and going to live in Wadi al-Nisnas, I discovered that what had happened in Lydda had been generalised to all the Palestinian cities, and that the inhabitants of al-Ramla, Jaffa, Haifa and Acre had lived in closed ghettoes for a whole year before the Israeli army decided to remove the wire. That year fenced in by fear etched itself so deeply into the Palestinian consciousness, however, that the ghetto became the hallmark of an entire people. Similarly, while the cities were ghettoised by the closing off of the Arab districts, into which everyone had been corralled, the villages of Galilee and the Triangle were transformed into closed spaces under military rule, which was only lifted eighteen years after the foundation of the state and whose objective – in addition to humiliating and impoverishing – was to paralyse movement and prevent people from going from one place to another in search of work without the permission of the military governor. By these means, they were to submit to their new fate and be rendered incapable of resisting the confiscation of their lands, which continued uninterrupted.

When Dalia reproached me during the final phase of our relationship for having lied to her and everyone else when I'd said I came from the ghetto, and insisted on being introduced to my true self, I explained to her that I hadn't lied to anyone. I really was a son of the ghetto, and my claims to Polish origins and to being from Warsaw were no more than an appropriate metaphor to describe my childhood in Lydda, my youth in Haifa, and my life in Jaffa.

The ghetto at Lydda consisted of a small piece of land fenced with barbed wire in such a way that it looked like an unroofed cage. It was set up in the area extending from the Great Mosque to the Church of St George and from there to the hospital, and a census of its inhabitants would show five hundred and three individuals, of whom two hundred were in the mosque, one hundred in the church, and one hundred and fifty in the hospital, these being the wounded plus the doctors and nursing staff. A further fifty persons were in the small number of houses next to the church. Manal was lucky, because Ma'moun was the first to react, and he asked her to join him at the Kayyali house, which remained her home for the next seven years. The other houses were occupied haphazardly, and the committee's decisions on redistributing them according to the needs of the inhabitants and the number of family members made no difference. Such a distribution was impractical because the ghetto was composed not of whole families but of individuals whom fate had led to remain in one of the three places where people had gathered and where they stayed, because after the massacre the Israelis didn't know what to do with all those people, so the military governor decided to fence the place in while waiting to see what would happen next.

Food was available from the stores of the houses in which people took up residence, but it soon started to run out. The only source of water was the ablutions tank. The people, though, were incapable of adapting to the new geography of the place. Many refused to live in the houses that had been deserted by their owners and preferred to stay in the hospital, the church or the mosque. It's said that people thought that by moving into these houses they might lose their original homes, while Najib Nafia yelled that he rejected the option because the houses had owners, who would return to them. Despite the insistence of committee head Iliyya Batshoun that their residence there would be temporary, as he had been assured by the military governor, and not last more than a few weeks, after which everyone would go back to his own house, Najib Nafia wasn't persuaded. He decided to stay in the mosque, as did many others. The ghetto's inhabitants were thus divided between two categories: the first, to which my mother belonged, decided to move into the deserted houses, and the second stayed at the Great Mosque, the church and the hospital. In these places, families set up boundaries between each other using woollen blankets fetched from the deserted houses. When winter set in, however, the inhabitants became conscious of how cramped the place was and how impossible it would be to go on living like that. It was a cause of conflict within the ghetto that was solved only a whole year later, when it was decided to ease military rule over the city and remove the barbed wire.

What I know is that we stayed on in the house Ma'moun found for us: Manal enjoyed the distinction of being the wife of a martyr who had fallen defending the city and none of the committee members dared to compel her to take a second family in with her. It is also said, though God alone knows if it's true, that Khalid Hassouna had his eye on my mother and had made up his mind to marry her a week after Iliyya Batshoun got married. This would explain why he refused vehemently to let anyone touch the house where she was living and convinced the rest of the committee of his view, claiming that this should be regarded as a way of honouring the martyr Hasan Dannoun, who had fallen at the side of the hero Abu Ali Salama.

The only thing I know for sure is that Khalid Hassouna hated me – it's something I was aware of throughout my years in the ghetto – and that he blamed me for Ma'moun, whom he called "the lady's young man". Naturally, I understood nothing about such things then, but I avoided the guy and was careful not to cross his path. It was only in our shack in Haifa that I heard the story of his attempt to marry my mother: after a beating from her husband, I heard her crying and bewailing her wretched luck for having refused to marry the respectable man who'd asked for her hand so as to take care of her in a decent way and be her second husband, and how it had all ended up in the misery she was living through with her husband Abdallah.

The inhabitants of the ghetto awoke to the fact that they would have to look after themselves, because the military governor had informed them that the state wasn't responsible for them, that they would have to make provision for food, water and medicines on their own, and that he wasn't prepared to listen to any more complaints on that score.

It was at this moment that the ghetto's first miracle occurred. The people decided to ransack the houses and search for food stocks. The head of the committee asked permission from Captain Moshe for the inhabitants to leave the ghetto for the old city and fetch provisions because he knew people had stocked up in preparation for the war. The captain hesitated and said he couldn't, because his orders said that the army wasn't responsible for feeding the inhabitants.

"I can't," Moshe said.

"What do you mean you can't?" Iliyya Batshoun said. "The people are hungry and soon they'll be eating each other. I can't control the situation."

"Okay, okay! Wait till tomorrow," Moshe said.

The morning of the next day, Iliyya Batshoun received the same answer. He then started shouting and seemed to forget he was a prisoner, and his pride came back to him, so he started to make threats. As soon as people saw the head of the committee raise his hand menacingly, they gathered in front of the gate to the ghetto and their voices began to rise. Moshe retreated and fired a shot from his pistol into the air. He also said that he'd allow four young men to leave to search for provisions – in the houses of the old city only and on condition that they wear Red Cross signs and that he wasn't responsible for their safety.

Ma'moun was the first to volunteer.

Khalid Hassouna told him off: "You're blind, boy. Go back!"

"I'm not a boy and you have no right to talk to me like that," Ma'moun answered in a loud voice. "Furthermore, I am not blind, I am bereft of sight, and go I shall," he continued, in literary Arabic.

Iliyya Batshoun intervened, mollified Ma'moun, and asked Ghassan Batheish to lead a group made up of four nurses, who appeared with a stretcher that they could fill with food.

The team's first accomplishment, in addition to the discovery of large quantities of stored provisions, was to come across eight old men and women who'd hidden themselves in their houses during the invasion of the city and stayed there, terrified and alone. These accompanied the team back to the ghetto, looking like a group of lost children who could no longer talk.

The provisions arrived and a haphazard distribution started, people taking whatever they wished. Things could not, however, go on like that. The provisions consisted of lentils, cracked wheat, chickpeas, oil, flour, sugar, tea and soap, so it was decided they should be put in a storeroom, and the room next to the church, which was originally where Deacon Niqoula, who had left with everyone else, had lived, was chosen, and Ibrahim Hamza was appointed as its keeper, to be responsible for the fair distribution of the provisions to everyone. Enforcing this decision wasn't easy at first. Fear of hunger drove people to hoard provisions in their houses or hide them under blankets close to where their bedding was placed on the ground. However, the abundance of food, and especially of chickpeas, oil, flour and cracked wheat, convinced everyone that there was no point in storing provisions individually.

Ibrahim Hamza formed three ladies' committees. The first was headed by Fatma, wife of the baker Jamil Salama, and its job was to make bread. There were also two cooking committees, one based at the hospital, supervised by Samira, wife of the priest Toma Niama, whose task was to make food for those living in the hospital and the church, and the other at the mosque, under the supervision of Khadija, wife of Khalid Hassouna, which was responsible for making food for those living in the mosque and the houses. As a result, the ghetto began to give an impression of cooperative labour, leading Shmarya Guttman, the city's military governor, to state to an Israeli newspaper that the Arab people of Lydda had "discovered today the benefits of cooperative life in the State of Israel".

In fact, however, the atmosphere of social solidarity and the healing of wounds quickly evaporated as collective life began to dissolve in the face of hardship and the impossibility of finding work or being able to move from one place to another. The ghetto thus came to resemble a prison yard, open to the sky, where people lived in idleness and fear.

How am I to tell a story that appears to me, today, like nothing so much as a tangled skein? And where should I start? With the water, or with the collecting of the city's corpses? With Iliyya Batshoun's marriage, or with his son Iskandar's visit to the ghetto to announce, before all, that he disowned his father?

How, too, am I to tell the story of Crazy Karim, or the cow that Hatim al-Laqqis came across? And who will believe the joy when four cows were discovered in the cemetery?

I'm at a loss because I'm incapable of understanding how the people were able to extract from death and despair the capacity to invent a life out of the putridity in the midst of which they lived. What is this amazing power that makes humankind able to adapt to death, and even live inside death itself?

I might say it's the instinctive will to live, for life resists death to the end, but I feel, writing these words, that what we call the will to live is just another name for people's capacity for infinite savagery. The killer is rendered savage by his thirst for blood, the victim by his refusal to die under any circumstances. The Israeli soldiers who guarded the ghetto's inhabitants were merciless – so said the Friday preacher at the assembly that took place in the square in front of the Great Mosque on Friday, 25 July. A little before twelve noon, the people had heard the voice of the muezzin rising from the minaret; it was the first time anyone had dared to climb it. "God is great!" rang out, and tears started to course over the faces of the men, who stood in amazement in the court-yard of the mosque, unable to believe their ears. At that instant, the people beheld God's hand in the form of a large cloud that blocked the sun's rays and brought with it a cool, refreshing breeze, and they smelled incense.

"It's the hand of God!" cried Sheikh Bilal, the preacher, from the top of the minaret.

The people didn't pray that day. They stood dumbfounded beneath the cloud that shaded the courtyard, eyes raised. Silence spread.

Once more the voice of the sheikh rose, and he said that God had commanded humankind to be merciful and show human feeling for one another. His voice was hoarse, as though he were both speaking and not speaking. He said, "Expect mercy from none but the Lord of the Worlds."

The sheikh fell silent. He was eighty and during the invasion of the city had fled to one of the citrus groves. Then, when the young men brought him back, he'd taken up residence in the mosque with a circle of his disciples and never again left it, living in the midst of the throngs of refugees who filled the place. He had tried to urge people to pray, but no-one had listened to him amidst the chaos of dying that had overtaken the city. Now, today, the sheikh had returned to his minaret, after first lighting incense and asking people to grasp hold of the ropes of God, because all other ropes had been cut and had failed them.

The people were silent under God's cloud, but they didn't pray, and when my mother told me the events of that day she said that prayer needed hope: "But we had lost all hope."

She said all the inhabitants of the ghetto – men, women, chil-dren and old people – gathered in the courtyard of the mosque.

Even the priest, Toma Niama, came out of his room, which abutted the church, and came running to the courtyard.

Iliyya Batshoun said that when he heard the sound of the call to prayer, he thought some disaster must have befallen them, so he came running and found himself in the midst of the silence of the cloud that cast its shade over all.

The sheikh had descended from the minaret and the crowd had begun to fidget, preparatory to dispersing, when Khadija's voice rang out. "O God! O God!" the woman cried, in a voice full of lamentation. "We want water, O God!"

Khadija had good reason for her entreaty: the ablutions tank had run dry after two days of use because it was the sole source of water, and all that was left was the well belonging to the hospital, whose water was polluted and gave off a foul smell. When Moshe informed the head of the committee that he was not responsible for ensuring a supply of water for the people and they would have to fend for themselves, Dr Zahlan suggested extracting the remaining brackish waters from the bottom of the well in the hospital's back courtyard and boiling it and using it only for drinking.

This solution, to which the people grudgingly agreed, proved to be unworkable, however. The water was green, as though full of verdigris, and even boiling it several times failed to get rid of the foul smell.

"We're dying of thirst!" Khadija cried. "And we'll soon die of hunger too because we're too weak to make bread."

The muttering of the crowd began to rise in a stifled cry. Khadija walked straight towards the wire and everyone joined her. The brown-complexioned, fifty-year-old woman, who used to cover her head with a black shawl, put her hands on the wire and started to shake it. Hatim al-Laqqis came forward and stood at her side and started shaking the wire too and shouting, "Shake the wire!" Suddenly, everyone was in front of the wire, rattling it violently, as though they meant to pull it free. At that instant, Captain Moshe appeared, and, standing behind him, a tall, bald man with a bandaged head. Moshe raised his rifle and silence fell.

Iliyya Batshoun and the other members of the committee advanced towards the wire and the people heard Iliyya say, "We're dying of thirst, mister."

One of the soldiers went up to the gate in the fence, opened it, let the committee members out for a meeting with Moshe, and told the crowd to disperse.

"We're not budging from here!" Manal cried. "We have babies. Our babies are drying up. Look at my son, everyone! His body's like a stick. What am I to give him to drink?"

Manal said, when she told the story of the thirst, that tears don't satisfy thirst. "If only tears could quench the thirsty!"

(3)

Hatim al-Laqqis said that the water gushing from the well was the most beautiful thing he'd ever seen.

Hatim, the Lost Lebanese, as Iliyya Batshoun called him, was the first volunteer to go with a group of the young men to look for water in the nearby citrus grove. The youth, who had worked from the age of nine as a newspaper vendor in Haifa, then switched to working as a mechanic in a garage before fleeing Haifa for Jaffa following a disagreement with his father when the latter decided to go back to his village in southern Lebanon, and who found himself alone in Lydda and trapped in the ghetto, came up with the idea that solved the water problem.

No-one knows how the stocky young man managed to slip through the gate of the ghetto, which had been opened, to find himself attending the meeting between the committee and Moshe, the Israeli officer.

The meeting began with threats. Moshe said he wouldn't allow such goings-on. Gathering in front of the wire and shouting would meet with one response, which was bullets.

"But we're thirsty, mister," Hatim said.

Iliyya Batshoun now suddenly became aware of the presence of the young man at the meeting. He looked at him angrily, but the youth put his finger to his lips to ask the head of the committee not to say anything.

Hatim said the children would die of thirst and that the

committee held the Israeli army responsible for the lack of water in the ghetto.

"We're asking for something very simple, mister," he said. "We want water."

Captain Moshe said that from day one he'd told the committee he was not responsible for them and they'd have to fend for themselves. "I told you, sort things out yourselves!" Moshe said in an Iraqi accent, after which he started gabbling in Hebrew.

"We're pleading with you, mister," Khalid Hassouna said.

"The water in the hospital well is almost used up and it's not fit even for animals," Ghassan Batheish said.

"We're dying!" Hajj Iliyya shouted.

"I don't have any water," Moshe said. "The city pipes have burst and I'm bringing water in for my soldiers from Ben Shemen."

"What do you want us to do?" Khalid Hassouna asked.

"I don't know," the officer replied.

"I know," said Hatim, and told them he'd found a solution to the water problem and was ready to supply the Israeli army too with sweet water on condition that . . .

"You're setting conditions?!" the officer asked.

"Shut up, boy!" Iliyya Batshoun said.

Instead of shutting up, Hatim explained his plan. He said he used to work in the Jaffa groves installing electric pumps for the artesian wells. The solution was to send a group of young men from the ghetto to search the groves, at which point the problem would be solved – "and you can send your soldiers with us, mister, to fill up with water for themselves."

"No-one's allowed to leave!" Moshe said. "Those are my orders."

Ghassan Batheish told Ma'moun, as they bathed in front of the well in the orange grove, that he'd felt the Israeli officer's embarrassment. "I swear he didn't know what to do with us. He hesitated and all the time his hand was on his cap, as though he was going to scratch his head, and his eyes wouldn't stay still. I don't know what had got into him."

Silence reigned over the meeting, as though a sentence of execution had just been issued. "We're thirsty because we were driven out of the city," Iliyya said. "Where are we supposed to go, mister? Our families got lost at Naalin and slept in the open country and we're not leaving here. You want us to die, we don't want to die. What the lad Hatim said is how it's going to be, tomorrow, at dawn. Everyone is going to leave for the groves and search for water and that way we can die from bullets and not from thirst."

Iliyya Batshoun stood, announcing that he was leaving, and so did all the members of the committee, but Hatim remained seated. "Get up, son!" Khalid Hassouna said.

"No-one leaves," Moshe said, and he asked everyone to wait for him for quarter of an hour.

Moshe left the hall and the committee members remained huddled where they were. Hatim now said that Ibrahim al-Nimr's grove was no more than eight hundred metres from the mosque and had a well and a pump, and that was the only solution.

When the Israeli captain returned, Ghassan Batheish told him they'd found a way out of the difficulty: "Ibrahim al-Nimr's grove is the solution."

The Israeli captain announced his agreement to the plan but wouldn't take responsibility for the security of the young men who went to fetch the water.

"Tomorrow morning," the Israeli officer said, as he ordered everyone back to the ghetto.

No-one slept that night. The young men discovered eleven empty barrels that had been used to store petrol and decided that in the morning they would take them to the grove and clean them. Thus, at 6 a.m., eleven young men assembled, Ghassan Batheish and Hatim al-Laqqis at their head, at the gate of the ghetto, barrels ready, awaiting zero hour. The gate didn't open, however, until ten. As soon as the long wait ended, the young men burst out, rolling their barrels, and Ibrahim al-Nimr led them to his grove. They were accompanied by a squad of four Israeli soldiers.

Oranges and lemons covered the grove. Fruit, some rotten, some shrivelled and wrinkled, carpeted ground that was covered with thorns. Ibrahim bent over and picked up an orange. He cut it in two with his knife and squeezed it into his mouth, the juice, gilded by the sun, dripping onto his beard and neck, the smell spreading everywhere. "These, the *shammouti*, are the best oranges in the world. God keep us, see how thin the peel is and how the fruit forms a cup overflowing with juice!"

He took a lemon, squeezed it into his mouth, and said, licking at the golden juice around his mouth, "Go ahead, boys! Help yourselves! Welcome to my grove!" Then he looked at the Israeli soldiers and invited them to pick the fruit.

As hands reached out to pick the lemons and oranges that nobody had harvested because of the fighting and the war, the young men heard the voice of one of the Israeli soldiers, who had aimed his rifle at them, ordering them to stop.

"It's my grove," Ibrahim said, "and everyone's invited, including you."

"It's forbidden," the soldier said. "This is state property."

"What state?" Ibrahim asked.

"Shut up, man!" Ghassan Batheish said. "We've come for the

337

water, not for lousy dried-out rotten oranges. Take us to the well, for heaven's sake."

Ibrahim seemed incredulous at what was happening. He began gathering oranges and lemons and making them into heaps. "The lemons are better, I don't know why, but a lemon can go for a whole year without anything happening to it."

A soldier approached and kicked over the yellow- and orange-coloured heaps that Ibrahim had collected, and said it was forbidden. "All land is now state land," he said, and ordered the group of young men back to their places.

At that moment, Hatim al-Laqqis shouted that he'd found the pump. Everyone, including Ibrahim, forgot about the lemons and they rushed towards the well, only to discover that the pump didn't work. Hatim tried in vain to fix it but said it was no use, because some parts had been stolen, which meant there was no hope of repairing it.

The young men returned with their barrels, carrying their disappointment to the inhabitants of the ghetto. Iliyya Batshoun, however, did not despair. He stood at the iron gate, asked to see the Israeli captain again, and told him the solution was to allow Hatim and two or three other young men to go to the groves that were scattered around the city and look for spare parts so that they could make the pump work.

And that is what happened. At 6 a.m. the following day, and in accordance with an agreement made with Captain Moshe, Hatim put on first-aid clothing and left with two young men on his personal responsibility, to look for a working pump from which they could take the missing parts. The captain said he wouldn't send soldiers with the group because the area was still unsafe and he wasn't obliged to expose his soldiers' lives to danger.

Hatim returned at 8 a.m., his clothes soaked, to tell everyone that the problem had been solved and they should take the barrels to the grove.

Ma'moun, who insisted on going with the young men, said he'd beheld the beauty of water. "Dear God, the most beautiful thing in the world is water, especially when it bursts out of the ground. It's amazing. It explodes in front of one's eyes like laughter and it flows and everything starts dancing."

"We have to clean the barrels first!" Ghassan Batheish shouted.

The young men though had been struck by water madness and the moment the pump began working and the water burst forth, they started leaping about around the pump, drenching one another, drinking, bathing, washing their clothes and laughing. The water even seemed to cast its spell over the four soldiers who accompanied the group and two of them began playing in the water with the young men, and the games only stopped when the sound of a bullet, fired into the air from the rifle of the corporal in charge, was heard and he ordered everyone to get back to work.

Cleaning out the barrels was hard. Getting rid of the smell of the petrol required large quantities of soap and water, and Hatim, Ghassan and the others had to take off their shirts to clean the barrels from the inside. In the end, they were filled with drinking water but before the young men could begin rolling them towards the ghetto, they saw Ibrahim rolling his barrel in front of him with a large jute sack that he'd filled with lemons and oranges on his back.

"What's that?" yelled the soldier.

"It's . . . it's from my grove," Ibrahim stammered.

"Throw everything on the ground and get going!"

However, the bald, fifty-year-old man, his lips glistening

orange, refused to throw away the contents of his sack.

"This is my land and my fathers' land, and this is my grove."

The soldier ordered everyone to stop and offered him a choice between the oranges and the water. "Throw them away!" the soldier yelled. "Either you throw away what's in the sack or there's no water."

"Throw them away and let us get on with it!" yelled Hatim.

But the man sat down on the ground, his sack in front of him, and put his head between his hands. His body began to shake.

Ghassan Batheish approached the sack and pulled it to one side. "It's okay, mister. Let's go now."

The soldier motioned with his rifle and the barrels began to roll but Ibrahim remained seated where he was.

"Go!" the soldier yelled.

The guy rested his weight on his hands in an attempt to get up, but fell to the ground and started to crawl towards the sack.

The soldier went up to the sack and kicked it; the oranges rolled out, and he trod on them. Some exploded beneath his feet but others – the ones whose peel had turned hard – remained resistant and the young men watched Ibrahim as he grabbed the hardened oranges that slipped out from beneath the soldier's feet and put them down the front of his shirt.

Manal said the arrival of the full barrels was like a wedding. "Everyone was in a state of delirious joy, except for Ibrahim, who went off to one side, cut an orange in two, looked at it, and asked me to come close, with Adam. He took an orange and squeezed it into your mouth, and that was the first drop of orange juice to enter your belly. He gave me all the oranges and told me, 'Take them for the boy who has no father,' and went into the mosque."

Three months after this incident, when the olive-harvesting

season began and the head of the committee tried to get permission from the Israelis to allow the owners of the olive groves to pick their harvest, the people of the ghetto realised what it meant when they said that the land had become the property of the state.

The city's military governor, Shmarya Guttman, whom Iliyya Batshoun and Khalid Hassouna met to ask to facilitate the people's going out of the ghetto to pick the olives, explained that the city's lands were now in the custody of the state because they'd been entered in the list of absentee properties.

"What absentees?" Khalid asked. "There are four men in the ghetto who have lands planted with olives and here we are, present, and all we want is permission to get to our land."

"Out of the question!" the military governor said. "You are, legally speaking, absent."

"You mean we're not here?" Iliyya asked.

"Exactly!"

"But we are here! You mean we've turned into ghosts?" Khalid Hassouna responded.

"Like you're ghosts," the military governor answered. "I believe you are going to be called, legally speaking, 'present absentees'."

"I don't understand," said Iliyya.

"Neither do I," the military governor said, "but that's the law, and you are forbidden to go to the fields and pick the olives."

"We can pick them and give them to you, but the olives can't be allowed to remain on the tree," said Iliyya.

"That's none of your business. The state knows how to take care of its property.'

(4)

After food and water came fear – a fear that traced itself on the walls of silence. The city, which, in the three months before it fell, had lived in the midst of the tumult of the refugees from nearby villages and the sounds of the battles raging on all sides, sank, all of a sudden, into the silence of desolation. During the first days of their residence in that small wire-fenced area, the ghetto dwellers failed to notice how heavily that silence weighed. However, once the celebrations – punctuated by staccato ululations – of the water barrels and the bringing in of food in sufficient quantities from the houses of the old city were over, the people awoke to the terrifying silence that enveloped their city, now that it had been emptied of its inhabitants. The people's fear took root in the sounds of silence that occupied the ghetto's long nights and days, and they were terrified. They began to talk as though whispering.

It is impossible for me to describe the life of the city without using the term "whispers of silence". Even the crying of babes-in-arms was transformed into a low moaning. I say babes-in-arms but I'm thinking of one specific baby, named Adam Dannoun. All the same, as I weave the memory of silence from my mother's words, I feel that the baby I was then wasn't alone. On the contrary, he was all the children of the world and those children had been struck dumb and forced to live and die in silence.

I didn't die. My mother told me that I'd been on the verge of death because I hadn't tasted milk for two weeks – the period from the fall of the city to the discovery of Abu Hasan's cow.

She said that discovering clean water and bringing it back from Ibrahim al-Nimr's citrus grove had saved my life; my body had gone dry and my crying was without tears. I had closed my eyes and entered the night of death, and when the water came and she sprinkled it on my face and gave me the juice of an orange and lentil water to drink, I opened my eyes and cried.

I didn't ask why she hadn't suckled me. The question didn't occur to me and I took it on trust when my mother told me that the ghetto had drained eyes of tears and breasts of milk.

The water was the first joyful moment after the days of fear and loss that followed the fall of the city and the fencing in of the ghetto. With the chuckling of the water in the rolling barrels, the people of the ghetto felt that in spite of everything that had happened, life had begun to flow again. They wiped their eyes with the water and saw they were still alive. At a meeting of the ghetto committee, Hajj Iliyya Batshoun wept as he said that the decision to allow the young men to fetch the water meant that "we will be staying where we are and not driven like cattle into the wilderness" that had swallowed the inhabitants of Lydda when they were driven with bullets from their city.

"When the young men saw the explosion of water," Ghassan Batheish said, "they went mad." Hatim al-Laqqis took off his clothes, knelt in front of the pump, and began writhing around under the cold, gushing water. He took a stone and scraped his body, emitting gasps that stirred in everyone the shuddering thrill of the encounter with water. Instead of cleaning the barrels, they rushed to strip off their clothes and began issuing mysterious noises from between their clenched teeth, as though they'd lost the faculty of speech.

Two Israeli soldiers threw themselves under the water fully

dressed in their khakis, as though they too had fallen under the water's spell.

"Drink!" yelled Ma'moun. "It's the best-tasting water in the world!"

Two bullets were fired into the air. The Israeli soldiers withdrew from the Lyddan baptismal celebration and silence reigned.

"Quickly! Quickly!" Corporal Naftali shouted at the half-naked Palestinians.

"Quickly, lads!" Ghassan Batheish said.

And the cleaning of the barrels began.

"Enough!" yelled the Israeli corporal, who ordered the young men to fill the barrels.

Then they started the rolling of the barrels, which proved to be exhausting. The distance separating the grove from the ghetto was no more than eight hundred metres, but it was an uneven earth track, full of stones. When the young men reached the ghetto, their naked chests were covered with sweat, and they felt the need to bathe again.

The barrels were placed at the three places of assembly – the mosque, the church and the hospital – and the people formed lines to the water, and drank and filled their containers.

Ma'moun was heard to shout that the barrel that had been placed in front of the church bell rope was for children only.

The people of the ghetto lived this way for an entire year. The young men would rise at 6 a.m., fill the barrels and roll them back, and at 5 p.m. they'd take the barrels back to the grove to fill them again.

There, in the water grove (as the people called Ibrahim al-Nimr's citrus plantation), they would rub their bodies with herbs and wash off the city's smell.

(5)

When did the smell go away? Or did it not disappear and the people just got used to it?

"People are dogs, son, they'll get used to anything," said the elderly man who'd been hiding out in the garden of his house when he heard the voices of the young men speaking Arabic and pushed himself over the ground towards them, supporting himself in a sitting position, using his arms.

"Get up, old fellow," Isam al-Kayyali said.

"I can't, son," said the old man, who was called Ahmad Hijazi, and when Isam took him by the arm in an attempt to get him upright, he heard him moan and whisper, "Mother!" but he couldn't stand.

The man wept, his cry of "Mother!" ringing hoarsely in his voice, and lost his ability to move.

The young men put him onto the first-aid stretcher which they used to transport the corpses and brought him to the mosque.

Isam told the members of the committee how they'd come across the man hiding underneath a sweet acacia tree, living off weeds he collected from the land and drinking dirty water that had collected in a small basin in the garden. The young man burst into a hysterical laugh as he recounted how the elderly man had called out for his mother, like a small child.

"Come on now! Could he really have thought he was still a child? Damn it, who clings on to life like that? It's ridiculous! I swear I couldn't believe it."

Dr Zahlan, who was making an inspection at the mosque, rebuked the youth and told him to be quiet. "We're all children, son. One is born a child and dies a child."

(Going over Dr Zahlan's words now, I feel terror. I write about a collective disaster only to discover in the end that what I'm doing now, which is restoring a memory that cannot be restored, is preparing to meet my second childhood here in my old age. My first childhood appears as though drowned in the fog of memory. Despite all the tragedies surrounding it, I feel tender towards it, as though the fog has served to veil its bitterness. The fog of memory veils pain, no matter how serious it may have been. But this second childhood, at whose threshold I have now arrived, has been aged by grief, makes the pain evident, and leaves me to face death alone. It seems that true death cannot be collective even if it occurs in the middle of a massacre. Every death is a unique event, and it may be that death's most eloquent statement is that its protagonists cannot recount it. I do not write of collective death in Lydda in order to gloss over individual pain: I ought to write each separate death as a particular experience, which is why, to be true to my project, I should write a book that has no end, each name that occurs in it forming a complete story with its many details, which is something neither I nor anyone before me has known how to do. That is why the prophets chose to write wise sayings and proverbs and why men of letters have ended up claiming to be prophets who write about others. Not me though. I, in all modesty, am writing my own story, and all these stories that I am recalling are my mirrors – and woe betide me, for my mirrors begin and end with death!)

I don't know the name of my biological mother. I'll call her Rawd so I can tell my Yemeni poet that even though I've abandoned the attempt to tell his tale as a metaphor, I've still taken him as a friend and a comrade. I won't allow the story of this woman to be merely a line in Ma'moun's narrative about a child moaning on the breast of a woman who looked as though she were sleeping. Ma'moun didn't pay the woman enough attention to be able to describe her to me, but I've decided she looked like Dalia, with her translucent duskiness, her thick eyebrows, her large, honey-coloured eyes, and her lips pursed like a rose. And now, as I write these words, I see myself as a child with pus-filled, half-closed eyes and small hands clasped about her long neck, whose crying she is the only one to hear. My real mother is a woman of stories, who vanishes into words, and my childhood, which began on her dry breast, will lead me to a death resembling hers. My mother Rawd died alone, a stranger surrounded by the throngs and the clamour of the displaced, while I shall die here, alone, a stranger in the midst of the clamour of this extraordinarily beautiful city that has decided to expel me from the circle of those who deserve to live.

I have, I swear, no desire to disparage New York: it is a home for those who have no home. But I feel the loneliness of longing. Only those who yearn can understand how longing splits their souls in two and casts them into loneliness.

I long for her so much I could cry out "Mother!" like Ahmad Hijazi when he saw the young men and understood that he was powerless and alone. I want to cry out "Mother!" so that I can die, my mouth filled with the taste of the juice of the oranges that Ibrahim al-Nimr gave me to drink when he returned from the water grove.

Ahmad Hijazi, who was sixty-eight years old, recounted how everyone fled and he'd found himself alone in the house. He said they'd forgotten about him in the terrified stampede.

347

"I heard shouting. I was sitting alone in the garden, picking up the sweet acacia blossoms that had fallen on the ground. Of course I was scared. I was scared because I couldn't understand what was going on around me. My blood seemed to have frozen in my veins, so I stayed put and listened to the ruckus and the noise. Israeli soldiers must have entered the house. I knew that from the wailing of Hasaniya, my son Maarouf's wife. I heard her crying, 'I beg you, mister!' I don't know what happened exactly but I heard a shot and the sound of running feet and then everything went quiet. Somebody in the house must surely have been hurt, because when I went in I saw the tiles were covered with red spots, but I couldn't find anyone. I sat down alone not knowing what I was supposed to do. My sons had forgotten they had a father and had run away with everyone else and I was here, with sounds of firing starting and stopping around me, and fear. I was afraid to stay on my own in the house and afraid to go out onto the street, so I went back to the garden and lived on my own."

Isam al-Kayyali said the elderly man was like a skeleton because he weighed nothing, and he rocked back and forth on the stretcher, moaning quietly.

At the mosque, he sat next to a pillar and spoke to no-one. At first, he refused to eat, claiming, when they brought him a plate of *mjaddara*, that he wasn't hungry. He dozed off for a few minutes, then he opened his eyes and quickly devoured the plate of food before curling up and going to sleep again.

In this first month of life in the ghetto, there was a corner in the mosque that the young people called "the old folk's corner", where there were three men and five women. Ahmad Hijazi was the youngest of them, and the guy, who recovered his strength within a few days, started behaving as though he was the only competent person in the group. He would negotiate on their behalf and take care to see that they were ensured enough food and water. Umm Fawwaz, who was eighty-eight, had the role of both mother and child. Those living in the old folk's corner called her Mama but this mother was as naughty as a little girl. Her senility had no impact on how energetic she was – a woman tall and slim, who, despite the slight stoop to her shoulders, walked with her back straight, got up early, prepared breakfast for her new family, and spent most of her time singing, weeping and wailing. No-one knew anything about her family because the only thing she could remember was her name, which was Umm Fawwaz, and when they asked her about her son Fawwaz, she would look into the distance and shrug as though she didn't care.

The young men had picked the group of old people up one by one from the roofs of houses or the gardens where they were hiding, and when Khalid Hassouna tried to question them about their families in order to fill in the Red Cross forms so that a search could be made for their families preparatory to their joining them, they all refused to cooperate. Ahmad Hijazi said he'd decided to stay in the city because it was their city and none of them would ever leave the motherland to become refugees.

When Ahmad had finished his patriotic speech, Munib al-Shayib, who was eighty years old and semi-paralysed, spat and yelled, "Screw the motherland and screw this life! Screw the children who leave their parents behind like dogs! No, I swear to God I don't want anything – not the motherland, not Palestine, not children, and not all this shitty food!"

The stupefaction that accompanied the first two days of the "ghet-toisation" of the population and their corralling into a narrow, barbed-wire-enclosed space quickly dissipated in the maelstrom of the shift to forced work that Captain Moshe imposed on the ghetto's young men and boys.

At 10 a.m. on Friday, 16 July, Moshe arrived at the mosque courtyard, fired three shots from his revolver, took the loudspeaker in his hand, and ordered all men and youths over the age of fifteen to assemble.

Moshe announced that five teams were to be formed to clean the city, each consisting of five persons. Two of the soldiers standing in the yard advanced and picked out the twenty-five youngest men and divided them into groups. The captain ordered all the other men to leave except for the head of the local commit-tee, Iliyya Batshoun, because he was to be held accountable for the youths' good conduct; he made it clear that any shortcomings in their performance of the work would have dire consequences.

The people understood that "dire consequences" meant they would be expelled from the city, and they made up their minds to remain. I, today, feel the same bemusement that the Israeli troops must have felt when faced with the mass of the ghetto's inhabit-ants. Why did they stay? Suppose they stayed by accident when they found themselves in the square formed by the Great Mosque and the church, which Israeli troops hadn't approached following the appalling massacre they had carried out at the Dahmash Mosque. All the same, why did they insist on turning the accident of their presence into a matter of life or death? In fact, those who left voluntarily following the establishment of the ghetto were a minority whose number could be counted on the fingers of one hand, while those who came to the ghetto after its establishment amounted to around a hundred, some being brought from houses where they'd been hiding, others coming from caves in the neighbouring villages, and some – the smallest number – sneaking in across the new border. They came to live the life of the ghetto and of exile within their own city. They preferred to stay there; indeed, they actually chose that particular "here", as though the homing instinct was stronger than any fears or the harsh conditions of life.

(Why would a person volunteer to live under the shadow of the ghetto, which would accompany successive generations of Palestinians from the first establishment of the Hebrew state? I confess I have no idea. Even after the move my mother and I made, following her marriage, to Haifa, where I discovered the stories of the dozens of infiltrators who had returned, at peril to their lives from the bullets of the Israeli border guards, I confess I still don't know! And when Ma'moun alluded in his lecture at New York University to the story of the clandestine return from Lebanon of the family of the poet Mahmoud Darwish to the village of al-Birwa, which had been demolished and bulldozed – a return that I regard as indicative of the instinct to stay put that may be observed in both groups and individuals – I sensed the absurdity of everything, and the impotence of language to express.)

The Israeli officer informed the people of the ghetto that work would commence on the morning of Sunday, 18 July. "Tomorrow's Saturday. The day of rest in this country is now Saturday. No-one may work. Work begins on Sunday morning. You will hear three gunshots at 6 a.m. The teams have to be ready then, and soldiers will go with you to begin the clean-up of the city." In a quiet, monotonous voice, the officer explained the tasks of the different teams and said that two armed soldiers would accompany each. He defined the work as falling into three categories: removing bodies from the streets and houses and burying them (two teams); collecting foodstuffs from the city's shops (one team); clearing the streets of barricades, stones and earth (one team). The fifth team would have the task of cleaning the Israeli military command headquarters which it had been decided was to be in the houses of Hasan Dahmash – a large house surrounded by a spacious garden – and Said al-Huneidi, opposite.

With the start of work, the people of the ghetto ran headlong into the truth of what had happened. The first days had been like a dream. Even the killing of the sparrow boy and his funeral had taken on, in the memory of the people, the shape of a phantom of vague features.

"Then, suddenly, we discovered we were living in a cemetery," said Ghassan Batheish on the return of his group from the fields of death that overlay the city's streets.

Ma'moun never spoke to me of those days. He abandoned me when I was seven and left the country never to return. Why did he tell me when we met in New York that he'd told me all the stories before he left and had hidden nothing from me except for the detail of how he'd come across me, which he'd left to my mother to tell me in her own way, as she'd promised she would? Was it because of that promise that my mother Manal seemed confused the night I left, when all she did was give me the will, hold back her tears, as usual, and whisper a few barely comprehensible words?

I don't remember Ma'moun telling me anything. Or at least, I do remember him telling me how Ghassan Batheish had come upon his mother and his crippled father dead in their house. I think – if memory doesn't play me false—that I'd returned to the house from the school the Israelis had opened after Ma'moun's was closed. I was sad and said, "I want my father!" and I cried. I don't remember exactly what had happened: probably one of my fellow pupils had said, "Poor guy! He's an orphan. His father's dead." That was the day that Ma'moun told me about my father's heroic exploits and his martyrdom and that the fate of Hasan Dannoun had been better than that of those whose bodies had been left to rot under the July sun in the city's streets because he'd been wrapped in a shroud and buried as a person should be buried. He also told me the story of Ghassan, who still to that day had nightmares because he'd come upon his parents, bloated with death, in his own home. The story etched itself into my consciousness and death for me thereafter was a swelling that afflicted the body. That day I was very afraid and asked my mother if I too was going to die. She answered me that everyone died in the end.

"Including me?" I asked her.

"For sure, son, but it's still early. You're still young."

"You mean children die too?" I asked.

"I don't know, son, but you aren't going to die. I'm with you. Don't be afraid."

But I was afraid. I remember that when I was six, I announced that I was Lord of the Wind. My favourite game at home was exercising my power over nature. It would rain because I had ordered it to rain. The sun rose because I had ordered it to rise. And my mother believed me, or at least pretended to. When I played Lord of the Wind with my comrades at school, they made fun of me, but that in no way shook my conviction that I could ride the wind and move the clouds however I wished. And I convinced myself that the Lord of the Wind did not die.

Ma'moun claimed to have told me everything. Maybe he meant he'd told Manal, I don't know! But, here in New York, when I read the few pages in Isbir Munayyir's book about Lydda in which he briefly describes the removal of the corpses by the teams the Israelis formed from the young men of the city, I sensed that some memory within me had awoken from a deep slumber, I know not how! Are these scenes that I see now before my eyes the sum of what Manal told me about the days of the ghetto when we were living in Haifa after her marriage? I don't know, but I can recount the entire story, with all its details – which today have become a tattoo drawn with the ink of memory – to any who want to hear. And I shall tell it, mercilessly. Who am I to be merciful to the victims? And what does mercy mean when the entirety of human history is fashioned out of cruelty and savagery?

At six in the morning of Sunday, 18 July, the inhabitants of the ghetto heard three shots fired, and in less than five minutes the five teams had assembled in the yard of the mosque, accompanied by Iliyya Batshoun and Khalid Hassouna. Before they set off, Iliyya Batshoun proposed to the Israeli officer that work should begin at seven, because about half the young men took part with other inhabitants of the ghetto in filling the water barrels at six. Captain Moshe, however, did not take the question seriously; he raised his eyebrows and said no. Then, at a wave from his hand, the groups went off to their jobs, while Batshoun and Hassouna returned to the home of the head of the committee to discuss how to reorganise the morning barrel teams.

Work in the group charged with appropriating foodstuffs

from the shops was easy. Ahmad al-Zaghloul, who led this group, recounted how he'd gone with his comrades and two armed Israeli soldiers to the beginning of the street, where Israeli lorries were waiting for them, and that he'd been amazed at the quantity of foodstuffs the city's shopkeepers had stored away in expectation of war.

"Tinned goods of every kind and grains and oil, and we were dying of hunger and had to load the Israeli lorries, which were headed for Tel Aviv. At the same time, we were forbidden to take anything because the eyes of the Jewish soldiers were trained on us and the Israeli soldier said we couldn't take even a piece of straw, or else . . ."

Ahmad al-Zaghloul's statement was inaccurate: the ghetto's inhabitants weren't dying of hunger, as he claimed, because the Israelis had allowed them to take the stocks they'd found in the houses bordering the barbed-wire triangle. They were, however, terrified of running out of food, and it never occurred to them that, four months after their ghettoisation and after the city's houses and stores had been cleaned out, they would be permitted to work as day labourers in the citrus and olive groves. You should have seen what it did to Iliyya Batshoun when, at the end of his days, he was forced to work as a labourer on his own land, and how "Hajj Sababa", as the ghetto's inhabitants used to call him, would carry the burden of his sixty years on his drooping shoulders, sluggish in his movements, exhausted by the work, and never ceasing to curse the fate that had turned him into a mere manual labourer standing in the morning line-up next to men who lived in the camps and had been brought in from the area around Nazareth.

Ma'moun said that the committee head, the bridegroom whose wedding had been the moment of greatest joy in the ghetto's night, had been transformed into a man of despair who trembled from grief and humiliation and cursed the hour in which he had driven away his son Iskandar when he came back to enquire why his father hadn't asked to be reunited with his wife – only to find that the old man, not satisfied with acting, at the end of his days, like a child, had also decided to change his religion!

It was Ghassan Batheish who invented the word that was destined to enter the Hebrew vernacular lexicon when he yelled in Iskandar's face, "Enough! Leave the guy alone! Go tell your mother *sababa*!"

"What do you mean *sababa*? This is divine anger!" Iskandar yelled, spitting on the ground as though in his father's face. "Screw *sababa* and screw this old bastard who's decided to behave like a child in his dotage!"

Sababa then became a Hebrew word, I've no idea how, even though it's classical Arabic. In Hebrew it's now a synonym for "pleasure" combined with English "cool" – a word plucked from the Arabic lexicon to which it belongs and which allots it the meanings of "love" and "passionate yearning" to be transformed into a Hebrew word that encompasses the senses of "pleasure" and "everything's fine".

Hajj Iliyya Batshoun's secret name thus became "Hajj Sababa". Whenever anyone talked about him, they referred to him by his new name – even his wife Khuloud was in on it, though she'd limit herself, when she heard the title, to making a gesture of connivance with her hand and giving an ambiguous smile without saying anything. All of them conspired to make sure that Hajj Sababa went to his grave without knowing his new name.

The story doesn't lie in this name that became a source of jokes about the old man who'd been stricken by passion and blinded by it to the difference in age between him and Khuloud, who was twenty-six, which is to say forty years his junior. It lies rather in the way the old man addressed his grown son, who'd crossed the border illegally to look for him.

"You're a grown man and I'm a grown man, so you have to understand me and not listen to your mother's ravings. See how my hands are trembling?" Hajj Iliyya Batshoun said.

"It's nerves, Father, and because of your age," Iskandar said.

"Listen, son, and try to understand," Hajj Iliyya Batshoun said. "Now, you tell me why, when I hold Khuloud, the trembling stops? Look, son, go and tell your mother I'm dead. I don't want to upset her, but what's happened has happened and there's no going back. I'm married according to the custom of God and His prophet and that's the end of it. I want to begin my life over again."

The son couldn't understand how the man could talk about a new beginning to a life that had reached its end in the midst of the total destruction that had befallen the country and turned Lydda into ruins. "Screw 'your grey hairs and your foolish airs'! What kind of a person changes his religion at the end of his life so he can get married? You're going to have a lot to answer to before God!"

With Khuloud, the old, would-be-young, man discovered the meaning of "the pleasures of married life", which his shyness and sense of guilt before his wife when they made love had hidden from him. With Khuloud, the man felt he'd never made love in his life before and that his previous marriage had been a kind of bachelorhood. Khuloud, whom the inhabitants of the ghetto had seen in ripped clothes, her matted hair covered with dust, and who had performed her sad dance in front of the soldiers, carrying her daughter, whose feet were covered with faeces, had become another woman. Her wedding to Hajj Iliyya was the ghetto's greatest moment of joy. It was autumn, and the city was preparing to celebrate the "Lydda feast", meaning the feast of St George, or al-Khudr, on 16 November, which was shared and which Christians and Muslims celebrated together. At this moment, people heard Iliyya Batshoun ask for the hand of Khuloud in the courtyard of the church. No-one remarked on the decision by the man who formerly had dedicated himself to his family and was known for his infatuation with the rites of the Christian religion, especially those of Easter. How did it come about? Why did no-one stand up to "Hajj Sababa" and tell him, "This is shameful! You're an old man! At your age, one should be looking to make a good end and devoting himself to worship, and forget the lusts of the body." Even the priest kept his mouth shut before Hajj Iliyya's decision to make a public declaration of his conversion to Islam so that he could take a second wife. Everyone indulged Hajj Sababa because they were looking for a moment of illusory joy.

The Orthodox patriarch of Jerusalem did not come, as was the custom, to the Lydda feast, which was the first to be held in the city following its destruction and the establishment of the new state. The patriarch was in the Old City of Jerusalem, which had come under the control of the Jordanian army, and his displacement to Israel would have called for special arrangements, so the matter was overlooked. At the same time, the Lydda church was packed with the refugees who were living in it and wasn't fit to receive the solemn patriarchal procession, while an inflow of people from the various parts of their new country to Lydda was an impossibility in view of the military rule that had been imposed on the villages and fenced-in ghettoes that had been set up in the cities. No-one, therefore, came. All the same, and in spite of everything, the feast of St George was not a sad occasion. The chivalric saint who slew the dragon proved capable of creating a festive atmosphere, and it was all the more so because the Israelis allowed the inhabitants of the Station District to come to the church – at which point the inhabitants of the ghetto discovered that they were not the only ones who had stayed behind. There was, in fact, another ghetto in the city, also holding about five hundred souls and made up of the men who worked on the railway, along with their families. It had been decided to allow them to stay because Israel needed to have the trains working.

St George brought the two ghettoes together. Three buses arrived at the entrance of the ghetto and the passengers got out and mixed with its inhabitants, who'd gathered at the gate. At that instant, the church bells began ringing and instead of the procession of priests that used to walk in front of the patriarch and cut a path through the crowd, dividing it into two halves, a phalanx of young men and boys formed in front of the priest, and scents of incense blended with Byzantine chants.

Amidst the sounds of the hymns, Iliyya Batshoun turned to Khuloud, who was standing at his side, and asked for her hand. The words, "Marry me, Khuloud, I love you," which Iliyya pronounced in a loud voice, came as a shock to Khuloud, who'd been living under the man's wing like an adopted daughter. However, the smell of life that erupted along with the incense and the ringing of the bells had inspired a sense of new beginnings in the sixty-year-old. He told Khalid Hassouna that life began with Woman, that life was female, and that this woman "has brought me back to life".

Khalid Hassouna tried to explain to his friend that people would make fun of him and that he would end up a wreck.

"Khuloud is a frisky mare and you're not the man to ride her. You're old and you'll never do it!"

But Iliyya asserted that a true horseman died in the saddle. He said he was going to die, because death was a reality, and he'd rather die with his head on his young wife's thigh than alone.

People said that Khuloud married him because she wanted his money and land, but the young widow would later recount, when she told Manal about her husband, who had indeed died in the saddle, that when she heard him asking her to marry him she felt a frisson of passion. "I swear, Manal, I'd never felt anything like it before. I'd married my cousin because he was my cousin and we had children because having children is part of being married but – I don't know how to tell you this exactly, it's mad – but with Hajj Iliyya, I went nuts. I swear I'd never seen anything like it – tenderness, and kindness, and then, when he screwed me and lay on top of me, I'd feel like I was a queen. Do you know what it means to be a queen? And he'd act like a young man and tell me stories and we'd laugh. Let me tell you a secret: laughter's the secret. Love means when you feel you want to laugh with the man. Like you were a tree, and the man is plucking fruit off you, and you laugh."

Khuloud told my mother the secret of Hajj Sababa's death in her arms – a secret that was known to all, but that, in my mother's book, could never be divulged.

Even the business of Hajj Illiyya becoming a Muslim went off without difficulty, as though he'd become a Muslim and remained a Christian: instead of going to the Church of the Holy Sepulchre, passing the three days of Christ's death there, and coming back carrying the holy flame from the tomb of the Messiah (which had become impossible after the establishment of the Hebrew state and with East Jerusalem remaining under Arab control), he took to spending the same three days in the church of Our Master al-Khudr and returning home filled with the joy of the resurrection.

The story of Hajj Iliyya's funeral, five years after he married, perhaps sums up the man's life best. The wire had been taken away a year after being put in place, some of the ghetto's inhabitants had returned to their original houses and others had found themselves renting from the Jewish National Fund a house that had belonged to one of the city's inhabitants who had been expelled. Most of the inhabitants of the ghetto, however, stayed there, as though they'd come to belong to a single tribe. Lydda, which filled with Jewish settlers coming from Eastern Europe, would be divided into two cities and would remain so: the city of the ghetto versus the city of the immigrant Jews.

Hajj Sababa's funeral saw the strangest rites performed. The Hajj was wrapped in a shroud in Islamic fashion and placed on a wooden bier, and the people prayed over him in the mosque. Then the young men carried the bier to the Greek Orthodox cemetery and there, at the grave, the mourners burnt incense and the sound of chanting was heard. The priest came forward, sprinkled holy water on the body that lay on the ground, and said, "You are from dust and to dust you return." The sound of the hymn "May His Memory Remain For Ever" arose and he was buried in the family grave.

At the Lydda feast, Iliyya Batshoun announced his decision to marry Khuloud and the joy blended with stupefaction because of the suddenness of the surprise. It was the ghetto's first wedding, and the groom was the head of its Popular Committee, while the bride, radiant with love, looked "like the moon at its fullest", as they say, and everyone was amazed at her beauty, her delicacy and her astonishing oriental dancing.

Ma'moun said that Khuloud's dancing had amazed him. He said he'd felt the undulations of love emanating from her full body and its curves. "True, I couldn't see anything, but I felt it. Circles of joy and desire scattered from her body and filled the place."

Khuloud said that she'd felt the man's heart beating in his fingers as she held his hand under the handkerchief with which the sheikh covered their hands, and said, "I give myself to you in marriage." At that moment, the woman's heart began beating in the soles of her feet, so she stood up, the sounds of the distant music tickling her ears. Suddenly, the sound of the *rababa* arose, and the bride drew herself up to her full height and began to dance.

She twisted to the still-distant music, her body fashioning its rhythms from its own curves and its sinuosity, and as the music grew louder everyone watched while the long red dress that she was wearing, embroidered with gold thread at the upper chest and the shoulders, was transformed into a fine shift that revealed rather than concealed, as though it had become a part of her – bending, retreating, clinging as she turned in the middle of the circle, she too kneeling, stopping, her torso pulling back till the sky embraced her navel, then hunching over herself, then stretching her arms upwards and climbing the air. Her feet turned, and with them the world. The robe rose a little to reveal translucent calves. A pulse ignited her eyes, tremors extended from the tops of her shoulders to the bottoms of her feet, colours fled from her long robe to the onlookers' eyes. It was as though Khuloud was not Khuloud but a woman intoxicated by her own body and intoxicating the people who stood, amazed, watching in silent ecstasy as they felt life begin to flow through their bodies and souls once more. Ghassan Batheish stood and entered the circle, and then everyone suddenly started dancing, the ululations rose, and Manal sprinkled rice over all their heads.

I close my eyes and see her now, the woman who danced twice, the first time for death, the second for love. Both times she traced with her dance the bewilderment, fear and promise of life. I sit behind the table, watching the blackness occupy the white paper in front of me, and from the viscous darkness Khuloud emerges with her radiant whiteness and her long black hair that covers her body. I see the woman who has become engraved on my memory with her long black robe, which she went back to wearing on the death of her husband Iliyya Batshoun and never took off again – a woman bursting out of the blackness radiating the love of life that she never betrayed, which is why, following her husband's death, she turned to worship and chose to be the keeper of the shrine of Sheikh Dannoun, cleaning it, lighting candles and living off the offerings of the poor, who found in the shrine of that Sufi sheikh a refuge and a cover for their nakedness.

As for me, I discover, as I write the story, that my years have been lost to me, that my wounds will never heal, and that as Dalia and I grew closer to the long-awaited moment of beginning, I feared, and she feared, and the two of us together were powerless to combine grief with grief.

Is not writing both a celebration of the years that have been lost and an elegy for them?

Only an elegy can stir sorrow, ignite the imagination, and toss a brand into the darkness of the soul. I, Hasan Dannoun of Lydda, now summon up the memory of another Omayyad poet, to elegise myself and to elegise and be elegised by my friend Waddah al-Yaman. Malik ibn al-Rayb was a poet – handsome, a dandy, brave and murderous, and a thief who slept with his sword slung in its belt across his chest. When the angel of death came for him, he found none to weep over him, so he composed his own elegy, which has become my companion in exile and whose words will be with me when the moment comes:

I thought, "Who'll weep for me?"
    and found none but my sword and my well-straightened spear.
They say as they bury me, "Go not far!"
    but could any place be further than here?

(7)

The story of all stories, though, will be the one whose heroes and victims are the young men of the two teams charged with gathering up and burying the corpses, whose number was increased during the second week to become four, composed of twenty youths. This story continues up to what Ma'moun named "the Appalling Moment", which was that of the implementation of the Israeli decree that the bodies, which had begun to disintegrate under the sun of death, should be burnt.

The story says that two teams were charged with gathering up and burying the corpses, the first under the command of Ghassan Batheish, the second under that of Murad al-Alami. Both were young men who worked at the hospital, the first as a nurse, the second, aged sixteen, as an orderly. The first had been unable to reach his family at the moment of the exodus, which was total chaos; the second had come to the hospital to give blood and stayed on, pretending he was an orderly; he hadn't left the hospital and he hadn't tried to look for the members of his family because he'd been seized by a fear that had left him too paralysed to take any action.

Ghassan Batheish's courage quickly evaporated when he returned from the first day's work unable to speak, his skin showing swellings from the bites of the blowflies, which had followed his group from place to place. Murad al-Alami, on the other hand, appeared unconcerned, as though he were just a machine for burying bodies.

Ma'moun was in Ghassan's team. When my mother asked him why he'd got himself involved, he replied that he'd joined because he wanted to see everything.

"So what did you see, you poor thing?" she asked.

"I saw everything," he replied.

Ma'moun spoke of that period during his New York University lecture, referring to the month when the corpses were collected as "the Days of the Corpses". I don't know how he managed to combine his personal story with literary criticism or how he entered Lydda's night via his analysis of the words "wherever the wind blows" in the poem of Mahmoud Darwish (the boy asks where his father will take him in their exile from his village, to receive the answer "wherever the wind blows, my son").

Ma'moun said that he'd discovered where the wind blew during his work of collecting the remains of the dead from the alleyways and houses. "Death and exile are two sides of the silence that creeps into the words of Palestinian literature. Take, for example, the story of the woman from al-Tantoura to whom Emile Habibi, in his novel *The Pessoptimist*, gives the name Survivor. In Habibi's novel, Survivor never tells her husband Said the story of the massacre to which dozens of the men of that Palestinian coastal village fell victim. She contents herself with talking of the treasure in the cave, thus proclaiming the language of silence to be the Palestinians' new language." Ma'moun's underlying thesis was that the issue was not the events of the Nakba, which were simultaneously well known and concealed.

"Don't misunderstand me, ladies and gentlemen. I shall not fall into the trap of saying that the Nakba was a unique historical event. History, ancient and modern, is a series of catastrophes afflicting numerous peoples. I might tell you the story of the corpses we had to collect from the alleyways, fields and houses of Lydda, or I might tell you about the men who were executed in al-Tantoura and how the soldiers of Israel's Alexandroni Brigade ordered the Palestinian men of the village to dig their own graves using their hands – but what benefit would there be in that? The issue isn't just the crime of the expulsion of the Palestinians from their land, because a bigger crime followed – the crime of the imposition of silence on an entire people. I do not speak here of the silence that follows what in the language of psychiatrists is called a 'trauma', but of the silence imposed by the victor on the vanquished through the power of the language of the Jewish victim, which dominated the world, meaning the West, following the crimes of the Second World War and the savagery of the Nazi holocaust. No-one listened to the cries of the Palestinians, who died and were dispossessed in silence. This is why literature came to forge a new language for the victim, or in other words to proclaim a literature of silence, and to take us, with Mahmoud Darwish, to 'wherever the wind blows'."

Ma'moun was right. Collecting reports of his "Days of the Corpses" was arduous and extremely difficult work, and I don't know why I got myself involved in that exhausting excavation of memory. People see no meaning in talk, and excavation of the memories of victims is a kind of gratuitous torture. I don't claim that memory is meaningless but I am convinced that memory is a process for the ordering of forgetfulness, and that I have to respect Manal's silence, as well as Ma'moun's. The man passed over the story in silence in his lecture, and I didn't get the chance to ask him on that tumultuous evening when I met with him at the hotel for the details of that time.

Despite which, I find myself obliged today to traverse Lydda's streets and alleyways because the story that I have been driven, in my folly, to write forces me to pass through the night-time of the corpses.

What took place during those days?

It is said, though God alone knows the truth, that the ghetto lived the Days of the Corpses in a strange mixture of grief and joy. I use the word "joy" well aware that it is inappropriate. How dare I speak of "joy" accompanying the fly-filled sky that covered the city?

For Manal, those days had one name only – "the blowflies". She said she covered every one of her child's limbs out of fear for his safety, and in the end had to cover his face.

"I swear, it was like I'd wrapped you in a shroud, and it wasn't just you, my dear: all the children were wrapped in shrouds and even the men put masks on their faces. Instead of being coverings for just the head, *keffiyehs* became coverings for heads and faces alike."

Despite this, Manal couldn't hide, even while telling the story of the blowflies, the moments of joy she experienced along with the other inhabitants of the ghetto during those sombre days, which were given tangible form in three incidents: the finding of the four milking cows; the finding of the sheep and goats and the stray mule and the cart; and the finding of the elderly persons who had hidden themselves in houses or gardens and were brought back to the ghetto. These moments of joy would have been impossible if the Israeli officer hadn't decided to employ the youth of the ghetto in the tasks of cleaning up the roads, looting the city, and collecting and burying the bodies.

I shall begin with the issue of the corpses because it lies heavily on my heart and I want to get it over with quickly so that I can get away from its nightmares, which paralyse me. The first puzzle I face is the number of bodies that were found. All the reports I've read speak of around two hundred and fifty dead, and that figure is reasonable for a military operation that lasted only two days. The information provided by Isbir Munayyir in his book on Lydda, however, indicates that the two corpse-collection and burial groups had become, after two weeks, four, and that the number of young men doing that work had risen from ten to twenty, not to mention that the work took an entire month! These items of information intersect with the expression that Manal repeatedly used when telling me of the torments she went through during my childhood and referred to those days as "the *month* of the flies", which is something Ma'moun confirmed when he recounted that he'd worked for a month burying bodies and remains. Twenty young men worked for four weeks to remove the bodies, meaning that what we have is a major massacre and that the number of the victims of the Lydda bloodbath in all probability exceeds the official number many times over.

But what have I to do with this numbers game? We have no Palestinian document relating to the number of dead, while the Israelis, from their side, weren't interested in documenting the numbers of their Palestinian victims. We find ourselves, therefore, faced by greatly varying estimates. For the single zero to the right of the number, we should perhaps write two, in which case we would be faced with a terrifying total, by the criteria of the day.

I will not, however, do that. I am both incapable of and unwilling to get into this game of numbers. It may be important to historians, but can never be more than a theoretical issue arousing much debate, given the absence of Palestinian documents, not to mention the disappearance of Palestine itself from the map. I also hate using the language of numbers when referring to the victims, because it robs the dead of their names and individual characteristics.

Murad al-Alami told Khalid Hassouna that he'd stopped the counting and the recording of names on the third day after the start of the operation. The deputy head of the local committee was the author of the idea of keeping tally of the dead and recording their names, but the difficulty of the task, the all-pervading smell, and the impossibility of identifying the victims because of the disintegration of their bodies, along with the Israeli soldiers' insistence that the young men finish the work quickly, made keeping count an impossible task that was quickly abandoned.

I indicated that each team had a leader, but that is inaccurate. Ghassan Batheish's nervous collapse made him incapable of exercising command, so leadership of his group passed automatically to Hatim al-Laqqis, who collapsed completely when faced with the scene of the incineration of the corpses during the final week, at which point Ma'moun took charge, and so on.

The third week of work was the great turning point, as Murad al-Alami related to Manal when he was telling her about the dead angel they'd found in one of the houses. Manal was anxious to know what had happened to Umm Hasan, her husband's mother, and questioned the young men daily about the progress of their work; it was this that allowed her to store away in her memory many of the details of those days, which passed in a fearful silence that enveloped the entire ghetto.

The things that are reported of those days are incredible. The work was debilitating and turned with time into a routine of exhaustion, sun and stench. Murad al-Alami recounted that the young men lost all feeling and that for them death became a tiring job, nothing more.

My main source for the following account is Murad al-Alami, whom I met in New York by chance. He was seventy, spoke fluent Americanised English, and lived with his wife in Brooklyn. The guy came to my restaurant to order a falafel sandwich. The clock said 4 p.m., and the restaurant was half-empty. He sat on his own behind the wooden table and began taking small bites from his sandwich. When he saw me smiling at his way of eating, he smiled and spoke to me in Arabic, saying he loved falafel but had stopped eating it in America because it gave him stomach pains. Then he added that he didn't like eating it in the Israeli restaurants that were all over the city because the Israelis' ability to fake every-thing, and specifically the origins of falafel, made him furious.

"You know?" he said. "They stole the country with their smarts and their strength – good luck to them, they can keep it! But falafel, no way! That's downright dishonest! Can you beat it – they call tabbouleh 'kibbutz salad' and hummus 'khummus'! Come on now! That's just low!"

I was amazed at a logic that could say "good luck to them!" at the theft of an entire country and then choke on a dish made from chickpeas. I made him a plate of hummus, fetched two bottles of orange juice, and sat down beside him.

"I didn't order hummus and juice," he said.

"They're on the house. Welcome to you and to the scent of Palestine!"

After a moment's silence, I told him, "But you're in an Israeli restaurant."

"Israeli shm-Israeli," he said. "I asked, and they told me you were Palestinian, so I came."

Then, when he knew I was from Lydda and was Adam, son of the martyr Hasan Dannoun, he rose and gave me a hug and said he'd made up his mind to forget everything about his city but he could never forget my mother with her baby in her arms and the blind youth standing next to her.

"Your mother was cute, my friend, cute and amazingly smart. What are you doing here?"

And so we got talking. In fact, we didn't talk about anything much. The words and the traditional phrases that say nothing beyond expressing the yearning for talk flowed. The guy finished his sandwich, I went back to my work, and the customer rush began so I didn't notice that Murad hadn't left. He remained sitting at his table, slowly sipping his glass of orange juice. At around 6 p.m., he came up to the till, where I was seated, and said goodbye, with thanks.

Murad became a regular customer and I came to find in him, as he ate in his bird-like fashion, a comrade come to me from my memory. I'd speak in what one might call "word crumbs" and he'd answer with signs from his eyes. I don't know why he said nothing, but he was cheerful and courteous and that was enough for both of us. He never asked me anything about my past; even his question about why I'd come to New York was one of those things one says without expecting an answer. Our friendship began to change, however, as a result of the crisis I went through and my decision to stop writing my allegorical novel about Waddah al-Yaman and turn to writing this present text.

One evening, as I was finishing my work, and because Sarang Lee was waiting for me so we could go to Fish, the restaurant on Bleecker Street that serves shellfish, octopus and crab, Murad entered and I apologised to him, saying I had to leave, but told him

I wanted to invite him to dinner at a fish restaurant on any day he chose because I wanted to consult him about something. He said he thanked me but that it was he who wanted to invite me to dinner, at home, because his wife was anxious to meet the son of the martyr Hasan Dannoun who owned the falafel restaurant.

At his home in Bay Ridge, I discovered how this seventy-year-old had turned retirement into an art form – a house surrounded by a green garden, a warm atmosphere, his work in the furniture trade now passed to his three sons, who lived with their families in apartments close by, the voice of Umm Kulsoum flowing quietly and enveloping the place, a bottle of white wine, a wife of around sixty still radiant with traces of beauty, a grilled fish lying on a bed of finely chopped parsley which the lady, with her exquisite bearing, placed on the table before us before quietly withdrawing.

When I expressed my surprise that his wife would not be joining us at the table, he said he'd asked her not to because I'd said I wanted to consult him on a private matter, or so he had understood.

"It's a misunderstanding," I said. "I need you to help me to write a novel, and the presence of your lady wife wouldn't disturb me in the least. On the contrary, I'd like her to be part of the conversation."

"A novel! I'm going to help write a novel?"

"Perhaps I didn't express myself very well," I said. "I mean that I'm writing a memoir and I want your help in remembering certain things."

"It seems you're still not expressing yourself well," he said, laughing. "How can you expect me to help you remember your life when I know nothing about you? Listen, I don't know anything about literature. All I know is I like classical poetry and I've memorised the poems of the Prince of Poets, Ahmad Shawqi, as sung by Muhammad Abd al-Wahhab, plus three lines from a poem by Ahmad Shawqi that no-one dared to sing, which is his poem about wine. Being the literary type who wants to write novels, you must know the ones I mean."

When I replied that I didn't know what he was talking about, he looked at me pityingly and declaimed:

> *Ramadan's over – go get it, cup-bearer!*
> *Let besotted maid come running to besotted master!*
> *Red or yellow, its noblest kinds are*
> *like young girls, each sweetheart with her special flavour,*
> *But beware lest its fragrant blood you spill –*
> *enough for you, harsh tyrant, the blood of the lover!*

He poured a glass for me, one for himself, and an extra one that he picked up and left the dining room with, returning after a few seconds in the company of his wife, Itidal, who raised her glass and said it was a great honour to meet the son of the martyr Hasan Dannoun, whose name was spoken of in Lydda and al-Ramla coupled with that of the hero Abu Ali Salama.

I seized on the opportunity created by Itidal to announce my objective, and said I wanted to write the story of Lydda and was looking for witnesses to the days of the ghetto.

Itidal said the Israelis had set up a ghetto in al-Ramla too and that the inhabitants of the al-Jamal quarter in the old city there still referred to it as such, but that she herself remembered nothing of those days because she hadn't been born at the time of the Nakba. She looked at her husband and said that Murad remembered everything because he'd been a young boy at the time and hadn't just experienced the ghetto but had tasted too the terrors of the prisoners' camp at Sarafand.

Murad, however, acted as though he hadn't heard us. He looked at me and asked if I'd memorised Shawqi's poetry.

I told him I had memorised the poetry of the ancients but of the moderns I liked the poems of Darwish, al-Sayyab and Saadi Yusuf, though I'd only learned a little by heart because that sort of poetry was written to be read, not recited.

"Alright then, let's hear something – a bit of the verse you've memorised," he said.

I felt I was falling into a trap and my visit would be a failure because it would go no further than exchanging verses, whereas I'd come with another goal in mind. Nevertheless, I felt obliged to go along with the guy, so I recited a short passage from Saadi's poem "America, America", where the poet says:

> *God Save America,*
> *My home, sweet home!*

> *America:*
> *let's exchange gifts*
> *Take your smuggled cigarettes*
> *and give us potatoes.*
> *Take James Bond's golden pistol*
> *and give us Marilyn Monroe's giggle.*
> *Take the heroin syringe under the tree*
> *and give us vaccines.*
> *Take your blue fingerprints for model penitentiaries*
> *and give us village homes.*
> *Take the books of your missionaries*

and give us paper for poems to defame you.
Take what you do not have
and give us what we have
Take the stripes of your flag
and give us the stars.
Take the Afghani mujahideen beard
and give us Walt Whitman's bead filled with butterflies.
Take Saddam Hussein
and give us Abraham Lincoln
or give us no-one.

"Well done! A forceful poem, though personally I only like the old stuff. Great poetry has to age, like wine, and this poetry of yours needs to be kept in the casks of people's hearts and breasts so it can mature. Memory is a wine jar for poetry, and poetry that the memory hasn't memorised isn't great."

I said I agreed, though in fact I disagree entirely with that theory. I seized, though, on what he said about memory being a wine jar for poetry to say that memory was a homeland that had no homeland, and that I wanted him to open the wine jar of his memory for me so I could replenish my own.

We were saved by Itidal, who told us the story of her parents, who'd lived through the bitter experience of al-Ramla, and recounted how the Israeli army, which had occupied the city, had expelled the inhabitants by forcing them onto buses, and how her father had succeeded in hiding in an abandoned well and had lived in the ghetto at al-Ramla and met his wife there.

"But Lydda was something else. Murad doesn't like to talk about it, but at Lydda, the ones who left drank the cup of humiliation while those who stayed behind drank a cup of poison."

376

The talk of Lydda vacillated between silence and speech. It was clear the guy didn't want to say anything. He said that when he'd decided to leave the city and emigrate to America, he'd gone to the shrine of Dannoun, buried his memory at the grave of the Prophet Salih, and left. "I decided not to look back and to build myself over again with this woman whose photograph, which my aunt had sent me from al-Ramla, I married before I married the woman herself."

All the same, words would seep through the wall of silence. He'd say a little, fall silent . . . Then he told me the story of the blind man who'd been unable to make it to Naalin, so he went back to Lydda.

"You're talking about Ma'moun," I said.

"Right, right, Ma'moun. He was a chivalrous and a noble man. I don't know where in the world he's ended up, but I'll never forget his beautiful soul and the Lydda Oasis school that he founded."

I told him everything about Ma'moun. I recounted how he'd taken part in the work detail that collected the bodies around the city, how he'd been taken as a prisoner to Sarafand, and then how he'd left for Cairo and completed his studies there. On hearing the stories of Ma'moun, the guy's memory exploded and he began to talk, jumping from one topic to another, weeping, falling silent and drinking wine. Between the silence and the wine, my plan of attack began to take shape. I took him back to the Days of the Corpses and questioned him relentlessly.

The man spoke with difficulty. His voice sank into the depths of his throat and he spoke as though suffocating. He'd look at me like a drowning man appealing for help but I'd lost all mercy. I was like an executioner who gets pleasure from torturing his victim and himself, as though some satanic *afreet* had emerged from within me. I'd beat him with the whip of questions and shock him with the electricity of words and his head was pushed down under the water of the memory of grief and by the time he got it out again he was on the verge of choking to death. Then I'd soften and tell him things I'd heard from Ma'moun or my mother. The tears would start from my eyes and the guy's heart would melt and he'd pull from the well of silence events of which no-one had ever spoken. I could see amazement, consternation and pain sketching themselves in Itidal's eyes, so I became fiercer because I realised that he'd never mentioned these events, even to his wife, who wept silently throughout that terrifying evening.

When I recall it, I feel ashamed of myself and sympathise with Murad's position. He stopped visiting the restaurant after that and didn't answer my repeated phone calls. I lost a beautiful and a noble friend to gain stories of what I'd lost and of my subjugation!

That night I drank wine mixed with sorrow and understood why our people call arak "the Virgin's tears" (referring to Mary, mother of Jesus of Nazareth). When wine mixes with tears, or turns into them, it opens the doors of the soul. I drank a lot that night and ate nothing. Not one of us took a bite of the sea bass (the American name for *luqquz* or "sea-wolf") lying there in front of us, and even though Mrs Itidal cast a look at the fish every now and then, she didn't dare invite us to eat.

At one point, Murad stood up from his seat, took the fish into the kitchen, and returned empty-handed.

"What on earth are you doing?" Itidal asked.

"I threw it away. It looked like a corpse to me, and I can't eat corpses."

The night the fish was transformed into a corpse, Murad told story after story. He would speak and then fall silent, close his eyes as though looking into the past, then open them, get up and fetch a new bottle of wine. He said he'd forgotten everything.

"Lydda, my friend, has become like a blank page in my memory. I've erased it and I've erased Palestine, but it's old age – old age takes you back to your childhood, life's end takes you to its beginning, and the memory of the past begins to take on incomprehensible shapes." He said his visits to the Palm Tree restaurant and his sudden devotion to falafel and hummus were the first signs of that return. "And now you want me to talk and I don't want to, but I'm talking all the same. See what I mean?"

Murad sketched with his words the details of those days. He gathered the bits and pieces that I'd heard from many people into a single narrative, and I saw the story as though it were unfolding before my eyes and forming itself into a succession of scenes. I shall, therefore, recount the story as I saw it and will not let my pen go near the tattered details with the intention of tying the different elements together in a logical way; on the contrary, I shall leave the scenes to speak for themselves, the way I saw them that night. I listened to him as though watching; as though I was before pictures that intermingled, intertwined and broke up in a series that had neither beginning nor end.

Scene One

He spoke of how people lost their features. "The cruellest experience is seeing the body of one of your relatives and not recognising them. Death is a mask. The features suddenly disappear from the face when the soul leaves it. That's why the dead have to be buried immediately: 'The dead are honoured in their burial.' When I think of those days, I don't see myself, I see someone who had lost his features just as the corpses had lost theirs – faces like masks, and smashed bodies breaking apart, as though a person was a wooden toy. Where had the succulence of the body gone? I swear I don't know! We were unable to recognise people: they were all wearing such similar masks that I could no longer tell whether death is a mask or our faces are masks for death.

"Listen, friend. You wanted to hear, so listen, if you can take it. It was hard at the beginning, then we got used to it, and the only barrier that remained was the smell. We could never get used to the smell, even though we covered our noses and mouths with cloth. An odd thing was that Jamil al-Kayyal, who would be killed later in the detention camp at Sarafand, had covered his face with a *keffiyeh* and an Israeli soldier ripped it off and yelled at him that that was Palmach gear. At the time, we didn't know who Palmach were or why its troops wore the Palestinian *keffiyeh* (before later deciding that the headgear of the Palestinian peasant wasn't appropriate for them). Jamil al-Kayyal struggled desperately to defend his *keffiyeh* and ended up being beaten with the butts of their rifles and left lying for a whole day on top of the pile of corpses that we'd collected, so his features disappeared and till the day he died he wore the face of a dead man.

"Death isn't just dying. Death happens when faces are erased and we can no longer distinguish between people, and all the dead resemble all the other dead.

"No! I bear no grudge against the Jews. They too die and as soon as they die become dead people just like us and cease to be Jews. We stop being us and they stop being them, so why the killing? I swear I don't get it. I don't have a grudge against anybody, but why?

"We were young and didn't understand what was happening. Or at least, I remember that there was just one thing in my head, and that was that I didn't want to die. Strange are the ways of humankind! We lived amongst the dead and all we cared about was not dying. I don't understand this instinct that we have inside our souls that will make a person trample on the bodies of his own parents to escape death."

He said the first day was terrifying.

"We assembled. I was the leader of the team and I didn't know what I was supposed to do. I was sixteen years old. Maybe my athletic appearance and muscles attracted the Israeli officer's attention, so he appointed me head of the second work detail. I was into bodybuilding and used to do it at the club in Jaffa. I was scared and couldn't think, but I had to take charge of a group of youngsters none of whom I knew. The fact is, I didn't know anybody in Lydda. I'd been living in Jaffa at my maternal grandfather's house. He was from the al-Hout family, who were originally Lebanese but lived in Jaffa. I was staying at my Lebanese grand-dad's house because the schools in Jaffa were better, and just before the city fell, my father came and took me to Lydda. My father, my mother, my brother Sadiq, and my three sisters Hind, Sumayya and Rihab fled along with everyone else and I got stuck in Lydda. I was at the hospital to give blood and I stayed there. I don't know why, but I just couldn't move. I was frightened and half-dead with terror at the sound of the bullets and the news, especially the news of the massacre at the Dahmash Mosque. My grandfather and his family stayed in Jaffa, then later went to Beirut by sea. My family went to Naalin and from there ended up in Beirut, and I stayed in Lydda, by accident. I felt I'd got stuck and I remained stuck to the end.

"I had to lead the team, and our first job was on Saladin Street. The bodies and the swarms of flies took us by surprise. People's bodies were strewn down the middle of the street and had bloated and gone rigid. The features of the bodies' faces had been erased and the smell clung to our skin. We were supposed to put the bodies on stretchers and move them to the cemetery, where they'd be buried. Our day began with sounds of moaning. I approached the first corpse with Samih, son of Sheikh Khalid al-Kayyali. It was a woman and her clothes were in tatters. Samih began by reciting the opening chapter of the Koran, while the soldier cursed him and told him to get on with the job. Samih recited the first chapter, and then we heard him sobbing and I don't know how it happened but we all started crying. We cried and sobbed and our bodies shook with fear. Feelings of nausea devoured us. 'There is no god but God!' yelled George Samaan, tracing the sign of the cross on his chest. The woman's body slipped out of our hands and hit the ground hard. We picked her up again, put her on the stretcher, and set off with her. And that, sir . . . that is how I came to know the people of Lydda. I met them corpse by corpse."

He said the work in the streets was the easiest.

"In the streets we didn't have to look for the dead. The bodies were strewn down the road, and by the end of the first day we'd got used to it. How can I put it? We'd learned how to pick up corpses without the limbs coming off. First, we'd get them together, meaning we'd gather them so that they didn't fall to pieces, placing the hands over the stomach, closing the legs, and lifting them by the shoulders, the torso, and the legs. A body took three people to lift it and there'd be two waiting with the stretcher to take it to the cemetery. In the time that they were away carrying one body, we'd have got another ready, and so on. After some terrible experiments, when three broke into pieces, we discovered a technique for loading them, though when a body fell apart, with an arm for example coming off, the process of gathering it together again and tidying up its parts was painful and difficult, especially when more than one bit was disintegrating. Because of this, the work took a long time, which made the soldiers angry."

Scene Two

Concerning burial of the bodies, he said:

"We discovered that burying the bodies was no easy task, especially as Samih al-Kayyali had decided that they were to be buried in the Islamic way, meaning we had to dig a grave for each one and place a stone under its head, which had to be pointing towards Mecca. I didn't object to the decision, even though I was convinced it would be impossible to implement given the circumstances in which we were working: the Israelis had given us only primitive implements for digging, and we had thirty bodies to bury on the first day of work. When the soldiers saw what we were doing, after we'd completed the burial of three of the corpses, they got angry and began cursing us out, and they ordered us to leave the bodies at the cemetery and took us back to the ghetto.

"The morning of the next day, we began the work at the cemetery and were told to dig a trench twenty metres in length and five metres in width. We spent the whole day digging it, and then they ordered us to throw the bodies in. What a terrible moment that was! No sooner did we try to lift the first corpse than the flies were everywhere. I swear to God, we were covered by a cloud of flies with wings on fire from the burning sun! But that's not the point: the flies were a natural part of working among the corpses. The point was the order to pick the bodies up on shovels and throw them into the trench. Dear Lord of All Worlds . . . can you imagine what that meant? I'm not capable of describing it, and anyway, why should I tell you? Telling is meaningless. My valued friend, you have to realise that at Lydda all telling came to an end."

Scene Three

He spoke of how they worked in silence:

"I swear to God, we worked at that job for a whole month, and there was only silence. I know you won't believe me, and to be honest I don't know why I'm running on like this. Ask my wife, she's right there in front of you, ask her! I don't talk much. I feel like the words won't come out of my mouth. I don't talk at home and didn't at work. Most of the time, I'd give my instructions to the workers with a wave of my hand and they came to understand me. I don't even know how to talk with my little grandson Umar, God protect him. The boy's five years old and he thinks his granddad doesn't speak English, though, in fact, he's the person I know best how to communicate with without using words. We speak the language of the eyes. Little Umar understands me and I understand him without talking.

"What have you done to me, man, to make me open the faucet of words? I swear to God, I have no idea what's going on! Maybe it's this French white wine. You know, white wine is the best thing in the world! We call it white, but it isn't really. It's yellow, or something close to yellow. People couldn't decide what colour it was so they gave it an imprecise name. Words never say what you want them to. That was the first lesson our bitter experience with our cousins the Jews taught us. They put us someplace where there's no language, and left us in the darkness of silence.

"I was telling you about the silence. To tell the truth, silence isn't a darkness, it's an attitude. We went a whole month, my friend, without speaking. We were like lifeless machines. We'd collect and dig and swat at the flies and no-one would let up long enough to look at his comrades. Our eyes were on the ground, our faces like the masks of the dead, and we worked.

"Just once, in our group, the silence was broken. We'd finished Saladin Street and gone into the side streets and now had to go through the houses. That's what Sergeant Samuel told us. Sergeant Samuel spoke Yemeni Arabic. He looked like us – brown and tall and with hollow cheeks, and his eyebrows were thick and met in the middle. And he was kind to us, meaning that from time to time he'd let us take a break, letting us sit down in the shade and giving us tea and cookies. There was something odd about his movements: whenever he saw a body fall to pieces, he'd touch his forehead to the ground. Once I thought I saw him cry, though I'm not absolutely sure if what I saw was tears or sweat. Anyway, Sergeant Samuel ordered us to go into one of the houses. He said he could smell something in there and we had to search it.

"The only time the silence was broken it was by a moaning that rose from deep within us. Nabil al-Karazon cried out, fell to the ground, and started to bellow like an ox with its throat cut and when we saw what we did, a moaning such as I can't describe to you came from within us. It seems that people have sounds hidden within their souls that no-one knows about and that only come out when it's time. The three Jewish soldiers who had stayed outside the house, waiting, came running towards us and when they saw what we'd seen, they turned and went back. Samuel started knocking his head against the wall and vomiting. I don't know how much time passed with us like that, but later one of the soldiers yelled at us and told us to get on with the work.

"After that, Samuel disappeared and they put a blond Ashkenazi sergeant in his place. His face looked as though it had been sculpted from rock. No breaks, no water, nothing. Just work, and making sounds or weeping was forbidden.

"Can you imagine? They forbade us to weep! Have you ever heard of an occupation army that forbade its victims to weep? We were forbidden to weep, and when you can't weep for fear of being killed, words become meaningless."

Scene Four

He spoke of the moaning:

"When we heard Nabil al-Karazon shouting and bawling, we ran towards him and found him kneeling on the floor by a bed on which lay a baby girl, her face distorted by death. 'My sister Latifa!' screamed Nabil, as he moaned. The scene was terrifying. I ran to cover the little girl, pulling off my *keffiyeh* and placing it over her fragile, rigid body, but Nabil removed the *keffiyeh* and started shouting, 'Behold the angel! Is this it, God? Is this what you do to us? Ahhh!' and with this 'ahhh' that emerged from his guts, our moaning – that of the five of us engaged in collecting the corpses – rose towards the heavens. The eaten-away face of the young girl became imprinted on my heart and has remained with me throughout my life. This is what people are. People are cadavers. Even children who look like angels are cadavers. Screw life and screw humankind!

"Then, after we'd calmed down a bit in the face of the sternness of the soldier, who cocked his rifle and ordered us to pick the child up and take her outside, Nabil was overcome by a fit of hysteria. He said, 'No-one is to carry her except me!' He went over to the little girl and picked her up, but her arm fell off. Nabil put her back on the bed, where she looked like a doll that had come apart. I went towards the bed, wrapped her in the sheet and picked her up. I held her close to my chest and felt death beating inside my heart. My tears fell on her corpse as though I was giving them

389

to her to drink. They were my gift to the young girl who had died of thirst. I gave her my tears so that she could pull the earth over herself and sleep quietly while the grass sucked her up.

"We placed the body of the child whom Nabil insisted was called Latifa and was his sister on the stretcher and set off towards the cemetery. Without saying anything, we decided to stop work and take the little angel to the grave. We found ourselves walking and didn't look at the soldier, who had raised his rifle and was ordering us to go on with our work. We turned our backs and raised Latifa on our shoulders, reciting the first chapter of the Koran and walking through the desolation. I don't know why the Israeli soldier didn't shoot us when we disobeyed his order. We heard shouts in Hebrew; the Ashkenazi sergeant was probably ordering the two soldiers not to fire and to go with us. We walked in a funereal procession, having first covered the body of the child with a white sheet like a shroud. When we got to the cemetery, one of the soldiers ordered us to throw her into the big trench that was used as a mass grave (I forgot to say that we'd dig a new trench every time the one we were using filled up and that our different teams took turns at doing the work) but Samih al-Kayyali screamed that we were going to dig her a grave and bury her as an angel should be buried, and that's what happened. We dug her a little grave and al-Kayyali led the prayer over her mortal remains. Then we settled her head on a stone and sprinkled dust over her.

"The weeping of Nabil al-Karazon filled the heavens, but nobody paid any attention to the fact that we'd buried a Christian girl according to Muslim rites. Even Nabil, who'd said she was his sister, made no comment on the matter and raised his hands as he recited the Koran.

"When we returned to the ghetto, we were surprised to hear

Hajj Iliyya Batshoun rebuking Nabil and telling him to stop crying. 'That wasn't your sister, lad. Why are you making such a fuss over her? You don't have a baby sister. Your sister Latifa is a young girl now, thirteen years old, and that's not your house. You know your family were all scared away and are in Naalin now, and your sister's with them. There's nothing for you to worry about, lad. You seem to have gone mad.'

"Everyone was convinced Hajj Iliyya was right, for the youth was odd and a loner and hardly spoke to anyone. He was always saying he wanted to leave and join his family in Naalin but was scared of the Jews' bullets. After the event, Khalid Hassouna encouraged him to go and reassured him that the soldiers didn't shoot at people who were leaving; in fact, that's what they wanted everyone to do. 'Put your faith in God, son, and go!' And that's what happened. The following morning Nabil disappeared. It seems he ran away from the ghetto, and he was never heard of again.

"But this story isn't about Nabil, or about the story he made up about his sister Latifa. This is about that little girl whose name no-one knew, and who became a holy woman whose grave people visited, because Our Master al-Khudr (or St George) appeared before her tiny grave, riding his horse and brandishing his sword."

Scene Five

He spoke of al-Khudr:

"Thus it was that we came to possess a new tomb for a holy woman, one of God's righteous wards. None of the inhabitants of the ghetto knew the girl's name, so 'Latifa' quickly vanished, along with Nabil al-Karazon, to be replaced by something strange, for the girl-child came to be known as the daughter of Our Master al-Khudr, and had a shrine built for her, which people called by different names. Some called it 'the Shrine of al-Khudr's Daughter', others 'the Shrine of the Angel'. As time passed, the second won out over the first and there appeared in our city, alone among all the cities of the world, a shrine to an angel, whose name no-one knew but which was always uttered with the definite article.

"Khuloud was the first to see al-Khudr guarding the grave. She said al-Khudr had appeared to her in a dream, standing in front of the girl-child's grave and brandishing his sword, and had ordered Khuloud to tell Hajj Iliyya Batshoun to build her a tomb, because al-Khudr had taken this angel to be his daughter. The clock said one in the morning. Khuloud awoke from sleep shivering with cold, her teeth chattering. Hajj Iliyya woke at the sound of her calls for help and hurried to the second bedroom, where Khuloud slept with her daughter. He pulled up the woollen blanket and covered her, rubbing her body to drive away the shivering fit. 'It's a summer cold,' he said. 'Tomorrow morning we'll go and see Dr Zahlan. You calm down now,' and he made her a cup of hot sage tea and sat down next to her, wiping the cold sweat from her forehead.

"When the shaking stopped, she told him that Our Master al-Khudr had come to her in her dream and ordered that a tomb be built for the angelic child and that he'd said he'd guard the tomb till the Last Hour. Hajj Iliyya told her to go to sleep and that things would be clearer in the morning and that they'd have to find a way to persuade the military governor to let them build the tomb. The next morning, Khuloud told her dream to everyone, and everyone believed her. Our Master al-Khudr appears only to women, and his orders have to be carried out. Of course, there was nothing we could do. The only thing that Ghassan Batheish managed to get done was to have a pile of rocks placed on top of the grave and plastered over with mud. In this way, the angel acquired a shrine unlike that of any other holy person – a heap of rocks that grew in size with time because people would fulfil their vows to the angel by placing more on the grave, leading to the growth of a shapeless cairn. And when, following the death of her husband, Khuloud suggested building a room over the grave, so that the place would look like a shrine, most people rejected the idea, saying that it had taken on its strange appearance because Our Master al-Khudr wanted it that way and that it mustn't be touched or a curse would fall on them.

"Imagine, my friend! We were afraid a curse would fall on us – as though we weren't living in the middle of a curse, or there could have been a disaster greater than the one we were suffering. But people are dogs. They're called 'human' because 'humiliation' is what they're used to, and they accept it and justify it. Imagine, we used to think that a pile of stones that we'd placed on top of the grave of an unknown girl-child was a sign of what Hajj Iliyya

Batshoun used to call 'divine visitation'. I never believed the guy had really become a Muslim. Hajj Sababa, as we'd come to call him, had been love-struck when he saw Khuloud dancing her little girl that savage way in front of the Israeli soldiers, and the only way open to him to marry her was to become a Muslim. But he used to use pious expressions that were strange to our ears, till we discovered they were used by our Christian brothers. Don't get me wrong! I respect all religions. All of us in the end worship God, but I don't like cosying up to holy men. To be honest, I was never comfortable with Khuloud's story and never believed that the Prophet al-Khudr had appeared to her, but I was forced to pretend to believe. In those terrible days, clinging to the ropes of illusion was all we could do. All the same, I told Ghassan Batheish that I had my doubts about how truthful Khuloud was, and the strange thing was that Ghassan who, like me, expressed his doubts about the appearance of al-Khudr to such an eccentric woman, who'd become the semi-public mistress of a man forty years her senior, began the custom of lighting candles in front of the stone cairn we'd erected.

"The appearance of al-Khudr to the young widow was a successful way to silence evil tongues, which had impugned the honour of the woman who'd lived under the protection of Iliyya Batshoun as though she was his adopted daughter, and who, the very day she completed the period she had to wait before she could legally remarry, switched from the status of daughter to that of wife."

Scene Six

He spoke of the sheep:

"I don't want to give a false impression of the first days of the ghetto. True, they were a tale of grief and silence, but nothing breaks silence better or makes people feel they're more alive than life's gifts."

He said that they'd often been forced to bury the dead where they found them because the corpses were too eaten away to move from one place to another.

"But we would call on al-Khudr for help. His appearances to women in the ghetto became the talk of all. Each evening, on our return from our exhausting work, drowsiness would steal over us to the rhythm of women's voices relating the appearances of al-Khudr and his angels. The ghetto now had its saint and righteous holy woman, and Muslims and Christians competed to tell their stories of the appearance of al-Khudr, or of St George, and to tell of the light that poured from the wings of a small angel that would stand on top of the mound of stones and dispel the darkness.

"We quickly began to forget the story of the miracle of al-Khudr, though, when the Lebanese boy, Hatim al-Laqqis, brought us the miracle of the first cow.

"Iliyya Batshoun said the cow was the gift of al-Khudr and we ought to slaughter it and present it as a sacrifice at the Shrine of the Angel.

"'The guy's nuts!' Manal shouted. Your mother was a brave woman. She stood up to Iliyya and the members of the committee and led the cow to her house, saying that al-Khudr had sent the cow as a mercy for the children, so they could drink milk.

"Hatim al-Laqqis wasn't part of our team, so I only know the story of how they found the first cow from what he told me. He said that after his team had finished burying its dead and was getting ready to leave, he'd heard a strange sound, so he decided to stay. He tricked the Israeli soldiers and disappeared among the graves. When everyone had left, he took his shirt off and waved it, to give a signal to the source of the sound. Suddenly, in the distance, he saw two phantoms coming towards him. They looked like two old men covered in dust. The phantoms drew closer to him and, sure that they were *jinn*, he exclaimed, 'I seek refuge with God from the devil' and began reciting the Throne Verse in a loud voice, and the phantoms heard and began reciting along with him:

God! There is no god but He, the Living, the Everlasting. Slumber seizes Him not, neither sleep; to Him belongs all that is in the heavens and the earth. Who is there that shall intercede with Him save by His leave? He knows what lies before them and what is after them, and they comprehend not anything of His knowledge save such as He wills. His Throne comprises the heavens and earth; the preserving of them oppresses Him not; He is the All-high, the All-glorious.

"At first, I'd been afraid they'd turn out to be Jews, then I thought they were *jinn* and became rooted to the spot; I couldn't even get to the end of the Throne Verse, so they finished it for me and then I understood." He said they'd come to him, each supporting the other so that they looked like one man divided in two. "'We're from the al-Hadi family,' they cried out, before sitting down on the ground. I pulled myself together, went towards

396

them, and sat down next to them. They couldn't believe that I was living in Lydda and that there was a large group of people living in the ghetto.

"They were twins, alike as two drops of water. The first was called Nabil and the second was called Kamil. They said they were from the Jerusalem area and that the fates had determined that they should flee their city for Lydda. They were about thirty but looked like old men. They said they'd bought a house in Lydda and opened a fabric store in the market, and when the Haganah invaded the city they'd escaped from their house and hidden in the citrus grove next door, and that that day they'd made up their minds to return, via the cemetery. They said they'd hidden among the graves when they heard the sounds of strange activity and hadn't understood what was going on. Then, when everything was quiet again and they'd decided to continue their journey, they encountered a stray cow grazing on the weeds that had sprung up around the graves, so they caught her and tied her to a gravestone.

"'And then we saw you.'

"A cow? 'And where's the cow?' I screamed at them, so they led me to her. I swear, the first thing I looked at was her udders, and I could see they were swollen with milk. 'It's a blessing from God,' I said. I bent over the cow and kissed her on the forehead. I took hold of the rope she was tied with and told the two men to follow me to the ghetto. They said they'd seen three other cows but hadn't been able to catch them. I said, 'Never mind. We'll come back tomorrow,' and I set off, holding on to the cow, and the men set off behind me."

Murad continued:

"With the first cow, there was general rejoicing in the ghetto, so the next day we decided we'd finish burying the bodies quickly so as to have time to catch the three other cows. There were four of us – me, a youth called Jamil who'd recently joined our group, and Hatim al-Laqqis and Ghassan Batheish making up the numbers. We hid among the graves until everyone had arrived but were surprised to find Blind Ma'moun with us. Ghassan ordered him to leave the place but the blind man refused, saying we needed him and he knew more than we did about cows. We found the three cows grazing on myrtle near the Shrine of the Angel, so we formed a kind of circle around them to make it easy to catch them. They seemed so docile, though, that it was as if they'd been waiting for us. We approached them and tied them up quietly; their udders too were swollen with milk.

"'This is the gift of the angel,' said Ghassan, bursting into tears. When we began the homeward journey, we discovered Ma'moun wasn't with us. We decided to look for him and began walking among the graves, leaving the cows in Hatim's keeping. Then suddenly we saw him: he was walking, carrying a sheep, and it was trying to get away from him. We ran and took the sheep from him. I have no idea how the blind man had been able to see the sheep, or catch it. Ma'moun indicated that he'd seen two head of goats and that we should look for them on the east side of the cemetery. And sure enough, we found them and caught them, with a lot of effort, because the goats were sly runners. Finally, we returned, bringing with us treasures beyond price.

"The people of the ghetto welcomed us with ululations of joy. The milk issue was solved and Hatim al-Laqqis took charge of distributing it to the children and the elderly, while Khuloud took charge of souring the milk and making *labneh*.

"Our Easter feast was the sheep and the two goats. The committee at first decided that the goats should be slaughtered immediately while the sheep should be kept for the Feast of the Sacrifice, but Iliyya Batshoun decided that the sheep should be slaughtered too, so that everyone in the ghetto could savour the smell of the fat as it cooked. I swear to God, I've never in all my life tasted food more delicious than the dishes made by the people of the ghetto from the meat and the bones! Manal made *kibbeh nayyeh* the way they make it in Eilaboun. Khuloud made tripe, shanks and heads. Meat with cracked wheat was prepared, people cooked Jew's mallow using the bones of the sheep, and tables were set. One young guy – I don't remember his name – even fetched a bottle of arak and many a cup made the rounds.

"We named that wonderful occasion 'the Night of al-Khudr's Angel' and it entered our memories as the first joyful night. No-one dared say the truth, which was that the cows and the banquet of meat were the product of our work in the cemetery. Thus, my dear sir, was life mixed with death as water is with wine, and the ghetto discovered that it could endure, and that we, who had survived the massacre by accident and had lived till then between the fear of death and the gathering of corpses, had stumbled onto life in the form of four cows, a sheep and two goats. And in the afternoon of the next day, our joy was made complete, when the group led by Marwan al-Kayyali, God rest his soul, came across a stray mule, which was brought to the ghetto, where it was hitched to a four-wheeled cart that had been abandoned next to the mosque. This provided us with a means of transportation that would greatly lighten the burden of dragging and rolling the barrels of water.

"Our joy, however, was short-lived, for once we'd finished collecting the corpses, we entered the maelstrom of the arrest and disappearance of the young men. The best of our youth went to Asqalan – they even arrested blind Ma'moun – where we were put in cages. Some of us returned to the ghetto, but others preferred to go from the detention camp to join their families in Ramallah."

(I didn't ask Murad about the twins because I know about the two men and know from Manal and Ma'moun the strange story of their escape from Jerusalem to Lydda: it's a story that, to be honest, no-one in his right mind would believe – and no-one did believe what they told us about the mad Jewish girl who accused them of raping her when she was twelve and they were fourteen, and how the accusation brought upon them the hatred of some Jewish youths, who threatened to kill them, and how scared they'd been because they were on their own, orphans, working in a small store that their father had left them in the Foreign Merchants' Market, so they'd been forced to sell it and ended up here in Lydda. Following their move to the ghetto, it was known of the two young men that they were models of cowardice and that they felt they were living in exile. They left the city for an unknown destination when I was six, according to what Manal told me.

I didn't believe the story until I read Amos Oz's novel *My Michael*, which tells of Hana Gonen and her tall tales about the two Palestinian boys. Could the story really be true? Could the Israeli novelist have changed the names of the Palestinian twins from Nabil and Jamil to Khalil and Aziz? Instead of recounting the tragedy of the two Arabs obliged to flee Jerusalem and live in the Lydda ghetto, he transformed his heroine's delirium and melancholia into a symbol of a city he dislikes. I have no idea – but then the relationship between the heroes of novels and the truth has always puzzled me and will continue to puzzle me to the last days of my life!

I don't want to accuse the Israeli writer of bias. When Oz wrote

My Michael, he turned Jerusalem into an allegory for his mother's suicide and he likely heard fragments of the story of the Palestinian twins and the Israeli girl's delusions and decided they would serve to reinforce his metaphor of Jerusalem as a city besieged by Arab villages. That is his right as an author – even if I can't understand how a novelist could write about Jerusalem without revealing the scale of the tragedy that befell the original inhabitants of the city's western districts, which the Israelis occupied, expelling their occupants from their homes. I both blame him and wonder at him for not seeing the light in the stones of Jerusalem, of whose gradations of colour the Palestinian novelist Jabra Ibrahim Jabra wrote at such length. Oz saw only a dark city clothed in the fog of his European memories, but anyone who visits Jerusalem knows that it is a city of light and that its roseate stones radiate and glow even in the darkness.)

Murad said he'd never forget the taste of the cauliflower upsidedown pot pie made by Hasaniya, the fifty-year-old who was the only woman to live in the mosque, behind a woollen blanket, and who spoke to no-one but herself.

"If only I were a painter, so that I could show you the beauty shining from the woman's eyes as she fried the cauliflower and fluffed the rice and how it was her platter of food that was the talk of the ghetto for ages! She would always ask us to bring her meat so that she could make the pie, but where, oh where, were we to find meat, when we were lucky to taste it once in a year?"

Scene Seven

He spoke of the fire and of the burning of the bodies, saying it was a moment he neither wanted to remember nor talk about.

The guy choked on his words as he told. He wrestled with meanings, so that he could speak of how he experienced the fire that burnt the last of the bodies and their remains. He produced the words like one who has lost the ability to produce words and wept like one who has no more tears.

(When I tried to write about this moment, which I did several times, I'd suffer a complete collapse. I'd be drenched in cold sweat and feel as though my heart had stopped beating. I'd be overcome by exhaustion, stop writing, throw myself on the bed and doze. This is my seventh attempt to write down what I heard. I drank half a bottle of vodka, sat down at the table, and decided to forget all the dreams I'd have when such exhaustion struck me. But I couldn't forget one dream that pursued me for seven days and seven nights:

We three – Itidal, Murad, and I – are sitting down. Murad drains his glass to the dregs and gets drunk. He pours another glass and drinks it, and the words come out of his mouth and turn into a rope that winds itself around his neck. The man cries out for help in words that come out as separated syllables, and with each cry the rope tightens around his neck and his words turn into a sort of rasp. Itidal and I never move from our places. We're like people watching a horror movie. The dream begins and ends without anything happening: the guy doesn't die and we make no attempt to save him. I'd wake up from this dream, light a cigarette and open my eyes as far as they'd go so that I wouldn't fall asleep again. Then, when the heat of the cigarette's little glowing tip reached my fingers, I'd get up in panic, then fall asleep again and enter a world in which delirium blended with the memories of that night. I became convinced that if I went on that way, I'd end up dying in a fire caused by my cigarette, so I decided to stop writing temporarily, but the decision did not release me from the maze of fires that Murad described as he choked on his words.)

Murad spoke of those days:

"Look, it's true that collecting the bodies and burying the remains were the hardest parts of the work, but during those days there were two teams of young men working on looting the city and clearing the roads. You were a baby and don't remember anything, so you can't help me remember the names, and you know that old age has its claims, which begin with memory, and memory forgets, and the first thing it forgets is names. First, the name disappears, then little by little the features evaporate, and finally the person vanishes into his name."

(I wanted to interrupt him to say that in that case the name was, at the end of the day, its bearer's grave, and that when the name was forgotten its bearer disappeared and the person along with it. However, I said nothing. I felt that the transformation of our names into our graves was the height of abomination.)

He recounted what the youth whose name he couldn't remember had told him about the orgy of looting that took place at the direction, and under the supervision, of the Israeli army.

"The youth whose name we've forgotten said his team was

403

made up of five persons and that its job was to clear the commercial establishments of their contents:

"'We entered the stores, whose doors had mostly been ripped off, and we emptied them of everything. We had to fill the small army trucks with canned goods, grains, flour, sugar, milk, everything. At first, we felt ignominy and shame. Why did we have to loot ourselves? Why did we have to rob our city for the benefit of these people? We knew that the trucks would go to Tel Aviv, and we worked with gritted teeth under the pressure of fear. After a couple of days of work, though, everything changed. We became full of enthusiasm and felt the ecstasy of thieves. We stole fearlessly because the army was protecting us, and we felt the pleasure of looting and enjoyed our work.'

"Screw us and what we'd become!" said Murad. "Can you believe it? You have to because I did. That's what puzzles me: how did we become looter and looted, thief and victim? It's amazing! Did you ever experience such a thing? No-one but us has ever tasted the moment of ecstasy felt by the victim when he flogs himself, and no-one can understand the feeling. Even I, who am telling you about it, can't understand it!"

The young man whose name we've forgotten said that after they'd finished the commercial establishments, the more difficult job began. This required joining the team that had cleared the streets and cleaned the military governor's office to theirs.

"That morning, we discovered that a new team had been added to ours and we were given orders to the effect that our new job was to empty the houses of every piece of furniture. The Israeli officer told us he wanted everything that was inside the houses and gave us to understand we must leave nothing behind. We were to go into each house, clear it out and clean it; even the doors and the windows we were to take off and load onto other, larger, army trucks. This new job was more difficult than the first. You might say we'd become porters, and we would return in the evenings, our backs broken from carrying furniture, all of which the trucks took away. The work was exhausting, but we didn't face any difficulties worth mentioning, and if we came across a bloated body in any of the houses, the order would come from the officer to get out of the house right away, and he'd splash kerosene around and set fire to the house, saying that it was better for the health of the city. We knew there were teams for collecting the bodies, so we couldn't understand why the officer would set fire to the house; he could just have ordered us to take the body to the cemetery and get on with the looting."

The young man told Murad that their group had faced two hard cases. In the first, the officer had almost shot the young man called "the Egyptian", and the second case was his own.

"We called him the Egyptian because he was dark-skinned, but he wasn't Egyptian. He lived with his parents and three sisters in the church and never stopped telling jokes. When we went in to loot one of the houses, though, the Egyptian discovered that it was his own. At first, he led us through the rooms showing off the beauty of the furniture, which his father had brought from Damascus. We began loading up, as usual, and got to a large mirror in the living room, about two metres tall with an oak frame topped by a wooden triangle resembling a crown that was inlaid with Damascene mother-of-pearl. The Egyptian held on to the mirror and shouted, 'No! I'm taking this to my family.'

"The soldier who was accompanying us inside the house didn't understand what was happening. He went up to the Egyptian, said something in Hebrew, and left the house. I, as head of the team, asked the Egyptian to step back and let go of the mirror, but he just clung to it more fiercely. The four of us formed a circle round him in an attempt to persuade him that such carrying-on was pointless. I told him we'd looted the whole city, 'so why this mirror? In a moment they'll make some dumb problem for us,' but instead of us convincing him, his attitude started to get to us, and the mirror became a symbol of all the impotence and shame we'd felt during those days of looting.

"The soldier came back accompanied by a sergeant who spoke Arabic and who asked us what was going on. I replied that we'd decided the Egyptian was right and we weren't going to take the mirror to the truck, we were going to carry it to the ghetto because they had no right to take it to Tel Aviv. I don't know where I found the courage to say what had to be said. Sergeant Roni – I think that was the name of the blond, blue-eyed sergeant – told us to load the mirror onto the truck immediately, plus a lot of stuff along the lines of our not having any right to take state property. He raised his stick and advanced with the soldier, who also had a stick, behind him, but instead of retreating, the Egyptian glued himself to the surface of the mirror, blending into its image, and we saw all of us inside it – five Palestinians and two Israeli soldiers inside a Damascus mirror. The soldiers fell on us and started beating us. Our concern was to protect the mirror from them, so we too glued ourselves to its surface, the blows from the sticks raining down on our heads while we screamed and cursed. The living room filled with Israeli soldiers who beat us with sticks and rifle butts and blood began to flow. Suddenly the mirror started to break into shards. I couldn't see clearly because my eyes were filled with blood, but I saw how our images in the mirror began to splinter and the colour red to consume us, and how when the Egyptian fell to the ground, the mirror fell on top of him and broke into little pieces. Our image disappeared and we and the Israeli soldiers were covered with blood, which oozed from our splinter-filled bodies.

"We ended up handcuffed walking down the empty street, our heads bowed and surrounded by the soldiers, who had their rifles trained on us. We weren't taken to the ghetto. They took us to an underground room which had been used in the past to store food supplies, in the house that had become the Israeli military command's headquarters in the city. We spent the night there without food or drink. I was convinced they'd throw us out of the city the next day, but the morning brought something unexpected."

The young man said the morning brought a surprise:

"And the surprise took the form of three nurses, who came in and cleaned our wounds. They put on them a yellowish medication that stung and that we discovered later was iodine. Our wounds were bandaged and we drank coffee that tasted like straw, made in the Israeli way, the kind they call *bots kafeh*, meaning 'mud coffee', which is a term for putting coffee grounds into a cup in the Arabic way, then pouring boiling water over them and stirring. The coffee doesn't dissolve but turns to mud, which is where the Hebrew name for this kind of coffee comes from. Even though we didn't find its taste to our liking, it was a good start and we took it as a positive sign, which would have been right, if I hadn't caught sight of that table."

Murad told us about the table:

"You know that they'd taken the houses of Hasan Dahmash and Said al-Huneidi as their military command headquarters. In the morning, we discovered we were in Hasan Dahmash's house, which was large, recently built, and distinguished by high ceilings

407

and a spacious living room where Captain Moshe, to whom they led us, was sitting, behind a rectangular wooden table. Moshe began by telling us off. He said he could refer us to a military tribunal on a charge of assaulting the soldiers, but that Sergeant Roni had interceded on our behalf. 'Do you understand what I'm telling you? Sergeant Roni, over whose head you broke the mirror with the intent to kill him, is the one who has asked me to pardon you! The condition is, though, that you apologise to me, because you broke a valuable mirror that is the property of the state. And to him, because you were rude to him. And Roni and I have accepted your apology.'"

The boy said that, at a gesture from the captain, the youths had begun to leave the large room, without a word of apology passing their lips. He, though, remained frozen in place.

"I didn't move. I was staring at the table at which the Israeli captain sat and could scarcely believe it. Everyone left and I stayed. The captain raised the back of his hand and said, 'Goodbye!' and when I didn't move he yelled at me, 'What's wrong with you, boy?' but I didn't answer. What could I say? I was devoured by fear and felt as though my tongue had stuck to the roof of my mouth. The officer stood up, came towards me, shook me by the shoulders, and asked me what I wanted. With difficulty I managed to get out that I didn't want anything, but the table . . .

"'What's wrong with the table?' he said.

"'The table . . . it's our table.' I tried to explain to him, stammering with fear, that it had been made by my father with his own hands and that he'd put it in the dining room and that it was made from the wood of an aged olive tree that had dried out in our field and my father had wanted the table to be with us for the rest of our lives because the smell of olive wood wafted off it . . .

'That smell, sir, is our smell. You've stolen the smell of my father.'"

(Did the boy really say those words, or had Murad's memory rearranged them in its own way? It doesn't matter. What matters is that the smell filled where we were, and I too suddenly smelled the smell of Lydda welling up from my childhood. I shall never be able to describe it, for the aromas of memory are hard to put a name to, but the coloured undulations in which silver blends with the green and blue that rise from the leaves of an olive tree under the sun took me back to the scent that is engraved in my depths, and I smelled the colour – a mixture of the scents of the olive and the fig, the two trees by which God swears in the Koran, when He says, *By the fig and the olive and the Mount Sinai and this land secure!* The two trees occupy a special place in the memory of my childhood, and especially of when I was arrested at the age of six for picking figs from a nearby garden that was part of the land owned by my grandfather and was put in jail for stealing state property and spent a whole night at the police station before being got out by my mother, who explained to me that I had to think of everything as lost and start from zero. The words "lost" and "zero" remained engraved on my memory even though I didn't understand. How can a child at the outset of his life understand that he has to begin from zero and from loss?)

The boy said the Israeli officer ordered him to pick the table up and take it home.

"The officer told me, 'Take it, boy!' and picked up his papers and files and put them on a small table that stood out of the way near the wall. He said he didn't believe my story: 'You're a nation of liars, but take it! It's not your table, but I'm going to give it to you. Tell your father, "This table is a gift from the Israeli army." Take it and don't let me see your face again!'"

But the boy said that that wasn't the end of the story.

"My comrades had stopped outside the Israeli officer's door to wait for me, and when they heard me say, 'I'll never take it!' they came in and carried off the table, and I found myself running with them outside, our feet barely touching the ground we were so happy. When we reached the hospital, Dr Zahlan took the table and announced that it would be put in the hospital's lobby because the hospital needed it, and that it would be safe there and would be returned to its owner as soon as the present mess was cleared up."

Murad said he'd told us these two stories to delay having to tell the one he was afraid of. He said that every morning he still smelled the smell.

"Can you imagine starting your day with the stench of burning corpses? I'm seventy years old now and it still goes with me everywhere. Every morning I have to go out into the garden, even if it's fifteen below zero. I go out to breathe in the air and get rid of the stench. The youth said they'd stolen the smell of his father when they stole the table, but my smell is the stench of death. What can I say? I think that's enough."

Murad leaned his chin on his hand, closed his eyes, and a voice unlike his own, the voice of a sixteen-year-old choking on the tears in his throat, came out of him, and through that strange voice I beheld the scene and smelled the fire and felt that I was choking and had to get out of there. I try now to recall what the man said the way I heard it and am smitten by a cold shiver, accompanied by a feeling that I am about to choke on the smoke that veils the vision from my eyes.

Murad said, "It was six in the morning of Thursday, the eighteenth of August. I'm not certain of the date but I'm sure it was a Thursday. The Israeli officer gathered the youth of the four teams that were working on collecting the bodies and informed us that today would be the last day of work. He ordered the leader of each team to have the bodies gathered together in the garden closest to where he was working.

"'There's no need to move them to the cemeteries or dig mass graves in the gardens of the various quarters. All you have to do is gather the bodies together in the place the soldiers who are with you specify. Your job will be easy and once it's done, this unpleasant and difficult work will be over.' The officer didn't forget to thank us in the name of the Israel Defence Forces, saying that through this work we had proved our loyalty to the Jewish State and our worthiness to be citizens of that state, which had been established to restore to those in exile their right of return to the land of their fathers and grandfathers."

Murad said, "What awaited us was more appalling than anything that had gone before. Two days after the end of the work, we found ourselves herded into detention camps, so we moved from a large cage into small cages and experienced the torments of the prisoner and the pain of the exile. As you know, the condition for immediate release was that we shouldn't return to Lydda but leave and go to Ramallah. Most of us refused, but I felt a loss when I saw Hatim al-Laqqis leave. With his cheerful spirit and amazing capacity for problem-solving, Hatim was more than a friend and a brother. He told us that Comrade Emile Toma, who visited us in the camp, had advised him to go back to Lebanon and had given him the addresses of some of the Lebanese communist comrades and that he'd agreed because he couldn't bear any longer to live in the ghetto as 'a broken-off branch' – with no parents and no family."

411

Of that day, when the sky poured down rain, Murad said, "Usually, it doesn't rain in August, but it did that day. It was rain unlike any other. It went on for just half an hour, as though the sky had opened a faucet and then turned it off. We'd piled the bodies in the garden, and the rain poured down, and you can imagine what happened to the thirty corpses or parts of corpses that our team had piled on top of each other. When the rain stopped, the two Israeli soldiers told us to gather the scattered parts together again with the shovels and then one of them gave me a gallon can of kerosene and ordered me to splash it over the parts and the fire started and the air filled with thick black smoke, to the sound of the crackling of the fire. And we, my dear sir, had to wait while the ashes dispersed into the air and then gather the bones and bury them in a small hole."

That was the end of what he had to say.

After a long silence, Murad filled his glass with white wine, raised it to me, and said, "Look, and tell me what you see!"

I didn't understand what he meant, but I regained my voice, with difficulty, to say that I saw a glass full to the brim with white wine.

"Do you know the poems of Suhrawardi the Slain?" he asked me.

I said I knew he was a Sufi and that he must have written verse, like all the other great Sufis.

> The glass was fine, the wine was pure,
>   the limits of each, in their resemblance, hard to divine –
> As though there was wine but no cup,
>   and a cup that held no wine.

412

I said it was beautiful poetry but I didn't understand what it meant.

He downed his glass at one go to announce that the meeting was over. I stood up.

He patted me on the shoulder and said, "Don't rush things. You'll understand soon enough."

Sonderkommando

I admit I felt something strange as I listened to the popping of the bones as they were devoured by the fire: Murad told, and I saw. It was grief. Grief squeezes the heart till you feel you're about to die and your heart is bleeding tears into your eyes. Thus it was, good folk, that I discovered a new source of tears – tears that don't emerge from the glands of the eyes accompanied by a gulping for breath but that emerge directly from the convulsing of the heart, so that they're as hot as blood and dig a groove down the cheeks.

My tears gushed without weeping, and I thought of my mother's face and the grooves of tears on her cheeks that nobody saw but I. And I understood everything.

Now I can say that I have understood the language of silence that was Manal's way of concealing her tears in the hidden grooves on her cheeks.

When I saw Claude Lanzmann's movie "Shoah", I was struck dumb. It was in 1991, at the house of an American Jewish doctor called Sam Horovitz who had decided to return to the Promised Land and had taken up residence in Ramat Aviv. The guy was a model of courtesy and good nature. He called me up to discuss an article of mine about Umm Kulsoum's song *"Ahl al-Hawa"* that had been published in *Kol Ha'ir*. Sam and his wife Kate were lovers of Arabic music and regularly attended video-screenings of Egyptian movies. He called me and we met more than once.

He declared his admiration for my articles, with their openness towards Arab culture, and said he'd never met another Jew so open to the culture of the region.

He asked me to explain oriental musical modes and the concept of the quarter-tone, and I was astonished by his love of Arabic culture. He said he'd read *Diary of a Country Prosecutor* by the Egyptian writer Tawfiq al-Hakim, translated into English by Aba Eban (sometime Israeli minister of foreign affairs), and had fallen under the spell of that writer, who had managed to present the social issues of the poverty-stricken Egyptian countryside in the form of a detective novel. He had daring ideas on the necessity of Israel's integration into the Arab region and showed sympathy for the cause of the Palestinian refugees living in wretched camps. Once, after a long discussion over coffee, I told him I wanted to ask him a question but was hesitant to do so and afraid of upsetting him.

I asked him why he had gone there. "You love Arabic culture but Israel is a project with a Western bent that despises the culture of the country's original inhabitants, so why did you come here?"

He answered me that he'd come because of Claude Lanzmann and spoke at length about the genius of that great leftist man of culture, friend of Jean-Paul Sartre and Simone de Beauvoir. He said Lanzmann's movie "Shoah" had changed his life and was one of the reasons for his adoption of his Jewish identity and his decision to return to the Promised Land.

"Lanzmann was the portal to my identity. Umm Kulsoum, though, is the magic of the East that captivated my heart when I came here.

"Have you seen the movie?" he asked me.

"No. I've heard of it, but the hype here in Israel made me reluctant to go and see it. I don't like blockbusters."

"This time, you're wrong," he said, and he invited me to his house, where I spent six hours transfixed in front of the small screen witnessing savagery in its most extreme manifestations.

"I'm bowled over," I told Sam.

A movie unlike any other, stories unlike any others, and one tragedy giving birth to itself inside another.

Despite Lanzmann's Zionism, his peacock-like personality, and his later movie "Tsahal", in which he glorifies the Israeli army with a blind partiality informed by a loathsomely romantic attitude towards an armed force that hides its amorality under claims of morality, my admiration for "Shoah" has never gone away. I regard it as a humane work in which the content is greater than the form, and one that succeeds in telling what cannot be told.

Nevertheless, I feel perplexed when faced by fate's coincidences and try to find an explanation for them, which I cannot. The coincidence of my meeting with Murad is understandable and logical: falafel, hummus and nostalgia led the seventy-year-old to the Palm Tree restaurant. But what possessed Claude Lanzmann to bring a group of Holocaust survivors and men who'd worked in the *Sonderkommando* teams to the Ben Shemen colony, just outside Lydda, to tell of their suffering when burning victims, victims who were of their own people? We may be sure that Lanzmann was unaware of the existence of a Palestinian ghetto in Lydda. Even if echoes of the great expulsion of 1948 ever reached him, it's certain that, if he'd had to choose between it and the stories of the Nazi holocaust that he decided to tell in his movie, he would have granted that marginal event no consideration. All that is understandable – or, let us say, something that I try to understand, having drunk that experience to its dregs, and adopted the identity; indeed, at one stage of my life I believed I was Jewish, the son of a survivor of the Warsaw Ghetto. However, my recall of scenes from that coincidental event fifteen years before my encounter with Murad al-Alami, who witnessed the transformation of the Palestinian youth of the ghetto into a new form of *Sonderkommando*, shook me to the core.

Why did Claude Lanzmann bring the Jewish men of the *Sonderkommando* to Lydda?

And would the Franco-Jewish writer and movie-maker have been able to imagine a possible encounter between those poor men and Murad and his comrades, who carried out the burning of the corpses of the people of Lydda in obedience to the orders of the men of *Tsahal*?

I have no idea, but what makes me angry is that no-one confronted the French director with this truth, which was known to all the youth of the Lydda ghetto. Maybe the tragedy has to remain enveloped in silence, because any discussion of its details would disfigure the nobility of that silence.

Murad was right to be silent.

Murad's silence resembles that of Waddah al-Yaman. Now I understand why Murad severed all ties with me and why Waddah al-Yaman rejected my attempt to identify with his story.

It's the story of the sheep that was driven to slaughter and never opened its mouth.

That is the story of the children of the ghetto.

I don't want to draw a comparison between the Holocaust and the Nakba. I hate such comparisons and I believe the numbers game is vulgar and nauseating. I have nothing but contempt for Roger Garaudy and others who deny the Nazi holocaust. Garaudy, who walked the tightrope of ideology from Marxism to Christianity to Islam and who ended up a mercenary at the doorsteps of the Arab oil sheikhdoms, committed the crime of playing with numbers, reducing that of the Jews who died at the hands of the Nazis from six million to three million. No, Monsieur Garaudy, in the Holocaust everybody died, for whoever kills one innocent person is like him who kills all humankind. As it says in the Mighty Book, *Whosoever slays a soul not to retaliate for a soul slain, nor for corruption done in the land, shall be as if he had slain humankind altogether*.

That said, what is the meaning of the chance encounter of these two incidents? Did they meet so that the banality of evil, the naivety of humankind and the insanity of history could be laid bare?

Or does their encounter point to the apotheosis of the Jewish issue at the hands of the Zionist movement, which transformed the Jews from victims into executioners, destroyed the philosophy of existential Jewish exile and, indeed, turned that exile into a property of its Palestinian victims?

I swear I have no idea! But I do know that I am sorrowful unto death, as Jesus the Nazarene said when he beheld the fate of humankind in a vision.

The Threshold

The ghetto didn't cease to exist when the wire was taken away towards the end of 1949: the wire remained engraved on people's hearts and the common name of the two Arab quarters – the Sakna Quarter, where I was born, and the Station Quarter, where the Israeli army allowed the railroad workers to stay and made them a ghetto like the one they made us – continues to be, to this day, "the Arab ghetto". And because the ghetto remains, its stories have remained along with it. Its men and women have today become the shadows of the memory of a crime and its stories have lodged in the walls of the city, which is now a city unlike itself.

All cities, and not just the occupied cities of Palestine, change. This was the lesson I had to get used to. Nazareth has changed, and New York, and Cairo, and Seoul, and Beijing, and so on. I have to pretend to myself that Lydda was subjected to a devastating earthquake and a rapid demographic shift. But why then does this city, which I left for ever when I was young, come awake again inside me at the end of my days? I am not a native of Lydda. True, I was born in that stricken city, whose old quarters, where the Palestinians live, are now overgrown with weeds, but my father's family has its roots in the village of Deir Tarif. Deir Tarif has been erased and in its place has been built the *moshav* of Bet Arif, meaning House of the Cloud, which was founded by Jewish immigrants from Bulgaria and then converted into a cooperative village for Yemeni Jews.

"My family lived in the House of the Clouds," I used to tell anyone who asked, "so why does the memory of my childhood drag me down today from my cloud and throw me into the alley-ways of Lydda?"

I've visited Lydda only twice in my life since I left. Once to help the nurse from al-Ghabsiya, who lives in Ramallah, to sell the house she'd inherited from her Bedouin husband, who was killed in a feud, and the second time with Dalia, who had decided to return me to myself.

Writing about Lydda, I have to adopt the stance of an observer and stop writing laments. Enough! The past is dead and I must deal with it without emotion. That is something I learned from the Abbasid poet Abu Tammam, who described the relationship between humankind and time in terms of a dream:

> Then that age and its people were done
> as though both it and they were dreams.

In "the language of the 'ayn", which is to say, the language of the Arabs, the "particles that are analogous to verbs" and the "defective verbs" occupy a magical status, as though they were somehow congruent with one another. Thus *ka'anna* ("as though"), a particle analogous to a verb, exercises government over both the inchoative and the predicate, the first being written with final -*a* and referred to as the "noun belonging to the particle", the second with final -*u* and referred to as its "predicate", while *kāna* ("to be") is a perfect defective verb that exercises government over the inchoative and the predicate, the first being written with final -*u*, the second with final -*a*! The act itself falls somewhere between *kāna* and *ka'anna* but it is an act replete with confusion: most of the time *kāna* turns the imperfect into the perfect, while *ka'anna* makes the perfect imperfect. A verb's consonantal root is, for the Arabs, a perfect verb, even if the act itself takes place before our eyes! In this language, verbs are used only as a past perfect to be invoked in speech and writing. When our forefathers wept over the abandoned encampments of their beloveds, they wept over the time, not the place.

The years and their people, who have become dreams, take me to the abandoned encampments of Lydda, and when I stand before the encampments of the city I feel as though I were standing before those of time. All cities are subject to desolation, but the desolation we lived, and still live, is that of time. This is the story that I have attempted to tell through the voices of its heroes and victims. It is a story that I had to tell in order both to remember it and to forget it, as a past that has passed but does not want to pass.

Lydda now has come to be as though it were not Lydda. Manal said that she had only left the city after she was sure that Lydda itself had left, and I believed her. We left the stricken city after my mother's marriage to Abdallah al-Ashhal and went to live in Haifa. But Haifa left Haifa too. That is what Abdallah reported, bitterly, as he bore witness to the loss of his first wife and his three daughters. There is nowhere left in Palestine that has not left its place. Even Nazareth, whose inhabitants weren't forced to move, left in a different sense, when it filled with those displaced from the neighbouring villages, which were demolished, and then had mounted over them the settlement of Upper Nazareth, which, instead of being a barrier between Nazareth and the sky, began to turn into an extension of the old Arab city.

I shouldn't have believed Manal, but I was young and incapable of crystallising words into speech. My sole reaction was that I cried when I left Lydda, but Manal refused to read my tears. She satisfied herself with taking me in her arms and weeping for my weeping.

The people of the ghetto watched as the Israelis took control of the time of the city. Their youth were driven into detention camps while the military administration imported young men from Nazareth and its villages to pick the olives and oranges – the poor stealing from the mouths of the poor, the poor living in a camp on the outskirts of the city and struggling to make a living when all other doors had been closed in their faces and the collaborationist class used them as a base for their political leadership. That's what Seif al-Din al-Zoubi says in his memoirs. The guy doesn't mention collaboration, but he explains at great length how he helped people to get work in Lydda through his relations with the Israelis. He doesn't refer in his memoirs to the desolation of Lydda. Maybe he didn't see, or didn't want to see, and that's an issue that deserves study, because no-one, as Ma'moun said in his lecture, was able to see things as they were.

And so the city became a kind of Tower of Babel. Languages barged into one another, strangers trod strangers under foot, and the influx into the city of Bulgarian Jewish settlers began, followed by that of poor Jews from everywhere. They took over the houses and lived in them, and Lydda became a "development city", to use the Israeli authorities' term, meaning a marginal city. Even the airport, which was expanded and modernised, came to be known as "Tel Aviv Airport" and "Ben Gurion Airport". Jewish settlers, and Bedouin too – because in 1950, the Israeli authorities expelled dozens of the Bedouin families of al-Majdal from the city and resettled them in Lydda. Bulgars, Bedouin and a ghetto. When they allowed the inhabitants of the ghetto to go to their homes in November 1948, to get blankets and winter clothing, the ghetto-dwellers discovered that their houses had been looted of everything.

The story isn't the emptying of the city of its original inhabitants, because an influx of people from the neighbouring villages in search of work began, and Lydda never became a purely Jewish city. It became a mongrel, its old quarters full of drug pushers, with things reaching a climax when the Israeli authorities settled Palestinian collaborators and their families in Lydda following the establishment of the Palestinian National Authority in 1994.

Neither my memory nor that of my mother can help me to describe the city's future. What I've written is merely an attempt to understand the beginning of things and, as you can see, what I call the beginning of things was the end of them for the vast majority of Lydda's people, who set off on a journey into the wilderness that continues to this day.

I'm not justifying anything here. I'm trying to describe what I saw and what I did not see, so that the words can help me to see better. But the fog of time surrounds me.

How am I to describe, and why?

Stories that I thought I'd forgotten resurface now. Stories that seem like ghosts wandering in the night of the memory turn into words, and words turn into memory.

I want to sleep, and I want these words to sleep too. I'm worn out and so are they.

But how?

I have no idea. The ghetto's stories have no end, and if I were to keep digging away at the memories of others to reconstitute my own forgotten memory, I'd have to write thousands of pages, which I am incapable of doing. Also, the imagination to which I resorted to write a truncated novel about my murdered poet Waddah al-Yaman aside, my creative powers collapsed when I reached the beginnings of my life, and I resorted to others to tell me their stories, or summoned up the fragmented stories that my memory had learned by heart from Manal and Ma'moun, and reconstituted what I needed to.

Now I understand the seductions of Scheherazade: the woman did not seduce King Shahriyar with her story so that he would spare her life, as is commonly supposed; she told stories to quench her thirst, which grew with the telling, causing her to start again and tell new stories. I think the character of the king with his insane desires is merely an excuse that became transformed into a fact with the construction of the frame story, which some writer must have added in recent times in the belief that by so doing he would give the stories meaning.

The meaning is the mistake. Scheherazade fell in love with her stories, and when she was victorious and, after giving birth to three sons, won the king's goodwill, she entered the lethargy that leads to death. Scheherazade discovered that the world of stories is the real world, that the story is not a substitute for life but life itself, and that victory and defeat are the same, both meaning the end of the story and the death of the storyteller.

I too wrote so as to delay my death, only to find myself horror-struck, because instead of moving away from death, I came closer to it.

The writer who added the frame to the stories of Scheherazade was as footling as every other writer who fears the story that comes to us for nothing, that explodes inside us as water explodes inside the belly of the earth. Who said we need meaning to tell stories? My never-ending ambition is to arrive at a meaningless text, like music, one whose meaning comes from the rhythms of the soul within it and which is susceptible to a variety of interpretations – but that's impossible. Language, from the day it became a means for the gods to communicate with man, has been crammed into meanings, and the one who uses it has been obliged to support himself on the meaning in order to arrive at the gratuitous kernel, which is literature.

I am incapable of doing that, which is why my beautiful poet Waddah al-Yaman abandoned me. I put him in the coffer of meanings and no longer knew how to get him out, so he escaped from me and hid in his story.

I don't want anyone to misunderstand me, for who am I to write my memoirs? I am no-one. I fear death and run towards it and for that reason have decided to fill the vacuum with a vacuum and to write whatever I wish, which would not have been possible without this frame made from the memories and the imagination of others. As for the stories themselves, they are free to flow where they will and take the course they desire. I shall be just the reporter of what I saw and experienced. I shall bathe in words as I did when I was small, when I used to tell my mother, as I ate grapes and squirted the juice all over my clothes, that I wasn't eating grapes, I was taking a bath in them.

And now I find myself at the threshold. The story awaits and I have to set off.

GLOSSARY

Ordering is by first element of the item as it occurs in the novel. Arabic and English definite articles are ignored.

the 8th (Armoured) Brigade	Palmach brigade formed in 1948 under the command of Yitzhak Sadeh and consisting of two battalions, the 82nd Tank Battalion and the 89th Commando Battalion
the 89th Battalion	see *the 8th (Armoured) Brigade* and *Moshe Dayan*
the Abbasid dynasty	dynasty of caliphs, descended from one Abu al-Abbas al-Saffah, that ruled much of the Muslim world, either practically or nominally, from 749 to 1517
Abd al-Rahman ibn Ismail ibn Abd Kulal	see *Waddah al-Yaman*
Abdallah	here refers to Abdallah I ibn al-Husein, King of Jordan (reigned 1921–51)
Abdallah al-Bardawni	Yemeni modernist poet, critic, and historian (1929–99)
Abla	cousin and beloved of Antar ibn Shaddad, a poet and folk hero (second half of the sixth century)

Abu al-Alaa' al-Maarri	sceptical Syrian poet and prose writer (973–1058); one of his most famous prose works is *The Epistle of Forgiveness*, in which the author visits Heaven and Hell and holds discussions with dead poets
Abu Ali Salama	see *Hasan Salama*
Abu Ammar	organisational name of Yasir Arafat, Palestinian political leader (1929–2004)
Abu Hasan Salama	i.e. Ali Hasan Salama (1940–79), son of *Abu Ali Hasan Salama* and a leading Fatah operative, assassinated in Beirut by Israeli agents; his statue once stood in the Shatila Palestinian refugee camp in Beirut
Abu Tammam	Abbasid-era court poet and anthologist (*c.*805–45)
Adel Imam	Egyptian stage and screen actor and director (1940–)
Agnon	Shmuel Yosef Agnon (1888–1970), Israeli Hebrew-language novelist, co-winner of the Nobel Prize in Literature 1966
Ahl al-Hawa	title (literally "Love's People') of a song (1941) sung by *Umm Kulsoum*, words by Mahmud Bayram al-Tunisi, music by Zakariya Ahmad
Akhmim	town in Upper Egypt, close to Sohag
Albert Camus	Algerian-French writer and philosopher (1913–60)
the Alexandroni Brigade	Israeli army brigade, responsible for the massacre of Palestinian villagers at al-Tantura in 1948

Ali ibn Sulayman al-Akhfash	scholar and grammarian of Baghdad (849–927)
Amos Oz	Israeli writer and public intellectual (1939–); his novel *My Michael* was first published in English in 1968
Andalus	those parts of the Iberian peninsula that were under Muslim rule from 711 to 1492 (and thus not the same as the modern Spanish region of Andalusia); more properly, in Arabic, *al-Andalus*
Antara al-Absi	pre-Islamic poet (second half of the 6th century A.D.) and chivalric hero of the folk epic *The Story of Antar*
Anton Shammas	Palestinian-Israeli writer, poet and translator (1950–); his novel *Arabesques*, written in Hebrew, was first published in 1986
the Arab Higher Committee	the central political organ of Arab Palestinians during the British Mandate (established in 1936, banned by the British in 1937, and reconstituted in 1945)
Arabesques	see *Anton Shammas*
Aref al-Aref	Palestinian, historian, journalist and politician (1892–1973)
Asqalan	coastal city in southern Palestine (Hebrew: Ashkelon)
Baalbek	city in north-western Lebanon
Bachir Gemayel	Lebanese politician and military commander (1947–82); co-founder of the Lebanese Front and supreme commander of its military arm, the Lebanese Forces

Barmacides	family of high officials at the early Abbasid court who, over three generations, amassed great wealth and power and were overthrown and either executed or imprisoned by the caliph Harun al-Rashid in 805
Battle of Latroun	the battle consisted of a number of engagements between 24 May and 18 June, 1948, during which Arab Legion forces around the strategic hilltop location of Latroun, west of Jerusalem and overlooking the Jerusalem–Tel Aviv road, repelled Israeli attacks
Battle of Meisaloun	the battle, near the town of that name in Syria about twelve kilometres west of Damascus, at which French forces defeated those of the short-lived Arab Kingdom of Syria on 23 July, 1920
Bayan Nuweihid al-Hout	(1937–), political scientist, author of *Sabra and Shatila: September 1982* (2004), which gives a minimum of 1,300 named victims as the number killed in the massacre at the Sabra and Shatila camps
Be'er Ya'akov	Jewish settlement established in 1907 in central Palestine, close to *Sarafand*
Ben Shemen	Jewish settlement (founded 1905) four kilometres east of Lydda and the nearby agricultural school, established in 1927 by Siegfried Lehman for youth from Eastern Europe
Benjamin Tammuz	Israeli novelist, poet, critic, and artist (1919–89)

Bialik	Jewish Palestinian poet writing in Hebrew and Yiddish (1873–1934)
the Book of Songs	twenty-volume anthology of poetry and songs, with stories explaining the occasions for their writing and anecdotes about their authors, by Abu al-Faraj al-Isfahani (897–c. 972)
the Cooper Union	the Cooper Union for the Advancement of Science and Art, a higher education institution founded in New York in 1859 by philanthropist Peter Cooper
Count Bernadotte	Folke Bernadotte (1895–1948), Swedish diplomat appointed by the United Nations Security Council as mediator in the Arab–Israeli conflict of 1948, assassinated in Jerusalem while in pursuance of his official duties by the Zionist organisation Lehi
dabke	traditional line-and-circle dance performed on joyful occasions
ḍād	fifteenth letter of the Arabic alphabet, unique to that language; hence, "the language of the *ḍād*" is used to mean "the Arabic language"
Dar al-Adab	Beirut publishing house
The Dove's Neck Ring	see *Ibn Hazm*
Edward Said	Palestinian-American professor of literature, cultural critic, and advocate of Palestinian rights (1935–2003), particularly well known for his book *Orientalism* (1978), a critique of the cultural representations that he saw to be the bases of Orientalism

Emile Habibi	Palestinian Israeli writer and politician (1922–96); *The Secret Life of Said the Pessoptimist* (1974) (referred to in the novel as *The Pessoptimist*), the best known of his seven novels, explores the duality of those Arabs who, like himself, did not leave their homeland during the War of 1948
The Epistle of Forgiveness	see *Abu al-Alaa' al-Maarri*
al-Farazdaq	Omayyad-era poet (*c.*640–728)
Fawzi al-Asmar	Palestinian-Israeli poet and translator (1947–); author, in English, of *To Be an Arab in Israel* (1975)
Galilee	the mountainous northern region of Palestine
Gate of the Sun	novel by Lebanese writer Elias Khoury (1948–) (1998; English translation 2005)
George Habash	Palestinian politician from Lydda (1926–2008) who founded the secular nationalist Popular Front for the Liberation of Palestine (P.F.L.P.)
Ghassan Kanafani	Palestinian writer (1936–72) and spokesman of the Popular Front for the Liberation of Palestine, assassinated in Beirut by Israeli agents. His novel *Men in the Sun* was made into a film entitled *The Duped*
Haganah	Jewish paramilitary organisation formed during the British Mandate over Palestine (1921–48), which became the core of the Israeli army
Hajj	literally "pilgrim'; a title awarded to a man who has made pilgrimage to Mecca (if Muslim) or Jerusalem (if Christian)

Hammad	Hammad ibn Abi Layla, called al-Rawiya ("the great transmitter") (695–772), regarded as the first to collect Arabic poetry and contextualising anecdotes, including the seven celebrated *Suspended Odes*
Haroun al-Rashid	fifth caliph of the Abbasid dynasty (reigned 786–809)
Hasan Salama	Palestinian leader (1913–48) of the armed struggle against Jewish settlement and British rule during the 1936–39 Arab Revolt, a member of the Arab Higher Committee in the war of 1948, and commander of the Lydda region during the latter conflict; organisational name Abu Ali. A statue honouring him stood in Shatila Camp until after the massacre there
Himyarite	member of the large tribal confederation of Himyar, whose roots lay in Yemen
Holy Struggle Organisation	Palestinian paramilitary organisation formed by Abd al-Qadir al-Huseini in 1931 to oppose Zionist activity and the British Mandate
Ibn Hazm	one of the most prolific and important scholars of Islamic Spain (994–1064), best known for his treatise *The Dove's Neck Ring: On Love and Lovers*, on the theory and practice of love
Ibn al-Kalbi	early Iraqi polymath (*d.*819), best known for his genealogical works

Ibn Zaydun	one of the most renowned poets of Islamic Spain (1003–70), known especially for his tempestuous love affair with and verses on *Wallada*
Ibrahim Abu Lughod	Palestinian, then U.S., political scientist, academic administrator and defender of the Palestinian cause (1929–2001)
Imru' al-Qays (al-Kindi al-Yamani)	pre-Islamic poet (sixth century) and author of one of the best-known of the "Suspended Odes" that legend has it were hung inside the Kaaba of Mecca; this begins with the words "Halt, O my friends!" using dual forms, i.e. those used to address two persons. Legend has it that Imru' al-Qays spent his life wandering among the tribes of Arabia, going as far even as Byzantium, seeking to avenge his murdered father and restore the power of his kingdom of Kinda; hence he was known as "the King Errant"
Isbir Munayyir	resident of Lydda and Postal Service official under the British Mandate who participated in the defence of his native city during the 1948 war and continued to live in Lydda after its incorporation in Israel until his death (1926–99). His *Lydda in the Mandate and Occupation Periods* draws on his personal recollections
Ismail Shammout	influential Palestinian painter (1930–2006), born in Lydda
Jabra Ibrahim Jabra	Palestinian writer, critic and translator (1920–94)

al-Jahiz	Amr ibn Bahr, known as *al-Jahiz* ("the Pop-eyed") (*c.*776–*c.*868), a diverse and prolific prose writer; his *Book of Eloquence and Exposition* is a pioneering attempt to describe Arabic rhetoric, with copious examples
Jamil-Buthayna	see *Jamil ibn Maamar*
Jamil ibn Maamar	renowned poet (*d.*701) of the Udhri tribe, famous for their celebration in verse of chaste love; according to legend, Jamil's unfulfilled passion for a certain Buthayna led him to add her name to his, so that he became known as Jamil-Buthayna
Jean Genet	French writer and political activist (1910–86); his visit to Shatila Camp in September 1982 following the massacre there resulted in an essay entitled "Four Hours in Shatila" (1983)
Jorge Luis Borges	Argentinian short-story writer, essayist, poet and translator (1899–1986); "Averroës's Search" (1947) in his short-story collection *The Aleph* treats of the difficulties faced by Averroës in translating Aristotle's *Poetics*
Jurji Zaydan	Syrian-Egyptian novelist, journalist and historian (1861–1914)
Kamal Boulatta	Palestinian artist and critic (1942–)
al-Khalil ibn Ahmad al-Farahidi	grammarian and lexicographer (718–91), whose lexicon, *The Book of the 'Ayn*, is arranged according to the point of articulation of the various letters; he was also the first to write a systematic account of the Arabic poetical metres

al-Khatib al-Baghdadi	Ahmad ibn Ali ibn Thabit ibn Ahmad ibn Mahdi al-Shafi'i (1002–71), known as "the Baghdad preacher", a scholar of prophetic traditions and historian, author of the fourteen-volume biographical dictionary *The History of Baghdad*
kibbeh nayyeh	minced raw lamb mixed with bulgur and spices
Kindite	member of the tribal confederation of Kinda, which established a kingdom in Najd (Central Arabia) that lasted from the 2nd century B.C. to the 6th century A.D.
kishk	cracked wheat mixed with yoghurt, formed into balls and dried for storage, then dissolved in water and eaten with onions, meat, etc.
knafeh	traditional Palestinian dessert made with cheese pastry soaked in syrup
Kol Ha'ir	local Jerusalem Hebrew-language newspaper
kubbaniyya	Palestinian Arabic (ultimately from Italian *compagnia*) for a Jewish settlement
Kuthayyir-Azza	Kuthayyir ibn Abd al-Rahman al-Mulahi (*c.*660–723), an Omayyad-era poet of the Udhri tribe, famous for their celebration in verse of chaste love; he is said to have linked his name to that of his unattainable beloved, a certain Azza
Labid	Labid ibn Rabia al-Amiri (*d. c.*661), a pre-Islamic poet, author of one of the seven celebrated "Suspended Odes", which are said to have been hung up inside the Kaaba of Mecca in pagan days

the Lebanese Forces	military arm, created in 1976, of the Lebanese Front, a coalition of right-wing Christian parties; commanded until his assassination in 1982 by Bashir Gemayel
Leila Shahid	Palestinian activist and diplomat (1949–); in September 1982, she accompanied *Jean Genet* on a visit to Shatila Camp in the wake of the massacre there
Lod	Hebrew name of Lydda (Arabic: *al-Lidd*)
Mad-over-Layla	see *Qays ibn al-Mulawwah*
Madyan	i.e. Madyan Shu'ayb, a town situated in antiquity near Tabuk in north-western Arabia
Mahmoud Darwish	pre-eminent Palestinian poet (1941–2008); his *Memory for Forgetfulness* is among his several prose works
al-Majdal	town in southern Palestine, about ten miles north of Gaza, depopulated between 1948 and 1950 and now incorporated into Israel's Ashkelon
makdous	small oil-cured aubergines stuffed with walnuts, red pepper, garlic, etc.
Malik ibn al-Rayb	a "brigand-poet" (*su'luk*) of the Omayyad era
manaqish	rounds of dough topped with thyme, cheese, etc. and baked in the oven
Mannin, Ethel	left-wing British novelist and travel writer (1900–84); her *The Road to Beesheba* was published in 1963

the Masked Man of Kinda	Muhammad ibn Zufr ibn Umayr ibn Shamar al-Kindi, an Omayyad-era poet said to have been so beautiful that he was obliged to wear a mask outside the house lest he be smitten by the evil eye
Michael Palumbo	journalist and author of *The Palestinian Nakba: The 1948 Expulsion of a People from Their Homeland* (1987)
Mireen Ghoseib	Lebanese translator of Arabic poetry into English
mjaddara	lentils cooked with rice and garnished with sautéed onions
Moshe Dayan	Israeli soldier and politician (1915–81); Dayan took command of the 89th Commando Battalion of the Palmach's 8th Armoured Brigade in June 1948
al-Muatamid	Abbasid-dynasty King of Seville (reigned *c.*1069–99) and poet
al-Muqaddisi	geographer (tenth century)
al-Mutanabbi	Abbasid-era poet (*c.*915–65) renowned for the virtuosity and innovation of his verse, much of which took the form of panegyrics written for various rulers; he was accused of claiming to have performed miracles and labelled "the Would-Be Prophet" (*al-mutanabbi*)
muwashshahat	strophic poems originating in Islamic Spain in the late ninth century that were often turned into songs with instrumental accompaniment

Naalin	village in central Palestine, eleven miles west of Ramallah; during the 1948 Arab–Israeli War, it was under Jordanian Army control
al-Nabi Salih	Palestinian village near Ramallah, named after the *Prophet Salih*
the Nakba	term (literally "the Catastrophe") for the dispossession of the Palestinian people as a result of the creation of the State of Israel in 1948 and the war leading up to it
Nuseirat Camp	Palestinian refugee camp south of Gaza City
Operation Dani	Israeli military offensive launched at the end of the first truce of the 1948 Arab–Israeli War with the objective of capturing Lydda and al-Ramla and lasting from 9 to 19 June
Operation Peace for Galilee	name given by Israel to its invasion of southern Lebanon, launched on 6 June, 1982, and subsequently of Beirut
Orientalism	see *Edward Said*
the Palestinian National Authority	interim body established in 1994 following the Gaza–Jericho Agreement to govern the Gaza Strip and Areas A and B of the West Bank
Palestinian Preventive Security	security apparatus of the State of Palestine (established 1994)
the Palmach	the elite fighting force of the Haganah
P.I.A.T.	acronym for Projector, Infantry, Anti-Tank (P.I.A.T.), a British man-portable anti-tank weapon that entered service in 1943

Prayers of Refuge	i.e. the last two chapters of the Koran, "Daybreak" (113) and "Men" (114), often used as prayers of commendation
present absentees	Palestinian internally displaced persons who fled or were expelled from their homes in Mandate Palestine by Jewish or Israeli forces, before and during the 1948 Arab–Israeli war, but who remained within the area that became the State of Israel; to this day, present absentees are not permitted to live in the homes they formerly occupied, even if they were in the same area, the property still exists, and they can show that they own it
the Prophet Salih	prophet mentioned in the Koran who was sent to the pre-Islamic Arabian people of Thamud only to be rejected by them and whose "sign", in the form of a sacred camel, they killed to show that his threats were empty; subsequently, and as predicted by the prophet, the people of Thamud were annihilated by a natural disaster
Qays ibn al-Mulawwah	Omayyad-era poet (mid-seventh century) of the Udhri school of chaste love, who is said to have been driven insane by his unfulfilled passion for his girlhood sweetheart Layla and to have lived and died in the wilderness, tolerating only the company of wild beasts; as a result he became known as al-Majnun ("the Madman") and Majnun-Layla ("Mad-over-Layla")

Qudama ibn Jaafar	Abu al-Faraj Qudama ibn Jaafar (*d. c.*948), known as al-Katib al-Baghdadi ("the Scribe of Baghdad"), philosopher, philologist and literary theorist; his work *The Assaying of Poetry* discusses the nature of poetry from a philosophical standpoint
Quraysh	the Meccan tribe to which the Prophet Muhammad and the caliphs after him belonged
Raja-e Buseila	Palestinian poet and writer from Lydda who taught English literature in the United States
Ramallah	Palestinian city six miles north of Jerusalem
Ramat Aviv	neighbourhood of north-west Tel Aviv
al-Ramla	town in central Palestine close to Lydda
Ras al-Ein	village near Lydda
Rashed Hussein	Palestinian poet, orator, journalist and Arabic to Hebrew translator (1936–77)
Sarafand	i.e. Sarafand al-Amar, a Palestinian village about three miles north-west of al-Ramla and adjacent to the largest British military base in the Middle East during the Mandate period, which contained a prison, where Palestinian nationalist activists were held. In 1948, Britain evacuated the camp and prison, which were taken over by Jewish armed forces
Sayf ibn Dhi Yazan	Himyarite king of Yemen (516–78), known for ending Ethiopian rule over Southern Arabia with the help of the Sassanids of Persia

the Second Intifada	period of intensified Palestinian resistance to Israeli occupation that took place between late September 2000 and 2005
Seif al-Din al-Zoubi	Israeli–Palestinian politician (1913–86); al-Zoubi fought with the Haganah during the British Mandate, was a member of the Knesset from 1949 to 1979 (with interruptions), and was mayor of Nazareth for several terms between 1959 and 1974
sheikh	literally "old man" but used without regard for age to mean both a Muslim cleric in charge of a mosque and responsible for providing cultic services, and a Sufi holy man regarded as capable of dispensing blessings to his followers. Also used as a title of scholars and teachers, ancient and modern, and, without religious signification, of certain modern rulers, such as those of the United Arab Emirates
Shmarya Guttman	before 1948, headed an intelligence unit of the Haganah; in 1948, military governor of Lydda; later, an archaeologist
Sholokhov	Mikhail Aleksandrovich Sholokhov (1905–84), Soviet-era Russian writer known for his descriptions of Cossack life and especially for his four-volume novel *And Quiet Flows the Don* (1928–40); persistent allegations that the latter was a plagiarism have been rejected by successive investigations

Sonderkommando	concentration camp work units composed of prisoners who were forced, on threat of their own deaths, to aid with the disposal of gas-chamber victims during the Nazi holocaust
the Songs	see *the Book of Songs*
Suhrawardi the Slain	Yahya ibn Habash al-Suhrawardi (1153–91), a philosopher of the mystical "Illuminationist" school who was either murdered or starved to death in Aleppo, where he had been imprisoned as a heretic
the Suspended Odes	seven long poems by pre-Islamic poets which are said to have been hung up, written in gold letters on cloth, inside the Kaaba of Mecca in pagan days
Taha Hussein	highly influential Egyptian writer and intellectual (1889–1973) and a figurehead of the modernist movement in Egypt and the Arab World, often referred to as "the Dean of Arabic Literature'; his controversial *On Pre-Islamic Poetry* argued that all or most of the poetry supposed to date from before Islam was forged centuries later
Tawfiq Fayyad	Palestinian novelist and Arabic–Hebrew translator
the Throne Verse	Koran, Chapter 2 (The Cow), verse 255
transmitter	i.e., transmitter of verse and associated stories. By memorising and passing on the works of the great poets, transmitters played a vital role in the preservation of poetry during

pre-Islamic and early Islamic times, when writing was little used and even mistrusted.

the Triangle	concentration of Palestinian towns and villages in the centre of the country close to the 1948 Green Line marking the boundary between Israel and the West Bank
Ubaydallah ibn Qays al-Ruqayyat	poet of the Omayyad era (mid-seventh to mid-eighth centuries)
Umm Kulsoum	renowned Egyptian singer, known as al-Sitt ("the Lady") and "the Star of the East" (1898 or 1904–75)
Waddah al-Yaman	Abd al-Rahman (or Abd Allah) Ismail (*d. c.*712), called Waddah al-Yaman, or "the Luminous One of Yemen", because of his beauty; a love poet known for his verses written in praise of a certain Rawda and of Umm al-Banin, wife of the Omayyad caliph al-Walid ibn Abd al-Malik (reigned 705–15)
Walid Khalidi	leading Palestinian historian (1925–) who has written widely on the dispossession of the Palestinians
Wallada	Wallada bint al-Mustakfi (*d.*1091?), poet and daughter of the Cordovan caliph Muhammad III al-Mustakfi; her affair with the poet *Ibn Zaydun* is reflected in some of her few surviving verses
Yalo	novel by Lebanese writer Elias Khoury (1948–) (2002; English translation 2009)

the Yiftach Brigade	Israeli infantry brigade made up of two Palmach battalions, with a third added later; commanded during Operation Dani by Mula Cohen
Yizhar	see *Yizhar Smilansky*
Yizhar Smilansky	Israeli writer and politician (1916–2006), pen name S. Yizhar; his novella *Khirbet Khizeh* (1949), in which he described the expulsion of Palestinian Arabs from their village by the I.D.F. during the 1948 Arab–Israeli War became a best-seller in Israel
the Zanj	term for people from eastern Africa, and especially those trafficked as slaves to Iraq to perform agricultural labour during the Abassid period; their fifteen-year revolt in Lower Iraq and Khuzistan between 869 and 883 has been described as the greatest servile insurrection in the history of the Islamic world

ELIAS KHOURY, born in Beirut, is the author of fourteen novels, four volumes of literary criticism, and three plays. Khoury is a Global Distinguished Professor of Middle Eastern and Arabic Studies at New York University and was editor in chief of the literary supplement of Beirut's daily newspaper *Al-Nahar*. He is now editor in chief of the *Journal of Palestine Studies* in Beirut.

Khoury was awarded the *Palestine Prize* for *Gate of the Sun*, which was named Best Book of the Year by *Le Monde Diplomatique*, the *Christian Science Monitor*, and the *San Francisco Chronicle*, and a Notable Book by the *New York Times*. *As Though She Were Sleeping* received France's inaugural Arabic Novel Prize. In 2012 Khoury was awarded the UNESCO Sharjah Prize for Arab Culture. In 2016 he won the prestigious Mahmoud Darwish Award for Creativity, and he was honoured with the Katara Prize for Arabic Novel 2016 in the category of published novels. Recently Elias Khoury was shortlisted for the International Prize for Arabic Fiction (I.P.A.F.) 2017, the most important literary prize in the Arab world, run with the support of the Booker Prize Foundation in London.

HUMPHREY DAVIES has been twice awarded the Banipal Prize for his translation of novels by Elias Khoury, in 2006 for *Gate of the Sun* and in 2010 for *Yalo*. His translation of Alaa Al Aswany's *The Yacoubian Building* was voted Best Translation of 2007 by the Society of Authors. He is affiliated to the American University in Cairo.

A New Library from MacLehose Press

This book is part of a new international library for literature in translation. MacLehose Press has become known for its wide-ranging list of best-selling European crime writers, eclectic non-fiction and winners of the Nobel and Independent Foreign Fiction prizes, and for the many awards given to our translators. In their own countries, our writers are celebrated as the very best.

Join us on our journey to **READ THE WORLD**.

1. *The President's Gardens* by Muhsin Al-Ramli
TRANSLATED FROM THE ARABIC BY LUKE LEAFGREN

2. *Belladonna* by Daša Drndić
TRANSLATED FROM THE CROATIAN BY CELIA HAWKESWORTH

3. *The Awkward Squad* by Sophie Hénaff
TRANSLATED FROM THE FRENCH BY SAM GORDON

4. *Vernon Subutex 1* by Virginie Despentes
TRANSLATED FROM THE FRENCH BY FRANK WYNNE

5. *Nevada Days* by Bernardo Atxaga
TRANSLATED FROM THE SPANISH BY MARGARET JULL COSTA

6. *After the War* by Hervé Le Corre
TRANSLATED FROM THE FRENCH BY SAM TAYLOR

7. *The House with the Stained-Glass Window* by Żanna Słoniowska
TRANSLATED FROM THE POLISH BY ANTONIA LLOYD-JONES

8. *Winds of the Night* by Joan Sales
TRANSLATED FROM THE CATALAN BY PETER BUSH

9. *The Impostor* by Javier Cercas
TRANSLATED FROM THE SPANISH BY FRANK WYNNE

10. *After the Winter* by Guadalupe Nettel
TRANSLATED FROM THE SPANISH BY ROSALIND HARVEY

11. *One Clear, Ice-Cold January Morning at the Beginning of the Twenty-First Century* by Roland Schimmelpfennig
TRANSLATED FROM THE GERMAN BY JAMIE BULLOCH

12. *The Shape of the Ruins* by Juan Gabriel Vásquez
TRANSLATED FROM THE SPANISH BY ANNE McLEAN

13. *Vernon Subutex 2* by Virginie Despentes
TRANSLATED FROM THE FRENCH BY FRANK WYNNE

14. *Stick Together* by Sophie Hénaff
TRANSLATED FROM THE FRENCH BY SAM GORDON

15. *The Tree of the Toraja* by Philippe Claudel
TRANSLATED FROM THE FRENCH BY EUAN CAMERON

16. *The Oblique Place* by Caterina Pascual Söderbaum
TRANSLATED FROM THE SWEDISH BY FRANK PERRY

17. *Tropic of Violence* by Nathacha Appanah
TRANSLATED FROM THE FRENCH BY GEOFFREY STRACHAN

18. *My Name is Adam* by Elias Khoury
TRANSLATED FROM THE ARABIC BY HUMPHREY DAVIES

www.maclehosepress.com